Between Two Bridges

Brian McHugh

Ringwood Publishing

Glasgow

Copyright Brian McHugh © 2016

All rights reserved

The moral right of the author has been asserted

First published in Great Britain in 2016 by

Ringwood Publishing

24 Duncan Avenue, Glasgow G14 9HN

www.ringwoodpublshing.com

ISBN 978-1-901514-35-3

British Library Cataloguing-in Publication Data

A catalogue record for this book is available from the British Library

Cover design by Jack McLean

Edited by Philip Amey and Philip Dunshea

Typeset in Times New Roman 11

Printed and bound in the UK

by

Lonsdale Direct Solutions

Praise for *Torn Edges*

'Brian McHugh's first novel *Torn Edges* is a magnificent tale bringing a Scottish dimension to an unjustly neglected era of recent Irish history. It sets us out on a voyage into a contemporary sea still in the eddies of what for many is a little known history – that of the Irish civil war of the 1920s. Wonderfully told, redolent with traces of Conrad, and too, of Rider Haggard in this tale. Action, history and a strain of the enigmatic, deftly drawn, courses throughout. This first book is unmissable and we much look forward to McHugh's next account of an enthralling journey.'

Jack McLean, Literary Critic and Commentator

'*Torn Edges* is a gripping story that alternates between modern-day Glasgow and 1922 Ireland of the Irish Civil War. This was a nasty conflict that split friends, families and former colleagues. Because of that it is often overlooked by Irish and Scots-Irish in their celebration of their proud heritage. Author Brian McHugh draws heavily on his own experience in the Gorbals, Govanhill, Mount Florida and Cathcart as he takes us along familiar streets and into well known pubs, restaurants and churches. All the while intrigue builds up as we try to find out why a Glasgow murder victim had a gold sovereign from the 1920s in his hand when he died. Can librarian Liam Casey unravel the connection between an old photograph of an Irish Free State soldier, a notorious massacre and a stabbing in a dingy city lane? A superb first novel from Brian McHugh. A great read, it seems certain it won't be his last.

Southside Press

About the Author
Brian McHugh

Born of Irish parents, and brought up in the Gorbals, Glasgow.

Attended a Glasgow secondary school and studied engineering at Strathclyde University.

Set up a small building company and returned to college to complete the engineering course.

Decided to become a teacher in the eighties and attended Jordanhill teacher training college.

Teacher of design, technology and graphics. An active trade unionist.

Main interests are current affairs, reading and the occasional game of golf.

Currently lives in the South Side of Glasgow.

His first novel *Torn Edges* was published by Ringwood in 2012 and is available from www.ringwoodpublishing.com, Amazon, Kindle and the other usual book outlets.

Acknowledgements

Big thanks to Ann Jarvis and Frank McGuinness for initial editing, proofing and support. I'd also like thank the staff at Ringwood, particularly Phil Amey and Phil Dunshea, for their help in the last few months. And finally to my wife Fran for her patience and encouragement.

Chapter 1

Whisky Galore

Charlie McKenna, with his hands in his pockets, was looking down to Herald Square from the corner window of his office on the eighteenth floor. To the right of the square the newly opened Empire State building towered over the whole area.

He had only ever opened the window once and that was to look down Thirty-Second Street in search of a quicker route to Penn station. He had put his head straight out looking left; then leaned forward, trying to see the station. The moment he shifted his head to look down directly at the street he suddenly felt he was being pulled out of the window and about to plummet to the pavement below. The feeling was so overpowering at the time that he immediately dropped onto one knee and grasped the window sill with both hands. It was all rather odd. Charlie had never considered himself to be particularly scared of heights – but he never opened the window again.

'Damned Italians!' said George, slapping the desk.

Charlie tilted his head. He pulled out his right hand and gently tapped the window. It was remarkable, he thought, that you could feel safe with a flimsy quarter inch thick piece of glass between you and oblivion.

'What was that, George?' he said distantly.

'These Italians are getting into everything these days.'

'Remember my brother-in-law is an Italian.'

'Joe doesn't count,' replied George Peebles with a dismissive wave of his hand. 'It's these guys up here in New York – Luciano, Genovese and the rest of that mob of Moustache Petes. They're trying to get into construction. I've already lost business down in Philly because of them and I can't afford it; that wife of mine spends money like there's no tomorrow.'

George had surprised everyone in Philadelphia by marrying Elizabeth Farrell, daughter of a wealthy Boston upholsterer that he met on a boat to France nearly ten years ago; they had three daughters that George doted on.

'Building trade has been bad for a couple of years; there's been a depression, George.'

'Why can't they stick to their usual rackets instead of muscling in on me? A few years ago they were knocking each other off good style.'

'They've been getting better organised past couple of years. Not so much the Italians, more the Sicilians.'

'Still Italians aren't they?' said George gruffly. He still insisted in pronouncing it as eye–talians. 'No matter where they come from.'

'It's a bit more complicated than that. Italy has many regions. Some of them speak almost a different language. Luciano calls Frank Costello a dirty Calabrian even though Calabria is just across the water from Sicily…'

Charlie stopped talking – George had already stopped listening.

'Who is this guy we're meeting anyway?' Charlie continued, walking into the middle of the room.

'Alex Davidson – they call him Sandy, for some reason.'

'Where did you meet him?'

'At a Lodge meeting or something.'

George collected lodge affiliations and memberships of political parties the way New York kids collected baseball cards.

'Which one this time?'

'Can't remember,' said George, shifting in his seat. 'In fact, come to think of it, I believe it was a charity ball last week. I've known Davidson for a while. He supplied timber for us when we were tunnelling for the subway from City Hall to the East River. We got chatting and he said he had a business deal that we might be interested in.'

There was a rap on the door and Mrs Greene poked her head round.

'There's a Mr Davidson in the front office – says he has an appointment to see you, Mr Peebles.'

'Show him in, Mrs Greene.'

Charlie took a seat in the armchair to the left of the large mahogany table leaving the other one for their guest. He gave George a guarded look.

Mrs Greene ushered Davidson through the open door.

'Come on in, Sandy,' said George, leaping out from behind the desk to grab Davidson's hand as he came through the door.

'Here, have a seat.'

'Bring us in a pot of coffee, Mrs Greene,' he continued with a quick look at his watch, 'in ten minutes.'

He bustled in behind the desk and nodded over at Charlie.

'My business associate, Charlie McKenna.'

Davidson took a couple of steps forward as Charlie stood up. He was about the same height and build as Charlie, but looked a bit older. His handshake was firm as he looked at Charlie, intrigued.

'Pleased to meet you, Mr McKenna, I've heard a bit about you.'

'Oh don't worry,' he added quickly, as he noticed a brief look of unease cross Charlie's face, 'nothing untoward, I can assure you.'

Davidson took his seat and settled back confidently.

'So how are we, George?' he asked. He had a neutral middle class accent with a hint of Bostonian twang. An accent that Charlie knew usually meant privileged money somewhere in the background.

'I'm fine but I'm afraid I didn't have time to brief Charlie on our little chat last week. I just got up from Philadelphia this morning. Could you give him a quick rundown on the business idea we discussed?'

Davidson sat back, he had quickly realised that, although George Peebles was the senior man, McKenna was the one that probably called the shots. He didn't regard it as an unusual arrangement in business, but he shifted his position so that he was speaking to Charlie more directly.

'In case you're wondering how I came to know of you, Mr McKenna,'

'Oh, Charlie will do fine'

'A couple of business associates know you from The Country Club. They say you run a square trade there.'

Charlie hesitated for a second. The Country Club was a speakeasy he ran on Seventh Avenue just above Forty-Third Street. In fact, he was more a sleeping partner than anything else. Not that he kept it a secret, but Davidson must have done a bit of digging around to know that Charlie was involved in the first place.

'It's not my main business but it's profitable,' he said with a shrug, 'in its own way.'

He was a bit irked but let it go.

'I'm more a construction man myself,' he continued, 'I have a few sub-contracting interests. George mentioned that you were a timber supplier. I'm afraid business in the building trade is a bit slow these days but it's picking up a bit.'

'Construction supply is not one of our main lines,' replied Davidson, 'It's a very competitive business and it's not particularly profitable for us, but we can sell off the less useful timber there. Perhaps if I gave you…'

He was interrupted by Mrs Greene pushing the door open with her back and turning into the room with a tray of coffee.

'Fine, Mrs G. Leave the tray on my desk and we'll help ourselves,' said George, coming out from behind the desk.

'You two carry on talking while I get the coffee.'

Davidson started again.

'My grandfather came to America some eighty years ago,' said

Davidson. 'He was a forester from Aberdeenshire, made a fortune supplying railway sleepers for the Boston and New York Central Railroads in the 1850s. Bought up thousands of acres of forest in upstate Maine. Most of it is white oak. My father expanded the company into a variety of timber enterprises – furniture, barrel making, that sort of thing. Construction timber is mainly pine wood, stuff we cut down to get to the oak. We sell it off cheaply. As I said, it's not our main business.'

'I'm not sure if...'

'Sorry, I'll come to the point. The most profitable part of our business was barrel-making. I say was, as you know things have not been that great these past few years, but we've managed to survive.'

George started to hand out the coffee.

'Sandy was telling me,' said George turning to Charlie, 'that his company had some contacts in the distilling industry around your old neck of the woods in Scotland. Cream for you, Sandy?'

'Yes please,' said Davidson.

'One of the ways the barrel-making business grew, was by exporting them to Spain,' continued Davidson, 'we also had a family contact in Scotland. A cousin of ours was involved in the distilling business – good quality Malt – and he needed old sherry barrels to mature the whisky. It was easy for us to supply old barrels from Spain to Scotland on the return journey to the States. Quite profitable at the time.'

'So what's the problem?' said Charlie.

'The problem, if it can be called a problem, is over-production.'

'Of barrels?'

'No,' said Davidson with a smile, 'of whisky.'

George looked bemused.

'You can sell good whisky in New York for $25 a case and they can't get enough of it, and someone has a problem with too much of it?'

Charlie was more cautious.

'Too much of anything can cause a price drop. Is that the way you're thinking?' he said.

'Partly,' said Davidson.

'But then again,' replied Charlie quickly, 'you're not claiming to be involved in bootlegging surely.'

'No, we never have been.'

'Just hold on,' said Charlie standing up. He took a few paces towards the window and turned round glancing over at George suspiciously.

'I don't know what George has told you but regardless of my association with The Country Club, I'm no bootlegger.'

'This is a different proposition,' said Davidson turning in his seat. He now knew, as he suspected, that the one to convince was McKenna.

'Look, don't take any of this personally, Charlie, and please hear me out before you jump to conclusions.'

Charlie was becoming interested. Things were becoming noticeably tighter in the construction business; he had lost money last year – not a fortune – but he had to lay men off for the first time before stemming the flow of cash leaving his account. A new direction might be worth listening to.

'Well then,' he said.

He sat down again, casually adjusting his trouser seams. 'Carry on, Sandy. I'm all ears.'

'As I said, cousins of ours, the Denholms, are in the distilling business. They have several small distilleries around the North East where my grandfather came from. Oddly enough, there's not a great market for individual malt whiskies these days and their main interest is blending them with inferior whisky to produce your run of the mill Scottish blends. When I say inferior I mean, of course, young whisky not substandard whisky.'

'You'd think there would be a good market for malt whisky,'

said George.

'Under normal circumstances, yes. The Denholms had a steady and prosperous clientèle before the war and were expanding their trade. The Great War almost put them out of business but they survived. By luck they acquired a bottling plant in Glasgow as part payment for a failed deal almost as soon as prohibition started in the States. They were able to churn out decent whisky by the boatload for the first three years and at the same time they exported barrels of pure malt to Canada.'

He stopped to take some coffee.

'They, of course, would be horrified if you said they were in the bootlegging racket, but their whole business depended on it – and they knew it. Trouble is that prohibition is about to end.'

'Don't be too sure about that,' interrupted George

'Can't be too sure about anything these days,' replied Sandy, 'but I'm pretty sure about that.'

Charlie was pretty sure as well. The Country Club wasn't quite what they called 'top drawer' but it attracted press men from the nearby Times building and middle management types from businesses around the area. The speakeasy also doubled up as a bookie's outlet. The bookie, Page Slavinsky, who also operated a small gambling joint over in Times Square, was a partner in the building lease but had no interest in the liquor trade. Part of the deal was to limit horse racing bets to a dollar in the bar. The bets were collected by a young street runner employed by Slavinsky. The limit was always exceeded, of course, but it gave Charlie an excuse to insist that the runner kept him informed who was betting heavily. In the demi-monde of the speakeasy, information, he had quickly discovered, was a much more potent commodity than violence. Word was that prohibition had run its course and politicians were already forming plans to get it repealed.

'I think you might be right there, Sandy,' said Charlie, 'but I'm not quite sure what this has got to do with us.'

'I'm talking about an investment. The American liquor trade won't have the capacity to cope when prohibition is repealed. If we buy stock now we can sell at a good profit when the Volstead

Act is repealed.'

Charlie sat up. He could understand the logic in the idea immediately.

'Yes, I can see that,' he said, 'but …'

He hesitated. *If it's such a good investment,* he thought quickly, *why does Davidson need George… or more to the point, why does he need me?*

'Let me continue,' Davidson said.

'To make it worthwhile, this needs investment, secure premises either here or in Canada, and importantly we need someone in Europe, Scotland specifically, that we can trust to carry out the deal.'

'What sort of money are we talking about?' said George.

Making money was the only thing George knew about. The intricacies of deals or investments did not interest him in the slightest. George once told him he had bought 10,000 shares in Drott Engineering and Manufacturing Company.

What was it that Drott Company actually made? Charlie asked him. George looked at him as if he was mad, 'Why it makes money, of course,' he had replied.

Charlie looked over at Davidson. He was interested to hear how he was going to pitch this; he was taken by surprise at his answer.

'I need $60,000 all in; I'm prepared to put up at least half myself,' he said in answer to George. 'I have two other investors committed for $10,000 each, three uncommitted as yet including yourself, but there's no immediate rush. What I'm here to do today, is to try to secure the services of your partner here, Charlie McKenna.'

Chapter 2

Old ground

In the long run, Des Capaldi had eventually concluded, there's something soul destroying about the death of a contemporary. After all it was not the natural order of things. It's not the same as losing a grandparent or an old aunt. Mike Hastings's murder had left Des bereft for some time, not only because he was a witness to it, but because it was the first time that someone he'd virtually grown up with, someone he knew really well, had died. He hadn't shed tears at any point, he never felt the need to show open sentiment, but for a while he felt a strange longing – an unusual emotion, a bit like the home sickness he felt as a child when he was sent to boarding school for a term. It was now well into February, several weeks after a sullen and uneventful Christmas holiday, and the days were still short and cold. It was Saturday morning just after ten and people were beginning to mill into town over the bridges that stretched above the wintry black waters of the Clyde.

'I was thinking,' Julie said, looking down at the scene from the small balcony. 'It might be a good idea to visit the grave today.'

Des looked up from the papers he was going through. He thought for a moment.

'I was thinking the same thing myself recently.'

He tidied up the papers; two or three job offers from magazines and newspapers for work after the busy Christmas period.

'Oddly enough I met Liam last week and he suggested the same thing.'

Julie closed the door to the balcony and came inside. 'I tell you what,' she said, 'I'll give him a ring now and see if he wants to go.'

'For heaven's sake, that's a bit sudden.'

'I know, but it's in my mind now; I think it might do us all some good.'

Before Des could answer she lifted her mobile phone, flicked down her contacts and dialled Liam.

She half expected to be put through to his answering service but he answered almost right away.

'Hi, Liam,' she said cheerily, 'how are we this morning?

'Two paracetamol and a large glass of water will usually do the trick I find… I take it that this is your Saturday off.'

Liam Tracey worked alternate Saturdays in the Mitchell Library. Julie continued her one-sided conversation.

'I, well I mean Des and I, were thinking of taking a journey up to the cemetery this morning. We pass your place on the way there, we could easily stop and give you a lift up… How about half past eleven? We'll park somewhere near your flat and you can come down when we give a blast on the horn… Okay, Liam see you later.

'That's that,' she said as she put down her phone.

Des ruffled his hair.

'You're a quick worker. I was thinking of sometime soon, not right away, not this morning.'

'So was Liam apparently. Best get these things done as soon as you can; if you don't go now, you'll leave it, and the longer you leave it the harder it becomes.'

Des lifted up some of his papers tapped them on the table and squared them off.

'I must ask some of the editors if they are looking for a part-time Agony Aunt,' he said with a smile.

Julie looked at her watch.

'We've got plenty of time, let's nip out and get some shopping now. I fancy a lazy afternoon later on.'

'Suits me. I've got a bit of work to do with these. I'll leave it till later,' Des replied, tossing the papers back on the table.

*

They managed to park about twenty yards from the front of Liam's close-mouth entrance.

'Jump out and give his doorbell a ring. I'll give the horn a blast as well.'

Des walked along then skipped up the half a dozen steps of the front entrance and pressed the buzzer. He walked backwards to the edge of the steps looking up at the bay window on the third floor as Julie pumped the horn. A few seconds later the large bearded face of Liam Tracey looked down and gave them a short wave. As Des turned and started going down the stairs, he saw Julie come out of the car and walk towards him.

'It's cold, I thought you'd stay in car,' he said.

'Sometimes it's better to meet someone standing up,' she said as she walked passed him. Liam was now coming out of the main door and was pulling it closed behind him as Julie quickly made her way up the stairs.

'Liam,' she cried, rushing towards him, 'how are you?'

He opened his arms and gave her a crushing bear hug.

'My God, Julie, it's a long time since I've had a welcome like that!' he said, disentangling himself.

'Oh, its ages since I've seen you and, well, it's nice to see you again.'

Liam looked a bit embarrassed.

'Yes, nice to see you too.'

They walked down the steps together towards Des.

'Des, old chap, how are you?' he shouted, extending his hand.

'Couldn't be better,' he croaked as Liam pounded him on the back.

'You get in the back, Liam, and we'll get going.'

From Victoria Road to the Lynn Cemetery all three chatted constantly. As they pulled through the gates Julie shook her head.

'This is our third visit here in as many months. I doubt if I've been to a cemetery as many times before in my entire life.'

'Consider yourself lucky then,' said Liam airily, 'I've been in plenty of them in my time.'

Julie parked on the larger concourse rather than try to weave her way through the narrow terraces of the main graveyard.

'We'll walk from here, it's only five minutes,' she said.

It was quite cold after the heat of the car, but it was turning into a crisp, clear day. The trees that surrounded the graveyard entrance were mainly alders and some evergreens like spruce and tall pines. As they walked through and turned to the left, there was a large copse of scrubby birch trees that suddenly reminded Des of Kosovo. He remembered the smoky stretches of silver birch shredded with gunfire, the acrid smell, the din of machine gun fire and the screech of the planes overhead, the riddled bodies of poorly clad men lying among the trees.

He suddenly shivered.

'You okay, Des?' said Liam, 'you're looking a bit pale.'

'I'm fine,' he replied, pulling his scarf round his neck, 'it's just the cold wind caught me there.'

Julie led the way, she seemed to know exactly where the grave was – she was good at remembering things like that, thought Des. They stayed on the footpath and looked down at the headstone.

'They don't usually get the headstone up that quick, it sometimes takes months,' said Liam.

'You're losing track of time, Liam, it's over three months.'

'Yes, of course,' he replied quickly, 'I was forgetting.'

They stood quietly in their own thoughts for a few minutes.

'Well,' said Des breaking the silence, 'you were right, Julie. I do feel a bit better for coming.'

He stopped for a moment.

'…although I'm not so sure why.'

'Strange thing – death,' said Liam. 'Hard to get over sometimes. I know it's an old cliché, but time truly is a great healer.'

'Maybe we should come again.'

'I think the next time I'll come myself,' said Des.

'Perhaps in a few weeks,' he added with a wane smile.

'Sure, Des,' said Julie.

'Come on, let's go,' announced Liam, 'before we perish up here.'

They walked back to the car chatting quietly in the pale sunshine. They were in a lighter mood: there seemed to be almost a spring in Des' step.

'Look at the state of that grave,' said Liam stopping in front of a gigantic gravestone shaped like a heart.

The area in front of the gravestone was cordoned off with a low white picket fence. Inside the tiny fence was an astonishing array of bric-a-brac. Plastic and real flowers were jumbled together. Spinning windmills and deflated helium balloons littered the outer edges. Inside, religious icons of every denomination jostled for position and every football team in Europe and beyond seemed to be represented in one way or another. For some unfathomable reason Star Wars figures and Snowstorm paperweights seemed to be surprisingly popular. A remarkably realistic, plastic Alsatian dog lay panting in front of a plaster statue of Saint Patrick. And there in the middle, one arm outstretched, the other forever holding a microphone to his lips – the piece de resistance – a four-foot statue of Elvis Presley.

Liam shook his head.

'Jesus, somebody must have gone in to a discount store for a hundred pounds worth of the most tasteless tat and emptied the lot in here. A hawker down in Paddy's market would be embarrassed to put out a display as bad as that.'

He thought for a second, then put his hand in his pocket and pulled a coin.

'Here,' he said, 'Do you think old Elvis would come alive and give us a song if I threw this in?'

Julie put her hand to her mouth to suppress a fit of giggling.

'Good job there's no one about,' Des laughing aloud, 'come on let's get out of here before we get thrown out.'

*

Liam sprawled in the back seat as Julie set off.

'I'm a bit peckish. I know a bar around here that's supposed to do decent lunches,' said Liam, lightly drumming his fingers on his stomach for effect.

'Now there's a surprise,' said Julie from the front.

'It's just over the hill and on your right hand side, can't miss it.'

A few minutes later she clicked on the car indicator and pulled the car into the small car park attached to the pub. They entered through a side door and found themselves on a small platform with a few steps down to the main floor. All three were quite tall and the platform was like a small stage. It could have been the dramatic entrance of three characters in a play. That is of course if any of the handful of customers lounging at the bar had bothered to lift their eyes from their newspapers.

'Let's sit over there,' said Liam pointing in the direction of a table underneath a window.

Liam sat with his back to the watery sunlight, Des slipped into the bench seat opposite.

'I'll get the drinks before we settle,' said Julie.

'Might as well order the grub as well. I'll have the gammon steak,' said Liam.

'How do you know …' said Julie picking up the menu, 'Oh, I forgot you've been here before.'

'Never eaten in here in my life,' said Liam, 'but I recognise a laminated pub grub menu when I see one. I'll give you even money that the gammon stake is somewhere between the traditional steak pie and the home-made lasagne.'

'Not bad,' said Julie impressed, 'almost true. How about you, Des?'

'I'm not that hungry, a snack or a sandwich will do.'

'Same here,' replied Julie.

'May I recommend you share a plate of freshly made nachos? I'll be surprised if they're not under the starter menu.'

'Spot on again, Liam!'

'Ah, the joys of being a bachelor!' replied Liam, rubbing his hands together, 'Tell me, does the gammon steak come with a slice of pineapple?'

'As a matter of fact it does – is that a problem?'

'Not a combo I take to as it happens, but I'll just put the pineapple to one side. I once made the mistake of asking for a gammon steak without the pineapple in a joint like this in town.'

'What happened?' asked Des.

'The waitress looked at me as if I had asked her to go outside, strangle a suckling pig, spit roast it and serve it on a bed of steamed wild rice,' rumbled Liam, 'when she recovered her composure she wrote down 'No Pineapple' underlined it and snapped closed her pad. "The chef," she said in a loud voice, "will not be best pleased."'

He sat back.

'I've never had the nerve to ask for a gammon steak without pineapple again,' he said, shaking his head.

'Might as well get me a pint of stout while you're on your feet,' he added.

'Anything for you, Des?' said Julie.

'A coffee for me. You have a drink and I'll drive home.'

'Sounds good. I'll get myself a gin and tonic,' replied Julie turning towards the bar.

'So how are things at the library?' said Des.

'Not bad. We've a couple of interesting exhibitions coming up now that Christmas is over. I quite like doing the research and setting the stuff up.'

'Talking about research did you ever get any further with that old postcard of Julie's Uncle Pat? You know, the one of him as a soldier in the Irish Civil War. You seemed quite intrigued by Julie's grandfather, Charlie McKenna, and his role in the affair.'

'Ah, yes. Charlie and the mysterious gold sovereigns. I must admit I kind of gave up after Mick got murdered.'

'Not like you. You're usually like a dog with a bone on these things.'

'True,' said Liam, 'it was quite interesting at the time. Maybe I'll have a think about it. Ah! A pint of stout.'

He took the glass from Julie hand before she set it down.

He held it up and admired the swirling foam.

'The stout is not quite settled yet,' he announced, placing the pint on the table.

'Oddly enough,' he continued, 'I'm heading over to Cork in two weeks' time. There's a conference for librarians. My boss said I might as well go, me being Irish and all that, and anyway no one else was interested. I suppose if it had been Paris or Berlin or somewhere equally fancy it might have been a different story. Head off on Monday, back on Friday.'

'Conference for librarians. Well now, that sounds exciting,' said Des with a nudge at Julie.

'Don't knock it... and less of your sarcasm, Capaldi,' said Liam a bit riled, 'some of these mature lady librarians can be quite adventurous.'

'Hold on a minute, Liam, before I forget,' said Julie. 'You've been invited over to my parents' house next Friday. It's my brother's tenth wedding anniversary and they've decided to have it at home with the family and some friends. My mother said she would like you to come along.'

'Thanks, Julie, and thank that mother of yours, the lovely Grace, for me. I'd be delighted to come.'

'About eight o'clock?'

'No problem. Now where was I?'

Before he could answer his own question the barmaid rushed over with cutlery, condiments and a coffee for Des. She returned a few moments later with the food. Julie had a quiet snigger as she spotted Liam trying to surreptitiously slip the slice of pineapple into a napkin without the barmaid noticing.

'Ah, yes, I was talking about Cork. Flying over from Prestwick, two weeks on Monday morning first thing. Big conference on Tuesday and only a couple of meetings the rest of the week. Back on Saturday,' he continued.

'I wonder,' said Julie, taking out her phone.

Des started picking at the nachos.

'I thought so,' she said, scrolling through her diary. 'I'm due a few days holiday then. Are you free, Des?'

'What?' said Des, trying to scoop some sour cream onto a chip.

'Could you take a couple of days off in a fortnight's time? I was thinking we could go over to see Liam in Cork. It could be good fun, and I've never been down to that part of Ireland.'

Des shrugged.

'Shouldn't be a problem.'

'Might be quite interesting,' Julie continued, 'I wouldn't mind seeing some of the places we talked about. You know, Tralee and that other place, where the mine was blown up. What was it called again?'

'Mmm ... I think it was called Ballyseedy Cross,' said Des.

'Well remembered, Des! I didn't realise you were paying so much attention. We might even find out more about Charlie's time in Cork.'

'Wouldn't get too excited about that possibility,' said Liam, 'it was a long time ago.'

He stopped eating and seemed to deliberate for a moment.

'Then again, you never know.'

'No problem with me going to Ireland,' added Des, 'but what about Liam? He might have some lady librarian lined up for the week.'

'Well, as long as it's towards the end of the week.' he said with a straight face, 'I might be busy on Monday and Tuesday. Anyway I'm away up to get another pint. Another gin for you, Julie?'

'Why not?' replied Julie.

'Nothing for me, Liam,' said Des, 'this coffee is still quite hot.'

Liam came back from the bar with the drinks in both hands and laid them on the table.

'Back in a tic,' he said walking over to the side of the bar. He was back two minutes later.

'Just noticed they have a juke box in here, thought I'd play us a tune.'

'Oh no!' groaned Des, 'not one of your daft Irish laments'

'Are you stone mad?' said Liam, shuffling into the seat. 'I don't mind singing them myself but I can't bear anyone else singing them. No, just something that crossed my mind up in the cemetery.'

'Nothing too maudlin, I hope,' said Julie, 'I could get a bit weepy after that visit.'

'Not at all! It's a great song – I just love the way he rhymes 'dwell' with 'hotel' in the first few bars.'

Julie and Des gave each other a baffled look. The music burst from the speakers:

'Well, since my baby left me,

Well, I've found a new place to dwell ... Kaboom!

Well, it's down at the end of lonely street

In Heartbreak Hotel ...'

'Ah,' said Liam, taking a large gulp of stout and leaning back in the seat, 'Elvis. *Heartbreak Hotel*. Now that's what I call a song!'

*

They didn't stay much longer but the sun was already beginning to drop down through the high trees in the hill opposite the car park as they left. An icy chill was returning to the air as they bundled into the car.

'Let me off at the corner,' said Liam, as they passed the park gates.

'Don't you want a lift down to Heraghty's Bar?' said Des.

'I've a few things to do at home, I'll pop down later.'

Liam pulled up his coat collar after closing the car door.

'I'll see you at your mum's next Friday then,' he said, '...eight o'clock, okay?'

'Fine! I'll see you there,' shouted Julie through the open window as Des pulled out to catch the traffic lights.

*

Julie turned on the TV as she came in. *Casablanca* was just starting on one of the movie channels.

'I think I'll have a lie down,' said Julie flopping on to the couch, 'that lunch and a couple of drinks have made me feel lazy.'

'Feel free, I'm going to finish off this paperwork,' said Des.

He stood in front of her and pulled his upper lip over his front teeth.

'Remember Paris?' He grimaced with a lousy American accent. 'I remember every detail. The Germans wore grey, you wore blue.'

'Oh, get out of the way,' she chortled as she snuggled down into the cushions.

Chapter 3

Perfectly legal

There was a short silence in the room. Charlie glanced over at George – he looked interested, which in Charlie's eyes meant he had no prior knowledge of Davidson's proposal.

'Perhaps you'd like to expand a little?' said Charlie.

'I don't want to overly complicate things at this stage. But I'll give you a name which you might know – Joe Kennedy.'

'Who doesn't know Joe Kennedy?' said George, with the hint of a sneer.

George looked over at a blank-faced Charlie and took it upon himself to explain.

'Kennedy's a big cheese in the movie business and the Democratic Party these days,' addressing Charlie, 'a millionaire's son who calls himself Irish. Hails from Boston.'

'He's also an astute businessman,' added Davidson, 'in the last few weeks he and James Roosevelt have imported a large inventory of liquor and managed to get the exclusive franchise for Dewar's scotch and Gordon gin amongst several other big players in the liquor business.'

'James Roosevelt? You mean the President's son?'

'Yes indeed.'

Charlie gave a soft impressed whistle.

'That's some connection.'

'Never heard anything about that,' said George, 'but makes a bit of sense, Kennedy put a lot of time and money into Roosevelt's campaign. I knew he and James were tight. After all, both were Democrats, both went to Harvard. Didn't think they would be up to any skulduggery.'

'No skulduggery, all perfectly legal and, anyway, Kennedy's old man made his fortune in the liquor business so there's nothing new here. Point I'm making is that if they're ploughing money into it, you can bet your bottom dollar that prohibition is sure to be repealed.'

'So, what is your proposition?' said George.

'Using my contacts in Scotland we could import whisky over here to the East Coast, Canada at a pinch, and store it in warehouses ready for release come the repeal. Remember, as I mentioned, there's a glut of good whisky over there. If we buy in bulk, we could get it at a knock down price.'

'Sounds interesting,' said George.

'Just a minute, Sandy,' said Charlie quickly, 'If it's such a good deal, why are you looking for investors?'

'Simple - I don't have enough spare capital. I probably could finance the whole thing myself but I'd be putting all my eggs in one basket. Regardless of what I've said, there still an element of risk involved.'

'Like what?'

'The law might not be repealed in the way we would like. They might repeal it only to allow real beer to be sold legally or they could ban specific kinds of booze like whisky or brandy or ban liquor of a certain strength. All highly unlikely, to be honest, but still a risk.'

'Anything else?' said George.

'Yes, well we could lose the lot in a storm at sea, but I've already formed a legitimate importing company to enable the investors to insure the cargo. Another slight risk would be some fraudulence or, more likely, some misunderstanding when dealing with the exporter. Things can go haywire when you're dealing with a large investment and relying on postal communication or telegrams.'

He looked over at Charlie.

'This is where you come in.'

'I'm not sure if I have the expertise for this sort of undertaking, there's a big difference between running a construction company and running an importing business.'

'True to a certain extent,' said Davidson, 'but I believe you have some knowledge of the import business.'

Charlie heard rather than saw George moving in his chair.

'Despite what you might have heard,' said Charlie, glaring over at George, who took a sudden interest in a couple of old envelopes lying on his desk, 'my knowledge is rather limited.'

'I have also heard,' replied Davidson, aware of Charlie's look, 'from other sources, I may say, that you are quite a resourceful sort of chap – a reliable kind of fella. You don't have to be an expert on company law or the intricacies of the import export business for what we had in mind.'

'And what exactly had you in mind?'

'Simply go over there and keep an eye on things, represent the investors, meet some of the guys in the business, you know, get the lay of the land. Don't get too caught up in prices or the legal aspects; we have a lawyer that we use in Glasgow - he'll look after those kinds of things. We'll also keep in touch by wire and telegraph. This is a fairly big investment for us and we've all agreed that we need someone on the ground. The pay is good – two thousand dollars plus all expenses paid for three or four weeks work.'

Charlie turned the figure over in his head.

Up to four years ago Charlie could clear four or five thousand a year easily; this past three years, even after laying off men, he was lucky to clear two thousand. It was tempting.

'When are you thinking of starting up?'

'Soon as we can. If you agree, we can get you over there in a couple of weeks' time, that's allowing for a six or seven day voyage. You shouldn't take more than a week or so to sort things out, then straight back.'

Charlie thought again. Two weeks was plenty of time to

organise his schedule and get someone to cover for his absence. More importantly he was walking out with a young lady in Philly for a few months now and they had become close, in fact, very close.

This shouldn't be a major problem, he thought quickly. Una was a senior nurse, a level headed woman who had occasion to be absent herself in emergencies. He'd be gone for three weeks, four weeks at most; *should be okay,* he half convinced himself.

'Give me a day to think it over,' he finally said.

Davidson stood up.

'Of course.'

Charlie lifted himself from the chair, walked over to Davidson and shook his hand.

'At the moment I'm inclined to accept, but there are one or two considerations to think about.'

'Sure. Here's my card, phone me tomorrow morning. I'm afraid I might have to head up to Boston later on in the day.'

*

'Okay, George!' said Charlie after seeing Davidson to the outer office door, 'What's going on here?'

'There nothing "going on" as you put it. I met Davidson and we talked for a while – mainly about timber supplies. Later on he mentioned that he was looking for investors for another business he was setting up.'

'What kind of business?'

'Oh, you know, just talked about his contacts in Scotland and opportunities to import some merchandise from there.'

'Really? So what merchandise was he thinking about? Some kilts perhaps? Maybe a few barrels of haggis? Oh no don't tell me, let me guess - some shortbread in fancy tins.'

'Goddamit, Charlie! There's no need for sarcasm.' said George, quite nettled.

'Whisky then.'

'So what! There's nothing illegal involved. It's all above board. Not only that, there is good profit involved.'

'I don't like this liquor business.'

'Are you kidding?' said George raising his voice, 'you're the one that's running an illegal speakeasy!'

He leaned across the table.

'The place is half owned by Slavinsky, and he mainly got involved for the bookie business he gets from it. He couldn't care less about drink. We employ a manager to run the booze part of it. I've got to do the rest. The cops from the local precinct have to get paid off; the local councillor is always at the tap for 'political donations'. And worst of all we have to buy our beer from that snake-eyed rat, O'Donnell. The reason Slavinsky wanted me in was because of my Irish connections, it made it look more 'authentic' he reckoned. What with all the kickbacks, I'm lucky if I get a hundred bucks a month from the joint.'

George gave a shrug.

'Nature of the business.'

'My point exactly,' said Charlie, 'If a two bit joint like The Country Club can attract a pack of wolves, like the O'Donnell's of this world, what do you think they'd do if they found out about Davidson's plan?'

'As I said, it's all perfectly legal.'

'These guys don't make subtle distinctions between legal and illegal. All they care about is easy money. In their eyes booze is easy money.'

Charlie saw George's eyes glaze over, he knew he was wasting his time.

There was a rap at the door as he turned away from the desk.

'Cablegram for you, Charlie,' said Mrs Green, 'Just arrived

this minute.'

'Thanks, Mrs G.,' he said, taking the brown envelope.

'Here, give this to the boy,' he added, handing over some change, 'and tell him to wait.'

He wasn't concerned about the cable, they were used constantly in business and occasionally required a reply, they were usually mundane rather than ominous.

He opened the envelope and pulled out the folded paper and scanned the message.

'Problem?' said George.

'No. Not at all,' Charlie replied, 'Una is asking if she could come up to New York for the weekend. I can't get back to Philly today; I have to go down to that job in Fulton Street tomorrow morning. I better give a reply.'

He went into the front office. The telegraph boy was sitting on the visitor chair swinging his legs.

'Can you take a quick message, Mrs G?'

'Sure thing,' she said pulling out a Western Union blank.

He wavered; he wasn't good at composing telegrams.

'Can I just tell you want I want to say and you can then translate it into a telegram?'

'Of course, Charlie, fire away.'

'Una is coming up to New York tonight for the weekend. She'll be arriving on the Royal Blue in Penn station around five o'clock. Just a minute,' he scratched his head, 'I'll need to book a couple of rooms…'

'How about the Lincoln? It's only a few minutes by cab from Penn station.'

'Good Idea. Can you do that for me?'

'Sure, I'll phone after I finish the cable.'

'Tell her to get a taxi to the Lincoln and I'll meet her there at, say, six o'clock. Give her a chance to settle in.'

He turned to go back into the office.

'Want me to book a show or a movie for tomorrow night?'

'Another good idea, Mrs G. I take it you have a recommendation?'

'There's a new Gloria Swanson over at the Paramount.'

He folded his arms and leaned against the door frame.

'Take it it's neither a cowboy movie nor a war movie.'

'No, but Una will love it.'

'Yes, and I'll hate it,' he said with a grin, 'might as well book it.'

He walked over to the stand to get his coat and hat and returned to the office.

'I'm off,' he said, 'I'll see you next week.'

'OK. I'm going back home tonight and I'll meet you here in the office on Tuesday around ten.'

Mrs G. had already sent the boy off with the cable and was phoning the Lincoln.

She put her hand over the phone.

'That's your rooms booked, Mr McKenna. I'll phone the Paramount in a minute.'

Charlie tipped his hat.

'You're one smart Patootie, Mrs G.'

*

Charlie pulled on his overcoat, and straightened his fedora in the elevator. He thought briefly about hailing a cab but decided to walk over to The Country Club. He had a few things to mull over. Tomorrow his squad, working from Fulton Street station, were blowing a wall in the subway to form a maintenance area. Not normally a problem but it could be a disaster if anything went wrong. He just wanted to be around to give the men a bit of support if nothing else. They were due to blast at 9:30. All going well, he could easily finish at noon. He also wanted to think over the Davidson offer. The proposition, he had realised, may have come at a rather opportune moment.

Returning to America in '23 had been a fraught time for him. His fiancé and one of his nephews had died from a sudden flu epidemic in the winter of early '23. He cursed himself for not keeping in touch. Yet it seemed the right thing to do at the time. He and George had cavorted about Paris while Charlie renewed his passport without leaving any forwarding address in case the Irish Free State authorities caught up with them. It never occurred to him that anything would happen in his absence; it was a decision that left Charlie riddled with guilt. It was the stoic forbearance of his sister and brother-in-law that kept him sane. He worked hard for the next few years gradually building up his own subcontracting business mainly with George but with several other contractors, especially in New York. The Crash hit him like everyone else but he invested most of his money building up the business. So, as luck would have it, he had very little money to indulge in stocks and shares or, indeed, not that much money in the bank – so he lost little and survived – just.

Until a few years ago he rarely attended anything other than formal social occasions, in fact it was at one such occasion that he was introduced to Una Fitzgerald. They met at a party given by the nearest thing to royalty in the Irish community in Philadelphia – the Kellys. It was a reception given for the Irish Free State ambassador a couple of years ago. Una was the daughter of a professional diplomat, a formal civil servant of Dublin Castle. Her mother was a Scotswoman from the Hebrides and Una herself was brought up mainly in Scotland and had trained as a nurse in a Glasgow hospital. It was this common thread that got them talking that night. Over the following months they started dating. Things started to get serious when her father was recalled to Dublin during one of the endemic Irish economic disasters of the late '20s and she decided to stay on in Philadelphia. She had a good job in the Pennsylvania Hospital and was part of an emergency team that was rushed to natural and man-made disaster points like floods and mine explosions. Their relationship had grown intense over the past year and there had been hints of marriage and a possible return to Europe. This Davidson business might give him an opportunity to look around and weigh up the possibility of leaving the States. Perhaps Glasgow could be a starting point.

It didn't take long to cover the ground from the office to The Country Club on Seventh Avenue.

From the street the club was a fairly traditional American restaurant with a vague Irish theme. The overhead shop sign was painted in what Americans regarded as Gaelic lettering with a few shamrocks thrown in for good measure. The premises had a central door on the street pavement that divided the shop frontage into two areas. To the left was the main restaurant serving area which was fronted by plate glass. Two thick gilded curtains, which opened in the middle, covered the outer edges of the window and an opaque lace curtain covered the lower half. This gave the illusion of openness to passers-by - they could see into the restaurant although in reality they could see very little. To the right was a full length display window featuring a couple of manikins sitting at a table being served by a waiter. This tableau was surprisingly artistic and drew customers to the large menu posted on the left of the window. The food was excellent and wholesome, if a bit bland. Steaks and mutton chops were standard, as were the popular 'blue plate' specials of slow cooked stews. At this time of day business was slow but steady. It usually started getting busy around five o'clock. Charlie walked through the central doorway. To his left was the main body of the restaurant shielded by a shoulder high wood panelled partition; to his right was a plain wall with a few soft drink adverts and some large photographs of the more illustrious diners like baseball players Mel Ott and Lou Gehrig. Towards the end of this short corridor was a left turn into the main dining area. However, a few steps on and to your right was a doorway leading to the bar. This doorway was accessed through two heavy curtains and manned by a pleasant young Irishman called Neil.

'Good afternoon, Mr McKenna,' he said with a lilting West of Ireland accent.

'And yourself,' replied Charlie.

The bar was agreeably busy, mainly men from The Times, some reporters, some office workers and some 'inkies', as the printers were called, took up a corner near the front door. There was a table with four or five young ladies in the other corner. At their back was a curtain which disguised the wall which formed the backdrop of the tableau in the front window. The whole undertaking was a shallow sham of course. A mere pantomime of going through the motions of legality which fooled no one, including the legislators of City Hall. The restaurant half was run legitimately by the hard working Sweeney family while the bar was owned by Charlie and Page Slavinsky and run by Peter Sharkey and his tribe of brothers and cousins of whom one of the youngest was Neil. Charlie organised the purchase of the booze and the backhanders. The hard drink was easy to arrange, two or three cases a week was enough to stock the bar; the same applied to wine. The beer, the most profitable commodity, was supplied by the local would-be gangster Manny O'Donnell. Charlie walked through the bar slowly; shaking hands, stopping to talk to known customers and introducing himself to newcomers. As he got closer to the bar, Peter Sharkey signalled him over.

'You've got a visitor, Charlie.'

'Who'd that be then?' he replied, smiling and nodding over to the local alderman.

'O'Donnell,' said Sharkey.

'I take it that he's in the office.' said Charlie, barely able to keep the contempt from his voice. O'Donnell irritated him on a variety of levels, most of all his ludicrous ham-acting performance of a movie screen gangster.

'I'll go up and see him.'

As he turned away Sharkey laid his hand on his arm. He whispered urgently.

'Watch it, Charlie, he's got Vincent McGhee with him.'

Charlie gave Sharkey a nod and turned his back to the bar. He tugged at his shirt sleeves, mainly to compose himself. O'Donnell and McGhee might be a dangerous pairing. This did not look good.

Chapter 4

The mysterious book

Liam had left the house a bit earlier than he thought. Looking at his watch, after he had walked down the front steps and turned left, he found he was about fifteen minutes early, but he was not too concerned. He looked skywards, it was dark, damp and a bit cold but not raining; it was simply a matter of taking a longer route to the McKenna's house just beyond Mount Florida. Those expecting sunshine, everglades or the blue rimmed Keys of Florida would be sadly disappointed at this typical Victorian urban village huddled around a railway station on Glasgow's south side. One or two half decent restaurants, a good butcher's shop and a couple of soulless bars just about summed the place up, Liam thought as he wandered through the quiet canyons of red stone tenements. He had been up early the past few days finishing off a photographic exhibition that opened that morning and was feeling surprisingly tired.

'Must be the first signs of getting old,' he thought glumly.

Not only that, but he hated house parties of any kind and decided that an hour, give or take, would be more than enough to pass himself. He consoled himself in the knowledge that Grace McKenna always put on a good spread.

The McKenna house was a sprawling Edwardian pile half way up a hill. Liam was on time and was greeted by Eddie McKenna at the door.

'Come on in. Give me your coat!'

The senior McKenna was a man best avoided; a man who, despite his educational achievements, was a perennial fourteen-year-old who could be both irritatingly cheerful and boringly juvenile. Liam handed over his coat and scarf cautiously and noted exactly where Eddie placed them on the coat rack; he was already planning his escape route. He wandered into the spacious drawing room where at least a dozen of the great and the good of the South Side were already milling around drinking from champagne flutes or nicely cut whisky glasses; he recognised most of them. The French windows opened out on to the lawn where a marquee had been erected.

'Ah! Liam, over here,' said Grace McKenna just loud enough to be heard across the room.

Liam sauntered over to the bar, nodding to one group and waving at someone he vaguely knew.

'I got in some of that ghastly stout stuff you drink.'

'Grace, you look lovely as usual, and my word, that dress shows off your figure perfectly.'

'Oh for goodness sake, Liam, cut it out!' she snapped, her neck turning a light shade of pink, as she patted the back of her hair. 'Here,' she said handing him over a can as if it was a dead rat, '… and don't even think about drinking it straight from the can!' she barked as Liam's hand hovered over the ring pull, 'Use this.'

She pushed over a fancy Belgian beer glass with neat lace doily underneath.

He wasn't too keen on any drink that came in a can; he made a face as he took a mouthful.

'To your son's tenth wedding anniversary,' he said.

'Indeed,' said Grace, lifting her glass.

'Where is he?' asked Liam, looking around.

'Probably talking to some oaf about rugby I'd say.'

'Em ... how is Richard these days?'

'Richard's a blockhead,' she said casually, 'fortunately he's a harmless and a rather affable blockhead. He has a post with the local authority promoting sports activities.' She looked vaguely into the middle distance. 'How he ever managed to find paid employment is still a mystery to me, anyway,' she said, flinging back the rest of her drink, 'I need to go. I'm afraid I've got to mingle.'

She walked out from behind the small bar.

'I'll see you later,' she added ominously over her shoulder.

Liam edged towards the French windows and the marquee.

'Excuse me,' said a small voice.

Liam looked to his left and down.

'You might not remember me. I met you a few months ago at the funeral.'

'Ah! Yes, you're …' said Liam, hesitating for a moment, he was good at putting names to faces, '…you're Julie's sister, Eileen.'

Eileen was flattered and taken aback that he remembered her at all.

'Yes that's right. Remember I showed you an old watch belonging to our grandfather Charlie McKenna? You seemed quite interested in it.'

'The one that your uncle Pat gave to you?' said Liam, 'Of course I do. I remember it had an inscription on the back… something like, New York 1920 with someone's name on it if I remember right.'

'George Peebles.'

'That's right. Well remembered.'

'Julie told me you might be here tonight so I brought something else that Pat gave me that might interest you.'

She pulled open her handbag and took out what looked like a box about the size of a very small paperback book.

'He gave me this about the same time, I think it's a box of some kind but I couldn't get it opened so I left it in an old cupboard in my room. I forgot all about it until you showed an interest in the watch. Here take it,' she said handing it over.

'Well I don't know…'

'Please take it. Just let me know if you find anything of interest.'

'Hi there, Liam,' said Julie coming through the French windows, 'glad you could make it.'

'Where the heck is Richard?' said Eileen, 'I've been looking everywhere for him.'

'He's out in the garden with some pals,' replied Julie with a sigh, 'they seem to be horsing around practising rugby tackles or some such nonsense.'

'Well, I'd better go and see him now. I'm heading off shortly.'

She turned back to Liam.

'I spent ages rummaging about that dusty old cupboard before I found that,' she with a quiet laugh, pointing to the box, 'I hope it's worth it.'

'Oh! What's all this then?' said Julie.

'Just something your uncle Pat gave to Eileen,' said Liam, slipping it into his pocket, 'I'll have a look at it later.'

'In the meantime,' he added, rubbing his hands, 'let's off to the marquee and see what's a'cookin out there.'

*

Liam went immediately to the top table and started lifting up lids.

'It's okay, sir, I'll do that,' said one of the two young ladies behind the table.

'Sorry I didn't realise…' said Liam with a short cough of embarrassment.

'That's okay. Now then,' she said, 'for the hot food we have three different kinds of curry.' She started to lift the lids of various pots. '…and we have Chilli Con Carne. We have Sweet and Sour. We have…'

'Hold on a minute, did you say Chilli Con Carne?'

'Made by my mother herself,' chipped in Julie.

'I thought as much. Well, that's the boy for me then.'

The young girl neatly dressed in a black uniform ladled out two heaps of chilli on a deep plate.

'Rice, sir?'

'Anything else other than rice?'

'How about some warm tortillas' She waved her hands like a conjuror's assistant over the table, 'or perhaps some nice crusty bread?'

'Is that mash potatoes there?' he said pointing to a bowl.

'Well, yes, well sort of, it's actually Colcannon, that's mash potatoes with kale.'

'And some spring onion by the looks of it,' added Liam, 'the very dab. Throw a couple of ladles of that on the plate as well.'

The girl dithered.

'Are you sure?'

'It's okay, on you go.'

With a shrug she did as instructed.

They moved back into the lounge.

'I got some good news,' said Julie, 'I've managed to get flights to Cork for a week on Wednesday. We'll be returning on Saturday on a later flight than yours.'

'That's grand!' said Liam, genuinely pleased, 'I thought you weren't all that serious when you first mentioned it.'

He started wolfing into the Chilli as he spoke.

'It should be great crack, there are some great pubs in Cork.'

They were joined by Des and another woman who Liam recognised as a fatuous and ludicrously ambitious primary school teacher.

They had just finished saying their hellos when she suddenly asked,

'Is that … colcannon you're having with chilli con carne?'

'It is indeed! All the rage in Dublin,' replied Liam confidently. 'Now surely you've heard of Tex-Mex, a combination of Mexican and Texan food?' he continued, hamming up his Irish accent.

'Oh yes,' she replied blandly.

'Well this here is...' he paused for a split second, 'Mick-Mex - a fusion of Irish and Mexican cuisine. Heard it's all the go in London as well now.'

'Oh really!' she said, looking at Liam briefly and with disinterest. Her eyes were already scoping the room behind him. She spotted a local councillor who was a big hitter on the Education committee.

'Sorry,' she said smiling and touching Liam's arm lightly, 'must dash!'

And she was off.

'Mary something or other,' said Liam twirling his fork in the air, 'McBride was it?'

'Used to be,' said Des, 'It's now Maria de Cardosi, she married some Paisley guy with an Italian surname apparently to further her ambition to become Director of Education. She reckons the Scottish Office considers anyone with an Irish surname as a bog trotter just off the boat. On the other hand Scottish Italians, she believes, are regarded as somewhat more assiduous and much more exotic.'

'Having an Italian surname yourself, Des Capaldi, no doubt you agree,' said Julie.

'For goodness sake, Julie, of course I don't. The woman is a half cracked, ruthless and deluded fool.'

'Should go far in Education then,' said Liam dryly.

'Anyway I've had enough,' he added scooping up the last of the chilli.

'I'm out of here within the next ten minutes if that woman is a sample of the guests your mother has invited. And even worse, I didn't like the tone of your mother's voice when she said she would speak to me later.'

In the course of the next five minutes a plan was hatched. Des would go back to the hallway and get Liam's coat and scarf and nip out the front door. In the meantime Liam would escape via an opening in the marquee tent when given the all clear by Julie that the area outside was clear of any lurking smokers. He would then make his way across the garden and down the west side of the house to the driveway where he would meet up with Des.

'Ah! Liam, I've been looking for you.'

All three turn around with a start.

'Julie was telling me…' Grace stopped and narrowed her eyes, 'what are you three up to?'

'Nothing,' said Liam blandly.

'Something to do with this trip to Cork I suspect.'

'Oh, that!' replied Julie with a little puff of relief.

'Yes that. I don't want you coming back here with any of your wild stories Liam Tracey. The last time you almost convinced me that Charlie McKenna took part in a gold robbery and old Uncle Pat was part of some sort of murder gang in Tralee.'

'Just a minute. I never said…' blustered Liam.

'You said near as damn it. Just a warning that's all. Now I need to go into the library to see councillor McNabb.'

She walked through the entrance to the library and gave them all a suspicious look before closing the door behind her.

The plan worked a treat and soon Liam was striding down Queens Drive towards home. But he was distracted. He slowed down as something that Grace had mentioned suddenly drifted through his head.

Where did she get the idea Charlie was involved in a gold robbery? I don't recall making remarks about the provenance of the gold sovereigns to anyone, let alone Grace.

He had often pondered about the appearance of several gold sovereigns before the murder of Mick Hastings. It was put down as some sort of McKenna family tradition for both Charlie and his brother Pat to hand out a gold sovereign on big events like weddings and births. Grace had shown him the remains of a roll of coins, four or five coins if he remembered correctly, that had had something like *Saorstat eEireann* – Free State of Ireland - printed on the roll cover. The coins he had seen were all in mint condition and all had the same date -1916 - which, as he had wryly pointed out at the time, was a remarkable coincidence. He was almost sure - he suddenly stopped walking. In fact he was positive that he had never mentioned, or even speculated, about the possibility of a robbery of any kind. If anything Grace was quite flippant about the coins. Why did she blurt out anything about a robbery?

He started walking again now deep in thought. Julie had once made a remark about Charlie taking two of his young sons, including a young Eddie McKenna, Grace's husband and Julie's father, on a trip to Cork around the early '50s. It wasn't long after this that, according to Eddie, he bought the house in Mount Florida. He didn't know too much about house prices but at a guess a house the size of the McKennas' would go for over a million quid on the West Side of Glasgow, perhaps a bit less over here, he thought. It hadn't crossed his mind before but he was sure Charlie McKenna worked as some sort of local authority middle management type in the building department - hardly the sort to purchase a piece of real estate of that value. Also, he reflected, in the '50s Charlie would have been getting on close to sixty years old - hardly an age when mortgage companies would be queuing up to hand over money for a property that size. Then again, perhaps he was reading too much into it all.

He took a sudden notion for a decent pint of stout to round off the day and quickly crossed the road beyond his own street to his local bar. It was pleasantly busy without being too overcrowded. He ordered a pint and retrieved the object in his pocket and turned it over in his hand.

It wasn't a box, as he had thought, but a small book with a locking device on the open edge, although he could immediately see why a mistake could be made as the pages were cut flush to the book's cover.

His pint arrived and he took a large hearty draft.

He leaned on the bar and looked closely at the locking device searching for a tiny aperture or keyhole ... nothing. He pressed the lock down but it didn't move, he tried upwards ... a slight give. He wrapped his index finger along the top and applied more pressure with his thumb and to his surprise the lock sprung open with a tiny click. Just as he was about to ruffle through the book pages, a deep voice to his left grunted.

'It's yourself, Liam.'

It was Sam Adams, an old friend of Liam.

'Yourself,' replied Liam nodding back. 'Another pint and a large whisky, malt, if you've got one, with one piece of ice – for Sam here,' he added as the barman began a search through the bottles on the well-stocked gantry for Sam's favourite malt.

Sam had what romantics call a nut brown voice, although others often referred to it as a smoke raddled croak.

'Thanks, Liam. What are you up to these days? Haven't seen you for a while.'

'Oh, this and that,' said Liam, locking the book and returning it to his pocket. 'Just opened a photographic exhibition up in the library.'

Liam had a lot of time for Sammy – they went back a bit. They fell into an animated discussion on the merits of various photographers as the rain starting pouring down on the street outside.

'Another pint?'

'No thanks, Sam, I'm for the off,' said Liam, looking towards the open door, 'the rain's easing a bit.'

Liam walked over and tested the weather by sticking his hand out.

'Down to a drizzle,' he said going back to finish off his pint, 'I'll catch you later.'

He heard Sam shouting goodnight as he hurried into the street. The rain started lashing down two minutes before he reached his front door.

'Damn the rain!' he said aloud as he hurried up the stairs and into the flat. He was not quite soaked through but damp enough to be annoyed. A quick hot shower before he went to bed would be ideal. He stripped off and padded into the bathroom throwing his wet clothes into a laundry basket. The shower revived him a bit but he still felt tired; he changed into some clean nightwear and headed for the bedroom. The sheets had a delightfully fresh aroma when he pulled back the duvet; he had forgotten that Mrs Wilson, his cleaner, always changed the bed on a Friday. He switched on the bedside light and hopped in with a satisfying sigh. The rain slashed against the window as he laid his head on the pillow. He was almost overcome by the fragrance of the sheets and the rhythmic beat of the rain. His head began to slowly sink into the pillow...

'The book!' he cried out suddenly.

He got up, went out into the hall and pulled the book from his coat pocket. On returning, he turned on his reading light, switched off the bedside lamp and puffed up the pillows. Lying on his left side he settled down in a pool of light, and started to flick through the book. It was acquired, it appeared, in Paris in late 1922. About half of it was a type of diary and, like all diaries, the early weeks were filled in and then gradually the entries became shorter and less frequent until they petered out around March. The other half was more like a notebook. This part was filled with neat, closely written text. Liam reached out and put on his reading glasses.

I was born Charles McKenna in North Donegal near the town of ...

Outside the rain had calmed down to a steady patter and Liam could hear the occasional and oddly comforting wet swish of car tyres on the street below.

He read on.

Chapter 5

The Country Club

Behind the bar in The Country Club, closed off by a heavy brocade curtain, was a back stairway to the rooms of the upper floor. Charlie used one of these as an office which he kept locked; an adjoining room was used as a waiting room for anyone who came to see him. Several of the other rooms were used by Slavinsky or his runners and were also locked when not in use. O'Donnell and McGhee were sitting in the comfortable armchairs in the waiting room nursing a couple of soft drinks.

O'Donnell stood up right away, arm and hand outstretched.

'Charlie! How the devil are you?'

'Great, just great, come on into the office.'

McGhee wavered, unsure if the invitation extended to him.

'Vinnie,' said Charlie, giving a discrete nod, 'why don't you go down to the bar and have a few drinks? On the house, of course.'

One thing Charlie knew was that hoodlums of McGhee's standing rarely refused anything that was free.

'Sure, Charlie,' said McGhee heading for the staircase.

O'Donnell was caught off balance; he would have preferred McGhee to have accompanied him into the office. To order him back from the bar would have been regarded as bad manners and, knowing McGhee's mental state and his inclination to take offence easily, possibly quite dangerous.

'Well then, Manny. What brings you over to this side of town?' said Charlie, as he settled into the chair behind his desk. The room was about 10 feet by 12 feet. In the corner was a roll top desk beside the large single window overlooking the busy Seventh Avenue.

'Oh, just passing, thought I'd put my head in to see if you'd thought any more about my offer.'

Charlie said nothing.

'Just bumped into Vinnie on the street,' added O'Donnell, 'I thought I'd buy him a drink, you know, have a chat about old times.'

Yes, I'll bet you did, thought Charlie grimly.

'Still thinking it over, Manny. It's a good offer, almost tempting.'

He had made him an offer for The Country Club a week ago. He hadn't thought about it too much and what with today's developments it had almost escaped his mind. O'Donnell, he knew, wasn't particularly interested in the bar or the restaurant but he had only recently discovered that the leasehold included the whole building including the rooms they were sitting in now. The upper floors could be easily converted to small bedrooms. They were close to Times Square and Broadway - almost, in O'Donnell's mind, an ideal position for a cathouse; the call girl business was one that O'Donnell was beginning to find more profitable over the past few months. This much was obvious from the amount of cash he was offering. Charlie knew all this but he was pretty indifferent to how a gangster made his money – it was always crooked, no matter what business they were in.

'What about the restaurant?' said Charlie.

'The restaurant and the bar are not a problem. They stay.'

'I still have to persuade Slavinsky to move out.'

'Persuade him?' said O'Donnell with a sneer, 'He's a goddamn two-bit bookie! Put a gun to his head – that'll persuade him.'

'Don't worry. He's my problem if we do the deal. Listen, I've got a bit of business to take care of over the next few weeks. How about meeting me in about a month's time. In the meantime, I'll get in touch with my lawyer and we can organise the transfer of the lease.'

'So you've made your mind up then?'

'Almost, depending on your side of the bargain. Get your

lawyer to draw up a formal offer and I'll do business.'

'Lawyers huh! What happened to good old fashioned handshakes to do a deal?'

'That ended in the crash of 1929,' said Charlie standing up. 'Let's go downstairs and I'll buy you a drink.'

*

Charlie did not encourage McGhee or O'Donnell to hang around, nor did he have to. They left after twenty minutes. For all their bluster and flash, The Country Club was just a shade too classy for them. It was outside their normal stomping ground and they were noticeably ill at ease. They were more at home a few blocks west, closer to Hell's Kitchen, where there were plenty of dingy bars they could visit and lord it over the local lushes, toadies and barflies in comfort.

Charlie was glad to see the back of them.

He wandered around for half an hour glad-handing the customers. There were no problems. With the Sharkeys on the bar, the place virtually ran itself.

He left around 5:00 and made his way up to the Lincoln.

A few things were turning over in his mind.

O'Donnell's offer would triple his and Slavinsky's investment in the four years since they signed the lease. Slavinsky would bite the hand off O'Donnell for that kind of return and now that he had built up a clientèle and a team of runners in the area he could operate from anywhere. It was obvious that O'Donnell had no idea of the value of the property ... and Charlie was not of a mind to enlighten him.

So, he figured, they should clear around a grand from the deal. The idea of upping sticks and moving out of the USA was becoming more attractive.

After he made his way through the revolving doors, he slipped

Arthur, the doorman, a dollar bill and told him to watch out for a young lady arriving in a taxi and to direct her to the booking desk. He hurried up the stairs to the reception area of the hotel and spoke to the under manager. The room keys were handed over along with a neat white envelope. Momentarily puzzled, Charlie opened the envelope with the paper knife on the hotel desk, and in it found two tickets for the Paramount for the movie *Perfect Understanding* - it even sounded awful.

Charlie took a seat opposite the desk, pulled forward a newspaper and tried to relax. He was still feeling uneasy about the appearance of Vinnie McGhee.

*

There was a slight kerfuffle as Una arrived. The doorman was looking around desperately for Charlie who had his head in the paper poring over some interesting events in Ireland. He looked up just as the doorman spread his hands in dismay to Una and he immediately stood up and signalled to attract his attention.

'Ah, there you are, sir,' he said, 'the young lady was earlier than expected.'

Charlie glanced at the lobby clock.

'Never mind, I'm here now,' said Una brightly, holding up her face for a welcoming kiss.

Charlie obliged.

'Una,' he said after giving her a warm hug, 'you're a sight for sore eyes. Come over here and have seat.'

'So, how was the journey?'

'Great, the Blue Line is terrific. Always on time.'

'I've booked a couple of tickets for the Paramount. Show starts in about an hour and a half; I'm not sure about having time to eat…'

'Don't worry about me, I had a late lunch on the train.'

'Fine. I'll book a supper in here for 10 o'clock.'

'Sounds good to me. What's the movie?' Una asked as she started taking off her gloves.'

'*Perfect Understanding.*'

'Swanson's latest!' said Una excitedly, 'It just premièred last week. How the heck did you manage to get tickets?'

Charlie looked a bit embarrassed, he wasn't quite sure what 'premièred' meant but guessed it meant something good.

'You give me too much credit. It was Mrs Greene, our secretary, managed to organise the tickets.'

'Well good on her!'

'Would you like a coffee?'

'No thanks, Charlie. Do you mind if I go upstairs and freshen up? I feel a bit grubby after the train journey.'

'I'll tell you what. I'll book the dining room and go back to my place, have a shower and change into a jacket and flannels. I only put this business suit on because George insisted on introducing me to one of his pals from downtown.'

'So, how did it go with George's pal?'

'Interesting. We'll talk about it at supper.'

He called over a bell boy and looked up at the clock.

'I'll send someone up to the room when I get back, let's say… half past six.'

He gave the bell boy a quarter to take up the bags and kissed Una on the cheek.

'See you in an hour.'

*

Charlie had an apartment on Forty-Seventh Street, a street to the east of Eighth Avenue and only a couple of blocks away from the Lincoln. It was an extravagance for Charlie as he spent a fair bit of time in Philadelphia these days. Thing was, he got it cheap two years ago at $35 a month for a five-year lease; it let him escape from the confines of the various lodgings and bachelor rooms on the upper west side. The lease was not a problem; he had made a few inquiries in the past few days and he could sell on the lease for a couple of months' rents - might even get a hundred or so for it. He took his time shaving and showering before setting out a lightweight tweed jacket and some cotton trousers. Again he was turning over a few things in his head. The recent events concerning The Country Club had made him uneasy. O'Donnell had few endearing features, it didn't worry Charlie, he had become used to dealing with bruisers like O'Donnell and could handle them. Most of the self-styled gangsters, he found, were not much smarter than the average street hoodlum. McGhee, on the other hand, was a different kettle of fish. At one time he was a hired assassin for one of the Irish mobs in Hell's Kitchen deep in the West Side before deciding to cut loose. Not content with the usual simple run-of-the-mill rackets of bootlegging and armed robbery he moved into a new area of business – kidnapping. Last year he was involved in at least two abductions, not the usual modus operandi of snatching famous people's children or their relatives, but those of notorious gangsters. In both cases he was said to have netted five thousand dollars. Anyone involved in that line of business, Charlie reckoned, was quite clearly not far from insanity. One redeeming feature was the fact that McGhee was originally from Donegal; from a windswept, rock strewn area known as Gweedore, a desolate, barren place even by West Donegal standards. Among some of the Irish, coming from the same county made you practically blood brothers. Not a fraternal notion that McGhee was likely to pay much attention to.

He turned his attention to the day's events. Charlie was never a great believer in blind providence but the offer of the trip to Europe seemed remarkably timely. By chance he and Una had talked over the idea of returning to Scotland or possibly Ireland this last few months. Una was missing her family badly and would return in a minute. Charlie on the other hand had liked living in America but he was becoming increasingly uneasy about New York. More importantly he had decided that Una's wishes were paramount; he knew that he wanted to be with her and where they lived was, to him, irrelevant. In several ways, he thought, Scotland might be preferable. He felt there was still a risk in returning to Ireland. The events of August 1922 had long since passed, but over time Ireland had bred a race of people with long memories. Why bother taking any chances? He had a considerable amount of money still tied up in Cork but that could wait. He left the apartment and headed back to the Lincoln and as he dodged his way through the excited bustling Friday night throng he felt his reservations drift away and he began to look forward to his evening with Una.

*

The Paramount was in Times Square and it was packed full. As he suspected the movie was drab and predictable; Una watched it closely and said she loved it, rehearsing and repeating chunks of dialogue as they left the cinema. More, Charlie suspected, to better impress her friends in Philly than anything else. Cab Callaway and his orchestra played before the movie show which saved the night for Charlie. *Minnie the Moocher* was a hot favourite among New Yorkers and the audience joined in the chorus with enthusiastic handclapping and cat calling.

The evening had turned to a light rain as they left the Paramount. Charlie turned up his collar and Una starting giggling as she struggled with her brolly. As they hurried through the crowd it turned into a regular downpour and they almost fell into the lobby of the Lincoln.

'Here let me take care of that,' said Arthur, taking the brolly from Una, 'I'll put it into the cloakroom to dry off and take it up to your room later.'

He turned to Charlie.

'I've arranged a table in your rooms; I'll have supper sent up in twenty minutes and I've left an ice bucket with some soda as you arranged.'

'Thanks, Arthur, good work.'

The Lincoln Hotel could not sell booze legally so various tiresome ruses were used to circumvent the liquor laws. Having supper or dinner in one's room enabled couples or parties of people to smuggle drink into the hotel. 'Smuggle' was hardly the correct word as the practice was commonplace and relatively open, even in the most hidebound of hotels. Before they left for the Paramount Charlie had handed over a few dollars to Arthur for the arrangement and the supply of some beers and wine.

Una threw her coat on the bed and walked over to the French windows leading to the small stone balcony.

'The rain's stopped,' she said pulling open the doors.

The balcony overlooked Seventh Avenue.

'What a view,' she sighed as she looked across the New York skyline.

She turned, looked back into the room and rested her elbows on the balustrade.

Charlie laughed.

'Easy seeing you're a movie fan, Una.'

'Damn! I thought you would never notice!'

She swayed into the room with exaggerated self-confidence.

'Open the bubbly while I …freshen up,' she said with an equally exaggerated Jean Harlow whisper.

Charlie laughed again.

The waiter brought in the food just as she was heading into the bedroom.

She looked over.

'Wow, fillet steak!' She immediately about-turned. 'I guess freshening up can wait for a while; I'm famished.'

*

They discussed several things over dinner, nothing major, mainly idle gossip about mutual friends.

Before dessert Charlie mentioned his possible trip to Europe.

'Nothing finalised yet, but it could all be arranged in the course of the next few weeks.'

'Sounds fun, do you want me to come along?' said Una casually.

Charlie was taken aback as the thought had never occurred to him. He was about to form an answer when Una cocked her head and replied.

'Hmm, come to think of it, that's not a great idea. I've put my name down for a course in midwifery. It starts in two weeks and if I miss it this time the chance might not come along again for another few years.'

'I didn't realise that you'd be keen on that side of nursing.'

'Not sure if keen is the word; I like to keep up to date and there's been some interesting developments in that field, that's all. It's not an intensive course – two or three weeks at most. In fact, some of it involves attending an upstate hospital near Allentown. I'll probably have to stay there for a week – maybe two.'

'Well then, looks like we won't see each other for a couple of weeks.'

'Ah well, as my mother says, absence makes the heart grow fonder,' said Una, patting the back of his hand. 'And what's all this about selling The Country Club?'

'Someone made me an offer a couple of weeks ago. To tell you the truth I had almost forgot all about it until today when the guy turned up at the bar.'

'Anyone I know?'

'Manny O'Donnell ... and I doubt if you know him,' answered Charlie. 'In fact if you did know him, I'd be worried,'

He pushed himself from the table and walked over to an ice-filled tub.

'I think I'll have a chilled beer – want anything?'

'No thanks, I'll just finish off the wine.'

'He's made a good offer. I'm seriously thinking of taking it up,' he said coming back to the table, 'Have to convince Slavinsky of course, but that should be no problem.'

'I always quite liked the idea of you running a New York speakeasy. It was always a good talking point at those endless cocktail parties organised by the Kellys.'

Una thought for a moment.

'It gave you a certain dangerous glamour,' she added with a wistful sigh.

'Glamour? Glamour was always a bit short around The Country Club.'

'Oh, I suppose so,' she replied, 'but you know what I mean.'

'Anyway, I'm going to give it some serious thought. I'm becoming convinced that prohibition will end shortly.'

'So why is this O'Donnell fella so keen to buy it?'

'It seems he has a different business plan for the place… not that he has discussed it with me,' he added quickly, 'in a way it's none of my concern.' He paused. 'Remember we talked about going back to Europe a while back?'

'Yes I do, but I kind of gave up as you didn't seem that keen at the time.'

'I've had another think about it. This little trip might be interesting. It'll give me an idea of what it's like back there.'

'Much the same as we left it I suppose.'

'You forget it's been a lot longer for me; I've been in America for nearly ten years now - you kind of forget places and people. Things can change in ten years.'

He stood up and paced across the room nervously.

'There's something else …' he said.

'What else?' Una replied, becoming alarmed.

He stood behind her and put his hands lightly on her shoulders.

'Do you think it would be a good idea to get married when I get back?'

Una turned around, putting her hand on his.

'Well then, Charlie McKenna,' said Una, with a combination of relief and delight, 'as marriage proposals go it's not exactly down on one knee with flowers and a diamond ring but it's good enough for me!'

She jumped up off the seat.

'And the answer is yes – I think it's a great idea!'

Chapter 6

The Conway Hotel

The sun had been up for a half an hour and Liam, leaning on the parapet of St. Patrick's bridge, had been watching the large black bird for ten minutes. It never moved. It sat on an upright blackened timber pile about six feet out in the River Lee. Liam was coming round to the idea that it was some sort of statue, some sort of feature in the river for gullible tourists like himself. The timber pile was slowly becoming more exposed as the tide was starting to wash out. Suddenly the bird turned and appeared to look Liam in the eye, at the same time he felt a shadow pass over him.

'Good morning, sir,' said a voice behind him. 'Sure it's a fine morning to be looking down at the river that gave the wonderful city of Cork its prosperity.'

Turning round Liam found a small elderly man, tidily dressed although a bit shabby, looking at him with the well-practised air of an expectant and happy leprechaun. His nose had the red glow of a constant drinker. Liam lay back against the bridge with one arm leaning on the parapet. He sighed. What was it about bridges that appealed to jakies and down-and-outs? What was it about rivers that drew them like iron filings to a magnet?

'You wouldn't ….' the little man faltered and looked around as if he was suddenly aware that it was very early in the morning, 'have the price of a cup of tea, would you?'

'Here,' said Liam pulling out a two Euro coin from his change, 'take this.'

'Kind of you, sir,' said the little man, 'you're not from round here are you? You sound like a man from the black north.'

'You're right. I'm from Tyrone, but I live in Glasgow now.'

'Glasgow you say,' said the man, rubbing his chin in a moment of reflection, 'I once knew a man who went to Glasgow - Joseph Gilmore.'

Liam thought for a moment.

'Can't say I know anyone…'

'Oh no! You wouldn't know him,' said the man, turning to walk away, 'he's been dead past thirty years, last I heard.'

The old man walked off, down to Bridge Street with a sprightly step.

Liam chuckled and shook his head as he turned and walked in the opposite direction. The Imperial Hotel was only a five-minute walk away, if that. He cut through to his left, down one of the narrow lanes near Patrick Street and threaded his way down to the South Mall. The sun was rapidly disappearing behind the large overcast clouds that hung over the city all week. At least, he thought, it wasn't raining. As he turned into the Mall his was view blocked by two enormous coaches dropping visitors at the entrance and he had to waltz and shimmy his way through the crowd at the foyer and then make his way to the breakfast dining area.

Helen was sitting in an armchair in a small ante-room before the dining area. She waved him over.

'It's okay,' she said, 'I've just arrived down myself. Good timing.'

'You haven't ordered yet?'

'No, not yet.'

'Right then,' he said, slapping at his coat pockets distractedly, 'I'll em… just pop up and put my coat away. Order me the usual and a pot of tea.'

'Here,' said Helen, handing over a small card. 'Is this what you're looking for?'

'Ah yes! The key or whatever these things are called nowadays. Back in a jiffy.'

It was still relatively early and the dining room was nearly empty. She ordered breakfast from a passing waiter. Some lightly scrambled eggs for herself and the usual mound of breakfast items for Liam. When someone else was doing the cooking, she had noticed, Liam, like most bachelors, ate like a primeval predator – filling up when the going was good.

She gathered up the newspaper she had picked up in the expectation of Liam being late and walked through to the dining area; she had spotted a table for two near a window.

Liam arrived minutes later.

'Here you take this,' he said handing over the card and pulling back the chair, 'I'm hopeless with these things. I'll end up trying to get money out of a bank or something equally daft.'

He shuffled the cutlery around as Helen poured out some tea.

'Lovely morning, well, for a while anyway. You should have come out for a walk.'

'I suppose so, but as you know, I'm not an early bird. Besides, this is the first morning I've had for a long lie-in. I've been up at the break of dawn since we arrived here. Where did you go?'

'Down by the river just as the sun was rising. Almost forgot what the sun looks like since we've been here.'

The waiter arrived with the breakfast plates and Liam tore into the food as if he feared someone would snatch it from the table before he was finished.

After five minutes he was almost done.

'Really Liam, must you attack breakfast with such … vim?' said Helen with a hint of exasperation. 'Your eating habits are quite normal at any other time.'

'Best meal of the day,' replied Liam, wiping up the plate with a piece of toast.

'Eating breakfast is a sign that the day has begun and good things can still happen … and, em … I can't remember the rest of the quote.'

'Oh, never mind,' Helen said, changing the subject. 'What time are we due at the airport?'

'The flight's due in at twenty past ten,' said Liam looking at the dining room clock. It had just turned nine.

'Plenty of time. The airport's only twenty minutes away from here. We'll leave at quarter to ten to be on the safe side.'

'I'm looking forward to seeing them. The only friends of yours I know, and see, are your fellow librarians,' she replied, scooping up the last of the eggs and buttering the remaining piece of toast.

'You'll like Des and Julie. I hope they like the Metropole. It's the only place I could book them in.'

'I'm sure they'll be fine,' said Helen, pulling away from the table. 'Listen, unfortunately I've got to talk to the event co-ordinator for ten minutes about this afternoon's session. You go and have a read at the papers and I'll see you back at the room when you've finished.'

*

'Just keep to the one-way streets until we get out of the town centre. The airport's well marked after that,' said Liam easing himself into the passenger seat.

They managed to weave their way out of the town centre and were quickly heading towards the airport.

'Do you know that during the crazy building boom they built another airport here? Apparently they demolished it because the runway was too short.'

'Did they really? I find that hard to believe,' replied Helen.

'And so you should, because it isn't true. It was a silly internet joke. What was frightening about it was the number of people who were prepared to believe that it *was* true. Turn in to your right after the roundabout.'

They parked up and strolled into the airport, they were ten minutes early according to the arrivals board.

'Let's get a coffee,' said Liam, 'by the time they get through formalities it will be another twenty minutes.'

After an espresso they stood at the arrivals gate and Liam

quickly spotted Des and Julie, looking a bit lost, coming out of the terminal.

'Ah, there they are,' said Liam, 'let's get over there before they go missing.'

Helen stood apart while the three off them hugged and kissed at their reunion.

'This is a good friend of mine—Helen Reid,' said Liam throwing his arm around her shoulders.

'Helen,' he said, 'this is Des and Julie.'

As they were shaking hands Julie's mind was working overtime collecting her first impressions. Helen was an impressively good looking woman. Possibly in her late thirties, mid-forties, but could easily pass for younger. She was dressed expensively, and carefully, in a neat, light coloured business suit with an open necked cream silk blouse. Liam had introduced her as a 'good friend'. Julie was unsure of the relationship implied. No wedding ring she noticed, so single or possibly divorced...

'Delighted to meet you both,' said Helen in a middle class Glasgow accent, 'I've heard a lot about you two these past few days.'

'Good things I hope,' said Julie laughing and waving a finger at Liam.

'Of course,' said Liam, bustling around, 'right then, let's get these two off to Cork!'

*

'I won't even bother asking if you had a good flight,' said Liam as they turned into the main Cork road, 'DanDare Airlines' are not renowned for their comfort. They would install hand rails and grab straps on the inside and nail seats to the wings if they could get away with it.'

'Oh, it wasn't too bad, quite a short flight anyway,' said Julie.

'True,' added Des, 'I've been on worse flights.'

'So, how has Cork been?'

Liam launched into a fifteen-minute monologue of the dinners they had eaten, the dances they had been to and the bars they had sung in.

'Get any work done?' said Julie as they parked outside the Metropole.

'Never halted!' boomed Liam, jumping out of the car. 'Did we, my dear?'

Helen gave Julie a knowing smile and a slight lift of her eyes to the heavens as she opened the back door to let her out. Julie knew they would get on well together.

'Not quite as swish as the Imperial but pleasant enough,' said Liam pushing open the foyer doors.

'After you've checked in have a wander about and get your bearings. Helen and I have a short meeting later in the town library. How long do you think …'

'I'm chairing the meeting,' said Helen, 'I'll break it up at two o'clock at the latest. How about we meet for a late lunch?'

'Let's go to O'Shea's'

Helen looked surprised.

'It's a bit …' she struggled for a word to describe the dingy restaurant, 'ethnic, is it not?'

'A bit heavy handed on the spuds if that's what you mean,' said Liam showing a bit of irritation, 'but nothing wrong with good old Irish cooking.'

'Sounds great. How do we get there?' said Des.

Liam marched up to the reception and took a city map from the pile on the desk.

'Get yourselves booked in and I'll show you how to get there.'

While Des booked in, Liam took Julie aside and drew a line from the Metropole to the English Market and from there to the library which he marked with a cross.

'Turn left when you leave here and walk down about two hundred yards to the crossroads then turn left again down to the bridge over the river.'

Liam stopped for a moment.

'I wonder if that damn bird is still perched there.'

'What?' said Julie.

'Oh, nothing,' said Liam, with a wave of his hand. 'It's about a ten-minute walk through town. Have a wander around the English Market; it's an interesting place if you like that kind of thing. You can then make your way up to the library, where I put the cross. We'll meet you there and then we can walk over to O'Shea's.'

*

By the time they packed away a few things and settled in it was well past noon. It was dry but a bit dull overhead as they crossed the bridge and into Patrick Street. They spent an hour wandering up and down the area. Julie liked the busy little side streets and the offbeat buildings. Des moaned about the modern street light system; 'Designed', he read from the street map and guide, 'to bring the harbour to the city centre'.

'I think they're quite cool,' said Julie.

'They look like half shut railway crossings to me,' grumbled Des, 'Let's head up towards the library in case we're late.'

They got lost a few times but managed to get there five minutes early. Liam was waiting in the main hall for them.

'Good. You made it then. Helen will be down in a few minutes.'

Helen appeared a moment later.

'Right then,' she said, 'let's go for lunch.'

O'Shea's was on a street opposite the library and somehow looked too large a building for a restaurant. Outside a chalkboard set out the lunch menu - mainly heavy duty fare like old fashioned roasts and fried chicken. The restaurant itself was up a flight of stairs that opened onto a single room with around twenty tables in rather regimented order. It was busy, but there were a few tables available.

'Crikey,' said Julie, 'this looks like a canteen set from a 1950s movie.'

'Good homely fare,' said Liam guiding them to a table beside the window.

A waitress with an ill-fitting uniform came over to take their order. The menu, she announced, was on the wall.

All, except Liam, ordered light salads. Liam decided on corned beef with veg.

'Why you insist on coming here is a mystery to me,' said Helen, 'the staff are surly, the whole place needs painting and refurbished and the food wouldn't be out of place in a shelter for the homeless.'

'For goodness sake! It isn't that bad; rather charming in its own way. Besides, I like the corned beef in here… and corned beef, before you ask,' he added, 'isn't that stuff you get in cans. In Cork it's cured brisket and it's excellent.'

'I'll take your word for it Liam,' replied Helen.

'Anyway,' she continued, 'what have you two been up to this morning?'

They talked and chattered throughout the lunch which, for all Helen's misgivings, turned out to be rather tasty and pleasant.

'We're all heading up to Tralee tomorrow morning,' said Liam as they had coffee, 'Helen and I went up on Tuesday for a couple of hours. There were a couple of things I wanted to check up on before I took you up there.'

'Yes,' said Helen, 'all very mysterious if you ask me. Liam said he would explain it all when you two got here.'

'All in good time,' said Liam finishing of the coffee, 'I'll get the bill. My treat for dragging you in here.'

As Liam paid the bill at the small reception desk, Julie took a wander around looking at some of the old photographs on the wall.

'That's us then,' said Liam leaving a generous tip in the saucer.

'Look here,' said Julie pointing to one of the photos, 'this place seems to have been a hotel at one time. Probably explains its appearance.'

Liam came over to look.

'I never noticed these photos before.'

'It seems to have been called the Corwell Hotel or something,' said Des looking more closely.

Liam stared at the photo for a few seconds.

'Well, well,' he said quietly as he took out his mobile phone and set it to camera.

He took two shots.

'Didn't take you to be a casual snapper,' said Des.

'It's quite incredible,' Liam replied, turning and looking around the room, 'it's not the Corwell Hotel, but the Conway Hotel. It happens to be the very hotel that your grandfather, Charlie McKenna stayed in whenever he came to Cork.'

'It that significant?' said Julie.

He looked at the picture on the wall again.

'Perhaps. I'm not really sure.'

He tapped at the camera.

'But it's another piece in the jigsaw.'

Chapter 7

Puttin' on the Ritz

Charlie hired a cab to take himself and a rather quiet and subdued Una down to Penn Station late on Sunday afternoon. It had been an eventful and strenuous Saturday.

During the morning and early afternoon Una had dragged Charlie almost through the entire length of Fifth Avenue to choose an engagement ring. Eventually she found one she loved in a small Jewish jewellers on Forty-Fifth Street; Charlie was relieved to find it was an affordable $50 including the small alteration to size. They were told to return at two o'clock for a fitting. Una, looking around, suddenly realised where she was, and insisted they lunched round the corner at the Algonquin. They had hardly crossed the doorstep when the maître d' instructed a waiter to show them to a corner table where Una tried to look nonchalantly bored as she tried to spot any famous faces from *The New Yorker*.

Charlie almost jumped as she snatched his arm.

'Don't look now!' she hissed fiercely, 'but Lois Long has just walked in.'

'Who,' said Charlie blandly, 'is Lois Long?'

'Shussh,' she replied, 'keep your voice down!'

As they ate, Una's eyes scoped the room endlessly, giving Charlie a running commentary of who was wearing what and what table they were sitting at.

Charlie, after paying a bill that would feed a family of six for a week, had to almost physically drag her from the dining room and back to the jewellers. The rest of the afternoon was spent in their hotel room making expensive long distance calls to her pals in Philadelphia and composing long excited cables to Europe. Between times she posed at the dressing table with the mirror at just the right angle to catch the light dazzling from the solo diamond of the ring. It was a perfect fit.

Later on, Una, swirling around the room, rattled off several well-known club places that they could go to for dinner.

Charlie looked up from his paper.

'You never struck me as one impressed by wealth.'

Una sighed, walked over and pulled him up from the chair. She hooked her arm in his and walked him towards the balcony.

'I'm not, you know I'm not.'

They stood at the open window. The light was beginning to fade as the sun started falling behind the skyline; lights were starting to flicker on in the tall apartments and office blocks around Midtown Manhattan.

'It's a special occasion. Not every day a woman gets engaged,' she said sweetly, 'is it Charlie?'

Charlie immediately felt guilty and a bit of a curmudgeon.

'Fair enough,' he admitted.

He turned around to face her.

'I'll take you to 21's.'

'Wow, now you're pushing the boat out! 21's is really Fancy Dan!'

'You get ready, I'll go down stairs and organise a cab.'

'Get ready!' she laughed. 'That's an understatement.'

She started to clap her hands and started singing –

> 'Dressed up like a million dollar trouper,
> Trying hard to look Super Duper,
> Come let's mix where Rockefellers walk with sticks,
> Or umbrellas in their mitts …'

She stopped and sashayed towards the bedroom and clicked her fingers. '… *Puttin' on the Ritz*,' she finished off loudly as she pulled the door closed.

Charlie was still smiling as he took the elevator down to the foyer, heading for the porter's lodge tucked in at the left hand side of the main entrance. He pressed the buzzer and put his head round the door. A young, black bus boy leapt guiltily from the corner seat trying to hide a comic book version of 'The Shadow'. He looked about thirteen or fourteen years old.

'Arthur around?' asked Charlie.

'I'll go get him, he's in the kitchen,' replied the boy in a southern drawl, 'back in a minute.'

Charlie wandered over to the main lounge and picked up a magazine. Arthur walked in sharply a few minutes later.

'Mr McKenna?' he said with a slight bow, just enough to be courteous without being obsequious.

'Can I be of help?'

'Perhaps. Do you know the 21 club?'

'I do indeed, sir, a fine establishment.'

'We intend to dine there this evening,' said Charlie, looking at the lounge clock, 'I realise it's a bit early for dinner by New York standards.'

'Nothing, Mr McKenna,' said Arthur, 'is standard in New York.'

'How true!' replied Charlie with a chuckle.

He slipped him a dollar bill.

'You look to me like an old military man,' he added.

'Third Division. Second battle of the Marne.' He held up his left hand; an index finger was missing. 'Could have been worse,' he said sardonically.

'After my time, Arthur, I was discharged in 1917.'

Old soldiers, as Charlie knew, don't have to say that much to feel an immediate bond.

'You'll know the 21 is a pricey joint. Fortunately, I know the Maître d' who does the early evening suppers, so I should manage the price of a dinner without ending up doing the dishes. Trouble is I've only been there once or twice and I don't have a card and I don't know the password, could you help me out?'

'Don't worry, sir, I'll organise that,' said Arthur, discreetly pocketing the note, 'do you require a cab?'

'In about a half hour?' said Charlie.

'I'll ring your room and leave a card with the password in an envelope at the foyer.'

'Thanks, Arthur, you're a pal.'

*

The 21 club pretty well exemplified the idiocy of prohibition, a private club that was open to anyone with enough money and clout. It was almost the reverse of the prohibitionists' utopian vision of a saloon-free non-drinking society. There was also a crazy paradox; before prohibition, saloon bar drinking was legal, but for a woman and the under-aged, it was illegal.

Now that all drinking was illegal, and there were no specific laws regarding gender or age, everyone started drinking. One of prohibitionists' main concerns was the damage that could be done to the youth of the country; now young woman flocked to illegal speakeasies and drank themselves silly. Getting arrested in a police raid, which was supposed to deter drinking, was regarded by young people as a badge of honour. Not that anyone in 21's at seven o'clock that night gave any of it much thought – they were far too busy drinking. Johnnie Flynn had received Arthur's message and kept a small table aside for Charlie.

Charlie was pleasantly surprised at the number of people he knew, mainly small time politicians of one sort and another. As George Peebles remarked some years ago ... 'For politicians, Prohibition is a flowing river of golden opportunities'. The band was loud and brassy. Una looked stunning; everyone wanted a dance. Una could hardly contain herself; she flew to the dance floor at any and every opportunity – by half past nine she was exhausted.

'I've had a wonderful day, Charlie, let's go home,' she announced half-drunkenly as she snuggled into his shoulder.

'I'll get a cab,' said Charlie with relief; he could only take so much of places like 21's. It was one of the many around Fifth Avenue and Broadway. At sixty cents a shot it was ridiculously expensive. A vacuous place where people went to be seen – by people who also wanted to be seen. George Peebles loved it but Charlie simply failed to understand the attraction of such places. He stood up to attract someone's attention. Johnnie Flynn quickly sidled over.

'Off home, Charlie?' he said.

Flynn was a Limerick man who was in the habit of coming into The Country Club when he was off duty. They had met briefly in Cork during the Irish truce of 1921 and got on well together. If the truth be told, Flynn had been more of a bookkeeper for the local flying column than anything else. Not that it stopped him from regaling the younger lads about his daring-do during the 'Troubles'. One evening he had been telling a group of teenage boys a colourful and dramatic tale of how he escaped from Cork Gaol with a company of Black and Tans snapping at his heels. When he turned to the bar to lift his drink, Charlie caught his eye. Flynn gave him a conspiratorial wink, opened his hands and gave the slightest of shrugs, smiled and turned back to his audience.

'Could you get me the bill and order a taxi?' Charlie almost shouted.

Flynn leaned over.

'Forget the bill, Charlie. Leave five bucks behind the bar in The Country Club,' he said quietly.

He straightened up.

'A taxi sir!' he said loudly as he started to weave his way through the tables. 'Follow me.'

Una clung onto Charlie like a limpet all the way through the dance floor, into the taxi and up in the elevator.

'You go on into the bedroom, I'll try and get this damn collar off!' he said as he switched on the lamp beside the mirror.

He went over to the French widows and pulled them closed – it was getting quite chilly. After wrestling with the stud for a few minutes he thought he heard a strange noise from the bedroom. He yanked off the collar quickly and threw it to the floor. He crossed the room and pulled open the bedroom door.

Una, fully clothed, lay face down spread-eagled across the bed.

Snoring like a rather contented warthog, thought Charlie, greatly amused.

*

Charlie had to buy a platform ticket from the machine to see her to the train and while he was briefly gone Una was waylaid by Sarah Kelly, one of the lesser lights of the Philadelphia Kelly clan.

'Una,' she screeched, ploughing her way through the crowd. 'How are you?'

She grabbed Una by the shoulders giving her exaggerated air kisses on each cheek then, holding her at arm's length, she looked at Una closely.

'Are you OK? You're looking a bit pale.'

'I'm fine, you should have seen me earlier.'

'A night on the town?' shrieked Sarah hooking her arm, 'come on, let's get on board, you can tell me all about it!'

'Just a minute, I'm waiting for Charlie.'

'Charlie who?'

'You know Charlie McKenna, he's a friend of George Peebles. You met him at…'

'Ah I remember him, the bootlegger,' replied Sarah with a crafty look.

'Oh for goodness sake! He's not a bootlegger he's …'

Just at that Charlie appeared with his ticket.

'Look who I've just met,' said Una quickly 'Sarah Kelly, you must remember her from the party last month.'

Charlie was caught off guard. He was about to say something when Una spun Sarah around.

'Sarah, be a dear and go on ahead. I just want to say goodbye to Charlie,' she said, putting her hand on Sarah's lower back and gently pushing her towards the ticket collector.

''Sure,' said Sarah giving Charlie an appreciative once over. 'Sure thing. See you on the platform.'

Charlie stood with the platform ticket between his fingers. Una removed it quickly and tucked it into his top pocket.

'You won't be needing that now,' said Una patting the pocket.

'Sorry, Charlie,' she said noticing his baffled look, 'I didn't want to go into explanations about the engagement and all that. She's very excitable and would have caused a scene. She would ask you a thousand questions if you appeared on the departure platform. I'll tell her on the train.'

She put her arms around his neck and kissed him.

'I better go. Sarah will be like a cat on a hot tin roof down there,' she said softy.

He looked at her, her face broke into a radiant smile as she turned and headed towards the collector.

'See you on Friday,' she shouted, blowing a kiss over her shoulder.

*

The early morning subway train in New York could be depressing, especially on Monday mornings. Fortunately, Charlie was too busy to be depressed; he was busy thinking of other things as he thumbed his way through *The Times* for the shipping section. He was looking for something in the following week preferably to Southampton via Greenock in Scotland, but he had only half a mind on it. He was considering the morning's work ahead on the Eighth Avenue line - another bit of tricky blasting, this time a bit closer to the East River. Should be done for 11 o'clock. He glanced at the station clock as they pulled in at Fulton Street station. *Just gone 7 am, might be a bit late* he thought; the guys in the blasting team liked to get started at 7:30. He also had the delicate problem of selecting someone to take charge of the blasting while he was gone. He had normally followed George's two basic rules for employing foremen:

'Don't let groups of men of more than five or six work together without a supervisor, appoint someone yourself or very quickly someone will emerge as leader – someone who you might not be able to control. Appoint someone who is competent, ambitious and more importantly, easily replaced; don't take one of the best workers – they're the guys who make you money.'

This was different. He needed someone who was highly skilled, at this stage it was too risky to leave it to the merely competent.

They worked without a break until ten o'clock. Charlie walked the length of the section with Lars Carlstrom, a twenty-five-year-old first generation Swede normally known as Larry. They carefully checked the fuses and the connections by hand before returning to the safety wall. Charlie gave the three-minute warning blast and started connecting the wires to the ignition dynamo.

'Here, Larry,' said Charlie stepping back from the T shaped firing plunger, 'Have a go at setting off the charges. Pull up the plunger and press down sharply when I pat your back in exactly one minute's time.'

He looked at his stop-watch and pressed the warning hooter again. Larry moved up and put one hand on the plunger, the other on the box to give more purchase. He licked his dry lips with nerves and anticipation.

The seconds ticked by. A nervy time for the squad as they hunkered down behind the wall. The biggest danger by far was in the failure to detonate rather than the detonation. It meant they had to go over the whole system to find the fault. Charlie leaned over and patted Larry on the shoulder. Larry turned the plunger to unlock it, pulled it up and snapped it down sharply in one fluid motion. Charlie was impressed.

The charge went off neatly with a muffled roar. Charlie could almost feel the sigh of relief behind him, they waited for a few minutes till the dust died down then they went off for a break. They would spend the rest of the day clearing up the rubble with loading machinery and the day labourers.

Charlie usually went home or attended other business after a blasting. He guessed that the labourers worked better with their own foremen without him standing around like an old fashioned 'Boss Man'.

He got cleaned up and decided to walk down to lower Manhattan, down near Wall Street where most of the major shipping lines were based. So far so good he decided. It looked as if he had solved one problem at least.

Chapter 8

Trip to Tralee

'How's the form this morning?' said Des.

'Spot on or, as some Glaswegians would say, Tickety-Boo,' replied Liam rising from the comfortable armchair in the lounge of the Imperial.

'And yourselves?'

'Great, enjoyed the walk over here. The weather was nice and it was a lovely view from the bridge,' replied Julie.

'I must say that was a great pub we went to after dinner, the music was excellent. Pity we had to leave a bit early; we were really bushed after the travelling,' said Des.

'Oh we weren't long behind you, we got back here just after ten and almost went straight to bed. Take a seat.'

As they lowered themselves into the armchairs Liam went on to explain that Helen would be down in a few minutes. They had permission to have the day off, but Helen had one or two things to sort out.

'I know you said Helen's a librarian like yourself, but …well, but she seems to be much busier than you are, Liam,' said Des.

'Ah! Of course, I should have said she *was* a librarian. Helen moves in greater circles than me I'm afraid. She's involved in the management of the 'Culture and Leisure Services Department', as they like to call it.'

He looked up at the ceiling.

'... or is it Sport and Leisure, or … even Culture and Sport these days? Anyway, one of these Byzantine empires that local politicians are fond of setting up. Quite high up I'm led to believe. Of course the system is all above the head of a mere book stamper like me.'

'I'm sure you do yourself an injustice, Liam.'

'I can't stand that old guff. Can you imagine me talking about economic, strategic and infrastructure performance plans with a straight face?' he grumbled with good humour.

Just then Helen breezed down the stairs waving to Julie.

'Hi there! That's me ready to go,' she said.

'Well, it's off to Tralee then,' said Liam jumping to his feet, 'Should only take an hour and a half or so.'

They waited on the pavement while Helen fetched the car from the nearby car park. The clouds beginning to thin out, small patches of blue were just about visible.

'Looks like we're going to have a good day for it,' said Liam as he squeezed into the front seat.

They talked of the previous night for a while and Helen turned on the local radio.

'You know something,' said Liam, 'talk radio was made for the Irish. It's hard to find a station that plays decent music on this car radio, they all seem far too busy chattering to one another.'

'Either that or they're playing Country and Western music,' added Helen.

'I don't mind Country and Western - a bit of a fan in fact. I started writing this song a while back…'

Liam burst into song.

'Ohhh … I'm just a cork in a sea of rye whiskey, headin' towards loneliness shore …'

He stopped. 'That's as far as I got I'm afraid.'

'Shows promise, Liam,' said Julie.

'Well it's not that easy,' said Liam peevishly, 'It can be difficult trying to write something that's essentially a parody of a parody. I remember hearing a song about a young bride who before going to her wedding service, decided to hop onto a tractor and plough the lower two acres 'cos her daddy wasn't well. As she finishes the last turn in the field she stands up on the tractor to wave to daddy and her flowing veil gets tangled in the rear wheel and chokes her to death– a tragedy of course.'

The other three started to laugh.

'Imagine following that song on stage. By the way,' he added, indicating a road sign on the left that had an old fashioned icon of a hand with a finger pointing towards Crookstown, 'we're just passing the road to Bealnablath.'

'Where?' said Helen.

'Bealnablath. It's the site where Michael Collins was assassinated in 1922. I've never seen it. Maybe we could call in on the way back if we have enough time.'

They sped on through the lush South Cork countryside. By the roadside the hedges were beginning to turn green with clumps of crocuses and some early daffodils showing on the verge. As they moved Northwest and upwards they passed the source of the river Lee in a series of loughs and reservoirs, through orchards and woods and finally through Macroom towards Killarney. The trees began to disappear after a time. The landscape became more rocky and windswept as they moved up through the mountains.

'Well, we'll soon find out if Killarney's lakes are blue,' said Helen.

'No we won't,' said Liam, 'for one thing this road bypasses Killarney and another thing – I've seen them. They're as black as the Ace of Spades. I know, you're thinking of the song …'

'Please don't ...'

Liam started singing.

> 'If you're Irish, come into the parlour, there's a welcome there for you,
>
> If your name is Timothy or Pat, so long as you come from Ireland there'll be a welcome on the mat,
>
> If you come from the Mountains of Mourne, or Killarney's lakes so blue,
>
> We'll sing you a song and ….'

'Oh for goodness' sake Liam! Must you sing so loud?' shouted Helen over the din.

'Sorry. Got a bit carried away there,' he mumbled, 'a silly music hall song written by a Welshman who had never set foot in Ireland'

The car started to turn down the steeper slopes of the Cork and Kerry mountains and they were soon in the green slopes of County Kerry and speeding along the road to Tralee.

'Here's another spot we need to stop at,' said Liam.

'Where is that?'

'Ballyseedy Crossroad.'

'Isn't that the place where the Free State Army blew up those prisoners? The place that you reckoned the photograph of Uncle Pat was taken?' said Julie.

'The very place. You'll see the monument on your right in a minute.'

They were going fast and the monument flew by.

'Don't worry. There's a parking area beside the monument, we'll stop on the way back. Over on your left is the infamous Ballyseedy forest.'

'Infamous for what?' asked Helen.

'Several murderous events took place around this area at the time of what the Irish call 'The Troubles',' said Liam, 'including the one Julie referred to.'

He turned in his seat to talk to Helen more directly.

'You know the background of the Irish civil war. I gave a short presentation on Monday afternoon and recommended a few books on the subject.'

'Yes, I know, but it seemed quite complicated to me. I was getting lost between regulars and the irregulars, the good guys and the bad guys …'

'You're not alone there, I'm afraid. Best way is to detach

yourself and treat it as a conflict with few winners and many losers.'

'Around March 1923, on the spot we passed,' he continued, 'a group of National Army soldiers took some prisoners, nine in all, to Ballyseedy Cross, tied them to a land mine and blew them apart.'

'Yes I remember you talked about that. I think you called it the Free State Army at the time and said the prisoners were irregulars.'

'So you weren't sleeping after all,' he replied with a laugh.

'Oh, listen to him,' said Helen, directing her comments to Julie and Des in the back, 'pretending he hasn't got the gift of the gab.

'As I said, it seemed a bit complicated,' she continued, 'but I got the impression that this event in Ballyseedy didn't take place out of the blue. It was some form of retaliation. But again I got a bit lost when you started mentioning place names like… Knock na something…'

'Knocknagoshel,' said Julie from the back, 'Liam gave us a written test on this a while back.'

'You're kidding!' said Helen.

'Don't listen to those two,' puffed Liam, 'prone to a bit of exaggeration from time to time.'

'I take it Liam hasn't shown you the photograph of Uncle Pat at the scene of the crime.'

'Not yet,' said Liam with a sigh.

'What photograph?' said Helen.

'All in good time,' he replied, turning to give Julie an irritated glare, 'I intended to show you it at lunch.'

*

They arrived in Tralee just after eleven and parked the car in Denny Street.

'Right then,' said Liam, glancing at a clock overhanging the street, 'I've arranged to meet someone this morning and I'm running a shade late.'

'Never mentioned a meeting to me,' Helen muttered.

'Pretty sure I did, but don't worry, I won't be long.'

They gathered on the pavement.

'You probably don't remember, Julie, but your Dad mentioned that they all stayed in a big guest house in Tralee when Charlie returned to Cork sometime in the '50s.'

'Did he?'

'Yes, he did, and I discovered… let's say from another source, that the house was not far from Denny Street, which,' he said, pointing up to the street sign, 'is exactly where we are now.'

'I reckoned that there couldn't be that many big houses in this neck of the woods. So, I mooched around and found an old guesthouse just off 'The Mall' on the off chance that someone might have remembered your grandfather staying there.'

'Crikey, that's some off chance! That must have been fifty or sixty years since Charlie McKenna was here,' said Julie.

'Some people in these places have long memories. Look around you.' he said, sweeping an arm. 'Looks like a sleepy seaside town in southern England, doesn't it? Eighty odd years ago this was like Beirut.'

'A bit of an exaggeration,' said Des.

'Not really, a small town like this was the centre of activity for rural guerrillas. The death and murder rate would have been proportional.'

'Anyway,' he continued, 'I got lucky. The present owners are an elderly couple who bought the place thirty-five years ago and still occasionally meet the previous owner who's now in her nineties. They said they would arrange a meeting with her at the guest house this morning at eleven. You guys find a nice place for lunch and I'll give you a phone when I'm finished – say an hour or so. Right, I better be off, see you later.'

He turned and disappeared into the crowd before they could say any more.

'Well that was all very mysterious and sudden,' said Julie

'Come to think of it he did wander off for half an hour on Tuesday when I decided to go and buy souvenirs,' said Helen, 'and I think he did chatter on about meeting someone when he came back. Not to worry, let's have a walk about, there's some nice shops around here.'

'Shoe shops?'

'Loads!'

'Sounds good to me.'

'Em … I think I'll give the shopping bit of a miss,' said Des, 'there are a couple of places I wouldn't mind seeing. Why don't we find a place for lunch, split up and meet back here at 12.30?'

*

Lunch was more like an old fashioned high tea. Neatly cut sandwiches with a tray of scones and cakes and, of course, pots of tea and coffee. They sat in a bay window overlooking the street; behind them the tearoom was awash with chintz and pink.

'Odd,' said Des, looking around 'everywhere we go we seem to wander onto the set of a 1950s movie.'

'I think it's rather charming,' said Helen.

'Agreed,' sighed Julie, 'delightful.'

'Enough of that old sentimental nonsense,' grumbled Liam, brushing some cake crumbs from his beard.

He took a photograph from his inside jacket pocket and put it on the table in front of Helen.

'Here's the picture we talked about earlier.'

He tapped the photo with his finger.

'This here,' he announced, 'is Julie's great uncle, Pat McKenna. Taken during the Irish civil war around 1922 or early '23.'

'Handsome young man,' said Helen.

'Yes, Yes,' replied Liam dismissing such trivia by waving his hand impatiently.

'Look at the boot to his right.'

Helen picked up the picture and looked at it carefully.

'Yes, I can see the boot … and?'

'If you could see it magnified it would appear to be a severed foot rather than an empty boot.'

She looked at it again.

'Could be,' she said with a slight shrug.

'Behind his right shoulder there's what looks like a soldier coming out of the woods and behind him there is a large white or shiny object.'

She squinted at the photo.

'Yes, I can see that.'

He reached over and turned the photograph in her hand.

'The reverse side. You can see the photograph has been made into a postcard.'

'Ah yes, that's quite interesting – quite common in those days I'm led to believe,' said Helen, 'I remember seeing an exhibition of them in the Burrell Collection.'

Turning it back over, he ran his finger down the right hand side.

'You'll notice this torn edge. Not on the postcard but on the photo. Torn down this edge, I think, to fit the postcard frame.'

'Is that important?' said Helen.

Liam placed the postcard back on the table.

'Liam,' said Julie suddenly, 'let me try to fill in the gaps.'

'Please do!' said Liam leaning back with a slight air of a man who had done his bit.

Julie sat forward.

'Liam is convinced that this photo was taken shortly after the atrocity at Ballyseedy Cross – the place we passed on the road down here, close to where the mine was detonated. The severed foot was part of the general debris and the reason for the torn edge on the photo is that it might have revealed something more sinister.'

Julie picked up the postcard.

'I'm told that reports on the event do mention body parts being scattered about and also that coffins were transported to the scene so the white or shiny object might be a coffin and the soldier might be coming down to join his colleagues. All perfectly plausible I suppose but, well … it all seems rather fanciful to me.'

'Nothing fanciful about it,' said Liam smacking the table lightly.

'What makes you so sure?' said Helen.

'I've found,' he stopped briefly to consider his words. 'I've managed to dig up some more information.'

'Like what?' said Julie.

'The old woman I visited at the guesthouse. She was the niece of the original owner of the place, a woman by the name of Mrs Conklin. She told me a rather interesting story. In fact, she let me borrow something for an hour or so … something very valuable, so much so that I insisted that she held my passport until I returned it.'

'Well, this is all very riveting. What is it?' said Helen.

Liam put his hand in his pocket and took out a coin. 'It was this sovereign.'

He placed it in the middle of the table.

'It's a George IV British gold sovereign dated 1916. The same as the ones Charlie and Pat had.'

*

Tralee, like many towns of its time and age, was not designed for car traffic. It took them twenty minutes to negotiate the intricate one-way system and narrow streets before they started back on the main Cork road. They reached what Liam reckoned to be the Ballyseedy Crossroad in another ten minutes. They pulled in at a small car park beside the monument.

'Probably only took five minutes to get here by bloody horse and cart a hundred years ago,' grumbled Liam as he stumbled, ill-tempered out of the car.

He stood facing the monument, map in hand, as the others sorted themselves out.

'Well then,' said Julie, 'give us the conducted tour.'

Liam faced the monument, rocking back on his heels.

'As you can see. A monument designed by committee,' he said, spreading his hands around enthusiastically.

'Originally it was conceived as a monument to the atrocity at Ballyseedy I would suggest. But it seems to have ended up a memorial to everyone in Kerry. The bronze figures were sculpted by Yann Goulet a French Breton, who was sentenced as a Nazi collaborator after the Second World War.' He turned and lifted his shoulders, 'Make of that as you will.'

He turned to face the sculpture.

'I think you'll find that …'

'Brrr … Cold out here,' said Helen drawing her jacket together, 'could we have the shorter version of the lecture, Liam?'

Liam drew her a look as he folded the map.

'The castings,' he continued tersely, 'are not to my taste. The dying man is rather theatrically posed and the child, for some reason, bares a remarkable similarity to the baby Jesus. As for the young man … he looks as if he's heading towards the nearest pub in search of a good drink and a decent punch up and I would also suggest …'

'Is this the actual spot of the incident?' said Des looking around.

'As a matter of fact it's not,' snapped Liam.

He turned round.

'Pearls before swine,' he muttered, opening the map again.

He orientated the map towards north.

'The original cross-road is over there,' pointing over the busy highway, 'Let's take a look.'

A large articulated truck thundered by.

'It's not too bad. It's a straight road and we can see traffic coming from both sides,' shouted Liam as he herded the small group across the wide highway.

They just made the other side as a large oil tanker whizzed by in a cloud of dust.

'For goodness sake, Liam,' coughed Julie, 'we'll all end up as human road kill at this rate!'

'Never mind that, come over here.'

They moved five yards to comparative safety in the corner of a short lay-by.

'Look down there,' said Liam.

'Oh yes,' said Julie, 'You can see the old road quite clearly. It looks more like a T junction of some sort.'

'Just beyond that wall over there is the River Lee,' said Liam, 'the only survivor was blown clear and ended up in the water. It's incredible that he survived.'

'Is this the same River Lee that goes through Cork?' said Des looking up to the hills, 'It doesn't seem to flow north.'

'Different River Lee. This one flows down northwards to Tralee. By the way Tralee simply means strand or beach of the Lee,' said Liam.

Helen had wandered further along the lay-by.

'Look at this.'

She was standing in front of a Celtic cross engraved with the name 'Seamus Taylor'.

'That's interesting,' said Liam, moving up to Helen.

He looked closely at the date. '14.3.1923'

'Mmm ... Fourteenth of March 1923, a week to the day *after* the original incident.'

'I can't see any sign of the house that's in the photograph,' shouted Julie peering down to the crossroad.

Liam walked back to the corner.

'I wouldn't have expected it to last this length of time. If you look at the photo it was pretty well derelict in the 1920s.'

He looked around.

'In any event this road covers most of the site, anything in the way would have been bulldozed to the ground.'

'Let's get back, I'm frozen,' said Helen.

'Anyone fancy a game of chicken?' said Des looking at the traffic.

'Hold on, there's a fairly big gap after that blue van,' said Liam.

After the van sped past Liam gathered them together like a sheepdog and chased them across the highway.

'Well that was interesting,' said Helen pulling her seatbelt, '... in a near death experience kind of way.'

'Still plenty of daylight left,' said Liam casually.

'Meaning?' replied Helen.

'We could pop into Bealnablath on the way back.'

'Bal na ... what?' said Des.

'Bealnablath,' said Julie, 'The place where Michael Collins was assassinated.'

'Well then,' said Helen pulling out into the road, 'Liam Tracey's "Lightning Tour of Famous Irish Civil War sites" continues.'

*

'Now that we've got time perhaps you can elaborate on the significance of that gold sovereign you produced at lunchtime,' said Helen, as they wound their way through the mountain range towards Killarney. 'I take it you managed to return it safely and get your passport back.'

Liam patted his jacket pocket.

'Safe and sound.'

'Now then, Helen, the sovereigns,' said Julie from the back, 'are still a bit of a mystery. It seems my grandfather Charlie and his brother Pat had some sort of access to gold coins. They used to hand them out on family occasions like weddings and anniversaries. I always thought it was a bit of a tradition of some sort; it never struck me as odd until my mother showed me a paper money tube that seemed to suggest that they all came from the same source.'

'Were there many involved?'

'Not really, probably about ten or twelve I think.'

'Yes, the whole thing started after a friend of ours, a policeman, found one of the coins at the scene of a murder,' continued Julie, 'but we eventually got a bit side-tracked by the photograph of Pat. That's the one that Liam is convinced was taken at the Ballyseedy bombing.'

'Yes, Liam told me about … Well, about the tragic end of your friend; it must have been hard for all of you.'

'Yes,' said Julie biting her lip, 'it was all quite traumatic. To be honest I'm not sure if I'm quite over it yet.'

She sat back and looked out the window.

There was silence in the car.

After a few moments Liam gave a discreet cough.

'I think I've managed to get some way towards solving the mystery of the coins and possibly Pat's role in Ballyseedy. I'll tell you about it over dinner tonight. By the way, I hope you don't mind but I booked a restaurant for dinner. It's quite handy, it's just opposite your hotel.'

Helen switched on the car radio.

*

Normally the drive through Kerry and Cork can be pleasant but in cloudy weather it can be hard going. The rain clouds that come billowing in from the Atlantic often lie low on the top of the hills and can give the impression of driving through a white fog. After the Killarney by-pass they started down the other side and soon the fog gave way to a steady drizzle. The car was comfortably warm and the radio hummed quietly as the chat show host encouraged phone-in callers to babble and cackle their way over a variety of bizarre topics. In the back Julie had curled up and was enjoying a short nap.

Liam peered ahead through the windscreen.

'It's getting a bit gloomy, Liam, do you think it's worthwhile?' said Helen.

'There should be a sign up ahead…' he said looking at the map, 'Ah, there it is … Crookstown.'

He tapped at the map.

'Take a right here, this should take us down to Bealnablath.'

Chapter 9

The Ghost of Michael Collins

Helen turned right at the Crookstown turn-off and within five minutes she was totally lost.

She stopped the car at the side of a farmyard crossing.

'Well then,' she said to Liam, 'what were those houses that we passed? Crookstown? Or were they "obviously an unmapped hamlet" as you put it?'

Liam wriggled restlessly in his seat.

'We came upon it so quick I thought couldn't possibly be a town.'

He looked at the map.

'I was wrong; we'll need to go back.'

'I don't think I can turn here, I'll drive until the road gets wider,' said Helen, turning the engine back on.

The road widened out after a couple of hundred yards to accommodate a few houses and a rickety service and fuel station. One of the houses seemed to double up as some kind of shop.

'I'll jump out and check to make sure we're on the right road here while you turn the car around,' said Liam.

Helen stopped outside the house to let Liam out and started the tortuous process of turning the car to face the opposite direction.

As Liam approached the entrance it became obvious from the signs outside that the house was either a pub that sold groceries or a grocery shop that sold drink. He looked through the dusty window on the left; the place looked deserted. A loud mechanical bell on a spring clattered as he opened the door. Two or three steps before him stood what looked like a long wide shelf or perhaps a large table covered in groceries of every kind in no logical order; below the shelf were open sacks of spuds of every possible variety.

At the far end of table was a chill cabinet filled with bottled beer and a freezer filled with ice cream. To his left was a counter – or perhaps, thought Liam for a split second, was it a bar?

A middle-aged woman seemed to pop up behind the counter like a pantomime character on a stage.

'Good day to you, sir,' she said leaning against the counter as if she had been there all day.

Liam, surprised by her sudden appearance, seemed unusually flustered.

'I'm ... I mean, we're ...'

'You're looking for Mick Collins's monument aren't you? Well, go back up the road and turn left at the pub on the corner,' she said, vaguely waving her hand behind her, 'a few miles down that road will take you to Bealnablath. The memorial is on the left; you can't miss it.'

'Thank you. We must have driven past the sign.'

'Don't worry about that; some eejit has probably stolen it. Happens all the time,' she said without moving.

'Thanks again.'

Liam opened the door to let himself out.

'Say a prayer for Micky for me when you're down there,' she added straight-faced.

The bell clattered.

'Sure,' he said.

He stopped and turned back round to the counter.

'I'll do that ...'

She was gone.

He squeezed into the front seat.

'Are you okay?' said Julie, now wide awake, 'You look like you've just seen a ghost.'

'I'm fine.'

Helen started the car again.

'We're on the right road. Just take a left at this corner and that will take us down to Bealnablath. The woman in the shop says the sign to Bealnablath is always getting pinched by tourists.'

'Was it a shop? Funny looking place,' said Helen.

'Not sure if it was a shop or a pub. It was quite odd; the owner seemed to appear out of thin air, gave me directions and asked me to say a prayer for Michael Collins.'

He seemed a bit jumpy.

'I'm not sure if I've just been blessed or cursed.'

'What are you talking about?' said Helen.

'Don't listen to him,' laughed Julie, 'That's just Liam's blarney. Making a story out of nothing.'

'Gave me a bit of a turn that's all,' he said grumpily, 'anyway we'll need get a move on if we want to get there and then back to Cork before dark.'

*

The road was a bit wider than a country lane with the occasional lay-by for passing; it seemed to be following a river through a shallow valley. Where it narrowed, the large beech trees and wild bramble bushes soared above them almost joining together to form dark gloomy arcades.

'Easy to see why they picked this road for an attack,' said Des, glancing from side to side, 'there's loads of ideal spots to ambush a convoy through this valley.'

'I wonder if we're nearly there. There seem to be no signs for this place,' said Helen.

'Something else I've noticed,' she added, 'I don't think I've seen another car on this road.'

As they turned yet another right hand bend the road widened

out dramatically. It seemed as if they had come across a giant empty car park in the middle of nowhere.

'There it is,' said Liam quickly, 'over to your left. Park anywhere here,'

'You can say that again!' said Helen, 'there must be room for scores of cars in here.'

'It's a bus park I would imagine,' said Liam, 'I think this place might be busy in the summer.'

Helen took the opportunity to turn the car around and stopped opposite the monument, leaving plenty of room for passing traffic should any appear on the road. They all left the car and sauntered over to the rather unusual looking red brick monument. It had a short staircase leading to the platform which measured no more than twelve feet by twenty/twenty-five feet. A large Celtic cross sat at the back and the platform itself was protected by a cast iron balustrade.

'Not very big is it,' said Julie 'I was expecting something quite impressive.'

'What? Like his profiled carved on the cliff side?' said Liam laughing, 'Nope, 'fraid not. Too much bad blood in Irish politics when this was built.'

'By the way, this isn't the exact spot according to this,' said Des who was now on the first level looking at a map on the monument.

Liam climbed up the stairs to take a look.

'It looks as if that white marker is the exact spot,' continued Des pointing over the road.

Helen and Julie walked up to the cross to look at the inscription.

It was a simple epitaph:

Miċeal Ó Coileáin
d'éag
22aḋ Luġuasa, 1922

Julie guessed that it must have read something like;

'Michael Collins died 22nd August 1922'

Julie gave a shiver, it was turning cold and a slight drizzle was beginning to fall.

She stood back.

The evening seemed still and silent. There was a pleasant balmy aroma in the air, a mixture of burning turf and pine forest. It was that time of evening when the light begins to fade—a time that the Scots refer to hauntingly as 'The Gloaming'.

'What a lonely and forlorn place to die,' she said, wrapping her arms around herself as she looked around.

Liam was standing with his hands on the balustrade.

'I must agree with you there, Julie,' he said quietly.

He looked moved by the hushed, eerie atmosphere around the valley.

His hands began to tighten on the ironwork.

'Come on, let's get going,' he added almost abruptly, 'It'll be dark soon.'

*

'Impressive or what?' said Liam with his arm outstretched.

'Isn't half!' said Julie.

'Not often you see a natural waterfall in a restaurant' said Des.

'Well it's not actually *in* the restaurant,' said Helen.

'I suppose you could sit out here and have a coffee when you've finished eating,' said Julie, 'rather pleasant I'd say.'

'What? In this weather?' said Helen pulling her coat around her.

'It is a bit chilly right enough,' said Liam, rubbing his arms. 'Let's go inside.'

There was an early-evening kind of quietness in the main

restaurant. They looked around and took a table beside the window that was close to a comfortable fireplace. Liam picked up the menu.

'Let's have a drink to start. I'll have …'

'… a pint of stout no doubt,' said Helen irritably. 'I'll have a dry sherry - a Manzanilla if you have it, but anything else will do,' she continued.

'Same for me,' said Julie.

'I'll just have a cold beer,' added Des.

There was a brief silence. Helen placed her hands on the table.

'I really must apologise. I'm sorry I seem a bit crabby, I just had a run-in with one of the event managers.'

'A bit ... crabby? Were you?' said Liam blandly.

'Can't say I noticed,' he continued, taking a sudden interest in the menu.

'Gallantly said, Liam, but I find that hard to believe. I've been barking at everyone since I left that meeting this evening,' she replied as the drinks were laid out on the table.

'Don't worry,' said Liam taking a huge draft of stout. 'A couple of drinks and a good tightener in here and you'll be as right as rain!'

'Too true,' she said, settling down in her chair and lifting her glass, 'Cheers everyone.'

The dinner menu looked excellent despite Liam carping about the overuse of French.

'Why is gravy always a "jus" or a "coulis",' he grumbled, '... and "mille feuille"; a Fancy Dan custard tart is what they mean!'

Helen asked for starters and finished the order with, 'Bring this man another pint.'

Liam was about to protest.

'… and stop moaning or you'll make me grumpy again,' she added.

The waiter laid out an elaborate array of starters.

'So,' said Liam, picking his way through some West Cork mussels, 'you never made much of the Collins monument, Julie.'

'I don't know, I suppose I didn't know what to expect,' she replied, 'come to think of it, you didn't look all that impressed either.'

'I think I was more spooked by the timing. I read that Collins was killed in the same kind of light as we had, you know, twilight getting dark but not quite night time. And, of course, meeting that lunatic in the shop.'

'Oh for heaven's sake Liam! The woman barely said two words to you – a bit harsh to label her a lunatic,' said Julie.

Liam looked unsettled.

'Maybe ... but I said a prayer, just to be on the safe side,' said Liam with a little cough, 'you never know about these things. Anyway, I found it an intriguing place. Apparently it took almost all night for the convoy to trek back to Cork. They didn't get Collins to a hospital until the early morning – he was well dead by that time of course.'

He fell quiet as he sopped up the juices with a lump of soda bread.

'I was half expecting you to tell us that Charlie and Pat were involved in the assassination somewhere along the line,' said Julie.

'No, not at all. Although they were nearby in Tralee at the time. I mean relatively nearby, of course.'

The waiters cleared away the dishes and brought in their main courses.

'So perhaps you can tell us about the mysterious sovereigns now,' said Des.

'Perhaps,' said Liam, eyeing up the fat duck breast on his plate, 'but that can wait till later.'

Chapter 10

A present from the USA

'Stop pacing about,' said George.

'I think better when I'm moving.'

Charlie stopped at the corner window, the one overlooking lower Sixth Avenue, and looked down at the elevated train track. He could just see Herald Square to his left.

He turned and sat on the window ledge.

'So,' he said, 'Davidson has made you a director of the importing company.'

'Me and the other investors of course, one thousand dollars start up, two thousand when the cargo is on its way, two thousand when the whisky is in the warehouse.'

Charlie said nothing for a moment, thinking it over.

'Sounds reasonable,' he said finally as he stood up.

He walked to his usual armchair and sat down.

'I've been busy the past few days,' said Charlie.

'You're telling me. Thanks for giving me warning about your engagement. Mrs G. told me this morning before I got halfway through the door. Always the last to know, that's me.'

'Sorry George, it was, well… a kind of spur of the moment kind of thing, but you're not telling me that it came as a big surprise.'

'I suppose not. I phoned Elizabeth about an hour ago. Even she knew before me; apparently Una phoned her first thing.'

'I was busy with other things as well. Yesterday afternoon I took a walk downtown to book a sailing. It looks like I could leave a week today by White Star to Southampton, dropping of at Greenock.'

'Greenock?'

'It's a town not far from Glasgow. I've booked provisional Second Class, and put down a small deposit.'

'Why not first class? Davidson will pick up the bill.'

'First class is too formal. Too many dinners and social events for a small select crowd, everyone soon gets to know everyone else. Second class you can move about a bit more and generally pretty well keep to yourself.'

He stood up.

'Not of course, as you insist on saying, that we're doing anything illegal,' he added.

'Can you get in touch with Davidson today? There's a few things I'd like to go over with him'

'Sure I'll get Mrs G. to get him on the phone. In fact I'll do that right now,' George replied getting up from his seat, 'I could be doing with a coffee.'

He returned a few minutes later.

'Mrs G. said Davidson was available and would phone back in about ten minutes.'

He put the coffee pot on a side table.

'Anything I should know about this trip?'

'Not really. I just want to organise payment for the voyage and my own fee. I also need a run down on who I'm supposed to meet, phone numbers, addresses and so on. Nothing exciting. I'll need to organise a meeting with him.'

George poured out some coffee for them both and they sat around chatting about the job down on the East Side.

Charlie glanced up at the clock as Mrs G. put her head around the door.

'Call for you, Charlie – Sandy Davidson.'

As Charlie closed the door, George picked up the early edition of *The New York World* and went back behind his desk. Settling down, he pushed the seat back then lifted one foot up, stopped, and slowly dropped it back to the floor, with Mrs G. still around he wisely resisted the temptation to put his feet on the desk.

Charlie came hurrying back in a few minutes later.

'By Jove that was quick! I haven't even got to the sport section yet,' said George putting down the paper, 'anything wrong?'

'No. I've got to get down to his office. He's leaving for Boston in a couple of hours and might not be back for a few days,' said Charlie shrugging on his top coat.

He looked at the clock again.

'I don't know how long this'll take and I need to catch Slavinsky later so I doubt if I'll be back today.'

He started putting on his hat as he moved to the door.

'I'll be back in here tomorrow around one o'clock. See you then,' he shouted from the outer office.

Mrs G. came bustling in.

'Finished with the coffee?'

'Leave it just now I might have another cup.' George gave his arms a stretch and suppressed a yawn. 'Listen. Why don't you finish for the day? I'm going out myself in half an hour and there will be no one here this afternoon.'

Mrs G. didn't waste any time. She had her hat and coat on and was out the door before George changed his mind.

George heard the outer door closing. He snapped open *The World*, pushed back his chair and slowly placed his feet on the desk with a contented sigh.

Once outside Charlie debated whether to get a cab, the subway or take Mrs G.'s advice. A veteran of New York transport, she told him it was quicker to walk and gave him brief instructions in her nasal Brooklyn accent.

'Down Thirty-Second ... Toyn right into Broadway ... Toyn left again at Twenty-Eighth ... the office is numba 234 West Twenty-Eighth Street ... D'y want me to write it down?'

'It's okay,' replied Charlie, 'I'll remember the directions.'

Looking around the street he realised that it was lunch time, a busy time in midtown Manhattan, Mrs G. was probably right – walking seemed the best bet. He set off at a brisk pace. He was there in no time.

The Brunswick and Portland Timber Company had their well-appointed offices in the second floor of the ten storey brownstone office building. The main foyer had an impressive wall map of the USA with each state picked out in various inlays of polished hardwood. Charlie asked to see Mr Davidson. An attentive office assistant came out to greet him and showed him into a large empty boardroom. He was directed to the far end where there were some armchairs and several small coffee tables scattered around. The young man took his hat and coat and arranged them on a coat rack.

'Mr Davidson knows you're here and will be down in a few minutes, please take a seat and make yourself comfortable. Coffee?'

'No thanks, I'm awash with coffee this morning, but thanks anyway. I'll just take a seat and wait.'

He picked up a trade magazine and had just sat down when a door opened to his left.

'Charlie! Didn't realise you'd get over so quick,' said Davidson extending his hand as Charlie stood up.

'I decided to walk; it's only fifteen minutes,' replied Charlie returning the handshake.

'Well, let's take a seat and talk this over,' said Davidson, 'but before we do I need to order something for us.'

'No it's okay, Sandy, I've already said I'm not bothered about coffee.'

'Who said anything about coffee?'

Davidson smiled as he left the room by the same door. He was back in a few minutes.

'So, Charlie, you said you had travel arrangements planned.'

'Possibly. I hope you and I can agree on some sort of reasonable timetable. I've put a small deposit on a second class berth for Tuesday week. That gives me a full week to get my own business in order. Hopefully a few meetings with you will fill me in on the business plan.'

Davidson was impressed. Someone who could work on his own initiative was a rarity in his line of business.

'Are you giving yourself enough time?'

'I've more or less decided on who to manage my East Side job. Elsewhere I've got reliable foremen for the other work I have and Mrs Greene can manage the paperwork. The Sharkeys will run The Country Club.'

Davidson nodded.

'You seem well organised.'

Another office assistant appeared, a young lady this time, and placed a tray with a bottle and some glasses on the sideboard behind Charlie. She lingered for a moment as Davidson continued to talk.

'Well, the sooner the better as far as I'm concerned. I just got word today that the distillers have rented out another bottling plant and are going into full production this weekend.'

Charlie gave a short shrug.

'I'm afraid I'm a bit lost here.'

'Sorry, Charlie. I'll give you a run down on how everything works.' He turned to the assistant. 'Joan, can you get a pad and write down some notes for Mr McKenna here?'

'Sure, back in a minute.'

'It'll save time if you can have some notes on times, names addresses that kind of thing. I'll get her to type them up before you leave.'

'Sounds good.'

Davidson stood up and walked to the table and brought back the tray.

'Not that I'm trying to ply you with drink at this time of day, Charlie, but I want you to take just a sip of this whisky,' he said as he poured two small measures into heavy crystal whisky glasses. He added a small piece of ice into each. He handed one over to Charlie.

'It's just to let you know how things work. The glass you're holding is what we call a single malt whisky that comes from the North East part of Scotland … sometimes known as Speyside.'

'It should be clear as a bell,' he said, holding it up to the nearest lamp. He swirled it around the glass and inhaled the aroma.

'Depending on the distillery, of course, it should smell of malt and honey.'

He finally took a mouthful, rolled around his mouth for a second or so before swallowing.

'Should taste clean and flavoursome and leave a pleasant aftertaste.'

Charlie followed the same ritual.

'I'm not a great whisky drinker,' he said, 'but I must admit that does taste very special.'

By this time Joan had settled down in an armchair behind Davidson with pencil and pad at the ready.

'That's a Denholm whisky, a Speyside malt. As you've noticed it's very much a connoisseur drink. Not one to be drowned with soda pop or thrown recklessly into a cocktail.'

'Expensive, I would imagine.'

'Yes indeed, but it can only be expensive if people are willing to pay the price. The problem is that the Denholm family have over produced, particularly in the mid '20s. Over fifty thousand gallons of the stuff – almost double what they require.'

'I don't know that much about whisky but I do know that it keeps. Surely they could simply store the stuff away.'

Davidson leaned back.

'Let me tell you a few things that I've learned about this

business. First of all alcohol is surprisingly easy and cheap to produce.'

'Not if you drink in 21's, it ain't!'

Davidson laughed.

'Too true! But think about it,' he continued, 'if rednecks in the Appalachians can make moonshine, then take it from me... it's easy to make. Some of the labourers we employ in our sawmills can hardly read or write, yet they can produce good quality liquor.' He held up his glass. 'A gallon of this stuff, can cost as little as 50 cents to produce. That's less than 10 cents a bottle - not much dearer than a couple of bottles of Coca Cola. In fact, the problem is storage. Whisky, unlike soda pop that can be sold straight out the back door, needs to be at least three years old. Not only that, it needs to be stored under the right conditions,' he said.

'And,' he added with emphasis 'can only be stored in either old sherry casks or ex-bourbon barrels and that, Charlie my friend, costs money.'

He paused for a second.

'However there is a solution. Most regular Scotch whisky is blended to have an *average* age of three years and Denholm's whisky blended with inferior or newer whisky can make a top notch brand. That's what I meant by the need for another bottling plant.'

'I take it that this is all a done deal then if they have already started to bottle the stuff,' said Charlie.

'More or less, although no money has changed hands yet.'

'I don't quite get it ... what's the rush?'

'Several reasons. One is the Denholms need to raise cash at the moment. They're not desperate but remember that the value of a commodity is made more attractive with scarcity; it would suit them to get this surplus off their hands. From our point of view anyone with a cache of good whisky, come the abolition of prohibition, could be sitting on a gold mine.'

'That still might be some time away,' said Charlie.

'True, but think of it as an investment. We're legally buying in 100,000 gallons of excellent blended Scotch whisky and storing it in a warehouse. The closer to the abolition the more valuable the stock in that warehouse becomes. In fact, we could sell the lot to another investor within days of it arriving here and still make a good profit.'

'Yes, I can see that,' said Charlie, in a tone that carried a lingering doubt, 'almost sounds too easy.'

'Don't worry, Charlie,' said Davidson, spreading his hands, 'just think of it as any other article of trade that increases in value through time.'

'I'm afraid,' said Charlie, holding up the glass, 'that there are some people out there who wouldn't regard booze as a simple 'article of trade'.'

Davidson gave a broad grin and finished his drink.

'Right again, Charlie,' he said.

'Now,' he added turning to Joan, 'down to business.'

*

Davidson spent some time discussing the people and contacts Charlie would probably need to meet. There were around about half a dozen at most. With each one he made sure that Joan took down all the details, the addresses and phone numbers, both home and office. He was careful to make sure the spelling was correct and checked it with his own diary entries.

'I've spent too much time chasing down wrongly spelled streets, and miswritten phone numbers in my day,' he said as a way of explanation.

He described some physical attributes of some of the ones he had met – this one had brown hair, so and so was tall. He added his own opinions on some of the people involved, mostly favourable. After twenty minutes he stopped and thought for a minute.

'Well, that's about all you need to know, Charlie. I don't think I can add much more. We're kind of depending on you to use your initiative in the unlikely event of something going wrong, but keep in touch by wire or you can book a phone call if you need particular details – Joan will give you my direct office number.'

He stood up.

'Finally, your expenses. Charge the return tickets to the office account – again Joan will give the details – she will also give you a hundred dollars in cash to cover any expenses on board. Use the same account for any hotel bills or extra travelling. We intend to give you one thousand dollars now and another thousand when the whisky…'

He gave a nod and a smile.

'… or should I say, the articles of trade, are in the warehouse, I hope that these arrangements meet your approval.'

Charlie shook his hand.

'Seems you have covered every angle, Sandy. I have no problems with the arrangements.'

'I'll get Joan to type up the details and to see you out.'

Charlie walked to the door.

'I know you're a busy man, Sandy, so I'll leave you to your business. I can't think of anything else we need to discuss but if I think of something, I'll let you know.'

*

Twenty minutes later Charlie was in a cab heading west along Forty-Fourth Street. In his coat pocket he had several envelopes: one containing some letters of introduction, the other the contact details he needed. He had a hundred dollars tucked into his wallet.

He ordered the cab driver to let him off at the corner of Sixth Avenue and from there he walked to The Country Club.

It was quiet as usual on a dull overcast Tuesday afternoon. There were half a dozen or so inkies from the Times who had finished off the lunchtime stop press reports. They were sitting around playing cards and he was aware of four or five people propping up the bar. Charlie was in a bit of a rush, but as he lifted the counter hatch to go up the stairs he heard a voice.

'Hope you're not too big time to talk to a couple of townies are you, Charlie?'

He turned around. Manny O'Donnell was sitting on a stool, drinking a beer. On his left stood Vincent McGhee.

McGhee appeared to be cleaning his fingernails with a small penknife, he looked bored and disinterested.

'Hi Manny... Hi Vinnie,' said Charlie affably, 'didn't see you when I came in.'

He lowered the hatch back down and walked over.

'So, how's it going?'

'Not bad, considering,' said O'Donnell.

McGhee grunted, hardly looking up.

'Heard you're heading back to the old country,' added O'Donnell.

Charlie was taken aback. He wasn't keeping it a secret; he had told several people he was taking a trip to Europe, but never specified any time or place. O'Donnell, being a two bit crook, thought Charlie could be up to something.

'Going over next week for a couple of weeks, on the Anchor Line.'

'Yes, I thought you might be. You'll be stopping at Moville in Donegal to let off the Irish passengers.'

'Could be, although it's not always the case,' said Charlie cautiously.

O'Donnell turned to McGhee.

'Vinnie, could you bring in the package from the car?'

McGhee stopped picking his nails and folded up the penknife. He gave Charlie a sneer as he turned away from the bar. Charlie's curiosity was tempered by a slight tug of concern.

O'Donnell ran his hand along the bar.

'You could do me a big favour by dropping off a package for me in Moville.'

Chapter 11

The Spotlight Shines

'So, that's two Espressos, one Americano and a pot of tea please, and I think we'll have some brandy. Three brandies and a pint of …'

'Excuse me!' sniffed Liam haughtily, 'I'll have whisky if you don't mind.' He stroked his chin thoughtfully. 'A single malt, Speyside. Denholm's 'Hidden Glen' if you have it, with one piece of ice.'

There was a moment of silence.

'Not often you touch the hard stuff, Liam,' said Des.

'… and rather specific,' added Helen.

'Just a notion,' said Liam casually, 'I've been reading a few good things about it; thought I'd give it a go.'

The waiter took a quick note and started to clear away the sweet dishes. The assistant manager threw some turf sods on the fire and used some iron tongs to get the fire ablaze.

'Lovely,' said Julie admiringly.

'Yes, very rustic,' added Liam trying to suppress a cough as the turf smoke caught the back of his throat.

The waiter dashed about with coffee cups and teapots. He rearranged the cutlery, added milk jugs and placed a tiny biscotto on each saucer while another waiter appeared at his elbow with the drinks.

Finally they settled back.

'Now then,' announced Liam after a sip of the whisky, 'to the story of the sovereigns…'

'Shouldn't we be taking notes …?' said Julie mischievously.

Liam gave her a scowl and continued.

'It appears that, for reasons that seem to be obscure, your grandfather Charlie McKenna and his younger brother, Pat, ended up here, in Cork, on the night of the 21st of October 1922. Charlie held some sort of rank, possibly as high as captain in the Southern Command in what was known at the time as the 'irregulars'. His younger brother Pat seemed to be a straightforward volunteer. Early the next morning they were dispatched in some type of commandeered armoured car, a Lancia I'm led to believe, down to a town called Passage West.'

'Ah!' said Helen. 'So that's why you wanted to go down there on Tuesday evening.'

'Yes. I just wanted to have a look about and see what was there, but as you recall it was just a small port with a quay for two or three medium sized boats. I don't think it was much bigger in 1922. I can only guess,' he continued, 'that someone, somewhere had gotten wind that the National Army were attempting to land troops there.'

'But I thought Pat was in the National Army?' said Julie.

'That came later. Let's just say that the situation was confused at this time. And remember that this was a Civil War and people often changed sides depending on circumstances. The situation in which they found themselves in Cork was as confused as any. The Irregulars, or the anti-treaty mutineers as some called them, were in disarray. They were continually outwitted and outmanoeuvred by a Free State National Army that contained many of their former colleagues. They also knew that landing by sea was a tactic used with spectacular success by the National Army over the previous two months. Only the week before they landed in a place called Fenet just outside Tralee and routed the irregulars in the well defended local barracks in a matter of hours. So it was a matter of urgency to get information on Passage West. Trouble was neither Charlie nor Pat ever reached there.'

He stopped to take some coffee.

'I'm not too sure, but I think they might have got lost. In any event they came across a vanguard unit of the National Army, it's not all that clear, but they seemed to overcome the unit either by ambush or trickery.'

'What, just the two of them?' said Des.

'No, I forgot to mention that there were another two involved, another two brothers as it happens. One's name was Declan …the other one isn't named.'

'Hold on. How do you know all this?' said Julie.

Liam put his hand inside his jacket and pulled out the small rectangular book.

'Charlie left this. It's a diary.'

He rippled the pages.

'Well, more a collection of thoughts and reminiscence; notes more than anything else really. It can be a bit confusing to read, but having wandered around Cork this week it's beginning to make more sense.'

'I don't understand,' said Helen, 'why would coming here give it more sense?'

'Well, for example, Charlie uses old street names and old place names. That's not a major problem, but it needed research. This street here, for example, McCurtain Street, used to be known as King Street.'

He looked at the little book.

'You and I are quite used to writing reports, recommendations that sort of stuff. Someone not used to writing usually makes assumptions. He takes it for granted that the reader knows the main characters and their political nuances; that they know, for example, how an army works. He even uses the occasional Gaelic expression … that kind of thing. Nor did he write in rigid chronological order either. I must admit coming here has added another dimension to me.'

He gave a short laugh.

'I could hardly believe my eyes when I saw that old photograph in O'Shea's, the restaurant we had lunch in yesterday. As I pointed out at the time, it was originally the Conway Hotel. Charlie mentions it in the diary. He stayed there a few times, it appears it was a place that he knew well.'

'So that's why you took a photograph.'

'Yes. I thought it was a remarkable coincidence, but when I thought about it, Cork is not that big and couldn't have had too many hotels in the '20s so I don't suppose it's that's unusual.'

'You mention that you think they got lost,' said Des.

'Yes, this is where it starts to get interesting,' said Liam leaning back.

'After they captured the Free State army patrol they discover that one of the vans was carrying a load of small arms ammunition and, even more intriguingly, Charlie discovers five heavy cases with the words 'Soarstat Eireann' stencilled on the side and below that 'An Roinn Airgeadas'.'

'What does that mean?'

'It means Department of Finance of the Irish Free State.'

'The gold sovereigns!' said Julie.

'Exactly!' replied Liam taking another sip of whisky.

'Wow! There were five cases of sovereigns, they must have been worth a fortune, how did ...' said Des.

'Hold on, all will be revealed,' said Liam, 'incidentally, in present terms, we're talking possibly millions of pounds here.'

By now the restaurant was beginning to fill up. A group of six well-dressed Americans took a table on the other side of the fire.

'I'm not sure how Charlie's plan evolved,' continued Liam, 'but I get the impression that he was making it all up on the hoof. They drove back to Cork via a town called Douglas ... why, I'm not sure ... but it seems that the landing of an invasion force convinced Charlie that the game was up. In Douglas he handed over the arms to the local militia and decided to carry on up to Cork. The Quarter Master of the brigade...'

'The Quarter Master?' said Julie.

'He's the officer who looks after the equipment and arms for the brigade,' explained Liam.

'This Quarter Master gave Charlie two hundred pounds for the van load of ammunition. Charlie split up the money in various ways. The two lads that were with them, for some reason, decided to stay on in the town of Douglas. Charlie and Pat must have arrived in the city around midday. By this time Charlie had hatched up the outline of a plan.'

Liam turned to the window and pointed over his right shoulder.

'Apparently he had a contact in one of the many bonded warehouses down the road here.'

'He decided he would lodge the cases of sovereigns in the warehouse on the pretext that they were expensive machine parts. This, it seems, was business he seemed to know a fair bit about. Apparently he and a fellow conspirator, a character by the name of George Peebles… more of him later on… had been smuggling arms into Ireland under the guise of mining equipment for a couple of years.'

'Charlie, an arms smuggler? Come on, you're making this up aren't you?' said Julie.

Liam leaned forward and tapped the book.

'It's all in here.'

Liam polished off the rest of the whisky, stood up and wandered over to the large picture window.

He pointed up the street.

'Imagine, if you can, the scene that afternoon. The sea landing had started in Passage West in the early hours of the morning with an exchange of gunfire. Charlie and his brother had been ordered to drive up to Passage West and had been on the road since dawn still not knowing what to expect.'

He turned for a moment to make an aside.

'You also should bear in mind that all those involved are young men, some no more than teenagers and it was a tense situation to say the least.

'They suddenly come across a patrol of National Army which would have been nerve-racking enough and could have ended in a murderous conflict. After that incident they then raced back to Cork via the town of Douglas, where the irregulars were hurriedly preparing to defend the streets. Their emotions must have been stretched to the limit. Coming into Cork they must have driven across the bridge below us and motored their way up to this corner on this very street before you. As I said, it was known as King Street in those days.'

He stretched his arm out to the left and swept it across the window and raised his voice.

'The acrid smell of burned out-buildings across the road here would still be in the air. Buildings put to the torch by the Black and Tans when they ran riot in the city the previous year and since left untouched. The sounds of distant gun blasts and the rattle of gunfire were coming from just a few miles across the river Lee. One must wonder at what was going through their minds...'

Liam stepped back and drew his arms dramatically across the scene outside.

'... as they raced hell for leather down this street with a load of hijacked gold bouncing around the back of the van – not knowing if an armed patrol of National Army had followed them into the city or not.'

He lifted his right arm and formed a cup with his hand.

'They must have ...'

Liam suddenly realised that the restaurant had gone quiet. The staff stood still and stared in disbelief. The group of Americans had all stopped talking and had turned around to face him. One had a drink poised half way to her mouth. Liam gave a polite cough and waved his hands in dismissal as he moved back to his chair.

'Sorry everyone, got carried away there.'

There was a short ripple of applause as he sat down.

'Well, well, Liam,' said Helen with a smile, 'seems you missed your vocation as an actor!'

There was a short silence before the restaurant patrons fell into a frenzy of excited chatter

'What was the name of that whisky again?' said Julie.

They had barely drawn breath before the waiter sidled over with a tray of drinks.

'Compliments from the nearby table, sir,' said the waiter nodding in the direction of the American table. He slid a card under Liam's drink. Liam gave a slight bow in recognition of the table's generosity.

'Can we still talk to his mightiness?' asked Helen.

Liam affected embarrassment.

'Sorry, folks, I was just getting into my stride there … didn't realise I had an audience.'

'Well, now that they've switched off the spotlight, how about carrying on with the story of the sovereigns?' said Des with a laugh.

'That's pretty much the end of the story about the bulk of the gold. They appear to have kept one case for themselves in the meantime and left the other four cases in the warehouse until they decided what to do with it.'

'How many coins in a case? Did he say?'

'Charlie mentioned a figure of 2,400 coins in a case, although it did seem a bit of an odd number to him. He later noted that it had something to do with the weight. Incidentally, at that time a sovereign would have little more than face value, perhaps an extra few shillings. In other words, they were a worth a little bit more than a British pound or four, maybe five, American dollars each.'

'Still a fair bit of money in those days I would imagine,' said Helen

'Indeed,' replied Liam, 'Gold coins were deregulated around 1935 or so I think. In today's market we could be looking at three hundred pounds a pop… so three quarters a million a case, at least.'

'Wow!' said Des, 'You mean they knocked off nearly…what? Nearly four million altogether?'

'A bit less I reckon, but who's going to quibble about a few hundred thousand quid?'

'So what happened next?' said Helen becoming more and more engrossed.

'I'm not sure if I've got this right ... but here goes ...'

He stopped talking to try the whisky.

'Slainte!' he shouted over to the next table.

'Cheers!' replied the older of the Americans, 'my pleasure.'

Liam settled back.

'The following day Pat and Charlie set of by train to Tralee. By some means or other Charlie had found out the afore-mentioned Mr Peebles had ended up in the Free State Army and was stationed at Ballymullen Barracks in Tralee. Peebles was a veteran of the US marines and signed up in America to join the Irish National Army at the rank of a Major ...'

'Is that plausible?' asked Des.

'Very plausible,' replied Liam, 'the National Army was desperate for ex-officers. When you think about it, English officers would have been politically unacceptable. Where better to go than to America? Charlie refers to seem some sort of debt owed to Peebles by the Irish Free State Government for an arms shipment, but it appears they – that's Charlie and Peebles I mean – were overcome by events, namely the assassination of Michael Collins.'

'Heavens!' said Helen, 'these guys lived in interesting times! Don't tell us they were involved in the ambush.'

Liam held up his hand and closed his eyes briefly.

'Please,' he said slowly, 'can I continue without these incessant asides?'

'Carry on! Mon Capitaine!' Julie said gleefully.

Liam gave a frustrated sigh and continued.

'Part of what happened next is a bit easier to unravel. The old lady I spoke to in Tralee was the niece of a Mrs Conklin with whom Charlie appeared to have some sort of financial relationship in so far as he financed a mortgage for her hotel – and she, in return, kept the remaining gold sovereigns in a personal strong box thus confirming to me the notes in the diary. Pat, I should tell you, had decided to join the National Army by this time and all this was apparently smoothly organised by Peebles. He, Pat that is, enlisted in the Ballymullen Barracks which I will come back to in a minute. It seems almost incredible, but as a result of Peebles using his rank, both he and Charlie were on the very boat that was used to ship the body of Michael Collins back to Dublin. They attended the funeral of Collins; Charlie watched from a tall building in Dublin - he doesn't mention the name of the place. Peebles believe it or not, was actually at the funeral service.'

Liam paused for a second.

'After the funeral Peebles seemed to have been settled up with his government debt and resigned his rank, which he was quite entitled to do after three months' service, and set sail for Paris with Charlie. Both of them subsequently show up in Philadelphia several months later.'

'I wonder why they went to Paris.'

Liam finished of his whisky.

'He alludes to a missing passport but nothing definite. Anyway, time we were off. I fancy a little walk to settle that grand dinner. How about walking into town for a nightcap? There's a nice quiet pub down by the riverside I'm sure you'll enjoy – no music or bands, no TV blaring away…'

Julie took it upon herself to organise the bill.

'Remember we've got travel arrangements to organise for tomorrow and Saturday,' said Helen, 'It might be good to have an early night.'

'Couldn't agree more. It's been a busy few days what with one thing and another, an early night sounds good to me,' said Liam, 'We'll stay for an hour or so then we'll head back.'

'Is there anything else in the book?' said Des.

Liam nodded.

Chapter 12

The numbers game

Manny called over young Francis Sharkey to clear an area of the bar. Frankie was a sassy seventeen-year-old who removed the heavy ashtray and wiped and polished the counter with exaggerated care.

'Okay, okay. Don't make a meal of it!' snapped O'Donnell.

He carefully took the cardboard eighteen by twenty-four-inch box from McGhee and solemnly laid it on the newly polished mahogany.

'I want to show you this,' he said to Charlie, who stood with a dozen different scenarios racing through his mind.

He took the lid of the box and uncovered a layer of cotton wool.

Charlie looked in.

'It's a photograph … a photograph of your wedding,' he said, trying not to sound too relieved.

'Yes indeed,' he said proudly. He lifted it out and held it in front of him like an orthodox priest holding a sacred icon.

'Yes, I remember, I was there,' said Charlie, 'the church was The Sacred Heart up in Fifty-First Street, wasn't it? About eighteen months back.'

'That's right. I want to send this to my old mother back home and I don't trust the damn postal service; it would be in pieces by the time it got there.'

He turned the frame around and looked at it admiringly.

'I haven't seen my mother for thirty years, not since she waved goodbye to me and my brother on the quay of Moville – I write occasionally. I'm sure she'll be delighted that I'm married and settled down.'

'There are indeed more things, but I think I'd like to have a word with Julie's mother before I reveal any more.'

'Why on earth would you want to speak to Grace about Charlie?' said Des.

Julie looked up.

'I have my reasons,' said Liam, 'let's say that Charlie's life in America might have had a darker side to it.'

He stood up and carefully laid down his napkin.

'There is also,' he added, 'the unsolved question of how Charlie got the rest of the gold sovereigns out of Ireland.'

Charlie could have sworn he saw Manny's eyes mist over for a split second. Married and settled down, he thought, that was stretching things a bit. He was about to tell Manny that Atlantic liners haven't stopped off at Moville with any regularity for decades but he thought better of it.

'Sure, Manny, I'll get your package over there. Get it wrapped up and make sure you put the address on the front and back. Give it in to Frankie here and I'll pick it up.'

Charlie wasn't concerned about whether the liner stopped at Moville or not. When he got to Glasgow he could easily arrange the box to go to Donegal, there was a regular sea route; people were going back and forward to Derry on a daily basis. He lifted up the hatch again.

'I'm sorry, Manny, I need to go upstairs for a while. I'll see you before I go.'

'That's okay, by the way, how is your side-kick George Peebles these days?'

Charlie stopped. There was something in the way he mentioned George that gave a slight tinkle of an alarm bell in the back of his head.

'Oh you know George, always complaining and grousing,' he turned and slowly dropped the bar hatch behind him ... *and probably talking too much*, he thought quietly.

'Tell him I was asking for him,' said Manny.

'Will do!' replied Charlie heading up the stairs.

He stopped at the top of the stairs to gather his thoughts for a moment. Manny was hardly a friend, he was just considered part of the community of semi-gangsters and would be-mobsters that he had to deal with. Okay, both he and George were at his wedding – big deal, nothing unusual in that – there must have been scores of people that were loosely connected to Manny at that wedding. No, it wasn't Manny that was making him uneasy; it was his sudden association with McGhee that was the problem. O'Donnell he knew to be street wise and cunning but not that smart; a pest at worst, but not a danger. McGhee, on the other hand, was clearly half mad and, rather worryingly, seemed to be gathering an unhealthy influence over Manny.

He gave a brief sigh. Perhaps he was making too much of it. This business, he thought, makes everyone paranoid. He walked down the corridor to Slavinsky's office.

'Charlie! Vi geyt es? Give me a minute,' shouted Slavinsky from behind his desk.

'Es geyt, a dank!' replied Charlie in Yiddish.

Slavinsky was nestling the phone earpiece in the crook of his neck. He waved Charlie over to a chair.

'Tell him 6 will get him 4 only if he places a hundred. That's my last offer.'

He rattled the earpiece back into the cradle.

'I got your message, something about an offer for the lease,' said Slavinsky straight to point, as usual. He folded over the racing section of the *New York World* as he spoke.

'It's a bit awkward. Manny O'Donnell has asked us to think about an offer for the lease. I've got to admit it might suit me; I've more or less decided to pack in the liquor business. In fact, me and Una are seriously thinking of leaving the US altogether...'

'... and going back to Europe? Are you nuts?' replied Slavinsky.

Slavinsky had a habit of finishing of other people's sentences and generally talked by asking rhetorical questions.

'Nothing definite yet, just thinking about it. I'm taking a trip to Glasgow next week and might have a look around.'

'Glasgow? That's in England somewhere isn't it?'

'Not really ...'

Slavinsky shrugged.

'Near enough as damn it. Anyway what's with the lease business?'

'O'Donnell is offering $1000 to take over the lease. The lease only has another eighteen months to run. Sounded good to me.'

'A thousand bucks for this place? What's he up to?'

'Who knows? He has his own ideas.'

He stopped talking for a moment and laid down the paper – unusual for Slavinsky.

'A thousand bucks ... not bad,' he said narrowing his eyes.

He ran his fingers over his mouth.

'It might suit me too. Horse racing and boxing are becoming so fixed that most of the high rollers have stopped laying bets. I'm thinking of opening somewhere up nearer Harlem and concentrating on the policy game. It's a nickel and dime racket but it's a no lose business. The blacks and the Italians love it.'

Charlie rarely gambled and wasn't too sure what the policy game entailed. He didn't ask. He would probably find out soon enough.

'What about the restaurant? Are the Sweeney's happy?' asked Slavinsky suddenly.

'The Sweeney's have been renting from us for two years. They pay the rent every month on the dot. Manny is keen to keep them, they're a good cover for ... well, anything. He's more interested in these rooms up here. Reckons he could build at least ten bedrooms in this space.'

Slavinsky looked up, rolled his eyes and gave a knowing grunt. 'Bedrooms? He's turning this place into a hotel? Yeah, and don't tell me,' he held up his hand, 'I know, he wants to become the next William Astor.'

Slavinsky leaned back and looked at the ceiling.

'Does it matter?' he mused, 'nothing to do with us after we leave, is it?'

Charlie continued.

'So I'll see the lawyer tomorrow and I'll ...'

'... make sure we get the money up front. When does he want to move in? I need a few weeks to get organised.'

Charlie stood up and walked over to the wall calendar. He flicked over a page featuring a coloured print of Blue Larkspur, the Belmont Stakes winner.

'How about Friday the Twenty First. That's six weeks away?'

'Sounds good. That's plenty of time. I'll head up to Harlem tomorrow, there's a few places I've got my eye on,'

The phone rang.

'Slavinsky here,' he barked.

'I'll get going. I'll see you on Friday,' said Charlie as Slavinsky snatched up the racing paper.

He almost knocked over young Frankie in the corridor.

'What do you want me to do with this?' said Frankie, holding up a tied package, 'I didn't want to leave it lying about the bar.'

'Has Manny left?'

'He and Vinnie left just this minute.'

Charlie took the package.

'Neatly wrapped,' he said.

He turned it over

The address was on the Port Road, Letterkenny.

'Neat writing too. I didn't think that Manny could write.'

'It's okay, I did all that. He gave me a quarter, told me to get myself a drink.'

Charlie halted for a second. He had a safe in the bar where he kept some important things but it would mean first rummaging in the drawer under the till to find the key, using the key and then using the combination number. He looked at the package again and turned it over, probably too big for the safe anyway.

'I'll just leave it in my office. I'll be down in a minute.'

Frankie was serving a couple of press guys when Charlie reappeared in the bar. He looked at the wall clock. Just gone half past one. Charlie was surprised; it seemed later.

'Here, I'll get these drinks,' said Charlie handing over a dollar to young Sharkey, 'could you do me a favour, Frankie, and get me a sandwich and a coffee from Sweeney's? Just the usual. Keep the change.'

'Okay, Boss,' replied Frankie snapping up the dollar, 'my lucky day, huh!'

'Cheers, Charlie,' said Hans Von Kaltonborn, who most people simply called 'HV'. Kaltonborn was a fifty something press reporter now trying to make a name for himself on radio.

'Don't worry, I'm about to pick your brains for the price of a beer,' replied Charlie, shoving a couple of paper mats under the beers.

'Any of you guys know anything about the policy game?'

'Yeah,' said Kaltonborn, 'They sometimes call it the numbers game. It's a bit like the lottery. You pick three numbers and if they match the last numbers of the daily take at the race track then you've won. If the daily take at, say, Vermont is $783.56 then the three numbers you need are 3, 5 and 6. The daily take is published by all the newspapers'

'Is that it?' said Charlie, 'I thought it was complicated.'

'Got to be easy to understand or people won't bet. You can also bet in small amount five cents, ten cents and so on.'

'But how much would you win?'

'Usually about 300 to 1.'

'Hey, that sounds not too bad for a return!'

Kaltonborn laughed and took a draught of his beer.

'Easy seeing you don't gamble, Charlie,' said his partner, 'any random three numbers in the correct order will give you a thousand combinations so the odds of getting the three numbers correct are not 300 to one but a thousand to one.'

The press man extended his hand to Charlie.

'Bob Best, just back from Europe.'

'That's over two hundred percent profit for the bookie and at hardly any risk,' continued Kaltonborn wiping his mouth with a napkin.

Frankie returned and placed a mug of coffee and a plate of chicken and cheese sandwiches with a side of pickles on the counter.

'Yes, now that you've explained it, I can see why they call it the numbers racket. Interesting, although I don't gamble much myself,' said Charlie lifting the coffee.

'Help yourselves by the way,' he continued pushing over the plate, 'Ann always makes way too much for me.'

'Mind you, if it's that easy why aren't more bookies doing it?' he added.

'Not as easy as you think setting up a racket like that,' said Kaltonborn lifting a sandwich, 'You need to gather up a decent amount of clientèle, and then you need runners you can trust or terrify to collect the bets.'

'… or better still people you can trust *and* terrify,' added Best, 'it's a rough old game, it may be small wagers but most people join local groups, like guys or women who work together – you know, in factories or shops, that sort of thing, and they make multiple bets – lots of money involved.'

'And unlike legalised betting, you can offer credit,' added Kaltonborn, 'that in its turn leads to loan sharking. And that's another whole bunch of easy money opportunities. Before you know it the vultures are hovering. The police reckon half the bodies fished out of the East River are involved in illegal gambling one way or another. Hope you're not thinking of taking it up?'

'No,' said Charlie, 'just curious, that's all.'

'Well just stay curious, that's my advice.'

'Don't worry, I've enough fish to fry as it is,' said Charlie, 'but I sometimes wonder how these mobsters manage to make a living. There must be dozens of bookies around the West Side alone. Yet, according to you guys in the papers, it's all controlled by a mysterious Mr Big.'

'Don't believe what you read in the papers. What the newspapers refer to as the 'underworld' is really a place of crazy anarchy; pretty much it's the survival of the fittest. A few of the Mustache Petes from Sicily and Calabria tried to muscle in on the more lucrative rackets but it ended in the usual bloody internal civil war. Criminals are too competitive to form monopolies.'

'Then they should form a political party, like the Nazis in Germany,' laughed Best.

'I've read a bit about them the past few years,' said Charlie, 'Where in Europe were you, Bob?'

'Austria. Vienna mainly,' he replied.

Charlie took some coffee.

'Sprechen Sie Deutsch?' he said.

'Ich spreche nur ein bisschen Deutsch.'

'I'm much the same, just a few bits of from the war.'

'I get by,' Best handed over a card, 'If you're ever in Vienna ...'

'Sure,' said Charlie sticking the card in his top pocket, 'as luck would have it, I'm going over to Europe next week; nothing as glamorous as Vienna though. Leaving on Tuesday.'

'Don't envy you. I'm not keen on sea journeys, just arrived in New York on Tuesday. Still feel as if I'm staggering about.'

Charlie laughed.

'I'm not too bad a sailor. Sorry, guys,' said Charlie finishing off his coffee, 'I've got a few things to do. Need to go.'

Charlie spent the next couple of hours firming up his travel arrangements and arranging the delivery of a new steel sea trunk to his apartment. He then had a pre-organised meeting with his new foreman, Lars Carlstrom, about the work schedule for the next couple of weeks. They talked over the drawings and material orders. They drank tea in the site office.

'This might be a bit of an opportunity for you, Larry,' said Charlie.

'In what way?' said Lars.

Charlie picked his words carefully.

'I'm thinking of selling up. George Peebles would probably buy me out but George has his hands full down in Philly. I'm pretty sure he would prefer to keep things as they are. How much money could you raise over the next few months?'

Lars was uncertain. He was far from being a fool but unused to business dealings.

'I'm not sure.'

'You should think along the lines of around a thousand.'

Lars was surprised, he was pretty sure he could raise a thousand. His father had a farm in Iowa, not exactly a ranch, but big enough. And he had ridden out the depression better than most. Lars had over a hundred dollars in the bank himself. He could....

Charlie stood up.

'Don't give me an answer now, just think about it.'

He walked towards the door and turned.

'Make a few enquires over the next few weeks ... and think about what you'd be getting yourself into.'

He gave a short wave as he left.

'I'll see you tomorrow about noon time.'

Chapter 13

One for the road

'Where did you say this warehouse was?' asked Des.

'We're walking in the wrong direction for that. The warehouses are behind us, down towards the river. I had a look during the week but most of them are gone, probably years ago,' said Liam.

'So where are we going now?'

'We're going to turn left here and go over the bridge. There's a nice little pub where we can have a nightcap.'

They walked down Bridge Street, a steep incline, to the start of Patrick's Bridge.

'What? A bridge with no jakies around?' said Des.

'A bit late for all that. Some old codger tapped me for a couple of Euros this morning when I was out for a stroll. Strange old guy, talked about someone in Glasgow that's been dead for twenty years.'

He stopped at the parapet.

'Just about here it was. I was just looking at ... Good God! It's still here!'

'What is it?' said Helen alarmed.

'That damn bird, an auk I think it's called.'

They all looked down to where Liam was pointing. A large black seabird sat passively on an equally blackened old timber upright mooring boom.

'Oh for heaven's sake,' said Helen, 'it's only a cormorant, probably roosting there for the night.'

'Are you all right, Liam? You seem to be getting spooked easy these days. So an old man tapped you for a few bob and you've seen a bird,' said Julie, 'hardly the portent of the second coming?'

Liam gave a slight shudder,

'What about the woman in the shop?'

Helen gave an exasperated sigh.

'Come on you! Let's get you a pint of stout to calm your nerves.'

Liam turned around and gave a grin.

'Now you're talking!! I feel better already.'

Liam walked ahead with Des pointing out the designer street lights across the bridge. Helen and Julie fell into conversation behind them.

'Liam's a card, isn't he?' said Julie, 'never a dull moment when he's around.'

'Infuriating at times though.'

'I didn't know he was seeing someone, came as a bit of a surprise, although he does keep his private life to himself I must admit.'

'Yes, discretion in one of his better qualities. I've known Liam for a few years now.'

'Have you?' said Julie, 'Sorry, didn't mean to pry.'

'That's okay, it's not a big secret. I live with my mother these days. I'm afraid she's getting a bit frail in her old age, needs a bit of looking after. Nothing arduous just the occasional bit of help now and again. Liam and I go out, you know, movies, dinner once or twice a month, the occasional exhibition; the odd weekend together, nothing too serious. We're not exactly teenagers, you know,' she laughed. 'I know that I snap at him occasionally but I'm really quite fond of him.'

'Did you meet at work?'

'More or less, I'd just come back up from London and managed to get a job with the local authority. I met him when he was organising a trade exhibition in the Mitchell. I must admit I was a bit vulnerable at the time. I had just ended a rather acrimonious affair with ...'

'Ah! Here we are,' roared Liam as they reached The Lamb's Gizzard.

Julie muttered an inward curse.

'The Lamb's Gizzard - what kind of name is that?' asked Helen.

'It's a pub name of course,' replied Liam, 'let's get ourselves in.'

The pub wasn't quite the slumbering tomb that Liam had suggested, but by Irish standards it was remarkably quiet. A radio played softly behind the bar tuned, no doubt, thought Julie, to some babbling phone-in show. The back lounge, only visible if you stood at the bar, contained about half a dozen men staring into a corner at an unseen TV set watching that other Irish obsession – English soccer. They sat at table in a raised area by the window while Des ordered some drinks.

'I must say this is pleasant,' said Helen looking out of the window at the moon reflected on the River Lee on a high tide, 'now then, how did you manage to find this place?'

'It was odd. I was looking through Charlie's writings and he mentioned hearing of Michael Collins imminent arrival in Cork a couple of days before he was assassinated. He said he was reading a paper in a pub down by the river, around here I guessed, when he overheard someone mention Collins name. I was looking around and I found this place.'

'Do you think ...'

'Highly unlikely that this is the same pub Charlie was in. This neck of the woods had loads of pubs and alehouses back then.'

'What's with the daft name?'

'God knows,' said Liam, 'it's one of these joke names that the Irish sometimes use for pubs.'

He looked uncomfortable.

'A bit like 'The Coughing Sheep' in Glasgow.'

'You mean the pub where Mick Hastings was murdered?'

'Yes. The Coughing Sheep is a silly play on words. A ship that left for America from Cork was often referred to as a Coffin Ship – hence the name 'The Coughing Sheep'.'

There was a silence as Des brought over the drinks on a tray and started to pass them around.

'Yes, a bit ironic given the events.'

'More like macabre, I'd say,' said Julie bitterly.

Liam gulped down a large draft of stout.

'Anyway,' he said dabbing his mouth with a napkin, 'At least we've got to the bottom of the mystery of the sovereigns – well almost. I'm still a bit in the dark about what happened to the rest of the consignment, although Charlie gives a few hints that it was recovered by the authorities some time later.'

'What about Pat and your theory about what happened at Ballyseedy Crossroads?' said Des.

'Still stands, I think. For a start, Pat is on the record as being stationed at the Ballymullen Barracks at the time of the incident. Mrs Conklin's niece gave me another bit of information. She said that Pat was transferred from Tralee shortly after the tragedy and it was heavily rumoured at the time that those who were involved were shipped out to avoid any further incidents. Not cast iron proof, I agree, but ties in with my thoughts on the matter.'

He took out the photograph again and laid it on the table.

'Look at the formality of the pose, then there's the soldier with the gun and the details of the coffins being there.'

'What about this large building on Pat's left, there's no sign of a building anywhere near where we were today.'

Liam waved a hand in dismissal.

'As I pointed out this afternoon, look at the state of the building. It appears as if it was ready to fall down even at the time. It stands to reason that a large building such as a pub or a small hotel would be at such an important crossroads. The new road that we were on would have demolished any sign of such a building. If you remember we had to look down a fairly deep embankment to spot the original crossroad. The new road is as straight as a die and pretty level, probably the engineers used what is called a Cut and Fill method and anything in the way would have been simply demolished or buried. If I've got time I might go over to Dublin to check the survey maps of the time.'

Julie leaned back.

'Since you told me this wild story, I've sometimes wondered if the memory of what happened down here is the reason why Pat went a bit crazy as he got older.'

'Possibly, but I wouldn't know. It could have been a number of things. By the way, I forgot to mention that your quiet and unassuming grandfather also had some sort of stake in that Tralee Hotel or Boarding House, whatever you want to call it.'

'Good God! No wonder he had so much money when he died!' said Des, 'Was it worth much when cashed in?'

'Don't know if 'cashed in' is the right word to use about the hotel but he certainly got a good pay off when, and if, he sold the sovereigns.'

'Why was that?'

'The gold standard was abandoned around 1937. It made sovereigns worth a lot more than their face value. Take, for example, around the early '50s. Each sovereign by that time would be worth around £35 or even as much as £40. That's somewhere in the region of £50,000 and in the early '50s that would constitute a large fortune.'

'At around £40 a pop surely the gold would be worth more than that,' said Des.

'Agreed,' said Liam, 'but think about it. It's not is if you could walk into a high street bank branch and hand over a large bag of gold sovereigns. Might have raised a few eyebrows I'd say.'

'So how did …'

'I think I know how Charlie managed it but let's leave it at that. I need to talk to someone else about it first.'

He lifted his pint and drained it in a gulp.

'As a matter of interest,' he continued, casually placing the empty glass in the middle of the table, 'did you know that there was a fairly large Jewish community in Cork?'

Julie looked at him bemused at this sudden change of subject, ignored the remark and sighed.

'I'm not doubting you for a minute,' she said, 'but there's a lot of speculation, and lots of ifs and maybes in all of this.'

'Och,' said Liam, 'you just lack a bit of imagination.'

'Something you certainly don't lack.' said Helen crisply. 'Anyone for a final drink? I think I'll finish off with an Irish coffee.'

'I'll have a Denholm's.'

'Oh no you won't. I don't to want to listen to you howling at the moon all night.'

'A pint of stout then?' he said hopefully.

'That's more like it. It's a deal – pint of stout it is!'

Chapter 14

The Stables

Charlie ended up almost running down Eighth Avenue then along Thirty-Sixth Street to Armstrong & Drever's fifth floor office. As it was, he was still a few minutes late. He stood with his hat in hands in front of the reception desk.

'I've an appointment with Mr Armstrong.'

The bottle-blonde girl behind the desk in the foyer carried on typing for a minute without reply. When she'd finished she ran her finger down the appointment book, looked up at the office clock and gave him a patronising look.

'I'll see if Mr Armstrong will still see you.'

She stood up, drew her vacant blue eyes over Charlie and shimmied over to the office door

Charlie was tempted to speak out. It infuriated him no end the way lawyers' secretaries expected the company's clients to turn up ten minutes early and then let them sit around clicking their heels until it suited them to inform the lawyer that they had just arrived. He kept quiet and removed his hat.

'He'll see you now,' she said with disdain as she returned to her desk.

'I'm sure he will,' he said through gritted teeth.

She started threading another sheet of paper into her typewriter roller without looking up. Charlie turned the elaborate brass door handle and entered the office. Armstrong was already half way across the room with his hand outstretched

'Charlie, old man, how the devil are you? Come on in, take a seat.'

'Good to see you, Harry. I thought that secretary of yours was going to heave me down the stairs for being five minutes late.'

'Don't worry about Vermillion, she's a bit over enthusiastic at times.'

'Vermillion?'

'Broadway actress. Between jobs, as they say. She likes to practise her roles in the office. I guess she must be practising Bette Davis today. It's good fun trying to guess the star of the day, besides all that I must admit she is pretty good at her job.'

Charlie grunted.

'To business,' said Harry, 'I heard you're giving up your lease to O'Donnell. What's he offering?'

'A thousand.'

Harry gave a low whistle.

'Not bad for a short-term lease. I'll do the paperwork for ten percent, sounds about right. Who's paying – him or you?'

'I'll get O'Donnell to stump up. I think he'll fall in with that as long as you don't inquire too much about the future use.'

'Which is apparently a …' he said, opening the file, 'small hotel.'

He closed the file and coughed discreetly.

'So, how are things these days?'

'Oh, not so bad.'

Armstrong started putting away the files as they talked. They had known each other for a few years now. Harry Armstrong had a few dealings and contracts with store owners and landlords who were affected by construction work on the subways and elevated railways of the local area. Their paths had crossed frequently. They spent the next ten minutes exchanging gossip about the local traders and hoodlums. Armstrong was that rarest of species - an honest lawyer. Although in New York that statement was only relative, he rarely took on any criminal cases. 'The money is never enough for the risk,' he always maintained and, as he put it, '… if New York's going to hell in a hand cart they didn't need him to give it a hand.'

'Well then, I'll leave you to it, keep in touch.'

'So you're off to Ireland next week,' said Harry as they walked to the door.

'Actually Scotland, if all goes well. I'll see myself out,' replied Charlie and gave a wave as he headed for the outer door.

Vermillion lifted her eyes and blew a stream of cigarette smoke in the direction of the window in what she regarded as a pensive manner. Charlie gave a nod in her direction; she did not respond.

*

Charlie asked Mrs G. to order a return ticket to Philly as soon as he entered the office and then spent the rest of the morning with her. They went over invoices, salary details and meetings which she could handle and which ones would be best to cancel for the coming three weeks.

Mrs G. started to fill up her diary quickly.

'Do you know when you're coming back, I mean, are you sure you'll be back in three weeks?'

'I'll be back. Well, unless the weather gets really bad. I'll cable or maybe phone you if things change.'

'Let's say you'll be back at your desk on Monday the fourteenth,' she said, writing it down in her diary. 'I'm going to type all this up and put it on the wall. I don't want George changing things on a whim.'

'Good idea. I'm going up to his new house on Sunday for lunch. I'll remind him who's in charge,' he said with a grin.

'I didn't know he had a new house. When did all this happen?'

'I suppose I shouldn't call it a house, he says it's more like a cottage with stables. His girls were harping on at him about getting some ponies so he thought it would be a cheaper option to buy something in Northwest Philadelphia.'

'Okay for the rich Irish, huh!' she retorted in good humour.

'That's me for the day,' said Charlie reaching for his hat. 'Lock up when you've finished.'

'Sure. I'll miss lunch and work till I finish this,' she replied holding up the diary.

He walked out to the outer door.

'I'll drop in on Monday morning to see if there are any problems.'

'Fine,' she shouted from the back office.

Charlie caught the early express to Philly the following morning. As usual it was pretty busy. He was early enough to manage a window seat in the Second Class carriage, also early enough to buy a *Philadelphia Examiner* that he flicked through disinterestedly. The train picked up speed and he started to gaze out the window at the spring countryside and farmlands of Pennsylvania. He started to think over the coming few months. He and Una had agreed that he should look around Glasgow for some property. Charlie was still in two minds about a return to Europe. He liked America, New York in particular, but he was becoming increasingly alarmed about the lawless and almost anarchic life in Manhattan. Gun battles and feuds were growing in intensity and the police and the law seemed to be unable to control anything. A recent 'War against Crime' resulted in dozens of murder prosecutions. Up in New York's state prison, Sing Sing, the electric chair was in daily use; they were virtually massacring dozens of inmates every month and it hardly made a dent in the crime figures. The Italians, particularly the new breed of Sicilians, were becoming increasingly well organised and more vicious. Prohibition was coming to an end, he was convinced of that, and started to wonder about what would replace the lucrative booze trade. Already one or two had muscled their way into the dope trade, traditionally the preserve of the Chinese and Mexicans in New York. The gangs and mobsters were organised and up and running; they were hardly likely suddenly to dissolve and decide to become model citizens. Prohibition, he thought grimly, had a lot to answer for. He wasn't too worried about his own future, he was resourceful and adaptable and compared to most he had survived the worst of the recession and he was relatively well off. He reckoned he could realise about ten thousand dollars all told. That was, he calculated quickly, about three thousand British pounds. He could easily afford to take his time and look around for opportunities, he hardly gave it a second thought. Una was keener, no doubt about that, she had no relatives to speak of here and she was anxious to see her family. Her father had a civil service post in Edinburgh and was now at an age where he was unlikely to start wandering again. She had a sister in Glasgow who had several young children she was dying to see. Perhaps, he considered, it was time to settle down and finish with the semi-legal and increasingly dangerous life he had created for himself over the past couple of years.

As the train pulled in to the chaos of Broad Street, Charlie pulled down a small carpet bag from the overhead package rack, alighted quickly and made his way down Thirtieth Street to catch a trolley. He had known from bitter experience that the worst way was by cab unless you were a rookie or loaded down with luggage. At this time of day, the journey by trolley rarely took more than fifteen minutes – twenty minutes at most. His sister surprised him by having his room ready when he arrived at the door. The indomitable Mrs G, she told him, had wired a short message as soon as she came into the office that morning. He was impressed; she never ceased to amaze him with her foresight. Charlie dropped his bag and headed back to Chestnut Street in an effort to catch George before he disappeared off the site.

George had the habit of dressing in working clothes when he was on site, not that he actually did any work, it was simply force of habit. He also hated shelling out for decent office furniture and any site office of Peebles Cons. Inc. was always filled with ancient stuffed sofas and armchairs that he found lying about the area; the only constant was an ancient drawing table that followed George around from job to job like a faithful, mangy dog.

'Have a seat,' he shouted above the din as he threw himself into an armchair behind his desk.

It exploded in a cloud of dust and cement.

'Are these the latest drawings?' said Charlie, diplomatically walking over to the window and picking up a blueprint.

'Just in. No alterations so far, thank God. What's the latest on your trip?' he added.

'Everything's going to plan. My trunk is getting carted down on Monday night and hopefully the ship should leave on schedule on Tuesday morning.'

'Have you organised a meeting with one of the Denholms yet?'

'I left that to Sandy. Latest is that the earliest meeting would be a week on Monday.'

George tried to mentally calculate the days. Finally he said, 'That's okay isn't it? The crossing usually takes five days to Ireland at most.'

'That's right, depending on the weather of course. I've temporarily booked a sailing home at the end of that week. So I shouldn't be away for much more than three weeks at most.'

'The modern world, eh,' said George with a romantic sigh, 'to think it took me a fortnight to get to America when I first came here. I came with ...'

'Good grief! Is that the time?' said Charlie looking at his watch.

'My sister has the address of a cousin of my father who has lived in Glasgow most of his life. I'll need it to send him a cable sometime today,' he added quickly; George could ramble on for hours about the good old days given the slightest opportunity.

'I just popped round to see what time you were expecting us tomorrow.'

'Tomorrow? Oh yes, tomorrow. Elizabeth has arranged dinner at the house for seven tomorrow evening. I'll pick you and Una up and take you over to see the stables, say about 2 o'clock?'

'That sounds good. Una is due back from Harrisburg tonight or tomorrow at the latest.'

'Harrisburg? Why is she up there?'

'Some sort of mining accident up near there. They were taking those injured to the hospital at Harrisburgh. No deaths apparently but a few serious injuries.'

'If anything goes wrong give me a phone here before I set out.'

'Sure, George. Listen, I need to get back. My sister's preparing a meal for me and a few of Joe's relatives and I've still got a few things to do. I daren't be late or there'll be hell to pay.'

'Ok I'll walk you down to the bus stop.'

*

Una had arrived early on Saturday and went immediately to her downtown apartment that she shared with two of her nursing colleagues. Like most well organised apartment blocks they had access to a couple of smart young boys who would deliver personal messages anywhere in town at negotiable rates. She sent one hot foot with a note to Charlie's sister and bribed him with an extra dime to bring back a return message.

She turned up outside Charlie's house at 1:30 dressed in fashionable leisure trousers.

'I hope you arranged for George to take me back to my apartment before we go for dinner.'

Charlie looked a bit confused.

'Why would he want to do that?'

'So I can get changed of course.'

'Oh! Never thought about that. Not to worry, I'll phone him at the house right now.'

Charlie's sister rolled her eyes and muttered 'Men!' as she walked back to the dining room with Una.

The cottage wasn't that far out of town but it took a while to negotiate the railway crossings and the raised tram track at intersections. As soon as he reached Germantown, George pulled down his goggles and started to race through the suburbs.

'For God's sake, slow down a bit, George. You're not driving a getaway car!'

'You're right, wouldn't want to knock anyone down,' he said, looking over his shoulder, 'even if we do have a nurse on board!'

'Just you keep your eyes ahead,' said Charlie, grabbing at the wheel to avoid a large dog that went crazy and proceeded to charge after them trying to bite the rubber tyres.

They reached the cottage in half an hour. George skidded the Chevrolet to a juddering halt at the front gate.

'A bit more than a mere cottage I'd say,' said Una looking up at the two storey building.

'It's not that big; it's only got four bedrooms.'

'What, in the whole house? Or is that just on the ground floor?' said Charlie with a laugh.

'It looks a bit bigger than it is because of the stables at the back. Come on I'll show you around.'

George was nearly right. The stables at the back did give the building the appearance of a large country house, although to call it a cottage was stretching a point.

'Stabling for four horses,' said George proudly, 'one for each of the girls and one for me.'

'Lucky girls,' said Una, walking into the nearest horse box.

'Costing me an arm and a leg,' he said to Charlie when Una was out of earshot, 'still, nothing's too good for my girls.'

'Hope you can afford it.'

'Just about. Must admit I got this place for a song. It's the upkeep that could be the problem.'

He turned to Charlie looking concerned.

'I could be doing with this whisky business working in my favour. I ... I might have overstretched things a bit recently.'

'You're not in debt, are you?'

'Nothing I can't handle but I could be in a bit of trouble if this goes wrong. I've just about enough to cover it…I mean, if the worst comes to the worst, and if I lose the lot.'

'Not like you to risk money you don't have. You might be putting me in a bad spot here, George.'

'It's not as bad as that. I believe this is a good deal.'

He shrugged.

'Even if I just get my money back there is no loss. If it goes badly wrong then I'll be in debt for five or six grand. True, it might take a couple of years pay to that off, but a risk I'm willing to take.'

He slapped Charlie on the back

'Don't worry. There's no pressure on you, Charlie, don't worry. You just do what you have to do, that's all.'

Saturday night dinners at the Peebles house could be elaborate affairs. Elizabeth Farrell had social aspirations that she acquired from her Boston upbringing. Her Irish Grandfather hailed from County Cork and was a cut above the usual immigrant insofar as he had some business experience, having run a small, moderately successful painting and decorating business partnership, before he decided to try his luck in Boston. He was remarkably successful and soon branched into a variety of enterprises including upholstery and interior design and latterly in banking and finance. He had two stunning granddaughters the younger one of which was Elizabeth; what she ever saw in George was always a source of wonder to Charlie. They married in Boston in a typically elaborate, Irish Catholic, middle class affair which George enjoyed immensely. It was, he was fond of saying, one of the few Irish weddings he'd attended that didn't end up in a fist fight. After a short honeymoon in Atlantic City they moved into a large apartment in downtown Philadelphia.

A soon as she arrived Elizabeth quickly acquainted herself with the local Philadelphia Irish society worthies including the Kellys, the highest in the pecking order. Dinner parties and charity events filled her social diary, and cocktail parties, which were technically illegal, were an everyday event.

Cocktail parties, Charlie discovered, were a bit of a grey area in the Prohibition Act. A peculiar anomaly of the Act was that, although the selling, transport and distribution of alcohol was illegal, strictly speaking, the actual drinking of alcohol was not illegal.

In any event the police never enforced the Act in middle class circles. Charlie had never heard of a cocktail party, no matter how rowdy, ever being raided.

The usual crowd had turned up. Some came for cocktails around six and later left for other dinner engagements, other guests, invited to dinner, stayed on. In many ways it was all rather informal and 'the bee's knees' according to Una. The young Peebles girls were constantly in attendance early in the evening, always keen to display their musical and dramatic skill to whoever was around.

Una was bombarded about her ring and the wedding arrangements, a discussion Charlie was wise enough to avoid. He gamely hung around the fringes of the male groups, chipping in occasionally when the discussion turned on sporting events, like boxing or the slow decline of the Philly 'Athletics' since winning the World Series three years ago. George was, as usual, noisy and gregarious, hinting that he had a good deal in the offing and, disturbingly, hinted that he had something to do with importing liquor.

Like most family dinners after coffee was served, the younger set decided to head down town to the jazz clubs and dance halls of Philly or nearby Camden across the river in New Jersey. Some guests went outside for a walk in the garden, several of the guests sat chattering in the drawing room while George and Charlie had a game of snooker and a cigar in the billiard room.

Charlie set up the table.

'You're getting me worried, George, I don't recommend broadcasting your deal with Davidson.'

George looked a bit hurt.

'You know what it's like, people ask how you're doing; I just gave a hint here and there, anyway, as you said, we're doing nothing illegal.'

Charlie bent down to take a shot.

'I know, but people are still a bit funny about the liquor trade. Remember we've had twelve years of prohibition. Most people read the papers, they think the booze trade is just like the Wild West. Not only that, but mobsters think that any business to do with booze must be illegal therefore fair game for anything. The rules don't apply to them. That's why they are in an everyday war with each other. That's why I think the less they know the better.'

'Fair point, Charlie, my boy!'

'From now on …'

He rubbed chalk onto the cue tip and blew off the excess. He pressed a finger to his mouth.

'… my lips are sealed!'

He leaned over the table.

'Now,' he said, 'just watch this shot!'

He hammered the white cue ball which, in turn, cannoned the red ball into the top pocket.

Chapter 15

A Wave of Streamers

Charlie had to leave Philly on Sunday afternoon to get an early start in the morning, he always had lot to do on Mondays. He appeared on the Eighteenth Street job at 7.00 and spent the first fifteen minutes going over the month's schedule to refresh his memory. Most of the men had arrived either before him or rolled in well before the official 7:30 start.

They sat around the rest area relaxing and drinking coffee before the shift began, the older guys were quiet for the most part, the younger ones joshed around telling exaggerated tales of their weekends. It was something that gave Charlie an icy shiver at times; it was almost like soldiers waiting to go over the top. In the office Carlstrom went over his own schedule; he could see no outstanding problems, he said. Charlie hung around with Carlstrom for another half an hour outlining some of the paper work he needed to supply to Mrs G. every Thursday – 'get it there before 2:00 at the latest,' he insisted, to give her a chance of organising the payroll before Friday evening. The risks of a payroll robbery in Manhattan were getting higher these days and reluctantly he started to pay his crew by cheque. The men could cash the cheque if they could get to the bank on time or, if they were desperate, Charlie allowed the cheques to be cashed in the speakeasy through the Sharkeys' account.

He paid a quick visit to the office to see Mrs G. He needn't have bothered, she was in her element. After ten minutes she shooed him out of the office to take a call from one of Charlie's trucking contractors.

Between one thing and another, Charlie was suddenly beginning to feel a bit redundant.

It was, he finally convinced himself, just the result of good forward planning.

Then it was back to the apartment to supervise the carting of his luggage down to the warehouse in readiness for the next morning's sailing. He spent a few hours in The Country Club mainly to give last minute instructions to Harry Sharkey the senior man in the speakeasy. Young Frankie was behind the bar.

'Do me a favour, Frankie, and haul down that package of O'Donnell's. I better not forget that or he'll bitch about it for years.'

Frankie dashed up the stairs and was back in a minute. He flicked the parcel up in air in a twisting movement and caught it deftly before laying it softly on the bar before Charlie.

'Your package, sir.'

Charlie grinned.

'Jeez! You're a cool one! I wouldn't have liked to have been in your shoes if anything went wrong there. O'Donnell doesn't take kindly to anyone fooling around like that.'

'What the hell,' he replied with a smile, 'no harm done.'

'Get me a beer and take one yourself,' said Charlie handing over a quarter and some small change.

Frankie disappeared through the back door to get a fresh case of beer.

'That young fella will come to a bad end one these days,' said Harry with a nod, 'way too lippy at times.'

'Dunno, looks like a smart kid to me. Is he staying with you these days?'

'No, he's staying with my sister Marge over in Brooklyn.'

Frankie clattered in with the beer crate.

'Didn't you recognise the accent?' said Harry, 'speaks like a Brooklyn tailor and he's only been here three years.'

'I noticed,' replied Charlie with a wink, 'see you in a few weeks.'

He took O'Donnell's package and went back to his apartment to finish his packing. Charlie insisted that he meet Una off the Blue Line in Penn station and get a cab to pier 36. She protested that she was quite capable of getting up to the Hudson quayside by subway herself. Charlie knew the subway system like the back of his hand and disagreed. After all, he pointed out, he had built most of it. Travelling to the West Side was not quite as straightforward as it seemed, he explained.

'One wrong platform and you could end up in Albany. Then where would you be?'

She was about to say 'Albany, of course,' but decided that this was not the time for such frippery.

Travelling by ocean liner was a bit of a trial at times. The stated sailing was 12 noon but passengers were always ordered to make sure they were aboard at least two hours before this; tides and sea traffic did not always coincide and ships occasionally had to leave before the given sailing time.

The cab dropped them off at the entrance of pier 36 on Eleventh Avenue. It was an unusual part of Manhattan, in so far as it was relatively crime free. The immediate areas around the docks were well protected by both police and private security outfits. It was mainly private guards; the area was too important and contained far too much wealth in the innumerable warehouses that lined the Avenue to be left in the unscrupulous hands of the New York police department. Only a couple of blocks east lay the Lower West End and the mayhem of Hell's Kitchen. Charlie found the shipping office and bought a boarding pass for Una and they both made their way up the gangway to the temporary boarding deck. The area was enclosed and had only one access to the liner's main passenger office. There was always an air of noisy excitement in the couple of hours before a liner left. A few licensed traders were allowed to sell coffee, hot dogs and soda pop before departure. One or two youngsters ran around squealing with excitement, exploring every nook and cranny of the deck. To save time Charlie checked in at the purser's office and received his sailing ticket. He also wanted to reassure himself that his main luggage was on board. The trunk had been stored in the hold and the hand luggage marked 'Wanted on board' would be delivered to his second class cabin sometime after the ship cleared Hudson River Bay. Satisfied, he returned to the boarding deck. Una had bought them some coffee and rolls and was sitting on a bench overlooking the pier below.

'You'll remember to go outside the main building and get a cab back to Penn station.'

'Of course I will, in fact I'll have to. I booked a day return and the next express leaves at one o'clock.'

She looked over at the large clock on the pier building.

'Plenty of time, it's only ten thirty.'

Charlie pulled back his coat cuff and looked at his latest purchase, a wrist watch, and gave it a tap.

'Can't get used to this thing,' he said

'Oh you soon will, believe me,' replied Una, 'I can't do without mine these days.'

He pulled his cuff down.

'When do you finish your course?'

'It's only two weeks, and I start on Monday. It means I'll be in Philly for the next few weeks.' She gave Charlie a sideward glance. 'Should give me time to organise the wedding ... that's if you're still keen on having it so soon.'

'Hey, that's a good idea,' he replied with sudden enthusiasm. If the truth be known, he had almost forgotten about the wedding in all the excitement of the voyage preparations.

They chatted about the wedding for nearly half an hour, mainly on whom they should invite. Una was quick to point out again that he shouldn't bother his head about other details, she would deal with that. That, she thought, was strictly her department... well, her and her friends.

It seemed no time at all before a deckhand rang the warning bell for disembarkation of visitors.

'Ten minutes to clear,' he shouted over the ruckus of noise, 'Travellers report to the purser's office now, the gate will be closed in ten minutes.'

The departure deck quickly became a noisy rabble as those travelling realised they had to move quickly or be herded off the ship with the visitors. Charlie and Una made their way to the gangway.

'I'll get going now,' said Una, her eyes welling up. She gave Charlie a big lingering hug and kiss,

She turned on the gangway quickly.

'I just hate long goodbyes.' It was an expression he had never heard her use before.

'I'll be back before you know it!' shouted Charlie as Una was almost swept down the gangplank by those desperate to get off before the gates closed.

Una made her way forward along the pier to roughly where Charlie said his cabin was. She stood patiently, knowing the ship could be as much as an hour before setting off. Perhaps not as long as that, she thought, as she spotted the tugs racing around in front of the pier entrance. Sailors were already throwing thinner ropes, heaving lines as they called them, from the bow … *or was it the prow?* she thought vaguely. One of the tugs had already reeled in one of the heaving lines and she could see the ship's sailors hailing up the heavy hawser ropes now attached to the heaving line. A funnel siren gave a sharp blast.

All this activity increased the anxiety of the crowd; you could almost touch the excitement. She suddenly caught sight of Charlie on the rails. He was scanning the crowd looking for her and she understood now why he asked her to wear a red scarf. She whipped it off and started waving frantically as she moved to the pier edge. The dockers were now lifting the stay ropes from the dockside capstans and throwing them into the river. Waves of coloured streamers were thrown by the passengers from the rails. Una caught one. In the next few minutes those on the pier side tried to exchange the streamer ends in the hope that eventually they would get the end of the one attached to a relative or loved one. It ended in an unholy tangle but no one cared. The ship was now being pulled into the Hudson by the tugs and the streamers were already pulling apart. A great roar went up as the last straggling streamers snapped. It was as if the ship had somehow lost its last connection with America.

Some cheered, some wept.

Chapter 16

Partner Whist

As the ship turned down the Hudson River, Charlie made his way over to starboard. The pier had disappeared from view. He was always impressed when he came close to the Statue of Liberty. While others considered its symbolism, he had mainly marvelled at the incredible construction problems of creating a gigantic copper statue, sailing it across the Atlantic and reconstructing it on an island in New York harbour. He never tired seeing it and often ribbed George Peebles about their trip to Paris where George was amazed to discover that 'la libertè' had been constructed in an enormous suburban workshop. The liner picked up speed and they soon passed Long Island Sound; Charlie returned to his cabin. It was a small affair, a double bed and a tiny bathroom with a hip bath although he quickly discovered that scalding hot water wasn't a problem; presumably it came from the engine room. He changed into more casual clothing, some light flannels and a woollen shirt and went for a stroll before tea.

First and Second Class passengers on Atlantic liners had their days arranged around endless eating arrangements from early breakfasts to late suppers. After strolling around for an hour or so he became aware that, despite all the hoo-ha on leaving the pier, the ship was far from being full. To his eye it looked like 20 percent of the accommodation was unused; changed days from ten or twenty years ago when most ships were packed to the gunwales. He sauntered into one of the several restaurants and bars available on the Second Class deck and took a comfortable armchair near the well-stocked library. There was also an excellent collection of magazines and periodicals available. When he ordered coffee the waiter raced to get him a small table, and placed it and the coffee pot at his left elbow. He then, unbidden, rolled over a small foot stool and placed it at the front of the armchair. Charlie picked up that week's *Time* magazine and planked both feet on the stool.

He could get used to this.

Over the next few days Charlie fell into a routine of spending most of his time eating and reading. There was a small gymnasium which he started using as soon as he felt his belt begin to tighten. He rarely ventured into the bar although buying a drink legally gave him a rather curious thrill. On the Friday night he noticed that they were holding a whist drive from 9:00 p.m. onwards. He was becoming a bit bored and it caught his interest as he fancied himself a good card player, particularly at Solo Whist. He signed up and duly turned up after dinner only to discover that it was Partner Whist, a game Charlie often found exasperating. Still he thought it might be of some interest. The cut had already been made and he found himself at a table partnered with a chap called Oliver Ward, who, as soon as he spoke, revealed himself to be Irish. Charlie guessed from somewhere in the North. He listened to him as he spoke to the middle-aged man to his right. It sounded almost like a Donegal accent but more eastern, possibly Fermanagh or Derry. The first points went to them; Ward it seemed had a good knowledge of the tactics. Within an hour they were ahead and seemed to be in touching distance of the final and some prize money. A twenty-minute break for tea and refreshments was called.

'Fancy a drink?' said Ward.

'Why not? I don't think I could look another pot of tea in the face. Let's stand up at the bar while we're at it; I'm getting stiff sitting on those hard chairs.'

'What's your poison?' said Ward when the barman approached.

'A small whisky with a drop of water. I'll try a malt, Denholm's if they have it.'

'Good choice. Make that two, barman.'

Ward took out a small cigar and offered one to Charlie.

'No thanks, but you carry on.'

'Well,' said Ward as the barman placed the drinks on paper doilies, 'You sound as if you come from my neck of the woods.'

'Oh, where's that then?'

'A place called Strabane in Derry.'

Charlie gave a short laugh.

'I'm from near Dromore in Donegal; we're practically neighbours'

There is usually a verbal courtship dance engaged in by people of the North of Ireland, a cautious game to see what side of the sectarian divide you come from. Ward cut it short.

'Here's to peace,' he said lifting his glass.

'Sláinte. To peace,' said Charlie.

They continued the card game to the final where they were outplayed and outsmarted by a couple of big bosomed middle aged dowagers - a couple of card sharks that would have been perfectly at home in the dollar poker games of the lower East Side. They celebrated their $10 win like it was first prize on a national lottery. Charlie and Oliver, as the losers, were given a bottle of Irish whiskey as a consolation prize.

'Well played,' said Charlie shaking Ward's hand, 'A night cap perhaps?'

'Sure, why not?'

They settled in two armchairs in an alcove not far from the bar.

'Heading to Glasgow?' said Charlie.

'No, not this time. I'm getting off at Moville.'

'That's interesting, I thought they had given up stopping there.'

'They only stop if they're ahead of time, this time of year they usually are.'

'You sound as if you've been on this trip a few times, Oliver.'

'Visit the U.S. twice a year normally. I'm a director of a linen company based in Derry but our main office is in Belfast. I'll catch a train in the morning, call in with a report to the office and then head back to our factory in Strabane.'

'There used to be a couple of linen mills round about our place, but it's been a while since I've been home,' said Charlie.

'Originally my grandfather started with a wool factory in the

South and then moved into linen about forty years ago. After 'the troubles' we sold up to one of the big fish. They employ me because of my contacts in America and oddly enough in Glasgow too. We had a mill in Lanark up until a few years ago.'

They got on like a house on fire. They ordered another drink, a double malt, and a pot of coffee to finish off the night. They talked of the Great War, the Troubles and Irish politics. Charlie explained his own business trip without giving too much away.

'Glasgow can be a tricky place to do business,' said Ward, 'not quite as bad as Belfast, but many of the business class have the same prejudices as their Belfast cousins. Not that I give a rap; I've no interest in religion.'

'Can't say I noticed it all that much when I was working there, I don't pay much attention to that sort of thing.'

'That's because you had a lowly job,' replied Ward, 'Commerce's different. I'm usually okay, and my name is a bit neutral so I don't get asked awkward questions. It can be amusing at times… and it's lucky I'm thick-skinned' he flicked some ash. 'By the way, I'm not sure if I'll see you on-board again, Charlie. We're due off the coast at Lough Foyle tomorrow and I'll get the transfer ferry first light.'

Charlie put his glass down.

'Just a minute, I've just thought of something. I wonder if you could do me a big favour.'

'As long as it doesn't involve money,' grinned Ward.

'I'll be back in a minute.'

He returned with O'Donnell's package.

'This is to be delivered to Letterkenny, the Port Road to be exact; the address is on the front. I could wait until we landed in Glasgow and get someone from there to take it over, but if you could…'

'Is that all? That's no problem,' said Ward lifting the parcel.

'It's not contraband, is it?' he joked.

'Nothing so adventurous, Oliver, just a wedding photograph that someone wants delivered to their mother.'

'I'll hand it into the Lough Swilly Bus service in Derry; in fact, I think the bus passes through the Port Road. I'm sure I could persuade the conductor to drop it off. It's something they do all the time.'

'That would be great, thanks. Damn thing is becoming a bit of a burden.'

Charlie reached for his wallet.

'Don't be silly, Charlie,' said Ward waving away Charlie's gesture.

Charlie smiled and leaned across the table and pushed the unopened bottle of Bushmills towards Oliver.

'We'll hardly drink this before you go. You take it.'

Ward grinned. He realised it would be surly to refuse.

'You got me there, Charlie! More than enough for the postage.'

They stood up and shook hands and walked out to the promenade deck.

'My cabin's toward the stern,' said Ward, giving Charlie his business card.

'I enjoyed your company, Charlie, I hope we meet up again. I'll probably be gone by the time you wake up.'

Charlie put the card in his top pocket.

'And I'll give a good tip when dealing with businessmen in Glasgow. If they ask if you're Irish, tell them you're an Ulsterman which of course, technically, you are…'

As he turned to walk away, he laughed.

'It always seems to fool them!'

*

Ward was right; he was well gone before Charlie had opened his eyes. In fact, it was the change in engine noise that originally woke him up. He must have dozed off for a while until he became aware of the silence of the engines. He could tell by the light in the port hole that it was early daybreak. Dressing quickly, he wandered out onto the deck. By that time, he could just see the ferry obviously moving away from the liner. He caught a glimpse of its navigation light glinting in the early dawn. Below his feet he could sense the vibration of the engines coming to life again. He was about to turn back to have a shave and get ready for his last day aboard when the rising sun appeared from behind a bank of cloud. It lit up the coastline in front of him and he could clearly see the low hills of Inishowen in front of the ferry. It gave him a bit of a start. He suddenly realised that this was his first sight of Ireland for what? Ten years? Although it wasn't the romantic thought of Ireland that passed through his mind, but the realisation of the quick passage of time.

Ten years.

He leaned against the rail and stared across. His mother and father had passed away three years ago both within a month of each other. His brother Pat had sent him a letter about his father dying quite suddenly after a short illness. He was seventy-five and never had a day's illness in his life. Pat had written the letter a week after the funeral. He had hardly got over the shock when a letter arrived two weeks later telling of his mother's death. She had taken to her bed shortly after the funeral and, as the old expression had it, 'turned her face to the wall', and died a day later in her sleep.

Charlie felt a slight shiver. It was cold on deck. The ship had started to move and the landline was now slowly disappearing. He had a quick look around, there was no one on deck except a few kitchen hands having a smoke beside the upper deck lifeboat. He turned and had a last look at the coast and quietly returned to his cabin.

The ship was due to dock early the next morning, possibly around 2 am. A couple of hours earlier than expected according to a Tannoy announcement in the lounge at breakfast time. Depending on the tide the ship could be tied up by 3 am. However, as the announcer added, the train service to Glasgow and other parts of the west coast didn't start till 6 o'clock and passengers should take their time disembarking. The return sailing to New York on this the ship was scheduled for Tuesday. Charlie spent the rest of the morning in the gymnasium trying to shake of his sudden bout of melancholia.

He finished his routine, showered, dressed and was more relaxed when he left the gym. He stood looking out to sea when there was a burst of excitement from the other side of the ship as passengers spotted Ailsa Craig, a small high cliff-faced island generally known as Paddy's Milestone, just off the Ayrshire coast. In the early evening the ship's engines slowed down as the liner manoeuvred its way past the island and up the Clyde estuary. The light was beginning to fade when Charlie went for dinner. The band had started its farewell dance in the adjoining ballroom when he suddenly felt quite tired, partly due to the early rise, his exertions in the gym and his decision to have a double malt with his coffee. He retired to his cabin to pack before turning in. He had finished packing and turned back the sheets ready to climb in when he suddenly remembered O'Donnell's package; he had left it on top of the wardrobe. He was half way there when it dawned on him that he had given it to Ward for delivery.

Well, that's something less to worry about, he thought as he closed his eyes.

Chapter 17

Stag's Breath

Charlie woke up as soon as the engines changed pitch. Rolling over, he picked up his wristwatch from the bedside cabinet. The luminous dial read 3:15. He let out a soft groan and lifted himself up on the pillow. As he was by nature an early riser, getting up at his leisure had become a bit of a bad habit this past few days and seemed to knock him off his stride. After a quick shake of his head, he lifted himself out of bed and started to dress in the semi-dark. It suddenly occurred to him that some sort of light was coming through the porthole. Peering out he could see the outline of the coast and what appeared to be a large town giving out a dull glow. He rightly assumed that it was the town of Greenock. The engines started up with a distant howl, the screw was now turning in reverse to slow down the ship as it reached its mooring point. He switched on the electric light and finished dressing without rushing, before he got down to packing his case.

The disembarkation process, as Charlie knew, was a slow process. Passengers milled around the boarding deck as if they had to leave at a moment's notice. Charlie took a leisurely breakfast and took a walk along the promenade deck along with some of the more seasoned passengers. They were moored in a line of several large ships about two miles off the coast in an area, according to yesterday's bulletin, whimsically referred to as 'The Tail O' the Bank'. It was now just after five and he could sense rather than see a faint glow of sunrise over to his right. The ferry would soon set off from the bank opposite.

Half an hour later Charlie stepped aboard the Passenger ferry with the rest of the First and Second class passengers. The ferry would return immediately to pick the luggage and then return for a third time to let the Third Class and Steerage travellers scrabble aboard as best they could. In the meantime the privileged passengers lounged around in railway waiting rooms picking up their main luggage and boarding the first train to Glasgow and the

West.

As they arrived at Glasgow Central a swarm of porters started milling around before the train had even stopped.

'Bags, sir?' shouted one slim, red headed youth in Charlie's direction.

'Follow me,' said Charlie and led the way back to the luggage carriage.

'I've booked into the St Enoch hotel, could you take me there?'

'Two shillings and sixpence?' said the porter hopefully.

'Done deal,' replied Charlie.

The porter manhandled the trunk and the case on to his barrow.

'Been there before, sir?'

'Kind of, but I don't really know the way.'

'That's all right, just keep up with me.'

He turned quickly and wheeled down a narrow tarmacadamed road which seemed to disappear into a tunnel and emerge in a street which passed under the main station. Charlie had to move along at a clip to keep up with him.

'Just a few minutes along Argyle Street, sir, and we're there,' he shouted as he slowed the barrow down and turned it on to the flat pavement before it reached the cobbled road.

It was a bit disorientating. They seemed to be in a darkly lit street but he could see bright daylight towards his left and right and he could hear a train slowly rumbling overhead. He realised that they were now under the main railway bridge.

As the train above them stopped and they passed into the open street to the left Charlie suddenly became aware of the silence of the streets; he and the porter appeared to be the only people around at this time. The large clock on the building opposite was indicating 7:30. Surely, he thought, there must be ... then it dawned on him that it was Sunday and he remembered - most towns in the world slowed down a pace on a Sunday but Scottish towns simply stopped. The rattle of the metal wheels of the barrow seemed to echo off the sandstone buildings like a machine gun. The porter was right, it took them no time to reach St Enoch Square, and Charlie recognised it right away by the small, baronial style building that housed the subway. The porter turned sharp right and started running to gain the momentum that would take the cart up the steep incline to the entrance of the hotel. Charlie was taken aback by his sudden change of pace. He would have offered the lad a hand but the boy, despite his youth, was a veteran; he had been on this route before. He was standing with a grin at the entrance while Charlie puffed his way up the short hill.

'Here,' he said handing over half a crown.

'And take this,' giving him another sixpence, 'worth every penny.'

*

After booking in, Charlie went up to his rooms on the second floor. It was a fairly big suite with a lounge and bedroom and looked comfortable. He decided not to stint on expenses; Davidson's newly formed import company would pick up the bill. He wandered over to the window and looked out. With the building being on a hill it was quite a panoramic view, although he could already see the beginning of a fog forming. He had planned to go out for a walk around to get his bearings but looking down he could see the streets were empty.

The hell with it, he thought as he threw his hat on the sofa, followed by his jacket. He was starting to feel the effects of his early rise. He moved into the bedroom and lay down. He was asleep within minutes.

He awoke with a start. The silence came as a shock. It unnerved him; the low throb of the engines had been his constant companion for almost a week. He threw his legs over the edge of the bed and stood up. He felt a bit dizzy but not physically sick - a good sign. A slight stagger as he walked towards the window made him reach out and grab the edge of the dressing table. His body was adapting to the lack of sea movement. He felt fine within a few minutes.

The fog, he could see, had intensified; he couldn't make out the buildings on the opposite side of the square. His suitcase was still to be opened and his trunk lay in the middle of the lounge, but the thought of starting to unpack right now disheartened him. He wandered over to the lounge window only to encounter the same dreary scene. Perhaps, he thought, a short walk would clear his head and help to shake off his sea legs. Guessing that it might be cold, he rummaged through his bag and found a scarf. In the lobby the hall porter asked if he would like him to order a taxi.

'No, I thought I'd take a short walk. Thanks just the same.'

As he was about to go through the revolving door he stopped and turned to the porter.

'Are there any shops around here? Somewhere I could buy some aspirin and maybe a newspaper.'

The porter went through the door with him

'The other side of the square, sir,' he said pointing across the street, 'you can just about see the light of the window from here. Best stick to the pavement in this fog.'

Charlie walked down the short slope and turned a sharp left following the pavement. There seemed to be quite a few small shops on this side of the square - mainly clothing shops, as far as he could make out. He was also keeping an eye out for Denholm's office building which he knew was somewhere on this square. He turned right at the end of the street to the second side of the square; nothing there either - a barbers, a couple of dingy bars that were closed. The subway building in the middle of the square seemed to be the only thing visible in the gloomy fog as he walked about. He turned right again along the longer side of the square. The buildings here looked more substantial with solid sandstone at the base and some with fancy office entrances. The small newsagent's that the porter had mentioned was now visible casting a murky light in the gloom. There was a pretty limited selection of Sunday papers and certainly nothing substantial as the *New York Times*, but he did manage to get some aspirin. He put the small box in his jacket pocket and tucked a newspaper under his arm. A half a block away he finally came to the Denholm Building. It was the last building on that side of the square, almost opposite the hotel

- only about thirty seconds away, he realised. Charlie stood back and looked up; he was impressed. It appeared to be a typically solid, well-built Victorian building, established, it claimed above the door, in 1872. He was tempted to continue walking around a bit more but the fog was going for his throat; he could wait till tomorrow. His best bet, he concluded, was to retire to the hotel, take it easy, read a bit, have dinner and an early night.

As soon as he entered the hotel the porter directed him to a pleasant reading room near the bar. The bookshelves were full of popular Scottish books and some heavyweight classics by Walter Scott and the like, none of which interested him. There was however a supply of the entire week's edition of the broadsheet papers and a stack of old magazines like *Punch*, *Time* and the *New Statesmen*. He had a quick look at the Scottish newspaper he had bought; it seemed to contain little more than reports on some football matches with a few grainy pictures of men sliding around in a mud bath. He threw it in the waste paper bin and flicked through some of the magazines. He selected a few, including one, a year old edition of *Time*, that had a much posed picture of Eamon De Valera in profile on the front cover. He ordered a drink and settled down in the armchair with a pile of papers and magazines.

He was stirred from a deep sleep before dawn by the distant but growing clamour of street noise which he guessed were workers heading for their places of employment. He lay quiet for a while planning out his day and by the time he got up and had a good stretch it was seven o'clock by the clock on the subway building. He had a quick breakfast in the busy restaurant and went for a walk around the town centre. The sun was up and it was a fine spring morning. The street names he found a bit of a novelty after being in New York and Philly for so long. The only streets in New York that had names were those in downtown business areas of Manhattan and the lower East Side around the Bowery. He walked through them: Waterloo Street, Wellington Street, Union Street, Princess Street, Queen Street and finally reached George Square, presumably named after George the Third, the one who denied Catholic emancipation in Ireland even after the union of parliaments in 1807. It had never occurred to him when he had lived here some fifteen years ago but Glasgow, it seemed, was very fond of English Royalty and the Union. He looked at the hotel opposite Georges Square – The North British Hotel. *North Britain – just about sums Scotland up*, thought Charlie with a degree of indifference. He turned and headed back to St Enoch Square for his appointment with the Denholms.

It took Charlie a frustrating half an hour to get as far as the office manager. Various personnel had looked at his credentials and papers with interest but seemed to lack any decision-making capability. He eventually found himself standing outside the office of an accountant with the name plate 'Mr Archibald Macpherson, Accountant and Office Manager'.

He managed to look like his name and occupation – tall, gaunt and pale, thought Charlie, as he sat on the hard chair opposite Macpherson's oversized desk. He had a hawk-like nose on which hung a *pince nez* which he adjusted as he read through Charlie's letter of introduction.

'I'm afraid Kenneth Denholm won't be available until eleven o'clock.'

'That's fine,' Charlie replied looking at his watch, 'I'll come back then.'

He rose from the chair.

'I see you're …' said Macpherson, looking back down at the letter, 'Irish.'

'Yes, I'm an Ulsterman, as it happens.'

'Ah!'

'I'll be back at 10:55,' said Charlie as he closed the door behind him.

*

Charlie took to Kenneth Denholm right away. A chubby redhead with an infectious laugh, as different from Macpherson as chalk is from cheese.

'Come in, come on in,' he shouted enthusiastically as he

grabbed his hand in a firm handshake. He dismissed Macpherson with an order to rustle up some coffee and biscuits.

'I take it your first introduction to Denholm's management was our resident Lon Chaney, Mr Macpherson.'

Charlie smiled.

'Don't worry about him. He's a stern-faced, old, Presbyterian curmudgeon. Remarkably efficient I must say and an inventive accountant. Now to business,' he said opening up a large file. 'We've already started loading the first consignment down at the docks at Finnieston.'

'But surely you are waiting for the first payment?'

'Should come through today. Ten minutes ago I wired Sandy informing him of your arrival. He's sending the release order for the funds which should arrive at the commercial bank…' he took out a half hunter and flicked it open, '… in about an hour. Incidentally, Sandy mentioned you've been in Glasgow before.'

'Well it was a long time ago, Kenneth ...'

'Call me Kenny.'

'I came here during the war in 1916, decided to join up and was off to France before I knew what was happening, I got myself wounded the following year and got sent home, well, sent back here to Glasgow, I mean. I managed to get sponsored by my sister in the US and went there at the end of 1917. Probably only spent a year and a half here at the most.'

'That's probably longer than I've spent here,' said Denholm, 'if the truth be known, I'm more at home in Aberdeen. I came down two weeks ago to supervise this contract.'

There was a knock at the door and Macpherson entered followed by a young girl with a tray of coffee and a plate of biscuits.

'Ah! Mr Macpherson. Mr McKenna and I will be leaving the office in fifteen minutes. We'll be gone for an hour or two. I'll leave you to,' he said and looked at Charlie with a smile 'to hold the fort, as our American friends would say.'

'Not an expression to which I'm accustomed,' replied

Macpherson stiffly, 'but I take it from the context you mean take decisions on your behalf in your absence.'

'Yes, something like that,' said Kenny, 'I'll let you know the moment we get back.'

Macpherson nodded formally and left the room without a word.

'My god, what a stuffed shirt that man is,' said Kenny light-heartedly, 'here take a seat and have some coffee before we leave.'

'Where exactly are we going?'

'I thought I'd take you over to see the bottling plant. It's only ten minutes or so, just over the river in an area known as the Gorbals.'

'Well, believe it or not, I know that area. A cousin of my father lives there; I remember going to see him a couple of times when I lived here. In fact I wrote to him telling him I was coming over. I must try to get in touch and arrange a meeting.'

Kenny passed over the coffee.

'I sometimes get lost when I venture into these tenement places. After a while one street begins to look like another.'

'I know what you mean. The streets of New York are numbered, upwards usually, from South to North and the roads that intersect them are avenues and numbered from East to West. A bit functional I must admit, but it makes it easy to get around.'

'Do you know the address? Not that I could help out; as I said, these streets all look alike to me.'

'He stays in Salisbury Street. I think I could probably find it from the main crossroad.'

'Right then,' said Kenny standing up, 'let's head over the bridge. We can have a look at the bottling plant then I can take you down to the Main Street and Gorbals Cross and leave you to your own devices for the rest of the day. I need to get to the bank after lunch and then I'll arrange a visit down to Finnieston quay. They've started to load up the other cargo on the steamer and they intend to leave on Wednesday. I want to get the first load away then.'

Charlie finished his coffee and stood up.

'I must admit I wasn't expecting such haste. I thought I'd be here at least a week. By the looks of it I could be off by Thursday.'

Kenny Denholm had already opened the door and was turning left towards the staircase.

'All going well of course,' Charlie added as he followed him out.

Kenny was half way down the first set of stairs.

'Don't worry,' he shouted over his shoulder, 'We'll have you home in no time!'

*

They walked about a 100 yards through the Square before they crossed a suspension bridge that Charlie had never noticed before. The river below them was in full spate. Turgid, brown waves tumbled over each over in a mad dash to the estuary and from there to the Atlantic. In the calmer parts, nearer the south bank, the water looked oil-slicked and a thin film of rainbow-colour grease caught Charlie's eye as he walked across. Not that it bothered him; it appeared no worse than the East River. Within ten minutes they were standing outside a large red brick industrial sized building on the corner of two streets of grey and blackened tenements.

Charlie looked up at the corner where the two streets met - Norfolk Street and Warwick Street.

'Ah! Yes, I get it now, all the streets around here are named after English counties.'

'Are they?' said Kenny, 'can't say I took much notice. Let's get to the office, it's just up here.'

He gave the doorman a cheery wave and raced up the stairs two at a time to the mezzanine that overlooked the packing area.

The plant manager looked harassed.

'I'm sorry, Mr Denholm, I can't take you around, I'm up to my neck here. We're working flat out on your order trying to get it ready and dispatched for tomorrow morning.'

'Och, don't worry about us, I'll just show Charlie around the main hall and we'll be off.'

For all his worldly experience, Charlie had never seen any kind of manufacturing process in his life. It took him by surprise.

'I didn't realise it would be so noisy,' he shouted to Kenny.

'This is the worst spot; this is where they fill the bottles with the blended whisky.'

Charlie had already lost his bearings. They had been up several staircases on one side of the building to look at the blending vats and then back down the other side. The noise was deafening as rows of bottles clattered out of one tunnel, then on to a variety of carousels before disappearing again. They came down yet another staircase to a quieter area which turned out to be a labelling unit.

'Highland Dew?' said Charlie, 'I thought it was called The Call of the Glen.'

Kenny shrugged.

'The marketing department deals with these kinds of things.'

'Is it all the same whisky?'

'No, not really, it depends what blend is used and that in turn depends on what malts we have available. We can do a run of 2,000 of one kind and then change over to another.'

'What about the names?'

'Over here,' said Denholm, directing Charlie to a corner office near yet another staircase.

The two office ladies stood up as Denholm and Charlie entered.

'Sit down. Sit down for goodness sake, we're not royalty you know! This here is Mr McKenna,' he continued, pointing in the direction of Charlie. 'He's the representative of the American company for our current order. Please ignore us. I'm just going to show Mr McKenna some advertising literature.'

The two women looked at each other nervously before they sat down. Denholm walked over to a large filing cabinet

'Yes, names! That can be fun. Making up names and labels seems to occupy a young woman full time in marketing,' said Denholm, pulling out a handful of files.

'They usually send a list over to me every week. It all seems to be Glen this or Island that.'

He started to spread some art work on a nearby table and picked up a sheet of label layouts.

'You get a mention now and again, Charlie. Prince Charlie's a recurring theme. Charlie's Nectar or Prince Charlie's Secret Glen or some such guff. Mountains and Stags feature as well. Although I did draw the line at one name ... Stag's Breath. There's a Jewish printer, Pensinsky, in Oxford Street,'

He stopped for a second.

'By God! You're right, Charlie. The streets are named after English counties!'

He scratched his head.

'How come I never noticed that before?'

'Anyway, as I was saying, this Jewish printer can hammer out labels, regardless how preposterous, in a matter of hours.'

'Strange, I never even thought of how or why certain whiskies were named. It never occurred to me.'

'Ah! But you would. Let's face it, would you take a drink of something called Stag's Breath or would you prefer something like Dew of the Glen?'

Charlie grinned.

'I see what you mean.'

'As for the art work...'

He spread some sheets across the table

'Glens, mountains and streams from every possible angle, stags in every position, highland cottages, claymores, bagpipes,

Glengarry bonnets, Royal Standards, and of course pictures, well paintings I suppose, of Prince Charlie. You name any Scottish cliché and we've got it. Simply arrange any of these and you've got yourself a label. Look …'

He pulled over a few bits and pieces and arranged them before turning it to Charlie. It had a colourful misty highland glen as a background. In the foreground a crumpled blood-stained Royal Standard lay over a claymore propped against a rock.

'Mysterious Glen – what do you think?'

'Not bad,' said Charlie, not too sure if Denholm was being serious or not.

Denholm slapped him on the back and grinned.

'Come on. Let's get out of here. The noise is beginning to get on my nerves.'

After descending a few staircases and negotiating a couple of corners they found themselves on the pavement a few minutes later.

'We'll walk down this street, Norfolk Street …'

He shook his head and muttered 'English counties – in this place.'

Before they reached the bottom of the street Charlie immediately knew where he was.

'This is Gorbals Cross, isn't it?'

'Correct, Charlie.'

He looked around to orientate himself.

'I'll find my way from here easy enough.'

'Right then, I'll leave you to it. I need to get to the bank. Come over to the office at ten tomorrow. Don't worry, I'll leave a message in reception telling them to take you straight up. Save you having to endure old Macpherson.'

'See you then, Kenny,' said Charlie as he took the road to the right.

*

Charlie thought he noticed a difference in the general area since he left, what was it ... sixteen years? The streets seemed more crowded with young children and women shoppers, but again he had seen worse. He found the address easily enough, it was a four storey grey tenement about half way up the street. The entrance, or the closemouth as they called it here, was a bit scruffier than he remembered as he made his way up the slate staircase. He peered at the name plates; he couldn't quite remember if it was on the first floor up or the second. The name J. CAROL, on a small brass plate, was screwed into the right hand frame of one of the three doors on the second landing. He had already written a short note this morning at breakfast which he anticipated posting through the door later in the afternoon. Still it would be bad manners not to knock just in case. He gave the door a few raps then pulled out the note ready to drop through the letter box. The door opened and a young lady looked out. She looked at Charlie and not recognising him, closed the door a few inches. Carlie reckoned she was of average height, taller than average, if anything. Dark, sleek, well-kept hair. She had an air of confidence. Late teens or probably early twenties.

'Yes?' she said defensively.

Charlie stood back a step and tipped his hat slightly.

'Sorry I ... I wasn't expecting anyone to be at home. I was just about to put this note through the door.' He showed her the note.

'I'm a relative of John Carol. He's a cousin of my father who is, well, *was* Michael McKenna, better known as Mick McKenna.'

'John Carol is my father. I'm his daughter, Theresa.'

Charlie looked surprised. He had forgotten about John's young family. Theresa looked at Charlie carefully, it was not often someone so expensively dressed appeared at the door of the Carol household.

She squinted her eyes.

'I think I remember you. You came here a few times when I was young. And I remember,' she said smiling, 'because you brought a bag of cakes – and cakes were in short supply in this house.'

She opened the door wide.

'Come on in.'

'Oh, that's not necessary,' replied Charlie.

He was well aware that the arrival of a sudden guest can cause embarrassment in poorer households. Tea, coffee and food supplies, things that well-off people take for granted, were often kept in meagre quantities.

'Actually I'm in a bit of a rush and I don't want to cause a fuss. I just want you to give this note to John.'

Theresa noticed his discomfort.

'If you're sure ...'

'I'll come back tomorrow evening, say about half six or so, if you think that will be okay.'

He handed over the note.

'My dad usually comes home from work around five, so that should be fine.'

She tucked the letter into a pocket in the folds of her skirt.

'Right, Theresa, I'll see you all then.'

Charlie turned and started down the staircase as they said their goodbyes.

As he turned back into the main street Charlie decided to hop on one of the endless stream of trams that seemed to pour down the main thoroughfare. He realised that it was only a straight fifteen-minute walk to the main bridge but thought of it as a bit of a pleasant distraction on the way back. He checked the change in his pocket as the car rumbled to a halt. The conductor picked out a few coppers from his hand and rattled out a ticket before directing him upstairs. Within a minute he realised he would have been quicker walking; the tram car travelled at a snail's pace through the busy lunch time street. Charlie relaxed and took in the surrounding street scene. The top deck of the tram was almost at the same level as the first storey flats. At this time of day most of the apartments were empty and the folk in the ones that were occupied seemed unconcerned about the lack of privacy. Some of them hung out the window, enjoying the activity below. As they passed the main crossroads Charlie became aware that the buildings were becoming more substantial. The tram stopped just short of a street he recognised. This was Oxford Street where the apparent wizard of the Printing Press had his business. The tram stop was just before a large, well-appointed bank at the corner and he could not help noticing the flat above. It had a large 'To Let' sign in the window, and below this and in smaller print, it read 'Four bedroom flat for rent'. As the tram moved forward he could see into the property and he couldn't help being impressed by the size and general condition of the place. Such a place, so near the city centre, he thought, would cost a fortune to rent in New York or Philadelphia.

He took a note of the address.

Chapter 18

How about you?

Julie was looking at some of the photos she had taken at the Collins memorial when she suddenly half remembered something about Liam wanting to get in touch with her mother. Was it something about her grandfather? Or was it something about that little book he showed them?

She decided to phone Liam right away before the thought left her. Even if he was busy she could leave a message. His answering service clicked in after a few rings.

'Hi Liam, Julie here. Did you mention something about wanting to see my mother about mmm ... something? Damn it, you know what my memory is like at times. It's just that I'm going up to Mum's tomorrow afternoon for an hour or so to catch up with the usual family gossip so I could get her to phone you or you to phone her or whatever ... Phone me later.'

She clicked the 'phone closed' button. *God*, she thought, *I'm hopeless at leaving messages.*

She was just settling down to flick some more photos when the phone rang.

Liam's name came up on the phone window.

'Crikey, that was quick,' she said.

'Just came into the office when the phone rang. I got your message.'

'Surprised you understood it, I usually start babbling when I'm asked to leave a message.'

'Sounded okay to me. About your mother ...'

'Yes, I'm taking a run up there tomorrow. Des is off golfing, or is it five-a-side football? Some such male bonding nonsense. Anyway, I'll see her tomorrow. Anything you want me to say?'

'Nothing really. Well, it's something I kind of wanted to run past her. I've been asked to contribute a piece to an online history site. They're running a series of essays on the Irish civil war and I quite fancied using something about Charlie in it.'

'Can't see Mum complaining about that. It's not as if you need her permission or anything like that is it?'

'No, I don't suppose so but I wouldn't like to go treading on any toes. There was something else I wanted to ask her about Charlie's time in America.'

'Yes, you mentioned something about some dastardly deed; I assumed you were being melodramatic as usual.'

'Probably too much stout taken I suspect. Tell her to phone me on this number.'

He had just given her the number when Julie heard a commotion in the background.

'Christ! I'll need to go ... some eejit has just fallen over one of my displays!'

'And here's me thinking that libraries are havens of tranquillity,' said Julie.

There was no reply.

*

Julie's mother phoned a few days later.

'Hi Liam, Grace McKenna here. Julie was saying you wanted a chat.'

'Thanks for getting back to me, Grace. Yes I just wanted you to have a look at something I rattled up for a History group I'm involved in. It mentions Charlie and I didn't want it, well, to cause any bad feelings.'

'It can't be that bad, surely?'

'No it's not, not at all … it's just well, I wanted to meet you and have ...' Liam was beginning to flounder. 'To be honest I just wondered if you had any knowledge of Charlie's time in America.'

There was a silence from the other end and there was a slight change of tone in Grace's voice.

'I know a lot about Charlie McKenna, Liam. Probably more than his own family does.'

'I'm not prying or anything. I'm just, well, sort of curious.'

'I'll meet you next Wednesday, would that suit?' she said suddenly.

'I've got some flexitime due. What time and place?'

'How about Bruno's? I could probably just about manage to totter down there. I'm not in the mood or of an age to go gallivanting into town. How about lunch, say about two o'clock?'

'Sounds good. Could you make it three? It means I could do a half day and leave here about two.'

'It's a bit late to call it lunch then, I suppose.'

'How about we call it an early tea?'

She laughed.

'Ok early tea it is, see you there at three.'

*

Bruno's restaurant is a peculiar place. It's on an island in the middle of a traffic intersection; it was originally a kind of bus shelter or bus terminus known locally as the Battlefield Rest which served the Victoria Infirmary, at one time a major South Side hospital. It later went through a bit of gentrification and then reappeared as 'Bruno's', an excellent Italian bistro which Liam had remarked 'wouldn't be out of place in Tuscany, either architecturally or culinarily'. Liam had hurried home from work at 2 o'clock to get changed into a fresh shirt and his usual misshapen suit jacket and was rushing along the road when he realised he was twenty minutes early. Not one to waste valuable time he nipped into a pub across the road for a pint of stout.

He took a seat and ran through his thoughts on how he would approach things. He had already more or less concluded that getting the gold out of Ireland would not have been that great a problem. 2000 sovereigns would weigh in at about 8 kilograms, much less than the hand luggage allowance on a modern airline, and could be easily distributed in various pieces of luggage. Getting it sold would be a much bigger problem; a few solutions were beginning to roll about his head. Liam was more curious to know what Grace knew of some of Charlie's associates in New York, particularly characters like O'Donnell and McGhee.

*

'Two dry sherries, if you don't mind,' he said a tad sharply to the waiter who had ambled over after a five-minute natter to his off-duty chum. The service was usually excellent but mid-afternoon, after a busy lunch time, an odd kind of lethargy falls upon the staff.

'Right away,' replied the waiter, quickly detecting Liam's chilly request.

Liam lounged back against cushions that formed the corner sofa. He had never been in the place at this time of the day before. He was struck with how remarkably quiet and calm it was. There were, at a guess, no more than ten customers spread through both levels. The place was so popular that it was normally heaving with customers. The waiter came darting back with a tray of drinks and a couple of menus under his arm. As he did, Liam spotted Grace coming through the front entrance and walking up to the bar. She looked remarkably sophisticated. She wore a tailored dark blue suit with a white silk shirt which almost glowed. A lustrous but discreet diamond necklace hung around her neck and she carried a small Gucci clutch bag under her arm.

'Thanks,' he said a bit more warmly, as the waiter returned with the drinks, 'And could you do me a favour and inform the lady at the bar where I am?'

The waiter turned around.

'No problem. Mrs McKenna is one of our regular customers.'

He raced off and guided Grace to the table.

Liam stood up to give Grace a peck on the cheek.

'My, Grace, you look terrific ...love the outfit.'

'I'm at an age where I buy less and spend more. By the way, you could have waited till at least I sat down before you started your old Irish charmer routine,' she replied as the waiter pulled out the seat.

The waiter fussed around for a few seconds before saying that he would give them time to look at the menu and that he'd return in five minutes.

'I took the liberty of ordering you a sherry.'

'Well done,' said Grace taking a rather unlady-like gulp, 'The very dab, I've had a busy day.'

'I'm a bit peckish,' said Liam running a finger down the menu. 'I think I'll have an Antipasto. How about you?'

'Sounds like the opening lines of a Frank Sinatra song. Not for me, I'll have a pick at yours, if it's half decent. And I'll have the Escalope of veal Milanese; tell them to go easy on the pasta.'

'Good choice, I'll have the same.'

Liam signalled over and gave the order and asked for a bottle of Barolo and a couple of glasses.

'Now then,' said Grace, 'what's all this about Charlie McKenna? You seem to be becoming obsessed with the man these days. Jetting off to Cork and trailing everybody up and down to Tralee.'

'Hardly obsessed, curious perhaps. The Cork thing was a coincidence; I was going to a conference there, nothing to get excited about,' replied Liam, a bit put out.

'I heard you discovered the mystery of the sovereigns, or so

Julie told me.'

'Well, the best part of it. There are a few missing links. I'm not entirely sure where this chap George Peebles fits into the scheme of things.'

Liam pulled out some sheets of foolscap from his inside pocket.

'I've written it down here with the usual guff about names having been changed to protect the innocent etc. It's only three pages long.'

He handed it over to Grace.

'I'll read it later, I'm sure it will be fine.'

She lifted up her bag and tucked the papers away as the waiter laid out a plate of antipasto with some bread. He had wisely brought over an extra fork and plate.

'You won't mind if I take the artichoke and a few olives,' she paused, '… that Mortadella looks nice and fresh.'

'Here take it,' said Liam.

'No, no, just a slither. I eat like a bird, as you know.'

Liam said nothing.

'Julie mentioned a book or some sort of … a diary you happened to come across,' said Grace, clearing up the remains of the plate with a chuck of rye bread.

Liam took out the small rectangular book from his inside pocket and placed it on the table between them.

Grace looked surprised.

'Lots of stuff in that pocket of yours, Liam - sheets of paper, a little book. Perhaps a rabbit up next?' she said, eyeing the book carefully.

The waiter took away the plate; there was hardly a trace of food left on the surface.

'The book was given to me by your daughter, Eileen, at that party of yours about a month or so ago.'

'Can I look at it?'

'Sure,' said Liam, 'I'll open it for you. It's got a strange little locking device on it.'

He unlocked it and handed it over.

Grace weighted it in her hand and opened the cover to the first page and looked at the imprint.

'Paris?'

'It appears he went to France with the mysterious Mr Peebles - something about a passport it seems. To be honest it is hard to read at times. He hardly ever puts down a straightforward fact. It's not really a diary as such. He seemed to write things down things more or less chronologically and then suddenly it becomes more a kind of notebook with interesting little facts he's picked up.'

The waiter returned with the escalopes. Grace put down the book and lifted up her knife and fork.

'Well,' she said, 'Let's tuck in!'

*

Grace rattled through the Veal Milanese and finished off with what she reckoned was 'just a smidgen' of chocolate sponge with a 'spoonful' of strawberry ice cream. Liam passed on the sweet and settled for a *doppio espresso* and an Italian brandy with a glass of sweet desert wine for Grace.

Grace sat back and dabbed her lips with a linen napkin.

'Well, Liam, let's hear it. What's your latest theory on Charlie McKenna? A pirate adventurer on the high sea perhaps or …'

Liam cut her short.

'Listen, Grace, you said you knew more about Charlie than you let on.'

He paused.

'Did you ever hear of someone called O'Donnell?'

Grace put her hands down on the table.

'Yes, I might have.'

Liam was watching her reaction closely; she didn't seemed too concerned.

'It's funny,' she said finally.

'There are some things I kept to myself for all these years. I was thinking it over last night. I never told anyone because Charlie started to confide in me a few years before he died. I don't know why me. I assumed because we had grown close over the years. We stayed with Charlie in the house we are in just now, after Una, his wife, died.'

She made a slight shrug.

'I used to make him dinner and kept him company in the evenings when the kids were in bed. You would have liked Charlie. Even when he got older he still had a bit of a sparkle. I didn't believe some of the stories at first but he showed me a few things he'd kept ... and told me about the sovereigns. To tell you the truth I was never sure about the photograph ...'

'You mean the one with his brother Pat?'

'Yes, of course. Your explanation about Pat's involvement with the Ballyseedy incident sounded crazy at first but now I'm beginning to think that it seems plausible.'

She stopped to take a sip of the wine.

'... and he showed me your little book. I had a quick look at the time but didn't take much notice. Never even noticed the Paris imprint on the front page. Oddly enough I thought it was completely lost; how it ended up in Eileen's hands I'll never know. I thought I was protecting his ... well his name, I suppose. But last night I thought, what the hell? Who cares? It was all a long time ago and anyone involved is probably now dead. Damn Irish are great ones for family secrets and for rewriting the past ...'

'Not the only ones to do that I can assure you of that, but I take your point,' said Liam quickly, 'actually I'm just thinking of writing up the whole thing so we can all have a better idea of what went on. What I do with it after that I don't know.'

'Give me a few days to read over your notes and I'll get back to you.'

'Sure, that's only fair.'

Liam took a sip of the *Vecchio Romagna* brandy.

'Just wondering. Did Charlie drink much?'

'Not to my knowledge. He went down to that bowling club not far from you. The Queens Park Club I think it was called.'

'Well, that's the first time Charlie's went down in my estimation. Wouldn't be seen dead in a bowling club myself. All those blazers and flannels.'

Grace ignored him.

'He had a few chums down there, war veterans and such like. I think Charlie had some dealings in France during the Second World War. He took the family over to Ireland in 1940 and they stayed there until the war ended. Eddie tells me that his older brother had an Irish accent for a while.'

'I'm beginning to wonder if there isn't anything Charlie wasn't involved in. I've started with three foolscap pages - wouldn't be surprised if there's not a trilogy in all of this.'

'Never mind all that,' said Grace, 'you asked me if Charlie drank and I'm just telling you that he drank very little.'

'Never drank whisky?'

'Rarely. The occasional malt …'

'Denholm's whisky?'

She looked at him curiously.

'Yes, but how did…? Never mind, I think I know what you're getting at. He told me that he ran some sort of illegal bar in New York for a while.'

'Yes, he mentions a speakeasy called The Country Club in the book.'

'You might be right but I can't honestly say that I remember him calling it anything.'

Liam was about to ask about a man called Vinnie McGhee when she suddenly looked at her watch.

'Damn! Richard, that son of mine, said he'd pick me up at four o'clock. It's now gone ten past.'

She picked up her handbag.

'Be a sport and look outside and see if he's about. He's got the common sense of an adolescent; it wouldn't cross his mind to come in to get me. He's driving one of those idiotic Jeeps or 4x4's or whatever they're called. Its bright red. You can't miss it.'

'No problem,' said Liam scraping back his chair and heading towards the door. As he manoeuvred around the tables he became aware that the place was now slowly filling up again. He stood outside and then quickly walked around the restaurant. Most people either parked in the hospital car park across the road or parked at meters in the nearby streets. The island, except for a bus stop and a couple of pedestrian crossings was surrounded by double yellow 'No Parking' lines on the pavement. He noticed a couple of local authority parking wardens wandering around the street on the left, but no sign of a red 4x4.

As he made his way back to the table it was obvious that Grace had settled the bill and was busy counting out some pound coins to leave as a tip.

Before Liam had time to protest she said, 'My treat, Liam. Not often a woman of my age gets taken out to lunch by a young, handsome ... well *youngish*, handsome man.'

Liam looked distinctly uncomfortable.

'See! Now you know what it's like to be sweet-talked!' she said.

'Relax. Take a seat. If Richard doesn't arrive within ten minutes, I'll get a cab.'

'Thanks for the lunch, Grace. My treat next time.'

'I was thinking about Charlie when you were outside and what you said about writing something about him.'

She closed over her purse.

'You know,' she said looking down at her nails, 'there's a trunk in the attic that has a lot of bits and pieces that Charlie left behind.'

She looked up.

'There's something in particular that I think you would like to see. Why don't we meet up next week about this time for tea? In fact, let's make it next Wednesday. I'll get Eddie to come round and pick you up at your flat at four o'clock, save you walking up that hill.'

'You've got me intrigued as usual. Sounds okay.'

There was a brief disturbance at the door.

'I can guess who that is,' said Grace without looking across.

Liam stood up and saw Richard talking to the waiter.

'You're right of course. Let's get going.'

Richard was hopping from one foot to the other by the time they reached the exit. For a brief moment Liam thought he was about to start a gymnastic 'running on the spot' exercise.

'Sorry I'm late. I got mixed up in the traffic. Come on, let's go.'

Bruno de Felice appeared at the kitchen door.

'For goodness sake, what's the rush?' said Grace as she turned to talk to Bruno. Bruno spoke with a strange mixture of English with an Italian accent that was peppered with idiomatic Glaswegian.

'Ah, Mrs McKenner! Howzit going? No see you for a while. How you enjoy your-a meal? I see you have a nice boattle of Italian wine with your-a dinner.'

'Very nice. Bruno, I'll be back again soon.'

Liam was never convinced of the authenticity of the accent; he was pretty sure Bruno was hamming up for Grace's benefit. In the meantime, Richard had vanished through the entrance. They said their goodbyes and followed him out.

Richard was standing on the pavement with his head in his hand.

'Damn, a ticket! I've only been here two minutes!'

He started to look about wildly for the wardens.

'I wouldn't make too much of a fuss, old man. Not only are you parked on a double yellow, but you're right in the middle of the bus stop. You'll be lucky if they haven't already got in touch with the police.'

'I'll pay the fine! Get in the car, Richard.'

He was about to say something.

'Now,' she added menacingly.

Richard scuttled into the driver's seat and started the engine.

Grace walked toward the passenger side.

'I'll see you next week, Liam ... that is, of course, if I manage to get home in one piece. Jump in the back and we'll give you a lift down to your flat.'

'No thanks, I feel like a walk after that big lunch.'

'Understandable,' she said with a knowing sigh, 'see you next week.'

Liam watched the 4x4 manoeuvre its way into the traffic before roaring down the street.

He took one step in the direction of the one mile walk to his apartment and stopped. Surely, he thought, such a walk required a pint of stout before being undertaken?

Satisfied with his justification, he walked across the road to the pub.

Chapter 19

Anchor Line

Like most port and harbour cities, Glasgow's main shipping lines and cargo carriers were concentrated in a few streets around the quays and warehouses. In Glasgow this was on the north side of the river, clustered around an area they called the Broomielaw.

Although the city still used many horse-drawn wagons there were one or two courtyards where management types could park their cars dotted around the places of commerce. Denholm managed to squeeze his car into one of the very few car park spaces in the area.

'Right, I'll pop into Norsk Shipping and finish off the paperwork and then I'll take you up to Anchor Lines.'

'If it's okay with you I'll just walk over to the Anchor office.'

'The Anchor office isn't around here, it's more up towards George Square. It's a good twenty minutes' walk at least from here.'

'No matter, I could do with the exercise. You won't need me until tomorrow morning and anyway I've got a couple hours to kill this afternoon.'

'Anchor has a whole city block for an office on St. Vincent Street. Safest bet is to walk down this main street and under the railway bridge until you get to St Enoch Square.'

'If I get that far I'll know where I am. I'll find it easy enough from there.'

'Right ho, Charlie, I'll see you tomorrow morning around the same time,' shouted Denholm as he disappeared into a labyrinth of offices and shop fronts.

Despite Kenny Denholm giving him a veiled warning, he decided to turn left through the Broomielaw and soon he found himself, in a moment of distraction, in a seedy area north of the main terminus for the Irish ferry sailings. He was suddenly aware that he had wandered into a red light district and he found himself the victim of a variety of barely disguised innuendoes and bawdy offers shouted from the doorways and first floor windows. Some might have thought this amusing, adventurous even, but Charlie knew, regardless of where in the world you were, such areas were usually unpoliced, chaotic and extraordinarily dangerous. He was also conscious that he was smartly dressed and was now beginning to attract a bit of attention, even at this time of day. Despite his semi-rural upbringing Charlie had a natural nose for danger. His street-wise instinct told him that the underclass of opportunist thieves and two-bit pimps generally target the timid and the unsure. He pulled back his shoulders with an air of confidence and put on a bit more pace. Using his sense of direction, he turned a sharp right eastward at the next junction and was relieved to see the glass top of the main railway station over the rooftops of the dilapidated tenements. Within a hundred yards a couple of ship chandlers appeared and a bit further on some gent's outfitters and one or two classier bars. He cursed himself for his lack of concentration. It occurred to him he had a fair bit of cash in his wallet and he would have bet all of it, he reckoned, on someone at some time being murdered in these parts for less than the loose change he carried in his jacket pocket.

Within a few minutes he was walking through the main concourse of Central Station and from there it was a short walk to St Vincent Street. The Anchor line building was an impressive late Victorian white granite building with the usual extravagant frontage; still reasonably clean despite the tons of coal soot, smog and industrial pollution that swirled around the streets of Glasgow. The foyer was formal with polished marble floors and red plush armchairs strewn around. A smartly dressed booking assistant dealt with his enquiries. They had only one of the more expensive second class suites left for the Thursday sailing he said, wringing his hands regretfully. Charlie doubted that this was the case and it was probably a well-worn selling technique but he wasn't in the mood to bicker. He booked it immediately and paid cash. Before he walked back to St Enoch square he popped into the main General Post Office by a side entrance and sent a short wire to Mrs G., telling her that he intended to phone sometime today.

He decided not to be too specific as he was not sure of the time difference. When he left the GPO building he decided to walk over to the square to have a better look. The Glasgow GPO was much larger and more practical looking than its Dublin counterpart or what was left of it the last time he had seen it in 1923. Oddly the Dublin version was by far the more impressive building with its classical façade, complete with Corinthian columns. Perhaps the British, he thought, needed to appear be more impressive in Ireland. He walked back towards his hotel, this time keeping to the main streets.

It was a ten-minute walk and he considered the day's events. The morning had been busy. Denholm had insisted on driving down to the dock-side to witness the loading of the final twenty thousand bottles onto the SS Rosario. The shipping agent looked anxious and was mopping his brow with a large handkerchief when they arrived.

'This ship's near enough fully loaded and needs to leave at noon,' he said shoving the handkerchief into his pocket, 'and there's no sign of your last consignment.'

Denholm took out his pocket watch and flipped it open.

'It's only ten o'clock man, the lorries are on their way.'

As he spoke a loud honking came from the main gate.

'See. There's the first one now.'

Far from being relieved, the agent was increasingly agitated.

'What about the rest?'

'The rest? It's only the last twenty thousand bottles for god's sake! That's only three or four lorry loads. Relax.'

'Come on, Charlie,' he added, 'let's have a nosey around.'

'Just a minute! You'll need these.'

The agent scrabbled about in a drawer on his office desk and finally produced two badges.

'Pin these on or you'll be stopped at the gangplank.'

Charlie and Denholm pinned on the badges and headed over

to the ship.

As they crossed over the cobblestone quay and walked up the gangplank the crane was already swinging out towards the lorry. The dockers had started peeling back the grey tarpaulin revealing the neatly packed boxes of whisky.

'I thought twenty thousand bottles would be a fair amount,' said Charlie.

'Not as much as you'd imagine. We've loaded up eighty thousand already this week. There are twenty bottles in an exporting box. When you think of it, a thousand bottles is only fifty boxes. A lorry can carry up to two hundred cases without any danger, two hundred and fifty at a pinch. I don't know why our friend is getting so excited.'

By noon the cargo had been loaded and various bits of paperwork flew around the office. The agent was beginning to relax. The pilot, who was to guide the ship down as far as Greenock, was greeted like minor royalty when he arrived through the gates.

'Have the hatches been battened down?' asked the pilot.

The agent solemnly assured him they had.

Charlie almost laughed aloud. He thought 'batten down the hatches' was one of these expression only Doug Fairbanks used in Hollywood pirate movies… like 'splice the mainbrace' or 'shiver me timbers'.

The agent and the pilot disappeared up the gangplank.

'What the hell does "batten down the hatches" actually mean?' asked Charlie.

'God knows,' said Denholm, with a show of disinterest, 'sometimes I think these sailor types make it all up as they go along.'

He pulled on his driving gloves.

'Come on. Let's head back to civilisation.'

*

Earlier that morning Denholm advised him to get in touch with his employers today at some stage.

'You could wire over a message or you could use our office phone but you might find yourself hanging around if the connection is poor. You'll want to keep it private anyway. Best use the phone in the Hotel and then if there is a delay at least you can hang about in comfort. Remember we're five hours ahead here,' he said, 'or is it six? I can never remember. Best make it around four o'clock to be on the safe side.'

Kenny dropped him in St. Enoch Square and, after glancing up at the clock on the Underground station, he decided to do a quick bit of shopping in the main shopping area. Something for Una and, equally importantly, some provisions for the Carol household. There was an enormous department store just past the square. He gathered up a packet of tea and a box of biscuits, nothing too fancy. He didn't want to embarrass them by appearing too generous. Across the road was an arcade which seemed to consist mainly of jewellers and watchmakers. He found playing the naivety card with a woman assistant usually worked a trick. It wasn't a hard role to play, his knowledge of women's fashion was almost non-existent.

'How about this thistle shaped brooch?' said the young assistant.

'A brooch?'

'Yes. It's a kind of decoration for an evening gown, sir,' she replied, placing the sparkling jewelled ornament on the upper left side of her jacket, 'very smart and ...' she added with sudden female intuition, '... and very fashionable.'

'Looks the very thing! I'll take it.'

'Would you like it in a small case? Only an extra two shillings.'

'Great! Could you wrap it for me?'

The hotel had a lazy mid-afternoon atmosphere as Charlie tried to seek out the under-manager. The porter dashed around the lower floors and finally appeared from the kitchen a few minutes later.

'My apologies, Mr McKenna, he appears to have taken the opportunity to grab a bite to eat now that the lunch crowd have gone.'

'Apologies from me also, Mr McKenna,' said the under-manger gliding silently through the open kitchen door. 'Now, what can I do for you?'

'No rush. I just wondered if I could put through a transatlantic call in the course of the next hour or so.'

'As long as you're prepared to hang around for a bit of time, but as we're not too busy ...' replied the under-manager, looking around the empty foyer to prove his point. 'In my experience they seem to operate some sort of queuing system and unfortunately it can be anything from twenty minutes to an hour. The longest was an hour and a half but that was a year ago. They seem to be better organised these days. Give the number to the telephonist and we'll take it from there.'

Walking Charlie over to the desk he added, 'It would be a good idea to keep your eye on the clock when making this kind of call, they can soon rattle up a large bill.'

'If it's a question of money ...'

'Oh no, not at all. Just a question of prudence. I've seen some of our customers turn rather ashen when they've been handed a bill after blethering for ages to an American colleague about some golf game they've just played. A ten-minute call can cost around £10. Just to give you an idea.'

'Thanks for the advice. I'll keep it in mind,' replied Charlie.

A young, smart-looking lady, the telephone operator, came to the foyer desk and asked for the New York number which Charlie carefully wrote down. At the back of the foyer there was a telephone switchboard about the size of a small wardrobe. The operator sat down and went through a series of complicated procedures with such confidence that Charlie could only stand back and admire.

Finally, she announced that the connection would be available in twenty minutes or, at the most, half an hour.

Charlie spent the time flicking through the papers. A lot of chatter about Germany and a politician called Hitler who appeared to model his politics on the Italian *Fascisti*. He suddenly remembered that newspaper guy – *what was his name again?* – had mentioned a new political party in Germany. He sat down and became engrossed in one of the larger articles in the papers.

The under-manger coughed to catch his attention.

'Your call is just about to come through. If you could follow me to the phone box.'

The 'phone box' was through a door which he hadn't noticed before. It was a small, well-appointed room with a lounge chair in front of a neat mahogany table. It was bigger, Charlie noted, than most of the bedrooms he had rented out in New York City. There was a notepad and some pencils beside a new-style Bakelite cradle phone. As he sat down the under-manager indicated to him to pick up the receiver. The operator answered immediately.

'Mr McKenna, operator here, your phone number has been answered. I'm putting you through now.'

'Hello? Hello?'

Charlie recognised the familiar Brooklyn accent.

'Hello, Mrs G. Charlie McKenna here.'

'Why, hi Charlie. Gee whiz! You sound as if you're phoning from next door.'

'Yes, I've got to admit it's very clear. Anyway how are you? How's everything going?'

'Everything's going swell; Larry and the boys are bang on schedule and there's no great problems with suppliers.'

She continued for two or three minutes in a very business-like manner without halting. Charlie took a few notes although he could see that everything seemed to be moving along smoothly.

She stopped suddenly.

'Are you still there?' she asked anxiously

'Yes, still here' said Charlie, 'listen I want you to take a couple of notes for Davidson. If you could type them up in some sort of logical fashion, I would be grateful.'

He proceeded to give Mrs G. some dates, quantities and prices that had been paid and one or two more technical details about arrival times and future shipping details.

'Got all that, Mrs G?'

'Oh sure! I'll get that typed up and take it over to Davidson personally.'

'Excellent. Is George around?'

'No. He left the office just before your cable came through.'

Charlie was still a bit confused about time.

'What time is it there?'

'It's just after eleven o'clock.'

'I thought if I phoned it would be ten.'

'No, five hours behind here, but never mind. George said he had an appointment with that creep O'Donnell.'

'With O'Donnell?'

'Yeah, something about The Country Club lease.'

'But why would George ...'

He stopped himself. There was little point in discussing it with Mrs G. It would only confuse matters.

'It's okay, Mrs G., I'll see George when I get back. I'm leaving on Thursday so should be back on Tuesday.'

'Gee that's quick. I've got you down as returning a week on Monday. You must come straight up here and tell me all about Europe.'

Charlie made a quick note - a present for Mrs G!

'I'll make sure I do. Now I'll say goodbye, or as they say here

– cheerio!'

'Cheerio ... how cute! See you later, Charlie.'

Charlie put the receiver back in the holder and looked at his watch as he opened the door – six minutes, not bad.

He allowed himself a few seconds to dwell on the appearance of O'Donnell on the scene. He dismissed it as probably something and nothing, but it settled in the back of his mind like an irritating itch.

The under-manager was at the door guiding some guests into reception. Charlie called him over.

'Do you require the phone payment now?'

'Not at all, sir, I'll put it on your bill.'

'Oh, by the way,' said Charlie as the under-manager turned to walk away, 'could I speak to the operator for a minute? I just wanted to thank her for the help she gave me.'

'I'll send her out to reception immediately,' he replied as he shepherded his new guests toward the foyer desk.

A few minutes later a rather anxious call operator stood before him.

'I hope everything went okay,' she said nervously.

'That all went exceptionally well, thanks to your expertise. Here,' he said discretely pressing a ten-shilling note into her hand, 'allow me to give you this small tip.'

Charlie moved toward the staircase quickly.

As she opened her mouth to say something he gave a broad wink and put his finger to his lips with a silent 'shush'. He turned and hurried upstairs.

*

Charlie decided to walk over to the Carol house. He reckoned that by the time he walked to the nearest tram stop and took a tramcar then crawled through the busy intersections he could be there. He briefly thought of a taxi, but dismissed it as impractical and, probably worse, an embarrassment to the Carol family. He suspected a taxi arriving in the area would be likely to arouse all sorts of speculation. To avoid getting lost he followed the same route as he had with Denholm. Across the narrow pedestrian suspension bridge then straight on until he reached the bottling plant then turning left and down towards the main cross. It was a pleasant evening and the streets were lively with people to-ing and fro-ing from the shops and pubs. Most of the shops were by now beginning to pull down shutters and, on the other hand, the pubs were getting busier. Glasgow was a town of singular drinking habits. The public bars and pubs opened at five o'clock and closed at nine thirty prompt. As a result Glaswegians had developed the habit of going for a drink in the early evening. He turned right at the cross into the main street. Here was even livelier as people queued up to go to the movies and musical theatres that lined the left hand side of the street. He reached the Carol house just before six thirty.

The door was opened on almost the first tinkle of the bell by Theresa. He could see Sadie, his father's cousin's wife, hovering anxiously behind her.

'Come in, Charlie,' she said cheerily.

The next few minutes were a mixture of handshakes and hugs as Charlie was introduced to what appeared to be a very crowded house. Chairs had been brought in and lined the walls.

The teapot was produced and tea and sandwiches were passed around in an excitement of chattering and babbling. Cigarettes were fired across the room at regular intervals. The tea and biscuits that Charlie provided were met with the usual cries of delight and approbation.

'You shouldn't have bothered ...'

'This is far too much ...'

The crowd, he finally deduced, was Mick Carol's immediate

family of five adults, that is themselves with two grown, young sons and Theresa. There was an older couple who were neighbours from Dromore and there were two bachelor cousins on his mother's side. A young newly married couple were lodging, god knows where or how, with the Carol's until they got a house of their own. Several children of unknown origin were shooed into a back bedroom.

The party, if it could be called such a thing, soon split into smaller groups. The older men talked of football and work, the younger ones tended to gather around Charlie, keen to hear all about America, and anything about gangsters and cowboys in particular. Eventually Charlie found himself talking directly to Theresa. She was an engaging young lady who seemed to talk passionately about world affairs and local politics, which had the effect of driving the other younger members off into a corner to discuss the latest movie they had seen at 'The Palace', a cinema that Charlie recognised as one of the busy movie houses he had passed on the main road.

'Do you get involved in politics in America? Do you know any politicians?'

'Only the ones I have to pay off. I leave the theory side to my business partner, George Peebles.'

'So you'll be a Democrat then?'

He hesitated, he wasn't sure if she was being tongue-in-cheek or not.

'Sort off.'

'I joined the Labour Party last year.'

Charlie was a bit surprised; he had little to do with politics when he was in Glasgow during the war.

'I always thought the Glasgow Irish were more inclined to the Liberals.'

It was Theresa's turn to be surprised.

'What on earth made you think that?'

'Well, they were the party of Home Rule when I was here.

Mind you, that was getting on seventeen years ago.'

'Oh I see. But that was such a long time ago.'

'Not to me it isn't!' said Charlie with a grin, 'and if I remember right, the Labour guys in Glasgow thought James Connolly was dangerous, small minded and a romantic nationalist.'

'Who was James Connolly?' she asked.

Charlie realised he was talking to someone whose grasp of politics would be enthusiastic, but verging on the naive.

'James Connolly was a radical socialist and one of the leaders of the Easter Rising in 1916. He had fallen out with the Labour party in 1912 and formed the Irish Labour Party with James Larkin in the same year.' said Charlie quickly. He stopped short, realising it would not be productive to go over old ground and possibly get into an argument with a young zealot.

'But I'm sure if you asked at your next meeting you might be given a different version of events.'

He opened his hands in a conciliatory fashion and discreetly turned his wrist to look at his watch – eight o'clock. He had been there well over an hour.

'But,' he added, 'such is the nature of politics. I have to go shortly but I wonder if you could do me a favour when I'm back in the states.'

'Of course I will. What is it?'

'I saw a house on the main street not far from the Clyde. It seemed to be for rent and I'm thinking of coming back to stay in Glasgow, well at least for a few months. I just wondered if you could make a few inquiries for me.'

'Yes of course I will,' replied Theresa with an unnerving enthusiasm, 'what's the address?'

'That's something I forgot to take a note of. It's the apartment above a large bank on the corner of ... I think it was Oxford Street and the Main Street. You'll see a large for let sign on one of the windows.'

She laughed.

'We don't call them apartments or flats, we just call them houses here. But I know the bank well enough, I can get some information for you I'm sure.'

'That would be great,' said Charlie handing over a small business card.

'If you get in touch with the person on this card.'

Theresa turned the card in her hand; she had never seen one before.

'This man here ... Kenneth Denholm,' she read.

'That's him. He's a business associate. I'm going to ask him to take care of one or two things for me when I'm gone.'

He noticed a look of uncertainty in Theresa's face.

'Don't worry, Kenny is a good guy, friendly, down to earth. Just leave a message for him in the office and he'll get in touch with me one way or another.'

He stood up, looked at his watch, a bit more obviously this time, and said the first thing that came into his head.

'Time to go I'm afraid. I need to be back at the hotel before nine o'clock.'

No one asked why it was necessary to be back at the hotel at a specific time. Hotels were a different world to them, perhaps hotels closed at nine o'clock, the same way as a pub closed at nine thirty.

It took Charlie, as he expected, about fifteen minutes to conduct a series of hearty goodbyes.

He walked back to the square by the same route. As he walked towards the revolving doors he suddenly decided that he would have a quick nightcap in the bar across the road.

The bar was busy but not overcrowded.

An elderly barman formally attired with shirt and tie and a large white apron came to serve him.

'What will it be?'

'A beer and a whisky, please.'

'Bottled beer?'

'Yes, that will do.'

'Do you want a half or a glass of whisky?'

Charlie was uncertain, he wasn't quite sure what he meant.

The barman was experienced enough to notice his difficulty.

'A large whisky or a small one, sir?'

'Small will be fine.'

Charlie paid for his drink and settled into a corner table.

Not that cheap, he thought. Much more expensive than The Country Club, which itself was hardly the cheapest bar in midtown New York.

He went over his schedule for the next few days. A full day tomorrow with Denholm and the dour Macpherson, mainly finalising payment dates and the like. It seems that Davidson's company had decided to order another consignment of the same volume. Denholm told Charlie that he needed to spend a bit of time tomorrow organising another cargo ship for next week if he could. They reckoned they could bottle another 100,000 bottles by that time. That's if we can think up another five or six brands names by that time, Kenny had added with a chortle.

That morning they agreed that Charlie had seen enough and had a good idea how the system worked. He could stay until next week if he wished, but in reality there was not much more he could do. McPherson had added that the Anchor line normally had a sailing every Thursday. They also agreed that the next payments would be one third of the total price payable when evidence of the ship departure was authenticated and full price on arrival stateside. It seemed his job was over.

He drank the small whisky in one draught and screwed his face slightly. A bit rough but passable.

He settled back to finish off his beer when he suddenly remembered O'Donnell. It occurred to him that he couldn't remember if O'Donnell knew where his Herald Square office was, *and in any event,* he thought, *why involve George? And how did O'Donnell get in touch with him and more importantly why?* He dismissed it. Again, he was worrying too much, and there was enough to think about as it was. The beer was nearly finished, he tipped over the last mouthful and walked out.

Chapter 20

... the old Ennui

On the fifth day out, while standing at the rail of 'Athenia', he became aware of two things; first that the Kipling aphorism 'He travels the fastest who travels alone' is a myth and also that travel is only truly glamorous in hindsight. The only thing that kept him sane was a small but rather smart cinema with a decent sound system on board where he caught up with a few of last year's movies he had missed first time round. 'Scarface' and 'Shanghai Express' were the best of the bunch. The rest of the time was spent avoiding a crushingly boring Irish businessman and trying to keep a few tables between himself and a couple of blue-rinsed spinsters who prowled and cackled their way around the lounges in the evening. According to the latest ship's bulletin they were some twenty miles east of Boston. They would pass the Statue of Liberty at seven o'clock tomorrow morning and for the first time in his life he did not intend to get up at the crack of dawn to see it.

Charlie caught a cab from Pier 57 and travelled back to his apartment with his trunk and hand luggage. As he put down his suitcase and threw himself on the bed he had that feeling of ennui that hangs around the bored traveller. He decided that he could snap himself out of it by having a cold shower in fresh water for a change. It worked surprisingly well and after towelling himself down and changing his clothes he rummaged through his luggage and found the few bits and pieces that he had bought for Mrs G. He lined them up on the sideboard and look at them apprehensively: a large decorative tin of shortbread biscuits, a pair of moderately expensive earrings and a rather classy tartan shawl. He thought himself hopeless at this sort of thing.

To his surprise and amazement, Mrs G. was truly ecstatic. Charlie had to fix up some coffee to calm her down as she whirled around the room in her shawl. After a while she was relaxed enough to talk about business. She rattled through a list. Everything went almost without a hitch, if anything the Eighth Street job was now in danger of getting a bit too far ahead of schedule. Larry Carlstrom, she announced, was running the operation with a military precision and it looked like his father had posted up the money if Larry wanted to buy Charlie out. And by the way, Una had phoned and said she'd come up on Friday night, probably get here in time for dinner.

'How about George?'

'I got in touch with George after you phoned from the dockside. He's coming up to New York tomorrow on the Blue Line. He should be here by two o'clock. Apparently he has some good news about the whisky deal. Incidentally the consignment arrived yesterday but it hasn't been unloaded. According to George, Davidson was down dockside and told them not to unload just yet.'

Charlie looked up.

'Odd. Sitting idle in port can be costly.'

'George said he'd tell you all about it tomorrow.'

Charlie thought for a moment.

'Do me a favour. Give Davidson's office a ring and see if you can get me an appointment for some time tomorrow.'

'Sure. Back in minute ...'

Charlie stood up and walked to the window and looked down. Herald Square looked unbelievably busy. Mrs G. came bustling in before he had time to think any further.

'Tomorrow morning at 10 o'clock,'

Charlie put his hand up and rubbed his brow trying to clear his mild headache.

'By the way, what's all this business with O'Donnell?'

'Don't know much about that. O'Donnell has been up here a couple of times. Not exactly the talkative type as far as I can see. He turned up with some ape last week but George wasn't in, so I sent them both packing.'

'Short haired man, mean-looking. Rarely looks you in the eye ...'

'Got him in one. Take it you know him?'

'Vincent McGhee.'

'That's right, I think I heard him calling him Vinnie at one point.'

She looked over at Charlie.

'Not normally your type, Charlie.'

'In this business you meet funny people ... and I don't mean witty and amusing comedians.'

He turned away from the window. He valued Mrs G.'s opinion; she had a good intuitive sense of character. There was something niggling him about the appearance of O'Donnell and McGhee.

'Anything I should worry about?'

She had her head to one side trying on one of the earrings again; it took her a second or two to reply.

'Those guys ain't got the brains to be smart ...'

She lifted the other earring and tilled her head in the other direction.

'... on the other hand, to my way of thinking, that makes them dangerous.'

*

Charlie was up and about at 6.30 the following day with a slight headache after Kaltonborn, the newspaperman, insisted on having a couple of Denholms 'Highland Cream' with him at nine o'clock last night in The Country Club. Charlie had brought back a couple of bottles, one of each, and he had placed them, almost as an afterthought, in the bag that contained Mrs G.'s gifts. He had stood and watched while 'Dew of the Glen' had been transformed into 'Highland Cream' before his very eyes – it happened in the bottling plant when they ran out of labels on the production line. Kaltonborn had insisted that of the two, 'Dew of the Glen' had much more depth with a just a hint of peat about it ... Charlie tactfully agreed.

He had originally intended just to pop in for a chat, a bite to eat and a couple of beers after finishing at the office. But the bar had been remarkably busy for a weekday evening and several of his regulars were keen to hear about his latest travels, and, as the old folks say ... one thing led to another. Young Frankie Sharkey was in good form, his skills in the bar and his one-liners were becoming so well-honed that he was in danger of becoming a stereotypical professional Irishman. The customers loved him. A neighbour and friend of his, Ned Ferry, had wandered in for a beer and found himself helping out Frankie for an hour when the bar got really busy. Charlie chatted to him for a few minutes as he downed a few free beers after his stint at the bar. It turned out he was a truck driver and a minor Teamster union official.

'Get many home jobs?'

'There's the odd day when I can take the truck home if I'm too far away from the base. I get the usual neighbourhood home removals and small market loads from the shop keepers.'

'Just asking, I thought I saw you delivering some beer here a while back.'

'Just a favour for O'Donnell. I usually keep away from that kind of work. Too dangerous for the money involved, especially for a skinflint like O'Donnell.'

Charlie was amused and slapped him lightly on the shoulders.

'Has a bit of reputation does our Manny.'

It was near ten o'clock when he finally opened his apartment door and almost fell into bed.

He leaned back on the subway seat. His head was becoming clearer after a few sips of the coffee that he just managed to grab from the vendor before his train arrived. At Times Square he changed lines and rode down to Fulton Street. On the Eight Street platform he ducked under scaffold that covered the main construction office and signed in with the site clerk. Larry was sitting in his chair when Charlie pulled opened the office door.

Carlstrom jumped up in embarrassment and came round to the front of the desk

'Charlie! How the devil are you! You're back early ... I hope you don't mind,' he mumbled.

'Not at all, Larry.' said Charlie, 'You don't need my permission to use the office, after all the company's practically yours these days according to Mrs G.'

'Yes, about that. My father has agreed to loan me enough money if you're still keen to sell.'

'I don't want to leave you hanging, Larry, as nothing is set in stone yet, but it looks more and more likely that we'll leave for Europe sometime after the wedding. Una's coming up on Friday. How about I give you a definite answer after the weekend?'

'Sounds okay to me,' replied Carlstrom, 'now, let me take you up to the exit point up near Second Avenue.'

*

Charlie left Fulton Street at ten o'clock after changing into his grey pinstripe suit in what passed for an executive restroom at the main contractor's office just above street level and above the main subway entrance. Earlier they had walked up to the new blasting area. It had been quiet. The night shift had finished an hour previously and the dust had settled down by that time. They had returned to the office in less than a half an hour and at least an hour before the next shift got going. All that Charlie required was a change of clothes, a hand wash, a quick brush of his shoes and his fedora and he looked like an advertising exec. from Fifth Avenue. Which was just as well as that is exactly where he was heading. He had decided to walk up to Davidson's mainly to clear away the last of the cobwebs and the slight unsteady residue of his sea legs.

The receptionist took Charlie's name and looked at a short list. She glanced up at Charlie somewhat impressed and picked the phone and appeared to phone Davidson directly. A few minutes later Sandy came rushing out of the elevator and greeted Charlie like a long lost brother.

'Right! I've got the coffee bubbling, let's go upstairs.'

As the door closed behind them Davidson said, 'I've got some interesting news about our cargo but I'll talk about that upstairs. In the meantime, I want to ask you about my cousin Kenneth. How is he doing? Still putting on the beef?'

'Looks well and he's in good shape.'

Sandy chuckled.

'Fatty Arbuckle always maintained he was in good shape, after all, as he pointed out, round *is* a shape.'

They both chuckled.

'No. Kenny's fine, although he's not one for hanging about the office. He plays golf a couple of times every week.'

'That's good to know, I've met him a few times and I took a liking to him.'

'I had an interesting time, he took me out for lunch a couple of times. I must admit Kenny's good company, seems a solid sort of guy.'

They sat in the office beside the fireplace. Nearby a young man was busy pouring coffee and arranging a plate of small sandwiches and cakes. When he left, Sandy settled back in his chair.

'I must admit our enterprise has gone even better than expected. We were offered $125,000 for the first consignment before the boat had reached half way across the Atlantic.'

Charlie whistled softly and leaned forward.

'A hundred and twenty-five thousand but that's …'

'Yes, more than twice as much as we paid Denholm's for the consignment, less expenses of course. Given that it was the first offer, some of the directors were keen to hold out for more. However, the second load is on its way and I suggested the same deal for the next cargo. That way we pay nothing for storage and get out while the going's good.'

'What happens if the price increases over the next few weeks? You'll lose out.'

Davidson spread his hands.

'A profit is a profit.'

Charlie sat back again.

'Always leave something for the next guy up the line, make them think they got a good deal. And of course we don't know how many people are now jumping on the bandwagon. There's only a certain amount of whisky you can put on the market before the price starts to fall. Remember, the reason we got a good price in the first place was because Denholm's had overproduced and we bought at the right time.'

'So where is the cargo now?'

'Heading for Baltimore.'

'Baltimore? I thought the 'Rosario' had tied up in New York.'

'The deal was completed yesterday afternoon. The new owners wasted no time in setting off on the last tide at seven o'clock.'

'The new owners?'

'Sorry, can't tell you who they are, but they're well connected and they're convinced prohibition will end in two or three months if not sooner.'

'What about the next consignment?'

'That's already changed course and is also heading for Baltimore.'

Charlie sat back and lifted up his coffee.

'I've got to say that's a good bit of business ... in fact that's probably an understatement.'

'It's always a good piece of business if everything goes well. There was a fair bit of luck involved in this enterprise. Remember that I had the inside information on the Denholm's and had wind of the schemes of Kennedy and Roosevelt. I also had a few investors lined up.'

Charlie had a smile.

'By this time next year George will be telling everyone that the whole thing was his idea.'

'Oh I don't care about that. Don't forget your own part in this business.'

'Oh, come on ...'

'Kenny wired me last week to tell me that he was impressed by your business-like approach. I've got to admit I've always valued Kenny's opinion.'

Sandy drummed his fingers lightly on the arm of the chair. 'As everything went so smoothly,' he continued, 'the rest of the consortium have decided to give you a bonus of a thousand dollars.'

'Very generous, thank them for me,' Charlie replied. Over all a total of two thousand bucks on a quarter of a million-dollar deal was small potatoes. It was an offer however, he thought wryly, that he was unlikely to turn down. It then occurred to him that he had made as much money in the past few weeks as he had the whole of last year.

Chapter 21

Wedding Bells

Charlie was caught completely off guard when he walked into the reception area of the Lincoln Hotel. Una ambushed him at the desk with two of her best friends, one on each side, clinging to her arms.

'Hope you don't mind but I invited Sarah and Dorothea up for the weekend. They're going to help me pick my wedding dress. And they'll pick their own bridesmaid's dresses of course.'

'No, not at all.'

'You've met Sarah Kelly, remember we met her at Penn Station last month.'

'Of course, how could I forget?'

'And this is Dorothea, I'm sure you've met at one of the parties last year.'

'Yes, I remember you, Dorothea. Nice to meet you again.'

Charlie hadn't the foggiest recollection of her at all.

'Run along now, girls, I need to talk to Charlie.'

Sarah and Dorothea clasped each and hurried upstairs giggling.

'Sorry about that, Charlie, and sorry I had to make light of it, but I was caught on the hop. Let's take a seat in the lounge.'

As they turned to go, the floor manager ghosted into view.

'Coffee for two? In the lounge?'

'Yes, please,' answered Una.

As they walked through the lounge and took a seat Charlie said, 'I don't know about you, but I'm beginning to find the service in this hotel borders on the servile. It's almost as if they're starting to read your mind in here.'

'Can't say I've noticed,' replied Una distractedly, 'I really hope you don't mind me bringing Dot and Sarah but everything has become so rushed. McBride has given us a booking for the twenty second of May.'

'But that's only two weeks away!' said Charlie, trying to sound surprised.

'Yes, I'm sorry, only found out on Wednesday, the day you arrived. I swithered about sending you a cablegram but I thought it best to see you.'

'Oh! Don't worry,' said Charlie.

He leaned forward and took her hand.

'Remember what I said about the sooner the better? Anyway George blurted it out yesterday to Mrs G. and she told me ... so I knew all about it. Just thought I'd string you along for a bit.'

'That big blabbermouth!' she laughed, putting her hand over Charlie's, 'I might have known he would have told someone.'

They untangled their hands reluctantly as the waiter slid the coffee tray on the table.

'Right then, to business,' said Charlie as he pulled out his cheque book, 'This will a cost a pretty penny no doubt.'

'You can forget about that. My father wired a thousand dollars as a gift towards the wedding last week. Unfortunately, my folks won't manage over. It's just not enough notice for them.'

'A thousand dollars! You didn't tell him we were getting married in the Ritz-Carton did you?'

'No I didn't, don't be silly. I believe they've put money aside for this. My sister's wedding in Dublin cost much more. They probably think that they have do the same for me.'

She leaned back and smiled.

'I suspect you have no idea how much a wedding costs these days, now do you?'

'Not really ... is a thousand dollars enough?'

'Yes, it's very generous in fact. So leave all the details to me.'

'You, plus Sarah and Dot, I take it.'

'Well, Charlie McKenna, you're getting the hang of this wedding malarkey already! Now how about some coffee.'

They spent a quiet contented half hour or so discussing wedding details, until Una glanced up at the clock.

'What will we do about dinner?'

'I'm not sure, have you made an arrangement with the girls? Or will we have dinner in the Polo restaurant here?'

'I never thought about it to be honest.'

Charlie had a think for a second or two.

'Look, I'll go back to The Country Club and have something there. I need an early night anyway, Saturday mornings and Sundays are the best days for closing down the track so Saturday is always a busy morning for us down in Eighth Street. Why don't you and your chums have dinner here and we can have a think about tomorrow later on.'

'Don't worry about tomorrow. I'll pack the girls off to Philly in the late afternoon, there's some big event at the Latham Hotel that they would apparently rather die than miss. We can have the rest of the weekend together.'

At that, Dorothea and Sarah fluttered into the lounge.

'Made that decision just in time by the looks of things,' said Charlie in a low voice, 'I'll stay for ten minutes and leave you to it.'

'It's a deal ... although you don't have to sound *quite* so relieved.' she added with a grin.

*

'So, how did it go today?' said Charlie as they sat down in the dining room of the Polo lounge.

'It was great fun I must admit. We were in Fifth Avenue almost before the shops had opened. Hard to believe but the wedding dress and bridesmaid outfits were all organised before lunch. Dot insisted on dragging us up to the Algonquin ...'

'Isn't that the same place we went to when we got engaged?'

'I know, but they had never been before, so I was able to pretend that the Algonquin was all a bit old hat and passé these days.'

Charlie looked at her blankly, obviously missing the point.

'So, when did they get away?'

'We went back to Henri Bendel's so they could get an outfit for tonight and then a taxi to Penn station for the four o'clock Blue Line.'

She looked at her watch.

'They'll be sitting with a cocktail in The Latham by now.'

Charlie toyed with the menu for a minute.

'It's a bit of a glamorous life they lead.'

'Not really. It's not glamorous, it's more ... it's all a bit.' She searched for a word, '... gratuitous. I don't know if that's the right word, perhaps vacuous, maybe. That crowd rarely have any jobs or occupations that are meaningful; they seem almost continually bored.'

'It's just that it crossed my mind that you might miss your life here in America.'

'Not sure about that, I like it here but I'm not sure if it really feels, you know, like home somehow. I know I'm not making much sense, but I'd like to give going back a chance.'

'I agree. By the way, one thing I have found out is that because I've been here over ten years, I can get an eight year permit which means I can come back without going through immigration. When we get married, it'll apply to you as well. So if things don't work out we can easily return.'

'Let's not think about it any more and start planning.'

'I'm glad you said that. When I was in Glasgow I spotted a

large apartment on the south side of the river, although they don't call them apartments. They seem to call any kind of living quarters a house over there ...'

'When you say big ...'

'It has four bedrooms which makes it large by any standards. I have some contacts and I made some inquires. I got a short cable yesterday. It seems it's rented out at eight pounds a month, that's about thirty-five dollars a month.'

'That seems reasonable,'

'I think we should take it for six months and then see what happens. I'll wire over the deposit tomorrow. It means we have somewhere to go if we leave, and if we change our mind,' he sat back and opened out his hands, 'in that case I'm only out a couple of hundred bucks.'

'Well, let's celebrate. I'll have a cocktail and then we can order dinner.'

They talked all through dinner, sometimes about things that seemed to go over Charlie's head. The invited guest list seemed to him to be a particular area of delicacy; apparently it was a minefield that required the skill of a diplomat. Una suggested he leave other practical concerns like cars, catering, photographs and the like to her and her friends. She also suggested they spend the wedding night in a nearby hotel and then head off for a two-week honeymoon in Niagara Falls. In the end it seemed all Charlie had to do was select a best man, get a suitable wedding suit and make sure he got there on time.

*

Charlie spent the following week tying up loose ends. He sold the construction business for the agreed sum to Carlstrom and George Peebles was happy to let Larry carry on with the contracts for the remaining subway undertakings which, he reckoned, should easily last until next year. His lawyer told him that the lease on The Country Club was coming along fine and he had agreed with

O'Donnell's lawyer to finish off the paperwork for a hand-over in four or five weeks' time.

Everything seemed to be fitting in and running like clockwork.

What, thought Charlie, could possibly go wrong?

Chapter 22

Afternoon tea

Liam looked out at the park opposite his lounge window. He had to lift his hand to shade his eyes from the late afternoon sun that was starting to go down over the large evergreen trees on the hills above. He was suddenly surprised to see that the inside verge of the park gates which were covered in crocuses, mainly purple and white the last time he looked, were now gone and replaced by young daffodils. Was it that time of year already? Or was he just beginning to notice them? He had hardly time to ponder this horticultural conundrum before the internal doorbell gave a loud buzz.

It was four o'clock on the dot.

He lifted the phone, 'Hello?'

'Hi, Liam, Prince Charming here, are you ready for the ball?'

Despite the intercom crackle Liam recognised the voice and the irritating jolly drivel of Grace McKenna's husband, Eddie.

'Down in a minute,' said Liam putting the phone quickly back in the cradle before Eddie made another inane crack. Eddie was waiting at the bottom of the stoop. Liam checked his pocket making sure he had his key before pulling the main entrance door closed.

'Your carriage awaits,' Eddie said with a grin.

Liam said nothing and pulled open the passenger door and squeezed in. Sometimes he had difficulty keeping his mouth shut when in the company of Eddie. He was irrepressibly cheery in a strange schoolboy fashion. He also had, like many of his ilk, the hide of an elephant. One of his many hobbies was building model aeroplanes of World War Two, which Liam thought, just about summed him up.

Liam replied to his banal ramblings with simple nods, or the occasional 'Yes indeed'. The journey was mercifully short.

Grace met Liam with a quick hug and perfunctory peck on the cheek.

'Glad you could make it,' she said as she led him into the large living room.

'I've set out a table in the garden. I'll take you outside and then I'll nip in to the kitchen and brew some fresh tea. Are you joining us, Eddie?'

'No, sorry, no time. I've got a tricky bit of gluing to do along the fuselage of a Messerschmitt Bf109.'

'Yes,' said Grace dryly, 'I thought you might have.'

Grace led Liam to a medium sized garden table on a patio beneath the shelter of a small bowery of ornamental maple trees. In the middle of the table was an old fashioned two tier cake-stand with a variety of tasty looking sandwiches on the base and some homemade cheesecake and éclairs on the top. It was set for three with classical ceramic teacups and side plates. It was a chilly afternoon and a gas garden heater hissed quietly nearby.

'Take a seat. I'll only be two minutes.'

Liam pulled back a chair and sat down. He almost had to slap his own hand as it crept towards a rather wonderful looking salmon and mayonnaise sandwich. He sat back and decided to take his mind off the cake-stand by reflecting on his theory on how Charlie converted the sovereigns into hard cash. *Did Grace know?* he mused, *and if she knew, would she admit it ... or was there some aspect of the acquisition of such a fortune that made her uneasy?*

He was brought back to reality by Grace clattering a large ceramic teapot on the middle of the table. The teapot, of course, matched the rest of the crockery

'You'll need to pour the tea, Liam, I'm afraid my wrists are not as strong as they used to be.'

Liam stood up and dutifully did as he was ordered.

'I see you like salmon,' said Grace as Liam sank the neatly cut bread finger sandwich in two bites.

Liam indicated that he couldn't talk with a full mouth.

'Delicious,' he said finally reaching out for another and wolfing it down.

'That was prosciutto and fig by the way, not that you appeared to notice.'

'Was it really?' he finally replied.

'Not to worry. Please carry on. I've probably made too many.'

Between them they polished off the rest, including some delightful little crabmeat with chilli and lemon pinwheels. They left only the Manchego and quince in toasted bread. Manchego cheese, they both agreed, was hard to digest.

They then started on the cakes.

'Well, that was an excellent spread,' said Liam pouring out more tea and trying to suppress a burp.

'Thank you, Liam. Nice to be appreciated. When it comes to sandwiches, Eddie and the rest of them are more your cheese-and-pickle type.'

The patio was well sheltered and warm from the heater. The sun was going down and the sky was beginning to darken behind them. They settled back in their chairs.

'As I was saying last week, at dinner in Greens I was overheard by a group of Americans when I was talking about Charlie's exploits. As luck would have it one of them publishes a Magazine aimed primarily at the Irish-American Market. The short piece I gave you last week was an outline. He has now contacted me again offering me a large article on the role of Cork during the Civil War.'

Grace interrupted, looking derisive.

'Overhear you? Not the way Julie tells it. Seems it was quite a performance.'

'I wouldn't say that,' he replied, shifting uncomfortably, 'anyway, I wonder if you could fill me in with a few details about Charlie. Can I ask you a few questions?'

'I'll tell you what I know ... if I can.'

'When did Charlie eventually come to Glasgow?'

'It was in May 1933. I'm sure about that. In fact I could probably get the exact date, I'm sure there was a post card with the date on it.'

'Yes, that ties in with a few things. I think I mentioned someone named O'Donnell last week. I was just wondering if the name McGhee rings any bells?'

'Both of them seem to be connected to the speakeasy, although I was never quite clear of the relationship. Both O'Donnell and McGhee came from Donegal so I assumed some sort of family connection.'

'Charlie mentions Atlantic City in the diary, does that mean anything?'

'Oh that's easy! Charlie and Una were married in Atlantic City on the twenty second of May 1933. The marriage certificate is in the trunk upstairs.'

Liam looked surprised.

'They were married and then came to Glasgow a week or so later?'

Grace appeared to waver.

'I don't see anything wrong in that, they moved into a large flat in Gorbals when they arrived here. Again I think I saw some sort of rental agreement in amongst his papers. He seems to have rented before they got married.'

'Is that likely? Marry, immigrate to another country and have a house conveniently rented before they arrived? I mean it wasn't exactly the age of the internet was it?'

'I don't know. Charlie was quite resourceful.'

Liam sat quietly flicking his beard. He sensed that Grace was being very cagey.

'What about this character Peebles? He features quite a bit, yet remains a bit of a mystery.'

'Yes, Charlie did mention someone called Peebles. George I think it was. Again there was some Donegal connection although I must admit I've never heard of anyone else with the surname Peebles in Donegal. They were friends and business partners as far as I know. It seems they spent some time in Ireland and France although nothing specific.'

'Oddly enough I did some research on the name Peebles and found that there were quite a few of that name in a small area just south of Letterkenny, indeed not that far from Charlie's hometown. Could be a logical connection. Most of them appeared to have left Ireland around the '20s and some changed their name from Peebles to Peoples but I can't find a reason for it. Perhaps most of them simply emigrated.'

He stopped to lift his cup.

'There seems to have been some tie-up between the four of them, I mean Charlie and George and the other two, McGhee and O'Donnell, but I'm not sure what it is,' he said cautiously.

Liam was getting the impression that she was not fully aware of Charlie's sudden decision to return to Glasgow. He tried steering the conversation towards the sovereigns to test his theory on how they were returned to Glasgow and disposed of.

'Talking of large places - you mentioned the flat in the Gorbals - I would think that someone working for the local authority would have been hard-pressed to afford a place this size.'

Grace looked uncomfortable.

Charlie felt her unease and rushed on.

'Let's not get tied up in the details of all this, remember that this was a long time ago. Let's put it this way, I suspect that in the early '50s Charlie went back down to Cork for two reasons. He had a business arrangement with a Mrs Conklin, an hotelier in Tralee. They had made a joint thirty-year mortgage arrangement around 1922 with Charlie providing the start-up capital, presumably with some of the gold he had acquired, which I'll come back to later. Mrs Conklin's niece, who I met on our recent trip, explained that her aunt had kept in intermittent touch with Charlie's brother Pat in Donegal. It seems they knew each other at least reasonably well and that she, I mean Mrs Conklin, also suspected Pat may have been involved in the incident at Ballyseedy Cross. To be honest, it was not conclusive. Then again what could be regarded as concrete evidence after all this time?'

He paused to brush a few crumbs from his trousers.

'I say 'kept in touch' but I'm led to believe it was no more than the annual exchange of Christmas cards. However, when the mortgage was finished she managed to get in touch with Charlie through Pat. I assume Charlie thought it was safe enough to return to Tralee by then and he made the trip with his two sons, including a very young Eddie. Mrs Conklin's niece was a bit vague about the gold but was pretty sure that Charlie received around two thousand pounds as part of the mortgage settlement.'

'Well, that would explain all this,' said Grace, looking around, 'a simple and profitable business arrangement.'

'Not quite. Back then two thousand would buy a decent semi-detached, but nothing like this. I suspect he took the gold that Mrs Conklin kept in the safe for him, after all it was part of the deal. In his writings he had mentioned that he had to sell some of the gold to get some capital for the hotel. He sold it to someone called Cohen, a Cork businessman, the man who owned a bonded warehouse, and, more importantly, was part of the Jewish community in Cork. Charlie was quite familiar with Jewish businessmen, his partner in New York, for example, was Page Slavinsky.'

Grace looked away as Liam continued.

'At one time a small area in the Gorbals had housed almost ninety percent of the Jewish community in Glasgow. By the standards of the time they weren't particularly discriminated against. However, they were hardly ever offered work in industry and it's a matter of record they were never employed in government posts. So they tended to stick to retail and trading and, by the '50s - the time we're talking about - they ran almost all of the jewellery shops in Glasgow. Getting the gold out of Ireland was easy enough. The boat from Dublin didn't check passports. Despite what some politicians tell you these days, Ireland is not considered, and never was considered, a foreign country. It came under an arrangement known as 'The Common Travel Area'. They hardly even bothered with Custom and Excise, as it was called at the time; all that was ever smuggled was the occasional pack of cigarettes. The sovereigns, or what was left of them, wouldn't even have been that heavy. They could have been easily carried and concealed in the luggage needed for a man on holiday with two young children. Okay, Charlie probably took a bit of a hit in the price negotiations with the jewellers, but they themselves were taking a bit of a risk. But hey, who's going to complain?'

'Got it all worked haven't you?'

'Am I right?'

'Near enough.'

Liam resisted the temptation to grin and give a high five.

'If this gets out it puts the family in an awkward position. This means this house was bought with the proceeds of an armed robbery.'

'Are you kidding? This all happened last century. For God's sake, don't worry. Hell! What are you thinking of? Selling up and giving the money back to the Irish Free State? A country that no longer exists.'

'I suppose you're right. I've been worrying myself silly. It's being going through my mind since you started your daft speculations, that you would eventually chip away until you got to the bottom off it.'

She glanced over at Liam

'It's one of the reasons I asked you over here. In a way you've lifted a weight off my shoulders'

Liam stood up.

'You know, I thought I knew Charlie, but with talk of McGhee and O'Donnell, you're beginning to make me wonder if something else was going on.'

She turned away.

'I'll take you up to the attic. Perhaps we could get some answers up there.'

*

Liam was standing by the small kitchen bin and just about to dispose of the Manchego and quince sandwiches.

'Don't throw them away!' barked Grace.

Liam gave a start.

'Eddie will take them. Put them to one side.'

She dried her hands on a towel.

'I'm going upstairs to change into some old jeans before we go into the attic. It's not that bad but it can be a bit dusty up there. I suppose I should have warned you.'

'Don't bother about me, these are just some old casual clothes I shoved on this morning.'

Grace turned round and looked Liam up and down.

'Yes,' she said briskly, 'I can see that.'

Liam furiously tried to think of a witty reply as she turned on her heel and walked out the door.

'Could you boil up the kettle while I'm gone?' she continued over her shoulder 'I'll bring up a mug of tea to Eddie.'

He gave out a mild cuss and put the sandwiches on to a plate and then continued to take in the tea things while at the same time trying to figure out how Eddie fitted in on a trip to the attic. Each time he went into the garden he seemed to interrupt a half a dozen small birds, finches he guessed, who were feasting on the bread crumbs around the table. Whenever he approached they fluttered back to the bowery with an oddly disturbing rustle of leaves.

'That's me ready,' announced Grace, pulling forward a large mug featuring Homer Simpson eating a doughnut, 'but first, a quick mug of tea for Eddie.'

She was wearing old jeans and a red woollen sweater that almost reached her knees.

'Here,' she ordered Liam, 'you carry up the plate and I'll take the tea.'

They marched through the living room with Grace at the rear shouting directions 'right here ... left again ... up the stairs, turn right at the top of the stairs and down the corridor.'

'I take it we're now in the East Wing,' said Liam, becoming bamboozled by all the directions.

'Nearly there ... open the door in front of you and you'll find a set of stairs that lead to the attic.'

'Right ho,' he muttered as he opened the door.

There was a narrow staircase to his right leading up to a half-landing.

'Ah! I see now why there's a fancy window on this side of the house. I often wondered why there was a stained glass window at the end of the building.'

They stood on the half-landing looking across to the window, even in the half light of dusk it was impressive.

'Yes, it's nice, isn't it? It's a smaller version of St Enoch from St. Margaret's church in London.'

Liam leaned back against the wall, folded his arms and sighed.

'It's strange, but you have to be on this spot to see it in all its glory.'

'You're not suddenly going through some ecclesiastic episode are you?'

'Just saying ...'

'Move over, I'll go up the stairs from here,' she said impatiently.

Grace jogged up to the next landing which was about eight feet long; there was a door in the middle.

'Eddie. It's me,' she shouted, rapping the woodwork 'I've brought you up some tea.'

'Come on in, the door's not locked,' said a distant voice.

I know Eddie's a bit loopy, thought Liam, *but surely they don't lock him up at night.*

He followed Grace up the stairs and into the room not knowing what to expect.

*

'Ah Liam, you've found me in my lair.'

The room was enormous, about thirty feet across and almost the full width of the house from the front to the back. At one end, the one overlooking the back garden, was an array of 5 or 6 high but narrow windows inside what is known as a mansard roof, the result of which gave a large, airy and light-filled room.

'This was designed as an artist studio in the early 1920s,' said Eddie, carefully putting down a small thin paintbrush, 'never did find out who had it commissioned, or why for that matter.'

Liam was a bit lost for words as he stepped into the room and looked around.

The ceiling on the left hand side dripped with model aeroplanes on threads, swooping and diving in various battle modes. Liam walked towards the window, almost in a daze, looking at the planes. They seemed remarkably realistic. The only one he recognised and could name was the Spitfire. The rest seemed to be a collection of old bombers and planes that he vaguely remembered seeing on those old British movies that were always shown on dismal rainy afternoons. He looked out at the vista before him. The sun, now red and going down below the hills to the west, cast a golden glimmer on the dark, altocumulus cloud formation above and filled the room with a coppery light. Below him was a maze of bare tree branches. Down to the right he could just make out the brown and red leaves of the small bowery that hung over the garden table.

Also on the right, near the window, where Eddie was leaning over what Liam took to be a model of the Messerschmitt Bf109, was a large workbench covered in bits of plastic, glue tubes and dozens of tiny paint pots.

He walked over to the workbench and placed the tea mug near Eddie and then, still a bit dumbstruck, wandered over to a large horizontal glass display case that was sitting against the wall, close to the work bench. It was the kind that you usually see in natural history museums. He placed his hands on the sides and looked in. After a few moments, he bent down closer.

'These look …' he said slowly, 'like ...'

'Bats,' replied Grace.

'Dead bats, to be more precise. Chiropterology is another of Eddie's interesting hobbies.'

'Amazing,' said Liam, clearly impressed, although he was not sure why.

'Yes,' replied Grace, arching an eyebrow, 'It certainly brings a new dimension to the expression "bats in the belfry".'

She, in turn, quickly walked over to the workbench and left the plate of Manchego and quince sandwiches beside the tea.

'Saved a sandwich for you.'

'Good. What's in them?'

'Cheese and pickle,' she replied, waving to Liam as she moved over to the door near the glass case.

'We can get into the rest of the attic through here.'

Chapter 23

Atlantic City

In Atlantic City a corrupt political system made alcohol more easily available during prohibition than any time before. In fact, the place was a bit of a madhouse even by American standards of lawlessness. Not that it bothered any of the tens of thousands of Philadelphians who descended on the New Jersey resort every day of the summer season. Those who stayed for a holiday were catered for by some of the largest and best appointed hotels in the world. The famous board walk, on the sea front, was a three-mile-long arcade of pleasant bars, cafés, fast food outlets, fun fairs and seemingly innocent penny slot machine joints. Those who promenaded along the Atlantic waterfront however, were mostly in the dark about the warren of illegal gambling dens, Chinese dope houses and brothels that lay a couple of city blocks to the North. The street life in these areas was a daily battleground of gangs of every conceivable ethnic origin involved in anarchic mayhem. The main task of the Atlantic City Police Department was not one of crime prevention, but to make sure they collected their pay-offs and, more importantly, to make sure none of the bedlam spilled over to the tourist area.

Other than that, the gangs could do as they liked.

Fortunately, 'The Tiffany', Joe McBride's hotel, was far enough away from the havoc of the North Side that it might have been in a different country.

They travelled down by train on the Monday before May 22 and took a cab to the Tiffany. It was Charlie's first visit to Atlantic City and he was impressed. McBride had already insisted on laying on a couple of coaches and cabs for the wedding guests who were coming by train on the day of the big event. This was not, as Charlie thought, an act of generosity by McBride but simply a practical consideration for the safety of his guests as the route to the hotel passed the outer edges of Atlantic Avenue. This rationale was never explained to Charlie or Una, nor indeed any of the paying customers of the Tiffany Hotel who just all thought that Atlantic City was a fun place to be.

They were escorted through the Tiffany by McBride himself. They were shown everything from the individual bedrooms to the 'Havana Ballroom' which had an impressive bandstand for fifteen players with a permanent baby grand piano. It was also, he assured them, fitted with the latest sound equipment. He had booked the swing band 'Victor Viscount and his Esquires' to provide the music for the 'wedding ball', as he insisted on calling it. The hotel even had its own photographic wedding studio with a variety of backdrops available. Outside, there were neatly trimmed lawns and flowerbeds of wild anemones. They giggled and laughed as they dodged the twirling water sprinklers. Una was enthralled.

Back in the office McBride asked about numbers. Una reckoned about a hundred at the main ceremony and the same again at the wedding ball. 'How about three dollars a head for the wedding and meal and, say, a dollar a head for the ball?' Una wavered for a minute, thinking it was expensive.

McBride threw in a glass of 'champagne' for each guest on arrival.

'Done deal,' announced Una, jumping up and shaking McBride's hand. Charlie had barely opened his mouth; he was about to, then thought better of it. He could learn a lot from Una he realised.

McBride ordered one of his staff to drive them over to the Ritz-Carton where Una had insisted that they stay for the two nights of the wedding before heading to Niagara Falls. After all, she pointed out, Charlie had talked of the Ritz-Carton when Una had mention her father's contribution.

'It was meant as a joke,' he complained lamely.

They organised their two night stay and had a cocktail in the lounge. Charlie lifted his glass in a toast.

'To Atlantic City – the only place in the USA where you can drink illegally without looking over your shoulder.'

They settled down in the plush armchairs.

'We have an hour before the next train home,' said Una, glancing at the large clock above the bar.

'So, what do you think of McBride's place?'

'I must admit I didn't think it would be so big. In Glasgow I stayed in the St Enoch hotel which is supposed to be one of the biggest hotels in Scotland and I reckon it's probably half the size of the Tiffany.'

He stopped and glanced about him.

'Then again compared to the size of this place, I suppose it could be described as middling.'

'Ideal for us I'd say,' replied Una, 'and quite reasonable under the circumstances.'

'What about getting up to Niagara Falls from here?'

'That's all squared up. Mrs Greene organised the hotel and all the travelling for us. That woman is a marvel! I've invited her and her husband to the wedding. Gladys and her husband can stay the night in the Tiffany.'

'Gladys?'

For a split second Charlie thought that Una was talking about someone else when it suddenly occurred to him that Gladys was Mrs G.'s first name. He was a bit taken aback and embarrassed. Not only did he always refer to her as Mrs G. but it never occurred to him there might even be a *Mr* G. on the scene.

He recovered well.

'Of course! Gladys! I'm that used to calling her Mrs G., that I don't think about it now,' he laughed, 'I must blame George for that.'

'… and talking of George Peebles,' said Una, 'he asked me to invite a few of your mutual friends down from New York.'

'Okay, give me the bad news.'

Una rhymed off a few names and nicknames as far as she could remember. About ten in all.

'I think I've only met a couple of them; O'Donnell, Sharkey and Slavinsky sound familiar,'

'I think you've met most of them at one stage or another over the past couple of years. I know all of them; they're okay. One or two like Sandy Davidson are mutual business partners, some of them are George's political cronies. The rest are old friends that have been hanging around New York for years.'

He thought for a minute – no real problems or potential clashes.

'No one called McGhee?'

'Not that I recall. Why, would that be problem?'

'No, not really. Just that he's made a few enemies over the years. Weddings can be a bit of a flash-point at times. Too much drinking, the usual, dancing with the wrong woman, that sort of thing. Old scores to settle ...'

'Not at any of the weddings I've been to!' said Una, alarmed.

'It's all right, don't get worried.' Charlie could have kicked himself. 'Just an observation I made at one or two Irish weddings in the past. It always involved family feuds but that's not likely to happen in our case, is it?' he added quickly.

'I'm beginning to wonder about your family.'

'Sorry I brought it up. Listen, don't worry about anything, everything will go fine. By the way,' he continued, moving the subject in another direction, 'Joe has agreed to be my best man.'

'Oh, I thought you would have asked George?'

'Joe's family. George knows about it and is quite happy.'

'Okay, let's finish our drink and order a cab. I'm dying to get back home. I've a million and one things to get organised before Saturday.

*

George and Elizabeth insisted on Una using their house for a display of the wedding gifts and a quiet drinks party for her pals while he and Charlie and 'a couple of the boys' went down to O'Malleys for a few drinks. Everything was civilised and remarkably sober considering the occasion. Charlie was back at his sister's house at ten o'clock; Una had her guests shooed out the door around the same time.

The guests made their way down to Atlantic City in a variety of ways. Charlie and his best man, his brother-in-law, Joe Di Dio left in a hired Chevrolet along with two of Joe's innumerable sisters, Dona and Rosanna, both of whom had a role to play in the upcoming wedding service. Charlie couldn't remember if they were flower-girls, bridesmaids or maids of honour or, possibly, a permutation of all of these roles. They decided, after a brief discussion and compromise, that they would have a Catholic marriage. Charlie was nominally a Catholic whereas Una was the product of a Scottish Episcopalian mother and a Church of Ireland father. As most of the guest were Irish or Italian Catholics, they thought a Catholic service appropriate. Joe and the sisters babbled in an excited mixture of Italian and English for the entire hour-long journey. Charlie heaved a sigh of relief as he rolled into the rear parking lot of the Tiffany. They were an hour and half early at the insistence of the sisters who were apparently given important, specific tasks before the wedding service started. Charlie was given access to a ground floor room which, he was told, he could use as a private dressing room until the ceremony began. He returned to the chevvy and raked through the luggage until he finally found the lightweight case containing his hired wedding suit; a morning suit with a white shirt and a white bow-tie. When he had tried it on in the outfitters he thought he looked like a dancing extra from a Busby Berkley movie. The salesman insisted that white bow-ties were all the rage these days and that anything other would look old fashioned. He took it reluctantly.

He had a wash and quick brush up and decided to go down to the bar and have a coffee. He was curious about the set-up and wondered if any of the guests had arrived. The bar area was quiet but within ten minutes it looked as if things were beginning to warm up. Workmen were carting flowers and chairs along to the main dining room where the reception was being held. He wondered about the service itself. Looking around, it dawned on him that the whole thing had a theatrical air and he was unsure of his part in it. Charlie suddenly and almost inexplicably started to feel nervous. Guests started appearing at the bar chatting and laughing without a care in the world. He was about to leave when he spotted the priest bumbling about the room with two young boys who he took to be the altar boys. He decided to have a quick word.

Charlie introduced himself to the priest.

'I'm Charlie McKenna, the bridegroom.'

'Charlie McKenna?' repeated the priest, who Charlie noticed seemed to be rather elderly. The old man scratched his head absent-mindedly.

'Ah!' he shouted out suddenly, 'the groom!'

'Well, how the devil are you?' he continued, grabbing Charlie's arm. 'Come over here 'till I have a look.'

He dragged him to a window, spun Charlie around and looked him in the face.

'A handsome groom you are too, Mr McKenna, bejesus!'

Charlie almost burst out laughing. In his adult life he must have met hundreds if not thousands of Irishmen and had never heard any of them use the expression 'Bejesus'.

'What's your name?' asked Charlie.

'Father Seamus ...' he hesitated for a second, '... O'Gready'

'Where are you from?'

'Oh! Just a little place you wouldn't know.'

'Try me.'

'Bally. Bally...' he hesitated again, '... gally.'

'Ballygally?'

'That's right. I said you wouldn't know it.'

'Look Father,' he said impatiently, '... O'Gready. I'm not that bothered about all that. All I want to know is what I've got to do during the ceremony.'

'Ah! Sure that's no problem. At all ... at all,' he announced, pulling out a small booklet. 'Go away and read this book, it has the full service ... Begora.'

Charlie put the booklet down on the nearest table.

'OK, O'Gready. Let's stop with the phoney Irish accent, it's about as authentic as New York's St. Patrick's Day parade. Not only that, I know where Ballygally is. It's in the North near the town of Larne.'

O'Gready looked crestfallen.

'You're kidding! Ballygalley is a real place? I just made it up a second ago.' He gave a sigh and continued. 'So, not fooled, huh? It's not my fault, blame McBride. He gets me to officiate at all his weddings regardless of what religion. I was a priest at one time but got slung out for pilfering the offertory money.'

'The offertory money? That's hardly a hanging offence.'

'Em ... That amongst other things,' O'Gready replied quickly, 'McBride prefers me to use the accent of the couple getting married.'

'And you get away with it?'

'Always. Hardly anyone speaks to me before the ceremony and by the time it all starts people are too excited to notice. Besides, I spent a bit of time acting in vaudeville around lower Broadway. Believe me, this is a cinch.'

Charlie was beginning to take to O'Gready.

'Anyway, for ten bucks a throw not to mention a day full of food and booze, I'm hardly in a position to argue,' he added with a shrug.

'Right, let's have a look at this book.'

'Just say your name where it says 'Groom' and you'll be fine. Don't worry too much, I'll keep you right.'

'What about Una?'

223

'Una?'

'Yes. Una's the bride.'

'Ah yes, the bride. Wouldn't worry too much about the bride. Ain't met a bride who didn't know the service procedure better than me.'

He looked around in an attempt to find the altar boys.

'As a matter of interest. What *is* your name?'

'Ira Cohen.'

'Funny name for an ex-priest.'

'It a long story. Just call me Father Seamus, it'll make things easier.'

He spotted the two boys standing having a cigarette beside the door to the garden.

'Now you get on. I've done hundreds of these things. Get yourself ready and enjoy the day.'

Oddly enough, knowing that 'Father Seamus O'Gready' sounded as if he came from the lower East Side made Charlie feel more confident.

It's the American Way, he thought with amusement, *better to have a professional actor than leave it to chance.*

*

He was right, of course, the wedding ceremony went without a hitch. Una looked stunning. Her wedding dress was a timeless, silk and lace affair and, although her face was partly hidden by a veil, anyone could see that she radiated happiness and contentment. Before the ceremony started, Cohen called them to the side to give the happy couple a final instruction.

'When I nod in your direction just say 'I do'.'

'Nothing else,' he added with a glare at both, 'I'll have no ad-libbing if you don't mind.'

With a loud cough he brought the congregation to silence.

He smoothed his hair; this was his moment; he was about to step on to his stage.

There was a small microphone near the altar that Cohen immediately placed between the couple making his own voice faintly muffled – 'Seamus O'Gready' hammed up the accent good style. The service itself was performed in a mixture of Irish/English with a fair smattering of mumbo jumbo Latin. It was punctuated with exaggerated Signs of the Cross and the occasional splash of Holy water. The altar boys nipped about looking busy, lifting up various props and then returning them when Cohen was finished. Towards the end he brought the couple together and asked a few questions which no one could quite hear.

Charlie and Una played their parts well, ringing out their 'I do's' clearly on the discreet nods of Cohen.

Finally, Cohen dramatically threw his arms apart.

'I now pronounce you man and wife.'

He beamed beatifically at Charlie and Una.

'You may kiss the Bride!'

The congregation stood up and clapped and cheered wildly.

*

The couple tripped down the aisle in a snowstorm of confetti and rice as they made their way towards the 'Wedding Studio'. The crowd were already heading to the bar and reception area before they reached the studio door.

'Well,' said Charlie, brushing rice from his shoulders 'that went smoothly.'

'Not too bad. I must admit I know little of the Catholic faith, but somehow ... well let's say it was hardly the solemn occasion I was expecting,' said Una cheerfully, 'and where in heaven's name did McBride get that priest from? He sounded half drunk.'

'Do you think so? I thought he was pretty good ... all things considered,' said Charlie avoiding eye contact.

The photographer rushed up and opened the door with a large important looking key.

'Come in. Come on in,' he ordered, as he switched on the studio lights.

'Have a look at the backdrops while I get set up.'

He started to fuss about with tripods and a couple of cameras that he pulled from the large and long metallic suitcase that he had dragged in. He was a tall, young looking man with longish floppy hair and an intense demeanour. The tripods were handled carefully and the cameras with the delicacy of important scientific instruments

In the meantime, Charlie and Una pulled the backdrops back and forward on a system of pulleys and rollers.

'What do you think?' said Una standing back.

'Well, this one is the Scottish glens ...'

'Yes, the large grunting stag in the background rather gives it away.'

Charlie pulled another one along.

'Cyprus trees? Mmm ... Italian countryside?'

Undeterred he tried another.

'Eastern Europe? Dracula's castle?'

The photographer looked up.

'That's us, ready to go.'

'We can't decide on a background.'

The photographer looked exasperated as he walked towards the painted hardboard scenes. He rattled around for a few seconds before rolling one of the scenes to the front. 'The Lakes of

Killarney,' he announced.

He jabbed at the scene as if he were stating the obvious.

'Look at it,' he continued with an edge in his voice. 'Irish.'

Charlie looked at the backdrop.

'Just a minute. That's just a scene of a waterfall, it could be anywhere.'

'Have you been to Killarney?'

'No, but I've been to Kerry and there are certainly no waterfalls that size ...'

'Oh, never mind, Charlie. Who cares?' said Una, 'Do you think anyone will notice?'

The photographer arranged the couple before the backdrop and hauled over a Grecian column topped by an urn full of artificial flowers which he placed between the couple. He ordered them about like a Hollywood stage director. 'Hold up the bouquet higher ... Turn to the left ... Move closer ... Place one hand on the pedestal. That's it ... now ... smile.'

The flair of the new-fangled electric flash system took them by surprise. Charlie thought his eyes had been incinerated and staggered back; Una screamed.

'Sorry folks, a little adjustment required,' the photographer shouted as he fiddled with some unseen control knob. 'Let's try that again ... smile.'

The next flash was a bit more subdued. Now satisfied with the technicalities he proceeded to shuffle the couple around. Charlie to the left, Una to the right; the urn to the left then the urn to the right. He took four more takes in rapid succession.

'Right, that's us.'

'You seem in a hurry,' said Una

'Yes. Another wedding. Up in the Ambassador. Saturday's a busy day for me,' he replied in a rapid staccato fashion.

He left a couple of business cards on the Grecian column.

'I can get some proofs down later on this evening. Call into my office tomorrow with the ones you want printed. Five bucks for ten copies. Lock up behind you. Give the key to back to McBride.'

He gathered up his gear and promptly disappeared.

By the time they found their way to the grandly named 'Banqueting Hall' the drink was in full flow. They had barely manoeuvred themselves into seats at the top table before McBride started rattling a glass for order.

'Silence for the best man.'

Joe Di Dio, like many of his class, was unaccustomed to public speaking and he did what most do in the circumstances, turned white and rushed through the toasts in a high-pitched panic stricken voice. After a few minutes and after two toasts of McBride's 'Champagne' he calmed down and soon became emboldened enough to end with a lewd joke in Italian which had those who spoke Italian in stitches. Charlie was next up and started with the usual, 'On behalf of my wife and myself ...' to great applause and raucous catcalling from his New York buddies.

He struggled on over a din of guffawing and laughter as those Italians who had a good grasp of English colloquialisms started to translate Joe's risqué joke. He wisely realised that his audience was getting excited and not of a mood to listen to any form of long speechifying; he finished quickly with a heartfelt thanks to 'Father Seamus O'Gready' who had somehow wangled a place at the top table, closest to the bar. He gratefully handed over to McBride.

McBride, a veteran of these events, demanded silence for a few minutes as he explained a few house rules which seemed to be fairly minimal. He finished with a snap of his fingers which ushered in an army of servers with large tureens of soup and boards of bread rolls.

The wedding feast had begun.

*

The wedding meal was an incongruous mixture of consommé soup followed by a small pasta dish and a huge plate of roast beef with potatoes and veg. The Italians complained that the pasta was overcooked while the Irish moaned that the spuds were undercooked; both sides agreed that the peas were like 'bullets'. Wine was poured freely and the meal finished with cake and coffee. But before anyone could start on the coffee George Peebles rattled his glass for silence. As he did, waiters positioned themselves at each table with ten glasses and a bottle of Denham's 'Golden Glen' whisky.

He raised his hand.

'Ladies and gentlemen, I would like you all to have a glass of whisky on me. And I'm going to propose a toast.'

At this signal each of the waiters uncorked a bottle and poured out an even measure into each glass and passed them around the table; a flask of chilled water was also made available.

George gave them a minute to organise themselves before standing up.

'A toast, ladies and gentlemen, to those fine purveyors of Scottish whisky ... the Denholm family.'

No one had ever heard of them but they all cheered and raised their glasses anyway.

'... and of course to the Bride and Groom,' he added almost as an afterthought.

Another loud cheer.

As the crowd made their way to the bars and the Havana Ballroom, Charlie had a quick word with Una.

'How are you bearing up?'

'It's been wonderful so far, Charlie. I must admit I haven't had a drink yet. I might just keep it that way.'

'Me too, I think we'll cut out early. Say about nine o'clock? What do you say?'

She grasped his arm and lay her head on his shoulder.

'I'll say its fine by me,' she said softly.

She was about to say something else when Rosanna charged up.

'Come on you two, you've got to be first on the floor for the wedding waltz.'

Victor Viscount and his Esquires made a decent fist of the waltz music although it had a rather fast beat and was more of a country and western polka than Viennese Waltz. The crowd enthusiastically bounded onto the floor before Una and Charlie had even finished birling round the circumference of the 'World Famous' Havana dance floor. Charlie was whisked away by one the bridesmaids while Una had to make do with a flushed looking Joe Di Dio's ungainly attempt at dancing a polka.

After doing the rounds of dance partners, Charlie and Una retired to a table specially reserved for them where they greeted many of the guests they hadn't managed to talk to during the course of the day. Many of them handed over gifts, most of which consisted of envelopes containing money which Una discreetly placed in a handbag sitting at her feet. It was more of an American custom than European, and an unusual experience for both of them. It felt as if they were holding court at a mediaeval banquet. Most of the Americans knew the drill and didn't linger too long, while the Italians made a great fuss and the Irish became maudlin and emotional. A teary Manny O'Donnell told Charlie that he would be ever grateful for getting the wedding photo intact to his dear old mother who had recently written to him wishing him all the best and asking if he would ever be home with his beautiful wife. Charlie was surprised that Manny had received a letter from his mother as he was sure he told him that hardly anyone could read or write in his family. He didn't pursue the point.

The dancing was at full pelt when Charlie and Una made their exit. It wasn't particularly difficult; McBride organised a taxi for them and spirited them out a side door and, as it happened, the secrecy was unnecessary as most of the guests were far too busy enjoying the band and the atmosphere to notice – either that or they were too drunk to care.

*

Charlie was awoken by a loud rattle at the door and a shout,

'Breakfast.'

He threw on a robe and staggered to the door,

'Morning, sir! Room service breakfast as ordered,' announced the porter rolling in a large trolley. 'Leave it by the table shall I, sir?'

'That's fine.'

He left the trolley and hovered by the door.

Charlie picked up some dimes and quarters from the dressing table and handed them over.

The porter grinned and gave a salute before disappearing.

'What time is it?' came a groan from the bed.

'Not that early, just gone nine. I didn't know you'd ordered room service breakfast?'

'Seemed a good idea at the time.'

'Are you getting up?'

'Not yet. Give me a while to gather myself together. Start breakfast without me if you like; I'm not sure if I could face too much.'

Charlie rubbed his hands; he enjoyed hotel breakfasts. He brought over a glass of orange juice for Una and then started on the kippers.

Neither of them had a hangover or anything like it. Una was simply dog-tired after all the work and preparation she'd put into the wedding day. She got up just after Charlie had poured his second coffee to take out to the balcony.

'You should come out and see the view, Una.'

She strolled out carrying her orange juice.

'Well, I wasn't expecting this.'

The tops of palm trees formed a lower edge of a panoramic view of the Atlantic before them: the sun was just above the horizon to their left. It wasn't quite a clear day but they could see the horizon in the distance. It was a spectacular view.

Una pulled the robe around her.

'A bit cold though. Still Spring I suppose.'

Charlie put his coffee on the table and sat down. Una left her juice on the balustrade and leaned over to look down at the lawn in front of the hotel.

'I can see the boardwalk from here.'

'Not that many places in Atlantic City that you *can't* see the boardwalk from.'

'What's your plans today?' he added.

'First off, I'm getting these envelopes out of the road. I might as well take them out here. Be a dear and pour me a coffee.'

Una came back with her purse and began to pull out some of the envelopes which she started to sort out.

'The girls said the best thing to do is to put them into two piles. One pile that doesn't have names and another with those that have names.'

'For any particular reason?'

'Well, the envelopes with no names usually come from people who don't have a lot of money. They are the ones with a couple of dollars, five or, at most, ten dollars. They don't put names on the envelope as they don't want to embarrass themselves by seeming tight-fisted so we remove the money and discard the empty envelope. On the other hand, those envelopes with names, are those who say 'Look at me'. We have to keep those envelopes and write the amount on the front. Then we send them a letter of thanks.'

Charlie looked a bit uncomfortable.

'Seems a bit ... mercenary, don't you think?'

She looked at him quizzically.

'All very practical if you ask me,' she replied already tearing open the named envelopes.

'Here,' she added, handing over a pile.

She shoved over a waste paper bin with her foot.

'You can start with the unnamed ones if your conscience is bothering you. Put the empty envelopes in the bin.'

Una set about her task with enthusiasm, stopping only to make the occasional and intriguing clucking and tutting noises. Charlie was more sullen, feeling that the whole exercise was a tad unsavoury for his liking.

She looked up.

'For goodness sake, Charlie. Stop acting as if we were rifling the pockets of the dead.'

'Nearly finished,' he replied with a hint of distaste.

Una turned back to her task, shaking her head and muttering under her breath.

She was down to the last three.

'Look,' she cried, 'a hundred bucks!'

'Well that's very generous, I wonder ...' he paused.

Una clutched the bill and envelope to her bosom triumphantly.

'Well then, Mr High and Mighty, you were just about to say 'I wonder who would give us a hundred dollars as a wedding present' weren't you? Well ... I'm not telling you.'

'Well, as I said, very generous.'

'Sandy Davidson, if you must know!' she cried.

'Lucky if we've got a hundred dollars over here,' he said, pointing to the pile beside him.

'Not that I've been counting or anything,' he hastily added.

*

'We'll take this money downstairs and put it in the hotel safe,' said Charlie, 'I've arranged to meet Mrs G. at twelve o'clock. She's going to give me a run down on the travel arrangements to Niagara Falls.'

'Fine, I'm going to meet the girls. Some of them are keen to go for a swim this afternoon before heading back to Philly later this evening.'

'A swim? Rather you than me. Have you ever tried swimming in the Atlantic?'

'No. Why, what's wrong with it?'

Charlie gave an involuntary cold shiver.

'Nothing. You'll love it.'

Chapter 24

Niagara Falls

Despite its popularity Niagara Falls had always been an awkward place to get to. Trains were slow and often held up as they struggled 400 miles upstate through the Hudson valley to Albany and from there on to Niagara. Or perhaps, thought Charlie, as he put down the luggage in the frontier style 'log' cabin that Mrs G. had booked for the newly married couple, its very isolation was part of the popularity among honeymooners. Mrs G. had also booked them on the Penn Station overnight sleeper which they both had loved. The Pullman carriage had proved to be a magic combination of romance and great fun. The cabin they now found themselves in was part of a small complex of similar looking accommodation in what the enterprising entrepreneur had called a 'Mo-tel'. The place was pleasant enough and not far from the falls and other tourist attractions. The first few days were spent in long walks, the usual boat trip to the Horseshoe Falls on the little steamer 'The Maid of the Mist', a name which, Charlie mentioned to Una, could be used as a convincing label on one of Denholm's whisky brands. They argued over which picture house they would visit; Una fancied the 'Armendola' which was showing *20,000 Years in Sing Sing* with Bette Davis and Spencer Tracy, whereas Charlie thought the title was ridiculous and suggested, without any apparent sense of irony, *The Penguin Pool Murder* showing in 'The Falls' cinema. They spent pleasant nights beside an authentic log fire drinking mulled wine. All very New England and all very cosy, even, as Charlie cynically thought, a trifle forced at times. Nevertheless, Charlie and Una enjoyed each other's company and were content to let the world drift by.

The cablegram that arrived on the Thursday of their first week did not alarm Charlie. He assumed it was a matter of business from Carlstrom or something from his lawyer concerning the apartment or The Country Club.

They were lounging around on the porch after breakfast as

usual. Charlie was reading the Niagara Falls NY Gazette on a rocking chair while Una half slumbered on an old-fashioned swing seat when a Western Union telegram boy arrived at the cabin. Charlie was about to go inside to look around for a paper cutter when the cable boy produced a little pen knife.

'This do, sir?'

'Well done, young man!' Charlie said as he sat down again, quite relaxed. 'Hang around I might need a reply form.'

The envelope was swiftly sliced open and the cable pulled out.

After a few moments his hand drifted toward his brow as he continued to read.

He looked up at Una.

'Are you okay?' she said anxiously, 'you look a bit worried.'

Charlie put the cable down on the table between them.

Una picked it up immediately and quickly read the message.

Something has turned up STOP you must phone George at this number as soon as possible, Mrs G.

'I wonder what's happened. It can't be that bad surely.'

'I don't know about that. If it was from George himself, I wouldn't be too concerned. George tends to make a mountain out of a molehill sometimes.'

He paused.

'... but Mrs G. on the other hand.'

He let it hang in the air for a second,

'I need to get to a phone.'

'I've not seen a pay phone around here, but there must be a telephone in the manager's office in the town.'

'The buses are every half hour into town,' he looked at his watch, 'Damn! Just missed one, we'll have to walk.'

'There's a phone in our office,' said the boy from the porch.

He gave the boy a quarter.

'Is it a public phone?'

'Sure, there's a public phone in the foyer. Follow me, it's just ten minutes along the highway.'

Charlie grabbed his jacket and hat.

'I'm coming with you,' said Una pulling on her coat.

*

The public phone was thankfully in a fairly large booth where both could squeeze in. Charlie managed to get a couple of dollars in nickels and dimes from the cable boy's stash of tips. Although he never mentioned it to Una, one of the prime reasons for Charlie's concern was the fact that he didn't recognise the phone number.

He was even more alarmed when the number was quickly answered by Manny O'Donnell.

'Hold on, Charlie, I'll get George.'

He could hear a commotion in the background. He had hardly time to speculate when an almost incoherent George was shouting down the phone about 'Sewer rats, scum, five thousand dollars, little Florence, Vinnie McGhee' ... followed by a catalogue of swearing and curses.

Charlie was startled by George's anger.

'Hold on, George, put Manny back on the phone.'

'What!' shouted George.

'Put Manny on again.'

There was a slight pause as the phone changed hands.

'Okay, Manny, what the hell's going on down there?' said Charlie, raising his voice.

'You're not going to believe this, Charlie,' said Manny, taking a deep breath, 'McGhee has kidnapped George's daughter in

Philadelphia and is looking for a five thousand dollars ransom.'

Charlie didn't answer directly. His first reaction was one of horror, followed by an immediate and instinctive assumption that Manny somehow had a role in all of this.

He cleared his throat.

'Let me get this straight, Manny,' he said keeping his voice calm, as he turned to face Una, 'are you telling me that Vinnie McGhee has organised the kidnapping of Florence Peebles, George's daughter, and is demanding a five thousand dollar ransom?'

Una immediately covered her mouth to muffle a scream; a look of utter fear crossed her face as she realised what was going on.

'That's right.'

There was an awkward silence as Charlie rolled over the facts in his head trying to figure out what to do next.

'I take it that McGhee has been in touch with George.'

He looked at Una before he spoke.

'Or,' he added evenly, 'was it just you?'

'He phoned George in the office just an hour or two ago and gave him the low down. Vinnie then phoned me, told me what had happened and asked me to be the go-between. I'm as shocked as anyone, Charlie, I didn't think even McGhee would pull a stunt like this.'

Charlie quickly placed his hand across the mouthpiece and closed his eyes.

He had almost blurted out something in anger. There was no doubt in his mind that Manny might be involved and was now trying to play the part of the honest broker.

He opened his eyes and gave his head a slight shake in disbelief before he spoke.

'Right, first of all, what are McGhee's instruction?'

'He wants George to get five thousand in cash, nothing larger than twenty dollar bills, and wait in his office until he phones. I think he's on his way up to New York. The girl is still somewhere in Philadelphia as far as I know.'

There was a brief silence while Charlie thought out his next move.

'Do me a favour, Manny. I needed to talk to George alone. The way he's feeling, he's likely to do something really stupid. I need to calm him down and reassure him for everyone's sake. Put George back on and leave the room for a couple of minutes. Tell George you need to go to the John.'

He heard a rustle as the phone has being handed over and there was some background noise.

'McGhee ... that dirty snake ...'

'Hold on, George, be quiet a minute and listen carefully.'

He could hear George taking a deep breath in an effort to contain himself.

'I'm okay.'

'Has Manny gone?'

'Yes, he said he needed the John.'

'So you're alone.'

'There's no one in this room except me.'

'I'm going to say this quickly. I'm going to leave for New York as soon as I can and I don't want you to do anything till I get there. There's a problem though. It could take as much as eight hours, even longer, to get down. It will be easy to stall McGhee for a day. Tell him that you agree to pay but it might take a bit of time to organise the money, especially if he wants the dough to be untraceable. He'll fall for that.'

There was a short silence.

'Don't mention any of this to Manny. Do you understand all of that?'

He almost sensed George looking around furtively.

'What's wrong with Manny knowing?'

'Nothing. Let's just keep calm. I don't want you or Manny to try and second guess things. Tell Manny I'm on my way down and should be there late afternoon or sometime this evening at worst. Go back to the office and stay there. I'll give you a call when I get to Albany. With a bit of luck,' he looked at his watch, 'that should be in around two or three hours from now, around one o'clock I guess.'

'OK Charlie, I've got that.'

'Try to keep McGhee cooperative. Don't get in touch with him directly in case you blow your top again, use Manny. I've always thought that McGhee was half cracked so don't make him suspicious. He's liable to do something crazy if he thinks there's a double cross.'

George seemed to calm down a bit.

'I'll need to get going, George, remember to stay in the office until I phone.'

'OK, Charlie, I'll see you later.'

Charlie put down the phone, leaned back against the phone booth and tilted back his hat.

His brow had a glow of sweat.

'Do you know what? In the back of my mind I thought there was something cooking in Manny's mind this past few weeks.'

'Let's get out of this box before I faint.' said Una pushing the door open.

The anxious looking manager came across to see them.

'Everything okay, Madam? Not bad news I hope.'

'Fine. I just felt a bit claustrophobic in the phone box.'

He wasn't quite sure what claustrophobic meant but carried on.

'If there's anything we can do ...'

'I'm okay now.'

They walked towards the door.

'Just thought of something,' said Charlie. 'We need to get a cab into town. Do you know any numbers?'

'I'll get one for you.'

As he scurried off into his office Charlie pulled Una over towards him.

'Don't say any more until we get on the road,' he said quietly.

*

'Hell,' said Una, her voice beginning to tremble, 'I thought these things only happened in the movies.'

They were walking along the road at a quick pace.

'Bootlegging is becoming less profitable, not only that, it's finished or near as dammit. People like Manny and McGhee are just trying out new markets, new ways of making easy money. They knew George had money. He couldn't help bumming about his clever deal with Davidson.'

'But you said it was all above aboard?'

'It was.'

He slowed down a bit to catch his breath.

'That's if you can consider any business transaction legal these days,' he added. 'Trouble is that McGhee and his like think that anything to do with booze must be illegal. To them George is a just another hood on the make. Someone who would be unlikely to call in police in a kidnapping.'

'What are you going to do?'

'I don't know. My first instinct is to let George pay the money and be damned. I know I need to get to New York before George has any thoughts of trying to outwit McGhee.'

Una stopped walking.

'Are you thinking of going alone? What about me?'

'From a practical point of view there a few things we'll need to clear up before we leave. I just can't imagine getting down there today if we've got to organise our luggage to Albany then transfer it all to the New York train. Plus another thing, we'll need to pay the bill for the Motel.'

They continued to walk; they were a few minutes from the cabin.

'We'll get the taxi down to the station together and organise train times and suchlike. I think we should try to get you on the 10 o'clock New York sleeper tonight.'

'That's OK by me,' said Una, 'by the time I pay the bill, get packed and organise moving the luggage I should have plenty of time to get the train. By the way, I thought you were being a bit optimistic about getting down there for this afternoon.'

'It'll be a matter of timing,' he said as he opened the cabin door, 'and luck.'

Una dashed in.

'You gather up some money and pack an overnight case. We'll need to get a move on,' shouted Una rushing into the lounge, 'the taxi will be here any minute.'

They got lucky. There was a train for Albany in twenty minutes with a connection to New York's Penn station. They booked a ticket for Charlie and managed to book Una on the sleeper in less than ten minutes. Charlie hurried along to the kiosk to pick up a newspaper for the journey.

Una took a minute to collect her thoughts. The detail of organising the trip had kept her mind busy. She was used to dealing with emergencies and disasters. She was always pragmatic and unemotional in a crisis and she coped by being organised and methodical, but she suddenly realised that she had never experienced anything like this. The whirlwind and the enormity of the last hour was beginning to get to her.

They walked over the connecting bridge and stood on the platform for the Albany connection. Niagara being a terminus station, the train was already sitting ready for its return journey. In front they could hear the engine puffing and wheezing as it made up steam; the platform was hectic and noisy as people wandered around to the continual background racket and bedlam of carriage doors opening and closing. They stood quietly making last minute arrangements until the guard gave the warning whistle and shouted the usual cry of 'All board'.

'Looks like you managed to get the local bone rattler this time,' said Una looking along the bustling platform with a wan smile.

'It'll do.'

They hugged for a moment.

'You be careful down there,' Una said.

'Hey, don't worry,' he said as he swung on to the carriage, 'I survived the Great War and a Civil War. I know how to keep out of the firing line.'

The train gave a lurch and moved slowly along the platform. As Una walked alongside, the engine blew the steam whistle, and Charlie raised his voice.

'Phone me at the office when you arrive in the morning. I'll be in there early.'

'Sure thing.'

She blew him at kiss as the train picked up speed.

'Good luck,' she shouted anxiously.

She stopped walking, gave a final wave and slowly turned away.

Survived the Great War? And a Civil War?

A sob rose in her throat; she quickly choked it back, lifted her head stoically and walked out of the station without looking back.

Chapter 25

The travel trunk

As he walked through the door Liam noticed that a long florescent strip light came on automatically; a second later, and further into the room, another twinkled, blinked and lit up, followed by a third.

'Woo Hoo. Very '70s sci-fi. Was Eddie thinking of recreating a nuclear bunker up here?'

'Some student of his decided to wire them up to look like that. They come on and off when they sense movement or some such nonsense.'

'Not as dusty as I expected,' said Liam, looking at the floor space, 'in fact, remarkably clean and tidy for an attic, I'd say.'

Grace walked into the middle of the attic space, her short heels making an eerie clicking echo. She glanced around with a frown.

'I haven't been up here for ages. Sometimes Eddie takes a mad notion and goes into a frenzy of cleaning and tidying up.'

She took a few steps forward.

'He seems to have surpassed himself this time.'

The centre space was cleared and most of the stored stuff was piled against the eaves. Liam found that the roof trusses were high enough to walk under without crouching and the whole area was covered with smooth chipboard flooring. At the far end was another white painted door.

'What's that door for?'

'That's another entry to the attic from the other side of the house and there's another staircase that leads down to the first floor. It's just a mirror image of the way we came up.'

Liam glanced around again.

'Quite a bit of space you've got up here. I've been in discos that are smaller than this.'

'Did you mention the '70s? And now Discos? Giving your age away there, Liam. I think young people just call them clubs these days.'

Grace walked over to the other end of the room and started rummaging around the right-hand side.

Liam moved towards the eaves on his immediate left-hand side.

'Amazing the stuff that people keep in attics,' he muttered, looking at half a dozen dusty boxes of old clothes. An old artificial Christmas tree stood in one corner surrounded by bags of decorations and lights. A couple of children's bikes were stacked up underneath the roof window. There was a massive red mahogany chest of drawers which looked Mid-Victorian to Liam.

'I wonder how the hell they managed to get that up here.'

'What?' shouted Grace from the other end.

'Nothing, just idle speculation.'

He sauntered over to the other side of the room, rummaged around then knelt down, pulled back a couple of tall boxes and peered into the gloomy recess below the eaves.

He heard a muffled voice.

'I need a hand.'

'Just a minute, I haven't come across the creepy rocking horse or the spooky tailor's dummy yet.'

'Never mind all that, come over here and help me with this.'

He crawled out backwards then walked over to the other end, near the door.

'Eddie must have shoved this trunk to the back to get it out of the way. Pull those boxes out of the road and we'll drag it out.'

Liam pulled one of the boxes out to the middle of the floor; it was surprisingly light.

'Take that other one away and we'll have a clear space.'

After he pulled it over curiosity got the better of him, he lifted one of the cover flaps and took out a cellophane covered box.

'Aeroplane model kits?'

'Ah,' said Grace without looking up, 'those must be Eddie's. He gets kits for birthday gifts and Christmas presents every year. It's being going on so long now that no one can be bothered thinking of anything else to get him. I often wondered where he kept them all.'

'Now, move that box out of the way and grab this handle.'

'What is this anyway?' Liam asked slapping the top of the large leather box.

'It's an old luggage trunk that Charlie had when he came back from America. His wife Una used it to store blankets when they lived in the flat.'

'Why has it got CEM on the side?'

'That's his initials – Charles Eugene McKenna.'

'Never thought of Charlie having a middle name. What's this? This label says "Not Wanted on Board."'

'On Trans-Atlantic liners some trunks like this were kept in the cargo hold and you couldn't open them until you got to the other side.'

'This one says ...'

'Look!' barked Grace standing up and placing her hands on her hips, 'are we going to pull this thing out or are we going to spend the rest of the evening just reading and discussing the labels?'

'Okay. Okay. Keep your hair on!' he ranted to himself.

The trunk was heavy but it slid along the floor once they got it moving. They pushed it out until it was directly below one of the lights.

'Wouldn't want to be carting that about on a holiday.'

'Different times. They had porters with trolleys and barrows back in those days. Anyway, they were usually only used for long journeys.'

Grace tried to lift up the lid.

'I think it's jammed.'

'Let's take a corner each and try it.'

With both lifting, the lid came up quite easily. They lifted the lid just over the back edge until the two stays on the side snapped into position.

Liam looked at the contents. It seemed to be full of old clothes.

'The top section is really just a shallow drawer or tray that we can lift off in a minute.'

Grace lifted up the first garment.

'This is Una's wedding dress on the top and there are one or two mementos that Charlie kept.'

She removed a red scarf from the dress.

'Shawls, scarfs and things. There's more stuff below the lid.'

Grace lifted up the gown,

'I've had this dress out a few times over the years. It's expensive material, feels like good quality silk.'

She pressed it against her body and looked down. The bottom hem was six inches off the floor.

'Una was not as tall as me as you can see, on Una the dress would have skimmed the floor.'

Liam dragged over a couple of old fashioned kitchen chairs from the corner.

Grace sat beside the open tray and pulled out a wedding album.

'You won't see many of these around, they were quite expensive in the '30s.'

She reflected for a moment.

'You know between one thing and another I've always thought that it was obvious Charlie and Una must have had a bit of money.'

'Probably something to do with the stash of gold coins he hijacked.'

'No need for sarcasm if you don't mind,' she snapped, 'I meant even before Charlie went back to Cork.'

She lifted up a larger framed photograph.

'This is their wedding photo. I remember seeing it the first time I came to this house. It had pride of place in the living room.'

'When was that?'

'Must have been in the late '60s or early '70s I think. Una was still alive.'

Liam took a seat and rubbed his beard.

'That gives me a bit of a shock.'

Grace looked at him curiously.

'Why should that give you a surprise?'

'I don't know.'

He thought for minute.

'It's funny how you begin to imagine people. I've been reading through that little journal of his where he talks of New York in the '20s and '30s, of speakeasies, of bootlegging, of journeys on Atlantic liners. It just seems like a different world altogether. It became almost fictional to me. You've just reminded me that they were real people.'

'I suppose you're right, I never thought about it that way. They were just Eddie's mum and dad to me. Una would have been in her sixties by that time, not that old really I suppose, but you know what it's like when you're young - everyone over the age of thirty is old.'

'You're right there,' he replied.

Grace held up the picture in front of her.

It was the bride and groom standing formally in front of some sort of country backdrop. The bride was pretty and carried a large and elaborate bouquet of flowers; on her right was a column on which stood a vase with more flowers. It was obviously professionally shot and crystal clear even after all this time. Liam recognised Charlie from an old army photo ... and the bride was wearing the dress that lay before them at that very moment.

'Here, that looks very good, very professional.'

'That's what I mean about them having money. They look kind of ... well ... classy, you know, wealthy in a sort of confident way.'

He was about to say that he supposed that knocking off the equivalent of several million would give you a degree of confidence, but he thought better of it.

Instead, he looked at the photo more closely, nodding his head wisely.

'Yes, I see what you mean.'

She tapped the backdrop.

'They went to Niagara Falls for their honeymoon and that looks like a waterfall back there.'

'Well,' replied Liam carefully, 'it's certainly a waterfall *scene*. I like the bouquet of flowers, and the, em ... the Greek column.'

Grace put it down by the side of the chest.

The album was quite thin with only a dozen or so photos.

'Some of these are not so good. I think they must have been taken by the guests.'

'You're probably right,' said Liam as he flicked through the pages, 'they're a bit fuzzy and they look as if they have been enlarged. Do you know anyone?'

Grace turned back a page. It was a group of people, half a dozen men and woman seated around a table; it was probably the clearest of the collection.

'The only one I remember Charlie talking about was this one here,' she said pointing out a moustachioed man lifting a glass.

'He said that his name was George.'

'George Peebles?'

'Could be, I don't think he mentioned his surname, but I got the impression it was someone he knew well.'

He looked at the photo closely. The man was older than Charlie, well built, almost portly. He had a pleasant, engaging smile.

Liam immediately knew who it was.

Well, well, he thought, the mysterious George Peebles makes an appearance at last.

*

'Right. Now we need to lift the box tray section off.'

Each end of the box had a short rope handle. They grabbed one each and lifted the tray clear and wide of the trunk and placed it on the floor. The trunk was about five-foot-long by two-foot-wide. Once on the floor, Liam stood on one side then reached down and, taking both handles, lifted up the tray by himself. It was fairly easy.

'What are you up to?'

'Just wondered how they managed these things. I can see now that one person could lift out the shelf by themselves.'

Grace gave him a withering look and sat down.

'Now that you've proved that you can, you can lift out that other box by yourself.'

Liam peered in. A polished wooden box about eighteen inches by two foot sat on the left of the trunk. It had a cast iron handle that sat in an insert making it flush with the top.

He prised the handle up and lifted out the box; it was almost as heavy as the shelf.

'Leave that to one side and we'll open it in a minute.'

Liam placed it on the floor near the shelf. Grace pulled a cardboard file and placed it on her lap and opened it up

'This has a lot of business papers in it which I don't think you'd find that interesting. But there's one or two things I found a few years ago that showed that Charlie had planned to leave the US around May or June of '33.'

'Like what?'

'Well there's a letter from one of his brothers in London dated March 1933 which talks of the rents in London. Obviously we don't have the letter Charlie sent but it's clear that they had considered London as another place to move to at one stage.'

'That's interesting. I assumed he intended to come here almost as a matter of course.'

'Might be something or nothing. Who knows?

'Anything else?'

'Well, as I told you, he prepaid the rent on a large house in the south side of Glasgow. The rent for this apartment, as the lawyer's letter kept calling it, was paid three months in advance - plus a hefty deposit. This was dated in May, so they must have decided by then.'

'Nothing really unusual in that is there?'

Grace tapped the file.

'There's something that doesn't quite add up.'

Liam pulled the other seat nearer the trunk and sat down.

'Carry on,' he said suddenly looking interested.

'Let's put the lid back down for a minute.'

They pushed the stays back, held the lid and let it fall gently until it closed with a satisfying clink.

Grace pulled a few papers and what looked like receipts from an envelope that was sitting among the papers and placed them on the trunk top.

'I put these aside a couple of years ago when I was arranging the trunk for storage. Charlie was surprisingly organized at times and these seemed out of sync somehow. It was only when you started ferreting around trying to research that business in Cork that I realised that it might make more sense now.'

She placed one of the letters and what looked like a receipt on the trunk.

'That is the Agreement for Rental,' she said, pointing to the letter.

Liam picked it up.

'If you look at the date you'll see the date of entry is June 26 1933. Two tourist class tickets on the SS California from New York on June 22 arriving in Greenock on June 29'

He then looked at the receipt for the tickets.

'Seems they timed it quite well, the place would be ready to move into by June 29.'

'But those tickets weren't used…'

She pulled out a set of tickets and put them in Liam's hand.

'… these were.'

*

The tickets were for Cabin class on the SS Britannic sailing on Friday June 2 for Liverpool via Belfast and Greenock. Arriving in Greenock on June 7.

Liam looked a bit bewildered.

'I'm not sure I get the significance ...'

'Don't you see? They originally booked tickets for the 22nd. You'll notice that it's just a receipt, they must have sent off the originals to get a refund. It means they left New York nearly a full three weeks before they intended. And look at this,' she said, lifting up the Britannic tickets, 'They went Cabin class, or first class if you like, look at the price ... $300!'

'Yes, I can see that.'

'That's nearly £5000 in today's money!'

'I didn't realize First Class Trans-Atlantic fares were that expensive.'

'Look at the receipt for the California, $135 tourist class ... less than half the price.'

Grace pulled out another two receipts for the St Enoch Hotel from June 7 until June 27 and put them on the table.

'Two hotel bills. One for 2 weeks at £33 and one for £15; that's about £2,000 in today's money.'

'I wonder why they did all that ... unless they had money to burn.'

'Charlie and Una weren't skinflints by any means but I can't see them squandering that kind of money just because they wanted to rush to Glasgow on some crazy whim.'

'So you think ... What?'

'I think something happened that made them leave New York in a hurry.'

Liam leaned back in the chair.

'I think you're right. I also think I know why and ...'

He nodded over to the polished box.

'I suspect I know what's in there too.'

*

They cleared away the paperwork and Liam lifted the wooden box on to the trunk lid. It was a nice piece of work. Some three inches deep with some intricate ivory inlays along the sides. It looked as if it had been French polished at one time but the patina was becoming dulled with age. There were two straightforward slide-clips at the front which pushed apart with ease, Liam lifted the top cover carefully and let it fall back until the thin metal chains at the side restrained the lid from falling over.

Inside was what appeared to be a piece of sackcloth or what the Americans refer to as burlap. Liam lifted the parcel out gingerly and placed it on the trunk lid and began to unwrap the cloth.

He looked at Grace.

'Well now. I suspected it might be something like this,' he said as he lifted the gun with both hands. Three or four bullets nestled in a fold in the cloth.

'Be careful!'

He took the gun in his right hand and flicked on the safety catch.

'It's a Webley revolver, it fires six ·45 calibre bullets. They started manufacturing this type, the Mark VI, around 1915 or thereabouts. Used as a service revolver by the British Army until the late '50s.

'It's a very powerful handgun. They called it a break top revolver,' he added as he snapped open the gun revealing the revolving chamber.

'No bullets loaded in there.'

He closed the chamber and flicked off the safety with one movement, and to Grace's utter surprise and horror pointed the gun at the floor and pulled the trigger.

She jumped up off the seat.

'For God sake! Are you out of your mind?'

Liam calmly broke open the gun, opened the chamber again and looked down the barrel.

'Just checking to see if there was a bullet stuck in the barrel.'

He snapped the gun closed, flicked on the safety, clicked the chamber back, gave it a spin and then placed the Webley back on the lid in one fluid motion.

Grace sat down slowly.

'You ... You looked as if you knew what you were doing there.'

Liam gave her a quick look and turned away.

'It's a long story.'

He put his hand near the gun, picked up one of the bullets and looked at it closely, turning it around in his fingers.

'Live ammunition, probably in a dangerous condition by this time.'

He put the bullet back with the others.

'Before we go any further I need to tell you that you can't keep this in the house. You have young grandchildren running around at times. I just wanted to show you how easy it is to fire a gun. It wouldn't take long for an adventurous soul to realise how easy it would be to place a bullet in the chamber with God knows what consequences.'

Grace looked flustered and mortified.

'To tell you the truth, I had almost forgotten all about it until you started taking an interest in Charlie.'

He leaned forward on the chair.

'I'll tell you what, Grace.'

He stood up and started pacing around.

'I tell you what I *think* I know. Maybe you can help me fill in some of the missing pieces.'

'Okay, I'll try, but I'm beginning to get the feeling you know more than me.'

'Right; the background. From what we both know, it appears Una and Charlie had decided, for whatever reason, to return to Europe. From the diary it appears Charlie was sent to Glasgow on some sort of business trip by George Peebles or one of the other business partners, possibly someone called Sandy Davidson, who seemed to have some sort of link with a distilling company called Denholm's. The idea was to buy up surplus whisky in the expectation of the end of prohibition. Not a bad idea under the circumstances and, may I point out, quite a legal and legitimate business deal. I don't know about the London thing, there is nothing in the diary one way or the other but, and I'm guessing here, I think Charlie made up his mind to come back to Glasgow during this trip.

'Why?' he asked rhetorically, opening his hands out. 'We don't know ...'

He stopped and picked up the framed wedding photograph.

'They got married in Atlantic City in May 1933. And it looks like the wedding was not a spur of the moment decision, it seemed to have been planned well in advance. Charlie had already sent the money for the flat in Glasgow and tickets for the journey had been paid for.'

He paused for a moment

'I didn't know anything about Niagara Falls but he mentions a trip to New York from Albany around this time so that might tie in.'

'Nothing in the diary about Niagara Falls? Is that not a bit odd?'

'Not really. I keep referring to it as a diary but it's not really a diary as such. As I've pointed out several times, its part diary and part notes, some of it is almost idle reflections at times. To be honest the scenario we're trying to unravel in New York only fills one or two small pages at the end of the book.'

He pulled out the book and flicked to the end.

'The last page is interesting. There are no entries after this page.'

*

'It's getting late,' said Grace, 'maybe we should get all this stuff back and head downstairs.'

'Good idea. Take the gun out and take it downstairs. You'll need to hand it into a police station or better still get in touch with them to uplift it.'

They put the wooden box back and left the gun and the sack to one side. After replacing the top compartment, they pushed and shoved the trunk back to its original position and repositioned the cardboard boxes. Grace picked up the sackcloth bag and walked over to the white door.

'We'll go this way, it's just as quick, plus it'll save us having to explain the gun to Eddie. I'm not sure I'm up to it at the moment.'

Liam looked around for the switch.

'The lights go off themselves when they don't detect any movement.'

The staircase was getting dark as the light was beginning to fade.

'I see the window on this side is not as fancy. Odd that I never noticed that before.'

'Never mind all that. Let's get down the stairs while we can still see.'

They opened the bottom door and Liam found himself at the far end of a familiar long corridor that led to the double staircase that, in turn, led down to the ground floor.

'You go on down to the lounge,' she said, holding up the sacking, 'I'll leave this in a locked cupboard in my bedroom.'

Liam was standing by the fireplace when Grace appeared in the lounge a few minutes later. She walked over to the bar in the corner.

'Time for a drink? I've got some of that awful brown stout you seem to be addicted to in the fridge.'

'Why not?' he replied, ambling over to the small bar.

She slid over the can of stout and, as usual, placed a cut glass beer tumbler on a mat. She poured herself a large gin, added a measure of Noilley Prat vermouth, clattered in some ice and then walked out from behind the bar and sat in one of the bar stools.

'Well then, Liam,' she said, taking a large draft of her drink, 'let's hear your theory about the gun.'

Chapter 26

Back to the City

Charlie was getting worried. Una's description of the train as the local bone shaker was proving to be right as it lumbered and trundled through the Mohawk Valley. It was plain that the shanty towns in the area had been highly industrialised over the years with a criss-cross network of junctions and crossings. Each siding they passed appeared to have at least one rusting hulk of a goods wagon stranded in the middle of the track. The sky was dark and dismal; an overhanging sheet of gun-metal grey. For miles it seemed like every possible type of commercial enterprise from logging mills to strip foundries had crawled up to the side of the railway line to die.

It was dreary and depressing.

He gave up reading and became restless. The thought that the connecting train would be delayed until they arrived in Albany gave him some comfort, but it would give him less time to get in touch with the office. A call would reassure George if nothing else.

Just as the thought had crossed his mind, they picked up speed just outside the town of Attica and started to rattle through the countryside at a fair clip.

There was twenty minutes to spare as he crossed over to the bank of public phones at Albany Union station. After the usual clicking and crackling he was finally connected to the office.

As he squeezed in a quarter he heard the anxious voice of Mrs G. behind the calm voice of the operator.

'... *that's for five minutes and then ten cents for each two minutes after that. No change will be given.*'

Mrs G now came through clearly.

'Charlie, where are you now?'

'It's okay, Mrs G. I'm in Albany, the worse part of the journey is over. I'm just about to get the train to Penn station ... should be in the office before five. Can I talk to George for a minute? It might be an idea to stay on the line.'

'Sure thing.'

He heard her plugging in the extension for the back office.

'There's a few things I want you to do this afternoon,' he said quickly before George had time to start a rant.

'I know you have several bank accounts and I want you to go to three or four banks and lift a total of five thousand dollars in twenties and fifties.'

'But I could lift it all from First American.'

'Better to spread it about, that way nobody gets suspicious, take Mrs G. with you.'

'Okay, I suppose you're right.'

'When you get back to the office divide the money into five bundles of one thousand of roughly equal amounts of twenties and fifties.'

'Why all the fuss about the money?' Mrs G. chipped in.

'No fuss. Believe me, it'll make things easier for us in the long run.'

No doubt it would, but Charlie was also keen to give them something to do in the afternoon instead of moping around. He discovered in the army that when things got tense, the men's anxieties greatly increased when left to their own devices. On the other hand, giving them even the most routine of tasks seemed to calm them down.

'Got all that?'

'I'll get ready and we'll head down to Herald Square. There's a couple of banks there that we have accounts in,' replied Mrs G., quickly answering for both of them.

'Take your time. Not all banks have mounds of cash lying around, if you can't get the money today don't worry, give an order for it tomorrow.'

'I never thought of that,' said George.

'Right, I've got to go. See you around five.'

He hung up the earpiece with a sense of relief. Mrs G. sounded, if not calm, at least composed and, so far, George hadn't become totally unhinged. He walked over to the railway office and upgraded his ticket to first class for less than a dollar; he had decided to try and relax for the shorter part of the journey. The newspaper kiosk was nearby, close to the entrance to the station, a couple of papers would pass the time. He selected *The Times* and the *New Yorker* magazine and walked down to his train platform just as the station Tannoy announced its departure in five minutes.

*

After a mediocre lunch in the dining car he retired to the first class carriage and took a window chair. The carriage was almost empty with only a half a dozen business types dotted around. He flicked through *The Times* but found it harder and harder to concentrate, in the back of his mind he kept on trying to work out O'Donnell's role in all this. By chance the paper was opened at the foreign news section with a dense piece on something called the Four Nation Pact that was headed up by a picture of Benito Mussolini; something about Mussolini triggered a memory. Charlie leaned back against the comfortable armchair, put down the paper and gave up all pretence of reading. His mind drifted back to the last time he saw O'Donnell – it was the night of the wedding.

After he and Una had met most of the guests Una thought it best to take her purse up to the room for safekeeping as the evening visitors were now arriving and the dance floor was getting busy. It was getting murky outside and some small floodlights in the garden came on as the waiters and the staff were pulling the heavy velvet curtains across the windows.

'You start circulating; I'll be back down in a minute.'.

The nearest table was occupied by his sister and her husband

Joe Di Dio.

Joe's extended family were in high spirits and roared out as Charlie approached:

'Congratulazioni agli sposi!'

'Congratulazioni per il tuo matrimonio!'

Charlie had very little Italian but got the gist of it. Almost all of Joe's relatives were Italian born and now, half-drunk, found it difficult to speak English. After a few minutes they ignored Charlie and started talking among themselves. Charlie chatted to Rose for a while until he finally noticed that Una had returned and was sitting beside George Peebles. He gave Rose a quick kiss on the cheek and made to rise. As he did so one of Joe's brother in laws stood up and solemnly said:

'Un brindisi al nostro patria! ... e el duce Mussolini!'

Charlie wasn't sure, but assumed it was a toast to the homeland and to Mussolini. To his surprise and disquiet the whole table rose, raised their glasses and shouted.

'El Duce! Mussolini! Evviva!'

He sat up in the armchair.

That was the connection. In the hubbub of the evening it passed unnoticed and by the time he reached the other table he had almost forgotten the incident.

George was in full flow. He had been down to Baltimore to see the warehouse where the liquor was now stored by a New York distribution company that bought the entire stock. He was pally with one of the directors who gave him a case of Gold Glen as a gift; a gift he was now sharing with his fellow guests. O'Donnell was on the periphery somewhere with his wife, Brede or Bridget as she was known as in America. George congratulated Charlie with an iron handshake and a slap on the back that nearly knocked him flying - sometimes George didn't know his own strength.

'Good man. I hope you'll be as happy as me and 'Lizbeth'

Elizabeth was too busy chattering to Una to notice. He remembered her daughter, Florence, was standing or sitting beside her.

What was she again? A flower girl or something?

She was half listening to the women but seemed preoccupied and quietly fascinated by Una's dress and wedding ring. It suddenly occurred to him that O'Donnell must have known that Florence was George's daughter. He also vaguely recalled moving away from the table as one of the Kellys insisted on talking a photograph with one of those new-fangled cameras with a built-in flash. Maybe he was jumping to conclusions, but it all seemed too much of a coincidence, but then again perhaps McGhee had strong-armed Manny into the caper. He kept turning it over in his mind until he was startled by the conductor's announcement that the next stop was Penn station.

*

Mrs G. greeted Charlie with great relief.

'George is in the main office,' she told him as he hung up his jacket and hat.

'How is he?'

'He's not too bad under the circumstances.'

She suddenly bit the knuckle of her right hand.

'I can't believe this has happened. That rat McGhee was swanning about here is if he was George's best pal! Then he pulls a stunt like this. The man must have a heart as black as hell.'

'Did you get the money?'

'Yes, didn't have much of a problem - excepting a few curious looks from one or two of the tellers. I've got it sorted out and it's in the safe.'

'Good. I'll go in and see how George is. Bring in the money when you get a minute.'

As Mrs G. had mentioned, George appeared, on the surface at

least, to be surprisingly calm. He was flicking through some bank statements as Charlie came in. He leapt up, came round the desk and threw his arm around Charlie's shoulder.

'By God, Charlie, you're a sight for sore eyes!'

'Have you been in touch with Elizabeth yet?'

He said nothing, went behind the desk and held his head in his hands. Mrs G. came in and placed a fat envelope on the table: she looked at George with concern and said, 'Elizabeth phoned the office just after ten; as you can imagine she was almost hysterical.'

'Okay,' said Charlie, 'That's understandable. How did McGhee get in touch? Did she say?'

'He sent her a note,' replied George, his voice rising, 'he grabbed little Florence as she was going to school.'

Mrs G. glanced at Charlie and took over.

'I took some notes,' she said, 'I'll go and get them. There's some coffee on the boil, Charlie. Might be a good idea if you brought the pot in here. I'll phone O'Donnell's number and tell him to get over here pronto.'

Mrs G. sat with a notepad on her lap.

'This ain't exactly what she said but nearest I could get. Around nine thirty a man came to the door and handed her a note and told her to read it right away, and read it carefully before she did anything or said anything. He turned and walked away quickly. Elizabeth had hardly time to figure out what he looked like.'

She looked at her notes:

'We have your daughter captive and she is safe for the time being. We want five thousand dollars for her release, the money is to be used notes in twenties and fifties and delivered to us in New York at a time of our choosing possibly tomorrow night. Do not get in touch with cops or you will never see your daughter again.'

'I got her to read it out twice so I could get it right.'

'That's the exact wording? Any mistakes?'

'If you mean spelling, there were one or two but nothing

significant. Is that important?'

'O'Donnell can't write, that I'm sure of, and I'd be surprised if McGhee can.'

'Probably one of the rats that McGhee has around him can write. Do you think we should get in touch with the police?'

'Are you kidding? The last thing we need is a bunch of bulls wandering around.'

'No cops,' said George suddenly, 'and I'm not interested in who's who. I just want Florence back. He wants five grand, he's going to get it, and there's nothing you or I can do about it.'

'I agree, George. Let's take one thing at a time. In a way things aren't looking too bad. You've got the money ready. All we need to do is sit tight and stay calm. McGhee won't harm your girl if we go along with his instructions; let's face it, he's only interested in the money. By tomorrow night this will be just a bad memory.'

The bell rattled in the outer office.

'That'll be O'Donnell, I'll let him in.'

Charlie knew right away that O'Donnell was well out of his depth as soon as he stuck his head in the door.

'Come on in, Manny,' shouted George.

O'Donnell looked sick.

'You okay? You look a bit peaky,' said Charlie.

'All this carry-on is getting to me. My ulster is playing up.'

'Ulster?'

'He means ulcer,' said Charlie.

O'Donnell rubbed his stomach, oblivious to the jibe.

'Right, Manny, has McGhee been in touch?'

'Got in touch an hour ago. Wants to meet us in The Country Club tomorrow night at nine o'clock. Have the money ready he says and he'll deliver the girl to George's house as soon as you hand it over. Make sure you have a long distance connection to

Philly for that time and George's wife can confirm that the girl is safe. He wants to be in and out in ten minutes. No cops and no funny business he said.'

'Well, that's pretty clear and straightforward,' said Charlie glancing, from George to Mrs G.

Charlie looked around at everyone again, stopped and looked at O'Donnell.

He opened his hands.

'One would be almost tempted to think he'd pulled off something like this before.'

The dry irony rolled over O'Donnell's head.

He was tempted to quiz Manny on his role in all of this but decided to let it go. The instructions were simple and pretty direct; he could think about Manny later.

Charlie asked Mrs G. to write everything down and type it up for him.

'Let's not make any mistakes here. Manny, I take it that Vinnie wants you at The Country Club tomorrow night as well.'

He squirmed on his seat, still rubbing his stomach.

'I'd rather not be but Vinnie is insisting. Look Charlie ... George ... I had nothing ...'

'Save it, Manny,' rapped Charlie, 'we've enough to be thinking about for the time being.'

'I've ... I've to phone Vinnie tomorrow morning about the transfer of the money and the girl.'

'You make sure you do that,' replied Charlie curtly.

He stood up.

'I need to get over to The County Club and make sure the Sharkeys have the bar closed and cleared for eight thirty tomorrow night. I'll get young Frankie to hang about in case anyone tries to come in by mistake while McGhee's there.'

'I've booked a couple of rooms in the Lincoln. One for you and

Una and one for George.'

'Good thinking, Mrs G. Una's travelling tonight but she'll be here at the crack of dawn tomorrow. Would you mind sending her a cable? Just tell her to make her way to the Lincoln, I'll leave a message in the foyer for her.'

He looked at his watch.

'It's getting late. Let's break it up now.'

He went to the outer office for his jacket and hat.

'We'll meet here tomorrow at lunch time, say one o'clock, just to run over things.'

He looked over at a pale-faced Manny.

'That includes you.'

*

'But Thursday's a good night for us, Charlie,' said Harry Sharkey.

He stopped wiping the bar and he stood with his hands on his large hips.

'How good?'

'A lot of the 'Times' guys come in after ten. The early Friday morning edition is always their best seller, not only that but the inkies get their weekly pay cheque late on a Thursday night.'

'You can open up after ten. Tell them the first drink is on the house. I'll square you up later on. Just let them know in time. I want the bar totally empty for eight thirty at the very latest.'

'What about the Sweeneys in the restaurant next door?'

'They're okay, it suits them. Thursday is a quiet night for them. They normally close around eight anyway.'

Harry Sharkey was a smart guy; he knew something peculiar was going on. He spoke out quickly as Charlie started to walk towards the curtain that led to the bar entrance.

'Charlie, is there something I and the boys can help you with?'

Charlie turned round and looked at him straight.

'Thanks, Harry, nothing to worry about, it's just a meeting I've arranged - nothing I can't handle. Thanks anyway ...'

He was about turn again when he suddenly snapped his fingers.

'Come to think of it, there is just one thing I need, now that you reminded me. I need someone here to look after the door just in case someone wants to come in. How about young Frankie?'

'Sure, I'll let him know.'

Harry thought for a moment and rubbed his broken, misshapen nose, the result of many years of New York bar-brawls.

'Look, Frankie is only seventeen and as thin as a rake. If there's any chance this turns into a rough-house ... maybe you'd be better off with me.'

Charlie gave a broad smile.

'Rough house? Come on, Harry, it's just a business meeting. Frankie will be fine, I give you my word. Remember, eight thirty sharp.'

He pointed with his finger to emphasise the point.

'Bar empty. No bar staff. No one except Frankie. You can get back in again at, say, five to ten - but phone first just in case.'

*

The afternoon meeting in the office the following day was quick and to the point. Una asked to come along and Charlie agreed. George had brought in an extra couple of chairs but Charlie stood over at the window with McGhee's message in his hand.

'Tonight, myself and George will meet up in The Country Club at eight. I want to make sure the bar is clear. I'm going to get a message typed up and pinned on the door saying the bar is closed for a private function. Young Frankie will hang around the main door just in case but he won't be at the meeting and the only people he'll let in is McGhee and Manny.'

He turned to Manny.

'What was Vinnie's phone call about?'

Manny still looked pale and nervous.

'Two of his men in Philly will be out in the street opposite George's house, one in the driving seat and one in the back with the girl. When Elizabeth comes to the porch front carrying a white handkerchief, the girl will be released. When the girl gets to her mother, Vinnie's men will leave right away. If Elizabeth doesn't appear by ten past nine they will leave with the girl and ...'

Manny paused and looked away.

'... he says they won't be back.'

'I think Vinnie watches too many movies,' said Charlie quickly.

He had noticed the intake of breath and tried to defuse the growing tension.

'The white handkerchief is a bit melodramatic, if you ask me. The handover is straightforward enough. I was half expecting the usual drop off points and money checking but it seems McGhee is confident enough to keep it simple. However, the thing is to get the business over and done with quickly. I'll contact Elizabeth shortly and go over the instruction carefully with her.

'Right, that's it. Let's not speculate on things that may or may not go wrong.'

He folded up the piece of paper as he moved away from the window.

'Everybody go home. Mrs G., take the rest of the day off. Leave the keys with me; I've got a couple of phone calls to make. I'll lock up and leave the keys in the doorman's office.'

'Phone calls?' said George 'What phone calls?'

'To my lawyer, I've still a few loose ends to tie up with

Carlstrom and also the lease on the apartment. I need half an hour to chew things over. No big deal.'

George grunted as he walked to the door.

Una was the last to leave.

'I'll see you back at the Lincoln for lunch.'

'Sure, meet you in the dining room, at,' he looked at his watch, 'let's say two o'clock.'

'Fine, I'll go and get ready.'

Charlie closed the door quietly behind her and sat down at the switch-board.

He picked up the phone and dialled 0 to connect.

'Good afternoon. Operator here.'

'Could I have a long distance?'

'Which town, sir?'

Charlie paused.

'Atlantic City, please.'

Chapter 27

Over one bridge

As promised the bar was totally clear well before 8:30. George turned up a bit earlier than Charlie instructed but kept well out of the road as bar staff tidied up and prepared the place for a later opening. The floor was brushed, furniture was tidied up and fresh ashtrays and water jugs were placed in the centre of the tables. Frankie had already pinned a typed message on the front door:

Closed Until Ten pm for Private Function

Harry Sharkey lingered before he left. He turned his bulky body towards the bar.

'Are you sure?'

'Come on Harry, get moving! It's nearly twenty to nine,' said Charlie.

When he left Charlie switched off all the main lights leaving only the front door illuminated. He placed a lamp on one of the tables in the bar and one at back of the restaurant.

Frankie was stationed at the door where he found he was starting to get a bit on edge; he couldn't put his finger on it but he sensed a tension in the atmosphere. Even the pool of light given from the table lamps seemed to give the place an air of menace. The top half of the front door was half-glazed with a painted sign of a country cottage. Despite that he could see out to the pavement quite clearly. Very few gave the place a second glance and no one even paused to look at the posted note. Frankie could hear some chairs getting moved around in the bar and George and Charlie talking quietly. After a few minutes he took a few steps up the corridor to have a look at the large clock on the wall; ten to nine. The sound of a car pulling up outside brought him back to the door sharply. A saloon with white walled tyres was sitting directly outside the door - an old '28 or '29 Packard, Frankie guessed. The man who came out of the front passenger seat wore a dark grey Fedora and Frankie knew him well - Manus O'Donnell. The one who come out of the back he only knew as Vinnie. He was bareheaded and wore a cheap pin-striped double breasted suit.

Frankie opened the door as they approached.

'Evening, gents.'

Except for a grunt from Manny, both seemed too preoccupied to acknowledge Frankie's greeting. He closed the door quietly behind them and drew his hand across his brow. To his surprise he found he was sweating.

Charlie stood up when they pulled the curtain open and walked into the bar. Vinnie narrowed his eyes and glanced about the room suspiciously, he looked even more rat-like than usual.

'Evening, Charlie ... George,' said Manny nodding to each of them in turn. He had regained a bit of composure but still looked bad.

McGhee said nothing and sat in a seat opposite Charlie.

'George,' said Charlie in a calm voice, 'get a connection to your house; I'll speak to Elizabeth in a moment.'

George looked pale but controlled, he left his seat and went behind the bar. In the darkened silence they could hear him talking quietly to the operator.

'Got the money?'

'Sure Vinnie, we've got the money,' said Charlie pointing to a large envelope on the table next to him.

'Take a seat, Manny, you're making me nervous,' he added.

Manny took a seat near the door.

Charlie lifted the packet and handed it to Vinnie.

'Want to count it?'

He stared at Charlie as he pulled out one of the doubled-over wads. He looked down briefly and rifled through it, put it back and pulled out another wad and did the same. He threw the envelope back on the table.

'Looks okay. I don't think you'd want to double cross me, would you, Charlie?' he said with a supercilious grin.

'Who would?' replied Charlie blandly as he stood up and walked to the bar. 'Fine, now you've got your the money, we can let your people know they should release the girl when the mother appears in the window as arranged.'

Moments later, George gave Charlie a nod.

'Can I make our phone call now? After all, you're the one that wants things done fast.'

McGhee lifted the envelope and casually shoved it into the inside pocket of his suit jacket.

'Sure, why not?' he said with a smirk.

Charlie walked around to the bar phone and picked up the earpiece.

'Elizabeth, Charlie here, the deal is done. Walk out the door as I told you and come straight back in with Florence. Pick up the phone as soon as you're back in,' he stopped for moment before adding, 'we'll be waiting.'

Charlie covered the mouthpiece and glanced over at McGhee who picked at his teeth and feigned indifference now that he had the money. Charlie stared straight ahead and drummed his fingers quietly on the bar. Along with some other instructions he had given to Elizabeth that afternoon, he told her it was essential to stay calm when on the phone; no chatter, no questions, no tears, no hysterics, everyone would be in danger at this point. There was an uneasy silence for a long three minutes. All of them became aware of the faint ticking of the clock in the hallway.

He uncovered the mouthpiece.

'Elizabeth, is Florence okay? Is everything else in order?'

She gave a simple answer ... '*Yes* ...' as instructed.

Charlie calmly put the earpiece back in the cradle, the soft click breaking the connection.

He then stepped from the bar.

'That's it, Vinnie. You can go now.'

'What? Don't you offer your guests a drink? We've finished our business and it ain't even nine o'clock yet.'

Charlie was taken aback; it was the last thing he was expecting.

'What'll it be?' he said going behind the bar again, 'whisky?'

'Sure thing, Charlie. By the way,' he added, with an oily sneer, 'I hear you and George do a good line of Scotch in here.'

Something played in the back of Charlie's mind; McGhee was becoming a bit sassy, a bit too smart-mouthed.

He poured out a generous measure of Golden Glen, walked back from the bar, handed it to Vinnie and took his seat. He didn't even bother asking Manny.

He looked at Vinnie closely, trying to work out what made him so menacing. McGhee wasn't particularly tall or well built; he had a decent middleweight boxing physique at best. He had a close cropped haircut like a college football player; a crewcut they called it. His dark eyes were sunk beneath two heavy eyebrows and his mouth was small and mean. There were several knife scars on his face but none that were too disfiguring. But it wasn't just the way he looked that made him feared, but his volatility and unpredictable moods. He was capable of taking even a minor bar fight to extremes regardless of the opponent or, in many cases, opponents. He fought without fear, like a man possessed and he lacked any conscience. He had mutilated, killed and murdered several men in his short life without as much as a second thought. McGhee revelled in his reputation. He wasn't that smart but, other than a tendency to be reckless, he had a great deal of lowlife cunning.

He took a swig of the whisky.

'I take it the girl is fine.'

'Everything went according to plan, Vinnie. Just like

clockwork.'

'I'm glad of that.'

Vinnie pursed his lips and then lifted the glass up to the light as if he was a connoisseur.

Charlie stole a glance at George; he looked tense, staring at Vinnie, his face a mixture of relief and anger.

'I had to leave her with that retard Salvatore Milazzo.'

Vinnie looked over at Manny with a twisted leer.

'You know what Sal's like. He likes them young ...'

He threw back his head and finished the whisky.

'... the younger the better,' he said with a lecherous snigger.

Charlie saw only a blur of light as the ashtray caught Vinnie under his nose, springing his head back violently. George leapt to his feet pulling the ashtray in an arc over his shoulder and just as Vinnie slumped to the side he brought it down a with a sickening crack on the side of his head just above his ear. The power of the blow knocked McGhee sideways and he slid off the chair and on to the floor. The ashtray had slipped from George's grasp and bounced against the wall.

Charlie had started to rise from his chair as young Frankie whipped open the curtain.

'What the hell!'

George's face was now contorted with anger and he was looking around for another weapon. Frankie rushed in before he managed to lift a chair.

'For Jesus sake! Are you crazy?'

Charlie had felt the blood literally drain from his face as he stood up. He quickly and instinctively grasped the corner of the table, his vision was going blurred. Something was happening to Charlie that he had never experienced before.

He was on the verge of fainting.

'Are you okay, Charlie?'

Frankie's shout brought him round to his senses. He shook his head trying to clear it. His mouth was so dry his tongue wouldn't move. He lifted up his right hand; it was trembling.

George suddenly went quiet and subdued. It was as if the exertions of last five seconds had drained him of life.

Frankie grabbed a glass from the bar and filled it from the water jug on the table.

'Here, drink this.'

Charlie snatched it with both hands and downed it in two gulps then he looked over at Manny. He looked as if he had been turned into an alabaster statue.

'Give one of these to Manny,' he said, handing back the glass.

He could almost hear the blood beginning to pump round his body and his head was starting to clear. Vinnie was still lying on the floor, his right leg started to shake; he was beginning to convulse.

McGhee's right hand and arm were lying outstretched and away from his body. Charlie bent down and grasped his wrist searching for a pulse.

In less than a minute he stood up.

'He's still alive,' he said.

Frankie looked relieved.

'Thank God for that. He's alive, that's good!'

Charlie looked down at McGhee and then back to Frankie, his face grim.

'Is it?' he said.

*

'Frankie, take these two next door.'

Charlie looked back down at Vinnie, then walked to the bar and grabbed the bottle of whisky and a couple of glasses in one hand. When he pulled back the entrance curtain he found Frankie standing in the corridor looking over the half partition, unsure of what do next. Manny and George were sitting at the small table near the back where the small lamp seemed only to illuminate them from the chest down

'Give them a small glass of whisky with some water,' he said quietly to Frankie, 'When you've done that go back and watch the front door, I'll be out to see you in a few minutes.'

He returned to the bar and quickly knelt down over the body, turning the head to the side to look at the wound around the ear. It appeared like the corner of the ashtray had caught Vinnie in one of the most fragile parts of the skull, possibly cracking through the skull into the brain membrane. He had seen severe wounds during the war and this one appeared to be as bad as he had seen, almost like a shrapnel wound.

He leaned back on his heels.

The wound and its depth might explain the convulsions and, if he was convulsing - then he was in bad shape, perhaps even dying. He felt the pulse again, definitely weaker but still there. If they could get him to a hospital...

He stood up and thought back to the war. He had seen soldiers with similar wounds die instantly; some survived with treatment, but then again ...

Vinnie's leg started to shake violently and Charlie made up his mind.

He walked round behind the bar and opened a small drawer under the till. It was full of all sorts of bits and pieces and he rummaged around until he found a key with a red disc. The safe was about four-foot-high but small enough to fit under the stairs leading to his office and the other rooms above. He heard the mechanism click into place as he turned the key to his left. Four concentric dials surrounded the lock, the outer one he quickly spun to the position 1 in line with the key, the next to 9, then back to 1 and lastly to 6; the door sprung open about an inch. The door was damned heavy. Charlie pulled; it needed both hands to open it fully. The top two shelves were stuffed with business papers, ledgers and invoices. Below them was a lacquered wooden box that he had picked up in Paris for less than a hundred francs, beside the box was a large canvas money bag where he kept a couple of hundred dollars in one dollar and five dollar bills for various pay-offs.

He placed the box on the bar counter and flicked opened the locks on the side and removed the burlap package inside.

The Webley still looked good considering it was over two years since he last took it out and cleaned it. It was a gun he had never liked and had never used for anything other than the occasional target practice; he had found it heavy and awkward compared to the Colt he had left in Ireland over ten years ago. He flicked it open and picked up two bullets from those spread out on the burlap. The first he placed in the top firing chamber, the second ... he dithered ... did the barrel spin clockwise or anti-clockwise after firing? He picked up another bullet, pushed one on each side of the firing chamber just to be sure, snapped it closed and clicked off the safety catch. The handle of the gun fitted neatly into his right palm; he curled his index finger carefully around the trigger. There was a small bundle of drying cloths beside the sink; he picked up a couple and started to wrap the first one around the gun with his left hand. As he walked around from the bar he wrapped the other one tightly around both the gun cylinder and over his right hand.

Until now routine had kept his mind from wandering but now thoughts were beginning to gather around like black crows. He became suddenly aware that he couldn't put a face to anyone that he knew he had killed. In the Great War he must have killed dozens of men, scores maybe, with a few sweeps of a Maxim machine-gun he commandeered in the battle of Torres; he was part of a battalion that placed tons of Amatol under Hawthorn Ridge which must have killed hundreds, possibly even thousands of Germans; he blew up a train bridge in West Tipperary that killed the driver and a passenger.

By now he had finished constructing the crude sound suppressor around his gun hand and was approaching the body of Vinnie - whose leg was still twitching - still alive. With an effort of will he forced all thoughts from his mind, leaned over the body and fired a shot from about four feet. There was a muffled bang and Charlie felt the thud of the bullet through his feet as it crashed into the wooden floor below Vinnie's head.

There was little point in checking the pulse this time, there was not a creature on the planet that would survive a point blank head shot from a ·45 handgun. He quickly unwrapped the cloths and placed them on the table. He folded one of the cloths over two or three times forming a pad that he placed under the shattered skull; the other he laid over Vinnie's head and face before lifting up the Webley.

Frankie was coming down the corridor as Charlie pulled over the curtain. Charlie walked straight through to the dining room where George and Manny were sitting at the nearest table; he held the gun loosely at his hip.

'What was that noise?' asked Frankie anxiously.

His eyes were drawn to the gun.

'Vinnie's dead,' he said in a flat voice.

Manny started to rise from his seat.

'Charlie, I had ...'

'Sit down, Manny. You're making me nervous again.'

George looked alarmed.

'For God sake, he couldn't have been that badly injured.'

Charlie placed the gun on the nearest table and turned to face all three.

He placed his knuckles on the table and leaned forward.

'I'm going to tell you a story about Vinnie.'

'When he was nineteen, Vinnie lost ten dollars in a poker game with Tony Borello, one of Dutch Schultz's bootleggers up in Harlem. Vinnie wasn't a good poker player and didn't play often. He later found out that he had been cheated and Borello was putting it around that Vinnie was a soft touch. When Vinnie heard, he was as mad as hell and the next day he walked into Borellos's speak-easy. The place was busy and Borello was sitting at a table with his back to Vinnie chewing the fat with a few of his cronies.

Vinnie stood behind him, pulled his head back and slit his throat from ear to ear, threw down the knife on the table and pulled out a gun and watched till the bootlegger choked to death in his own blood. Not one of the gang moved a muscle when Vinnie left the joint.'

Charlie stood up straight.

'All for a lousy ten dollars.'

Except for the ticking of the bar clock there was silence.

'Vinnie McGhee is what is known as a psychopath, he has no fear nor does he have a conscience. He has no regard or concern for the consequences of his actions ... in other words, and in plain language he is crazy and should be locked up in a nut house. If he had survived that blow to the head, he would have come after every one of us. We would be looking over our shoulders for the rest of our lives.'

*

Manny O'Donnell sat silently, almost scared to catch anyone's eye. He saw Charlie enter with the gun and he seemed to be almightily relieved not to have been shot out of hand. When Charlie started talking and not shooting, Manny's face gained a bit of colour. That's if you could consider going from chalk white to light putty grey to be a colour change.

'Manny, you and Frankie go out to the car and send the driver home. Tell him that you and McGhee have decided to stay for a drink,' he pulled out a five-dollar bill, 'and tell him to have drink on me.'

'Sure, okay.' said Manny in a dry, hoarse voice.

They both started to walk towards the door.

'When you come back, stay in here with George for ten minutes. Frankie, when you come back, go into the bar.'

Both nodded and said nothing.

Charlie heard the front door opening and closing as he got to work back in the bar. From the same drawer under the till he pulled out a ball of twine and a small penknife and placed them on the bar counter. From the safe he pulled out the canvas money bag. He opened the door to the right of the bar which led to a small six-foot by four-foot room, used both as cloakroom for the staff and an area for general cleaning equipment and material. He took off his jacket and replaced it with one of the bar tender's aprons, lifted out a bucket and mop and left them on the floor beside the still body of Vinnie McGhee just as Frankie pulled the curtain back and walked in.

Frankie stared at the body as he walked in.

'I need a hand, Frankie, but only if you feel like it.'

Frankie lifted his eyes and looked straight at Charlie.

'I'm okay. What do you want me to do?'

Charlie emptied the money-bag and left the cash lying on the bar. There were two 100 dollar stacks of five dollar bills, one thin envelope of a 100 dollars in twenties and a smaller wad of mixed bills held with an elastic band. He threw over the ball of twine and the penknife to Frankie.

'Straighten his legs and tie them together. Join his hands and tie them at the wrist. I'll deal with the rest.'

He walked around the bar and stood beside Vinnie's head. Kneeling down he opened Vinnie's jacket, pulled out the envelope and threw it on the nearest table. He then wrapped another towel round the gunshot wound and took away the pad. It took a minute or two and a bit of effort but he managed to slip the empty money-bag over the head. He pulled the drawstring around the neck.

'What are we going to do now?' said Frankie as he finished tying the wrists together.

'We need to get rid of the body somehow.'

Charlie started to pace up and down.

'I was thinking of putting it in the store room in Sweeney's kitchen until I thought of something.'

Frankie stood up and ran his hand through his hair.

'I know this sounds a bit crazy ...'

Charlie stopped pacing and looked at Frankie closely.

'I'm listening, Frankie'

He continued hesitantly.

'You remember Ned Ferry? I think you met him in here, he sometimes delivers beer for Manny.'

'A young, well-built kind of guy, helped you out one night. Yes, I remember talking to him in here.'

'I know him well; he lives in my neighbourhood over in Brooklyn. He came in here about eight o'clock this evening just as Harry was closing up. He said he had a small truck belonging to some outfit over in New Jersey that he was keeping overnight and asked if he could park it out the back.'

Charlie started to look interested.

'I was just thinking, if we could persuade him to take...' he stopped and looked down at the trussed-up body of Vinnie McGhee, 'to take ...' he thought for a second, 'a delivery across to Brooklyn.'

'Where is he now?' said Charlie sharply.

'He said he'd have a beer up at Smiths and he'd come back here at ten.'

Smiths was a small Irish speakeasy at the end of the block, no more than two or three minutes away.

Charlie leaned over to the bar and took fifty in five dollar bills from one of the packs.

'This might help you to persuade him. He'll get the same again when he's finished.'

'A hundred bucks!' said Frankie, totally awed at the thought of almost two months' wages.

'You'll get the same.'

Frankie wasted no time and headed towards the fire exit that led to the side alley.

'I'll go this way, it's quicker.'

'Wait! Just a minute. What will you do when you get to Brooklyn?'

'You can dump anything into the East River around the Brooklyn Naval Yard. There are dozens of alleys and backstreets that lead straight to the river.'

'Hold on. We'll lift Vinnie closer to the door then I can finish cleaning up.'

Charlie slipped his hands under Vinnie's shoulders while Frankie lifted his legs. It was a bit of a weight, probably around 150 pounds at most, but manageable over a short distance.

'I'll be back as quick as I can.' said Frankie, as he pushed open the panic bar on the fire exit. He was gone before Charlie could say anything else. He left the door ajar for Frankie's return and then set to it with the bucket and mop. After rinsing and mopping the floor several times and using the sink in the cloakroom to get rid of the gory water, he put the mop and bucket at the end of the bar. He then walked over to the table, lifted the envelope and tucked it into his back pocket as he looked at the bar clock; he could hardly believe it, it had just turned quarter after nine.

*

He had hardly finished putting the equipment away and removing the bar apron when Frankie rushed in through the fire exit.

'Ned Ferry said he'd do it. He's gone round to the parking lot to get the truck. He'll be here in a minute.'

Charlie tidied up the bloodied towels and the bar apron and shoved them into an empty brown paper shopping bag and put it on top of the body.

'Get rid of this as well.'

He could hear the truck pulling up outside and pushed open the other side of the fire door so they could manoeuvre the 'delivery' into the alley.

Ned jumped out of the truck and came round to the door. He looked a bit red in the face and nervous. If anything, thought Charlie, he looked even younger than Frankie.

'Is this it?' he said, nodding at the body.

'Come on, Ned, give's a hand here,' replied Frankie, grabbing the legs.

Ned went to the top of the torso and lifted it up with much more ease than Charlie did.

'Charlie, pull down the back flap.'

Charlie walked past them quickly, held the back flap, pulled out the pins, and let it down carefully.

Ned and Frankie lifted the body up and lay it across the edge of the truck. Ned rolled the back canvas down, slammed up the flap and replaced the pins.

'Right, that's it. Let's get going.' said Ned slapping the truck.

It was clear that the boys' initial, uneasy fear was now beginning to turn to a kind of exhilaration.

'We'll be back as soon as we can, maybe a half-hour,' shouted Frankie as he raced round to the passenger door.

Charlie pulled the fire doors closed leaving the one with the panic bar slightly ajar as before.

Half an hour was leaving it tight.

He walked through the bar and into the dining room. To his surprise George and Manny were chatting almost casually as he walked in. He didn't bother asking them the topic; there was still too much to do.

'George, could you tidy up in here and take everything back to the bar. I'm going to phone Elizabeth again just to make sure everything is okay.'

He turned to O'Donnell.

'Manny, you can get going, but I need a word. I'm going to walk you up to Forty Fourth Street.'

He lifted his hat from the rack.

'... and we're leaving right now.'

He pulled the front door closed and turned the key and popped it into his pocket.

'I don't have a lot of time so don't start any flim flam.'

Manny said nothing as they started to walk up Seventh Avenue.

'Who and just how many were involved with Vinnie down in Philly?'

He dropped his head and answered.

'Just two. A local guy that Vinnie knew from Philly, a small-time punk, Paul Duggan. Vinnie gave him fifty bucks to take Salvatore Milazzo down to Philly on Tuesday and drive him back to New York tonight, drop off Milazzo and then get lost.'

'This Salvatore Milazzo, the name sounds Sicilian.'

'No, he's Italian.'

Charlie glanced at O'Donnell but let it pass.

'I never heard of him, is he connected?'

'He does some work for the Genovese mob. Mean-looking guy and a bit of a creep, but I'm not sure how high he sits, these guys keep everything to themselves.'

Charlie was quiet for the next couple of minutes while he turned this over in his mind. If Milazzo was Sicilian, then it changed things a bit. Sicilians had a habit of holding grudges, some of them carried family feuds for generations. He had to think quickly.

'Okay. Now tell us your role in all of this.'

O'Donnell stopped and turned round.

'Charlie, I had nothing ...'

'I told you, Manny, no flim flam,' he said raising his voice.

He took him by the arm and tugged him forward.

'And keep walking, I don't have the time and, incidentally, neither do you. So start talking.'

Manny talked.

'It started when I came back from your wedding. George kept on bumming about the big deal he had just made. He reckoned he made about fifteen thousand dollars smuggling all that booze in from Scotland.'

'It wasn't smuggled, but never mind.'

'I was just talking about the wedding with Vinnie and he asked me whereabouts in Philadelphia did George live. I told him and he said he knew the area well. Had he any family? he asked. Sure, I said, three girls. Vinnie said nothing at the time but the next day he asked where exactly George stayed, you know, the address and all that. I never thought that much about it but he sends down Sal Milazzo to check it out the next day. Next thing I know he snatched the girl, honest, I knew nothing until he phoned me yesterday.'

There was no point in debating with Manny, he would go round in circles and get nowhere.

Charlie had made up his mind, Milazzo could be a problem,

'I'm leaving New York tonight. You tell Sal a disagreement broke out after the money was passed over and the girl was released. I pulled a gun and a shot was fired. Vinnie managed to get out but might have taken a bullet. He disappeared and left you in a bad spot. You had to smooth things over. George went crazy with me for putting his daughter at risk. You tell him that when I heard Salvatore Milazzo was involved I took fright and decided to leave town.'

'You got all that?'

'Sure, Charlie. A fight broke out; Vinnie might have got hit. You took off when you heard Sal was involved.'

'You talked to George after the dust had settled. George let it slip that I had talked about going out West, to Los Angeles to work for an old friend called Regan.'

'Ok, you decided to high-tail it to LA to work with a guy called Rogan.'

'Not Rogan ... Regan. Terrance Regan. Listen, I know you guys like nicknames. Terrance Regan is usually known as 'Rocky' Regan.'

'Okay, Charlie, I'll remember that, Rocky Regan.'

They came to the corner of Seventh Avenue and Forty-Fourth Street.

'I'll leave you here, Manny.'

O'Donnell thought for a moment before sticking out a hand.

'You're a regular guy, Charlie. I'm sorry about all this.'

Charlie shook his hand.

Manny gave him a brief, haunted look.

'Good luck,' he said and turned left towards the slums of Hell's Kitchen.

Chapter 28

Another day, another bridge

He held the little book and turned to the last entry.

'Read this,'

'I need my glasses.'

Her hands delved into some mysterious part of her jumper and produced a small pair of gold-rimmed reading glasses, held them up to the light, then perched them on the end of her nose.

'Now then. Not a lot here, I see,' she said, holding the book at arm's length and the page with her thumb.

'Meet at nine with Manny McGhee.'

'No, that's with Manny *and* McGhee'

'$5,000?'

She squinted at the page.

'Florence and Milano?'

'Florence and Milazzo.'

'Sorry, looks like Milano.'

'Milazzo is a common Italian name, particularly in Sicily. I looked it up.'

Grace gave him a look over her glasses.

'G. hit McGhee with an a.tray?'

'George hit McGhee with an ashtray. I think.'

'M. badly injured I plugged him.'

Grace looked up.

'Is that it?'

'There was a meeting. It seems someone called Milazzo who,

on McGhee's orders kidnapped Florence, that's George Peeble's oldest daughter - she appears to have been eight or nine years old at the time. McGhee demanded a ransom of $5000 dollars. At the meeting some sort of fracas broke out and George hit McGhee with an ashtray. He was so badly injured that Charlie shot him at close range.'

Grace took off her glasses and put them on the bar. She looked at Liam and then threw her head back and laughed loudly.

She put her hand back in the hidden pocket and pulled out a handkerchief and started wiping her eyes.

'Excuse me, Liam, I can't help it ... all that from a couple of lines in an old diary!'

She laughed again.

'Ashtray? Gun? Did you miss out the Lead Pipe and Colonel Mustard?'

Liam was quiet for a minute and then had a smile.

'Does sound a bit like something from Cluedo, I must admit.'

'But you can't be serious.'

'It all ties in. Think about it. The last page was written in a hurry and he never made another entry even after ... what? Fifty years?'

He stood up, took a drink of the flat stout and scowled.

'I had a look through some online editions of the 1932 and 1933 New York Times. It appears that there was someone called McGhee who was alleged to have kidnapped children of local gangsters and successfully ransomed them ... and Peebles and Charlie had a connection. McGhee came from a township called Gweedore in Donegal. In addition, Peebles had recently made a lot of money importing whisky into the States. To someone like McGhee, drink meant bootlegging, and bootlegging was illegal. Therefore, George was a gangster and thus fair game. I can't be totally sure of course but I get the impression that something hellish happened that night which ended in Charlie killing McGhee. Or as he put it, plugged him.'

'It doesn't say that. Okay, McGhee might have been badly injured; perhaps he was just giving him first aid.'

It was Liam's turn to laugh out loud.

'First Aid? Are you kidding? People who use guns are in the habit of using euphemisms, they knock people off. They throw the lead. They rub people out. And they plug people. Much more pleasant than saying "I blew his brains out at close range with powerful handgun", don't you think?'

'Okay, no need to be so graphic,' snapped Grace getting off the stool.

'You missed out a bit,' continued Liam.

'Where?'

'The date at the top of the page.'

'1st June 1933.'

'That was the night before he and Una sailed for Glasgow. A journey that you said was unexpected and seemed to be unplanned.'

She put the book down.

'You've got the irritating ability to make all your tall tales sound,' she tapped her hand on the book, '*almost* plausible.'

Liam could see that she was starting to look emotional; her eyes were becoming moist. Perhaps, he thought, the idea of Charlie being involved in something as outlandish as this was too much, a bit of a shock even.

He looked at his watch.

'Need to get going in a minute.'

'That's okay.'

She stood up, quickly gathering herself together.

'I'll need to start making dinner shortly. By the way I was wondering if you'd like to come over a week on Saturday, we're having a party for Eddie.'

She picked up her reading glasses and put them away.

'You could bring ... your friend.'

Liam gave her a glance.

'Ah! You mean Helen.'

'Oh, is that her name?' she replied, trying to sound surprised. 'Julie mentioned that she met her in Cork.'

Liam thought about it. It wouldn't be a bad idea; they didn't have that many mutual friends. It might make a nice change.

'I'll ask her. I'm sure she'll be pleased to come.'

'And another thing. This damn gun. I'm going into town to pay that parking fine for Richard.'

'What parking fine?'

'You remember last week – outside Bruno's.'

'Ah yes, of course'

'I can pay the fine in the sheriff court. Do you think I should take the gun down there and hand it in?'

'Sounds ideal to me. Come to think of it, I'm working on Saturday for a while. Maybe I could meet you and help with any explanations and ... em ... that sort of thing.'

'*Explanations*. Not sure I like the sound of that. But never mind. I intend to get down there early. Town is usually mobbed if you leave much later. Nine too early?'

'Fine. I'm going in around seven to supervise some last minute alterations in a new exhibition. I'll take a break about then and meet you at...'

He thought for a second.

'Do you know that café in the old subway building in St Enoch Square?'

'Yes I know it. Meet you at nine or thereabouts. I'll get your coat.'

He shoved the book into his coat pocket as they said their goodbyes.

It was now dark and a light drizzle started as Liam hurried on; what with one thing and another he was beginning to feel a bit melancholy and looking forward to a decent pint of stout in his local bar. He returned by a route that took to him through Queens Drive, and past Queens Park. He reflected on the names around the area: Albert Road, Prince Edward Street, Victoria Road. For a city that called itself home of the Red Clydeside and that prided itself on its radical past, it sure had a love affair with the English Royal family. As he passed by his own apartment block, named Balmoral Terrace after the Royal castle in the Highlands no less, he looked up at the small Liberty statue, standing high on the east corner. Through the gloom he could just make out the torch of freedom and equality in her right hand. She faced the Queens Park.

At least, thought Liam with quiet satisfaction, the builder had a sense of irony.

*

Liam started walking down through an area called Anderston at eight thirty. He managed to get the first bus into town at six twenty and was more or less finished at the exhibition. Helen had turned up and gave him a hand and everything was well under control for the eleven o'clock opening but he said he'd be back before ten, just in case.

It was sunny but cold, as he walked along Argyle Street towards the large railway bridge that leads to the Central Station. Around the station area, like most large railway stations in the world, was a seedy part of town. It had the usual scruffy, dingy bars and hotels where low-end hookers hung around in the early evening. There were loud and rowdy sports bars, fast food outlets and greasy spoon cafés with of course the odd trendy restaurant for the travelling hipster to 'find'. It was the kind of place that upbeat travel writers like to call 'vibrant'.

Even hardened Glaswegians gave the area a wide berth.

However, on Saturdays mornings when most of the large shops didn't open until ten or thereabouts the place was quiet, pleasant almost. He walked under the railway bridge and onwards towards the Square; he was deliberately a bit early. On his right hand side was a building he wanted to look at. It was a Victorian office block which he passed by on many an occasion, but took little notice of. It was, he could see, smaller than the neighbouring buildings, in both height and width, and was built in blonde sandstone.

He stood at the entrance and looked up. It was surprisingly ornate. There was no brass plaque around the door to explain the building's history or its origin. As he walked to the corner to explore further he heard a yell.

Grace walked over briskly. She was wearing a long length, dark blue Crombie style coat with a light blue, silk scarf and leather gloves.

'Sorry to shout. Very unladylike of me,' she said looking embarrassed, 'but you looked a bit preoccupied.'

'Well, you're dressed for the weather, and bit early.'

'The train times on a Saturday morning are a bit wonky.'

They walked over to the old subway station, now a coffee bar.

'Think it's a bit chilly to sit outside?'

'No, I'm fine,' said Grace, 'get me an Americano with some hot milk on the side.'

'Anything else.'

'A Danish would be nice.'

For the next few minutes Liam paced in and out with various cups, milk jugs and pastry plates.

He finally sat down with a croissant which he started to cut open and fill.

'See that building over there,' he pointed over with a knife slabbered in jam and butter.

'The one you were standing beside?'

'Yes. That building used to belong to Denholm Distillers, that's the company that Charlie dealt with when he came here in early

1933. He probably had meetings in there.'

Grace removed her gloves and looked over with disinterest.

'It changed hands a long time ago as you can see.'

He turned around to look behind him.

'Charlie stayed in the hotel that was here at the time, the St. Enoch Station Hotel. Gone now, I'm afraid.'

'I remember that place! Very fancy I recall.'

'I didn't come to Glasgow until the '90s, so it's a bit before my time. There's a bit where he mentions going across a bridge to see some sort of bottling plant. I've not managed to track down a photo of the place yet.'

Grace had started on the Danish.

'Did Charlie ever mention what he did when he came here? You know, did he get a job?'

'Una told me that he owned a bar across the river, somewhere in Bedford Street I think it was. He gave up after a few months. I remember him saying it would have been easier to run a bordello in Dodge City. He then worked in construction and after a while got a manager's job with the local council; apparently some female cousin of his became a City Councillor.'

Grace was picking crumbs off the plate and started to get ready to move. She gave a slight shiver.

'You're right. It is a bit cold. I think we should get going.'

Liam finished his coffee and rose from his seat.

'Are you going to leave that?' she asked, pointing to a piece of croissant.

'Well ...'

'Sin to waste it.'

She lifted it up and popped it in her mouth, dabbing at her chin with a handkerchief to clear off the flakes while they walked through the square. As they walked down to Clyde Street, Grace started to pull on her gloves and chat about the weather.

'The bridge looks nice at this time of the morning,' said Liam as they approached the stone towers.

'Yes, I suppose it does,' she replied, still distracted

Below them the river was dark, almost black. Except for the sound of a bus purring along the road bridge far to their right hand side it was almost eerily quiet. There was no one about, not a soul. The bridge swayed imperceptibly as they approached the middle.

Grace stopped and looked over the side. It was where the hand rail joined the suspension cables and together they made a wider ledge at this point. She took her large Hermes bag from her shoulder and placed it on the hand ledge. A small flock of Blackhead gulls, about a dozen strong, bobbed half asleep in the water. On the south side of the river two swans floated elegantly near the bank.

Suddenly Grace unclasped the Hermes and pulled out the burlap bag, lifted it over her shoulder and heaved it like an Olympic shot putter over the hand rail.

'What the ...'

Liam stood with his jaw almost at his chest as he watched the sack birling lazily through the air. A few small objects dropped out of the sacking as it started on its downward journey, *That'll be the bullets*, he thought.

It turned once more in mid-air before plummeting down towards the gulls.

It crashed into the river with a tremendous splash just missing one of the nodding seabirds.

The bird leapt vertically in the air screeching like a banshee followed by his mates who immediately joined in the screeching as they starting flying in circles. Being seagulls, of course, one or two had to investigate the splash on the off-chance that it might have been something to eat.

'Good grief,' said Grace calmly, 'what a commotion!'

Liam was still speechless as he looked around to see if there was anyone to witness what had happened. A jakie had wandered under the north arch and was tying a dog to the railing. After a few seconds the dog lay down, gave a bored yawn and put his head between his paws. The man busied himself arranging a cardboard notice and a polystyrene cup; he never even glanced up. To him, it seemed, there were more important things in life. The strange little tableau gave Liam a weird sense of deja vu.

He turned back to Grace.

'Why on earth did you do that?' he sighed finally.

'I'm not sure I could be bothered with all the 'explanations' as you put it.'

'The gun, well, it was an important historical ...' he tried to think of a word, '... artefact.'

'Oh really?' She lifted an eyebrow in amusement, 'on Thursday it was a murder weapon, now it's an important historical artefact?'

She started to clip up her handbag.

The seagulls settled down and were floating about preening their feathers.

Grace looked at Liam with some sympathy.

'Sorry about that, Liam. I suppose I should have said something but sometimes it's better just to get it over with. I really couldn't face a load of silly questions from some teenage policeman about where it came from and all that.'

Liam had relaxed a bit and thought it over.

'Perhaps you're right.'

'There's no need for you to come over to the court now, is there?'

'I'll head back. I might as well jump on the subway.'

'Did you remember about next week?'

'Next week?'

'At the house, you know, Eddie's party.'

'Oh, yes, of course. I saw Helen this morning. She says she'd be delighted to come.'

Grace started to arrange her shoulder bag and began tightening up her gloves.

'By the way, what's the occasion?'

'It's Eddie's birthday.'

'No problem thinking about what present to get him then.'

He rubbed his beard.

'I wonder if he has the Bristol fighter F2?'

'A what?'

'A Bristol Fighter F2. Used by the Free State Army in 1922.'

Grace gave a quiet groan.

'Okay! Okay!' he laughed, putting his hands up in surrender.

Grace gave the gloves a final tug.

'How's it going with all this Charlie stuff anyway?'

'Almost ten thousand words so far.'

'You're kidding! From an old photograph and a couple of sovereigns?'

'Not a lot to go on I must admit.'

'What about, you know, the bits in between?'

'Oh don't worry about that,' he said, waving goodbye as he turned away.

'I'll just make up the rest as I go along.'

Chapter 29

The Big Sleep

Charlie retraced his steps back to The Country Club where George was tidying in the bar as he walked through the curtain.

'I'm going to phone down to Philly. Give me a couple of minutes.'

After the usual debate with the operator about who was paying for what, he was put through.

'Hello,' said a cautious male voice.

'Is that you, McBride? Charlie here.'

'Hi Charlie. Is everything okay?'

'Didn't go quite as expected, but I'll ask George to get in touch tomorrow morning. Are Elizabeth and Florence alright?'

'A few tears at first but Elizabeth is getting her ready for bed and making some supper. I'm going to make my way back to Atlantic City in about half an hour.'

'Did your boy follow the car?'

'Yes, just back a minute ago. Just as you thought, the car went north and onto the ramp to Route One and the New Jersey Turnpike. They're on their way to New York.'

Charlie gave a slight grunt of satisfaction He looked over at George who look dazed and bewildered.

'Could one of your guys stay the night? Not that I'm worried but, you know ... just in case.'

'No problem.'

'Could you put Elizabeth on? I think George wants a word.'

'I'll go get her, she's upstairs, be back in a minute.'

Charlie placed the earpiece on the counter and signalled

George over.

'Elizabeth will be down in a minute.'

'What the hell is McBride doing there?'

'Just a precaution. As I told you, Vinnie is ... was ... half cracked. It's difficult to know what he would do, how he would jump. I asked McBride to hide out in the house in case anything went haywire. I also asked him to have one of his men follow the car to make sure it left Philadelphia. I didn't want any of Vinnie's crew hanging about down there.'

He could hear a crackle on the earpiece.

'On you go, that'll be Elizabeth,' he said, walking round to the front of the bar and over to the fire exit.

He pulled out the cash left over from the money bag and started sorting it out.

As George started talking, there was a rattle at the fire doors as one of the side doors was pulled open.

'That was quick,' said Charlie, glancing up at the clock. It was just gone nine forty.

Ned and Frankie almost tumbled into the bar.

They talked together, almost as one.

'Keep it low, boys, George is on the phone,'

'We were travelling along the Brooklyn Bridge, it's usually quiet after six.'

'Yeah, but this time hardly anyone around at all.'

'I pulled over at a maintenance area near the middle of the bridge ...'

'We jumped out and threw Vinnie over ...'

Ned clasped his hand to his mouth to suppress a giggle.

Like most youngsters who think they have got away with something dangerous, they were over-excited and on edge.

'Okay boys, let's take it easy.'

He had to get them out of the bar. They would be unable to contain themselves from talking and babbling.

'Are you sure no one spotted you?'

'We turned off at the ramp and came back over to Manhattan slowly. There was half a dozen cars and trucks passed us on the other side, not one of them stopped.'

Charlie handed over another banded fifty-dollar bundle to Ned.

'And here's yours,' he said, folding five twenties and tucking them into Frankie's top pocket.

Frankie pulled them out and looked at them. He had rarely seen a single twenty in his life let alone a bundle of five.

'Gee, thanks Charlie,' he said with something approaching amazement.

As he started to put them back, Charlie pulled out another ten.

'This is your wages for the rest of the night and tomorrow's shift, don't come in here until Saturday night. I'll fix it with Harry. That goes for both of you.'

They looked at each other.

'I'm leaving town tonight. I'm heading to Los Angeles.'

Ned looked confused.

'Is that in Mexico?'

Frankie punched Ned on the top of the shoulder.

'No you numbskull, it's in California. Where they make the movies. Hey Charlie, you thinking of becoming a movie star?'

'No. But I need to get out of town for a while.'

The boys became serious for a minute.

'Take the truck back to Brooklyn now and park it somewhere handy.'

'What do we do then?'

'Don't do anything. Nothing. You're finished for the night.'

Charlie looked at them both.

'Know any good taprooms in your neighbourhood?'

'Only O'Neil's.'

Ned snorted in disbelief.

'O'Neil's, are you kidding. He charges 20 cents for a beer!'

Charlie grinned.

'Here,' he said, pulling out another five, 'the beers are on me. Now get going, before I change my mind.'

*

George put the earpiece back on the holder.

'I feel a bit better. Elizabeth is calm and Florence appears to be safe, sound, and ... unharmed.'

He leaned over the bar and rested his head in his hands.

'My God, this whole thing is like a hellish nightmare.'

Charlie quickly told George what had happened to Vinnie's body, then he pulled out the blackmail money package and put it on the counter.

'Your money, George.'

'Jeez, I had forgotten all about that,'

'Here,' he said pushing it back, 'you keep it, you deserve it.'

'No I don't.'

'Yes you do. Keep it.'

Charlie looked closely at George then finally opened the brown envelope and placed the money on the bar top.

'There's a drawer under the till behind you. Open it. You'll see some plain white envelopes, there should be a pencil in there as well. Take them out.'

George found them at the side of the drawer and handed them over. Charlie took an envelope and wrote a name on the front, smoothed out one of the thousand dollar bundles, opened the flap and tucked the money inside, flattened the whole lot down and sealed it.

'I'll give you this later,' he said, sticking the envelope into an inside jacket pocket.

He pushed two thousand dollars over to George.

'Buy the girls a couple of ... horses, or something. I'll take the rest. I'll probably need it. I've decided that we're leaving tomorrow if I can get a sailing to Europe. Though it shouldn't be much of a problem with this,' he said, lifting up a bundle and slapping it into his palm.

'Funny how they're always fully booked until you mention a first class cabin. Might even get one to a British port if things go well.'

'You never said ...'

'We were going anyway, a couple of week's early won't make a bit of difference. It'll take the heat off everyone.'

'What about your business, the apartment?'

'All fixed up near as damn it. I've told Manny that I'm worried about Milazzo and I'm heading off tonight to Los Angeles.'

'You're worried about Milazzo? I thought you'd never heard of him?'

'I haven't. But I've a good idea that saying I'm scared of him will boost his sense of self-importance. I also told Manny that Vinnie took a bullet but survived and disappeared during the fracas – with the money of course.'

George was impressed.

'How the hell did you manage to think of all that!'

'I told Manny I was going to work for Terrance Regan, remember him? We met him on the way down to Cork. Red headed loud mouth, "Rusty" he called himself.'

'Yes I do come to think of it. Lived in Chicago, said he commanded a flying column in Tipperary.'

'Yeah,' Charlie said without emotion, 'in his dreams maybe.'

George came round to the front of the bar. He looked weary and needed a seat.

Charlie had a sudden chuckle.

'With a bit of luck when Frankie and Ned start talking,' he said with a grin, 'Milazzo will probably believe I'm off to Mexico to become a movie star.'

'What?'

'Never mind,' he said taking a seat beside George, 'want a drink?'

'No thanks, not now.'

George looked around at the table and the chairs and gave an exasperated sigh.

'Even though Vinnie was a rat it's hard to believe that he was alive just an hour ago.'

'He's probably lying at the bottom of the East River by now.'

George glanced up.

'The big sleep.'

They heard the front door opening. Charlie turned around, irritated.

'That must be Harry. Damn, told him to give me a ring before he came back.'

He looked back at George.

'What was that you said?'

'Death.'

George had a faraway look.

'... it's what the wise-guys call death. They call it the big sleep.'

The curtain swished open as Harry stepped into the bar.

'Everything go okay, guys?'

His jacket was half off when he suddenly stopped and looked down, he poked at a hole in the floor with the toe of his shoe.

'An accident, Harry, George dropped an ashtray.'

Harry narrowed his eyes and looked at both of them but said nothing and walked on.

After Harry changed into his apron in the little cloakroom, Charlie moved to the bar.

'I need to leave town for a short while. There's a couple of things you need to know before I go.'

Harry put down the glass he was about to polish.

'I gave Frankie the rest of the night off and told him to come in Saturday. I squared him up with his wages.'

Harry nodded at Charlie. He looked over at George. He knew something had happened; his face gave nothing away.

'That's fine by me. He's been busy lately, could probably do with time off.'

'And there's this,' he said handing over the key ring with the red disc. 'It's the key to the safe, you can have it. I never used it much. There are some account ledgers and receipts on the top shelf. I kept a float on the bottom for any unexpected expenses. It's also handy for overnight money if you can't get to the bank.'

Charlie continued explaining how to open the safe.

'You put the key in the lock, and turn it until the first lock clicks. About quarter of a turn to the right. There are four dials on the lock rim. Start on the outside and turn until the number one aligns with the key, move inwards, use the next three numbers nine, one and six. When they are all aligned the door clicks and unlocks. It will spring open about an inch.'

'Sounds easy enough, what were the numbers again?'

'1916 – it's a year, a date.'

'I'll remember that year.'

'Won't we all?'

'Yes, indeed. That was the year Frankie was born, 1916, I'll remember that alright.'

In a way Charlie wasn't surprised. He picked the date because of the Easter uprising in Dublin but Harry was like most Irish Americans. To him, over in Ireland, there was no deadly politics, no uprising, no war of independence, no civil war. It was all just simply 'The Troubles' where brave Irishmen fought the dastardly English Black and Tans. Keep it nice and uncomplicated. Charlie had come to believe that most Americans thought the entire history of America was about Cowboys versus Indians. Even the British press, over the years, had reduced the Great War to England versus Germany. It was as if the death and mutilation of millions of men were the equivalent of a soccer match where England scored the winning goal before the final whistle.

Charlie put twenty dollars on the bar.

'As I promised, the first drink is on me.'

Harry eyed him suspiciously.

'Twenty dollars. That'll go a long way, you must think we get hundreds in here on a Thursday night.'

'I'll leave it to you.'

He picked up the wooden box.

'Let's go, George.'

'And take that notice off the front door on your way out,' shouted Harry as they passed through the curtain and into the corridor.

There were a couple of inkies already at the door as they were leaving.

'Is the bar open, Charlie?'

'Sure is,' he said, prising off the tack holding the notice, 'here, take this into Harry. He'll give you a free drink.'

The two guffawed as they went down the corridor.

'Harry Sharkey give anyone a free drink – that'll be a first!'

George had already hailed down a yellow cab; they were at the front door of the Lincoln within five minutes.

Charlie walked up the front stairs as George paid the cab. As he went through the revolving door he spotted Arthur the doorman. He was about to talk to him when Una flew into his arms.

'My God, Charlie. Is everything alright? I've been worried sick ...'

She spotted George coming through the door.

'George! How is Elizabeth? How is ...'

Charlie pulled her close.

'Not now, Una,' he whispered in her ear, 'everything's fine. Go into the lounge. I'll be in in a minute and tell you how it all went.'

Una pulled away looking anxious.

'Okay, I'll see you over at the bar.'

Charlie handed over the wooden box to Arthur.

'Could you put this in the strong room overnight? I'll pick it up in the morning.'

He put his hand in his pocket and slipped him a dollar.

'And a couple of Whisky Highballs would go down a treat.'

Arthur gave his usual, hardly perceptible nod.

'I'll arrange that, sir,' he said and glided away.

George was at the bank of elevators to the left of the porter's lodge.

'Say goodnight to Una for me. I don't think I could stand an interrogation at this time of night.'

'I think you've been through enough the past few days. It's a good night's sleep you need.'

'If I can sleep,' he said wearily as he stepped into the car.

Charlie pulled out the white envelope from his pocket.

'By the way, do you mind delivering this?'

George looked at the name on the front - Mrs G. Greene.

'Mrs G?'

'She told me at the wedding that she and her husband were saving for a retirement house in Coney Island. That should help them out.'

The elevator girl coughed.

'Which floor, sir?'

'Sixth, please.'

'Why don't you give it to her yourself? She'll be in the office in the morning.'

'Mind your feet, sir.'

'I don't have the time.'

'Besides,' he said as the doors were closing together, 'I don't like long goodbyes.'

*

The SS Britannic was towed from Pier 24 out into the Hudson by three tugs that tooted and wailed at each other in a language only their captains understood. Charlie and Una were on the stern watching the last of the streamers break from the quayside; they didn't have a streamer; there was no one to see them off.

The tugs managed to get the Britannic into mid-stream before they could hear and feel the turbines pick up revs as the ship got under way. Two tugs followed the ship down towards The Battery, giving her the occasional gentle nudge to keep her away from Jersey harbour. It had been a hot day for May in New York and the warm air and the ice-cold water of the Hudson had combined to start a fog about an hour ago. Una had met an old friend from college and she was busy chattering to her and someone, who Charlie took to be her husband, on the starboard side.

'Charlie, we're heading up to the promenade deck to see Liberty. Are you coming?' shouted Una.

In a minute, Charlie signalled waving his hand to tell them to carry on.

As the ship rounded Battery Park it started to pull to starboard and Charlie could see the Brooklyn Bridge quite clearly through the mist for a few minutes. He had never taken much notice of it before; from this distance it looked quite magnificent with its illuminated towers and elegant slim suspension cables. There was something beautiful but ominous about the view; to the right he could just about see the welding flashes from the Naval shipyard on the Brooklyn side. He looked down, suddenly fearful, it was quite a drop to the water. It reminded him of the sudden bout of vertigo he took when looking out his office window.

For a brief instant, he imagined he could see something floating

...

'Are you coming up?'

Una had appeared at his side.

'Are you alright,' she said, looking at him quizzically

'Fine, I just felt a bit giddy looking down at the water.'

'We're about to pass Liberty, don't you want to see her?'

'Seen it a million times.'

They walked over to the starboard.

'Hope you don't mind but I've asked Mr and Mrs Campbell to dinner with us in the First Class lounge. I know Hilda from college in Glasgow. She's going back home to a job as a welfare supervisor on the Health Panel. Her husband John is a banking accountant; he has a new job as well.'

'No, I don't mind meeting them at all.'

Liberty appeared like magic through the haze. Charlie walked to the rail and stared at the enormous figure. He remembered how excited he was on his first trip to America in 1917 – it seemed like a lifetime ago now.

Getting the train from Penn station to Philadelphia; meeting George Peebles for the first time at his sister's wedding; back and forward to Ireland and France during the troubles. Prohibition, the bootleggers, Cab Calloway singing Minnie the Moocher, *The Country Club, the would-be gangsters like Manny, the pimps and spivs and hard boiled bookies like Slavinsky ...*

'Will you miss America?'

Charlie turned around, thinking before answering.

'I know a part of me always will.'

He turned back to see Liberty slowly disappearing in the mist.

Then she was gone.

Charlie turned again, looked at Una and suddenly gave her a dazzling smile.

'So, dinner with the Campbells?'

He linked arms with Una.

'An accountant and a social worker, you say?'

He took a step forward.

'I can't wait.'

The End

Some other books from Ringwood Publishing

All titles are available from the Ringwood website and from usual outlets.
Also available in Kindle, Kobo and Nook.
www.ringwoodpublishing.com

Ringwood Publishing, 24 Duncan Avenue, Glasgow
G14 9HN

mail@ringwoodpublishing.com

Torn Edges

Brian McHugh

The prequel to *Between Two Bridges*, *Torn Edges* is a riveting mystery story linking modern day Glasgow with 1920's Ireland.

When a gold coin very similar to a family heirloom is found at the scene of a Glasgow murder, a search is begun that takes the McKenna family, assisted by their librarian friend Liam, through their own family history right back to the tumultuous days of the Irish Civil War. The search is greatly helped by the discovery of an old family photograph of their Great-Uncle Pat in a soldier's uniform.

Torn Edges is both entertaining and well-written, and will be of considerable interest to all in both Scottish and Irish communities, many of whom will realise that their knowledge and understanding of events in Ireland in 1922 has been woefully incomplete. *Torn Edges* will also appeal more widely to all who appreciate a good story well told.

ISBN: 978-1-901514-05-6   £6.99

Dark Loch

Charles P. Sharkey

This is an epic tale of the effects of the First World War on the lives of the residents of a small Scottish rural community. A crucial central strand is the long-running romance between tenant crofter Callum Macnair and Caitriona Dunbar, the beautiful daughter of the local laird.

The story is initially set in the fictional village of Glenfay on the banks of Loch Fay on the west coast of Scotland. The main characters are the tenant crofters who work the land leased to them by the laird, Lord Charles Dunbar, and his family. The crofters live a harsh existence in harmony with the land and the changing seasons, unaware of the devastating war that is soon to engulf the continent of Europe.

The book vividly and dramatically explores the impact of that war on all the main characters and how their lives are drastically altered forever.

'*Dark Loch* is a powerful exploration of the momentous impact of the First World War on a remote Scottish crofting community. A fitting memorial and a gripping read.'

ISBN: 978-1-901514-14-8   £9.99

The Volunteer

Charles P. Sharkey

Born in the same hospital room in Northern Ireland in July 1960, Danny Duffy and William Morrison will never meet again. But their lives, and the lives of their families, will be tragically intertwined by politics, secrets and blood.

As the country teeters on the brink of civil war, all must decide what part they will play. While some choose to strive for peaceful, ordinary lives, Danny finds himself standing in front of a panel of IRA men, ready to take up arms and join them; but what is he fighting for, and how far is he willing to go?

Against the violent and fearful backdrop of the Troubles, *The Volunteer* paints a thoughtful picture of how history intrudes on every life, and how our beliefs are shaped by the world we live in, for better or worse.

ISBN: 978-1-901514-36-0   £9.99

The Activist

Alec Connon

When Thomas Durand embarks on a cycling trip around Britain with two fellow students, his life changes forever. A chance encounter inspires Thomas to leave home and drop out of university. As he roams, his eyes are opened to the harm inflicted by humans on the natural world. Driven by an increasingly passionate interest in marine conservation, what begins as a typical gap-year turns into a decade's worth of activism on the open ocean. Here the stakes are highest of all: Thomas enlists with Sea Shepherd, a controversial organisation dedicated to the protection of marine life. It is a commitment that will soon place his life in danger.

The story follows Thomas, from his first tentative steps into the life of an activist in Vancouver, to his battles with a Japanese whaling fleet in the Southern Ocean. An ecological thriller, *The Activist* will shock and inspire anyone with an interest in marine life, conservation and the splendour of the natural world. Without preaching, it is also a clear-eyed demonstration of why this cause is worth fighting for.

"Alec Connon's extraordinary adventures into the world of the whale epitomise the vast disconnect between the human and natural world. In this heartfelt novel, he explores the outer edges of the world which we have dominated, and the price it has had to pay for that domination. In picaresque episodes which are by turns funny, tragic and deeply moving, Connon addresses, in a highly personal and evocative manner, the ways by which we might make amends for what we have done."

Phillip Hoare, Samuel Johnson Prize winner and author of *The Sea Inside*

ISBN: 978-1-901514-25-4   £9.99